The Miner's Wife

By Diane Allen

For the Sake of Her Family
For a Mother's Sins
For a Father's Pride
Like Father, Like Son
The Mistress of Windfell Manor
The Windfell Family Secrets
Daughter of the Dales
The Miner's Wife

DIANE ALLEN

The Miner's Wife

MACMILLAN

First published 2019 by Macmillan
an imprint of Pan Macmillan
20 New Wharf Road, London N1 9RR
Associated companies throughout the world
www.panmacmillan.com

ISBN 978-1-5098-9520-5

1 3 5 7 9 8 6 4 2

A CIP catalogue record for this book is available from the British Library.

Typeset by Palimpsest Book Production Ltd, Falkirk, Stirlingshire
Printed and bound by CPI Group (UK) Ltd, Croydon, CR0 4YY

Dedicated to the Dalesfolk of Swaledale
and Wensleydale and to the lead miners
who lost their lives in those remote dales

1

Swaledale, the Yorkshire Dales, 1877

Meg Oversby sat enjoying the warm sunshine of the June day. She leaned back and turned her face up to the sun, and smiled as she watched a skylark dip and dart in the blue sky as it sang its tune. Her father had arranged for her to get a lift into Swaledale to the little village of Gunnerside with the local butcher, although he would have had something to say about it, had he known how the man had enjoyed glancing at Meg's ankles as he helped her up to sit next to him. But she had been thankful for the lift, because her heavy basket of butter was no longer weighing on her arm as his two horses struggled to climb the steep hillside out of the village of Hawes and the small hamlet of Simonstone. Carefully they had picked their way along the track, which snaked and turned following the fell contours, with a horrendous drop to their deaths if the animals put a foot wrong.

Once in the village, Meg had made her delivery of butter to the small shop that the local lead-miners' wives used, run by her ailing surrogate aunt and uncle, before making her way back home, out of the long green valley. Now she was enjoying a little freedom as she sat on the edge of the limestone chasm known as the Buttertubs. It was deep enough for the Devil himself to live in, and many a stray sheep had fallen to its death down the hole, but it was a beautiful part of the world, with the winding pass between Great Shunner Fell opening up to beautiful, remote Swaledale at one end and to the village of Hawes and Wensleydale at the other. The chasm had reportedly been given its name by local women who, like herself, delivered butter and had found it a cool place to rest and chill their produce in the deep cavern, before carrying on their way.

Meg could well believe this, and she enjoyed the warmth of the day, picking some of the sweet-smelling wild thyme that grew around her and placing it behind her ear before she stood up. She gave a backward glance at the dale, which was also home to two lads who had taken her eye, brothers who worked at the Owd Gang lead-mines. She'd hoped for a sighting of them, but knew they would be working at the mines high up in the fells above Gunnerside. Not to worry, she thought to herself, there would always be the following week, when her next delivery was ready to be hawked to the small village shop. Next week she would as usual travel the ten miles with her father in the horse and trap, and while he had a jar at the King's Head to quench his thirst and catch up with the news of the dale, she would quickly make her way up the steep fellside to the lead-mines above

2

Gunnerside Gill. There the workers of the Owd Gang mines toiled, looking for the mineral ore of galena, which was then smelted into lead.

She knew Jack and Sam Alderson would be working there, Jack in the smelting mill and Sam as a 'deadman', removing the 'deads', or useless rock, from the working mine and refilling an older, disused mine. Both brothers had danced with Meg at a local event in Hawes Market Hall a time or two since the Christmas dance when they had all first met – much to her parents' disgust, as they were not the sort of men a wealthy farmer's daughter should associate with. But Meg's head was turned by their good looks and the attention that both of them had shown her, albeit briefly. She had watched both brothers for a while and had noticed them flirting with other girls; and then one evening they had spotted her and had come to talk at first, and then dance with her.

She smiled now as she remembered both lads with their arms around her waist, guiding her around the dance floor as she had never been held and danced with before. All three had enjoyed their evenings together. The trouble was that she couldn't make her mind up which one she preferred. She mused over each brother as she stepped out onto the rutted road that took her back to her family home at Appersett. Jack was charming, but serious; however, Sam was the better dancer and was always joking. The brothers looked alike, with dark brown hair and bright blue eyes, but they were complete opposites when it came to their characters. Both had taken her eye, and both had argued with each other for her affections. She really shouldn't be thinking about either, Meg told herself as she made her way along the road home. But then she broke into song, feeling a spring in her step as she remembered their smiling faces. She'd do as she liked – and not even her father would stop her.

'Well, you've taken your time, young lady. I hope you haven't been trailing up to those lead-mines and fluttering your eyelashes at the men. None of them up there are worth owt, they've none of them got a penny to their names.' Agnes Oversby looked up from her baking and shook her head as her daughter came sauntering into the kitchen at their home, Beck Side Farm. 'You can take that thyme out of your hair and all, especially if one of them gave you it, madam.' She looked at her slim, dark-haired daughter and shook her head. Meg was a bonny lass with a glowing complexion, and Agnes knew that many a man would soon be wanting to court her.

'I've not been anywhere near the mines, Mother. I've taken my time because the day is so warm and, after all, it is a fair way there and back – my legs feel like jelly. I'm glad Father will be taking the horse and trap as usual next week.' Meg slumped into the Windsor chair next to the fireside and took the wild thyme out of her hair, then played with the purple flowers in her hand.

'Aye, well, you needn't think you are going to sit there for long. You can take your father a jug of ginger beer. He'll be dying of thirst in this heat while he's scything the top meadow. I'm busy baking and haven't time to see to him. You'd both complain if there wasn't anything to eat

4

in the house.' Agnes scowled at her daughter; Meg had been out all day, and while she knew it was a good distance, she should have been back sooner. 'Has Harry paid up? Did you tell him there would be a few pounds more butter next week, now the cows are milking well?'

'Yes, the money's in the basket, and he's glad you can supply him with more butter. He says there's a new influx of miners moved into the dale, after a fresh vein of lead was found at the Sir Francis level.' Meg yawned and leaned back in the chair, showing no inclination to get up and walk to the high meadow with a drink for her father.

'That'll mean more rubbish coming into the dale. They've ruined those hills with their mining and damming of the becks. That land's going to be worth nowt, if they are not careful.' Agnes cut out the scones she had been making and placed them on her baking tray, before brushing them with beaten egg, then walked over to the fireside oven. 'Stir your shanks – get gone with your father's drink, and on your way back you can bring me the eggs from the hut. While you are about it, have a look in that clump of nettles next to the cowshed. I saw an old hen making her way out of them this morning, and I bet she's nesting there.' Agnes placed her scones in the oven and nudged Meg's legs, to get her to move.

'I've always got to be doing something – you never let me be,' Meg growled as she went to the big earthenware bowl of home-made ginger beer, specially brewed for haytime, and filled a pottery jug to the brim for her father to drink out of.

''Tis the Devil that makes work for idle hands. It's

better that you are busy than sitting there romancing over them useless lads. Now, get gone, and don't forget to look for that nest.' Agnes flicked her tea towel lovingly at her nineteen-year-old daughter. Meg was a grown woman who knew her own mind now, and Agnes feared she'd lost her little girl.

Meg walked through the farmyard. The sun was still hot and the smell of the dry earth and the chickweed and groundsel crushed beneath her feet filled the air, as she opened the yard gate and walked up the wooded outrake to the meadow that her father was mowing with his scythe. She knew it was hard work, but her father had put his foot down when her mother suggested that he pay one of the neighbour's lads to help him, saying that he could manage it himself and needed no one. So when she saw him covered in sweat and swearing at his lot, she didn't feel much sympathy.

'Are you hot and bothered, Father?' Meg passed him the jug of ginger beer and looked around her.

'I bloody well am, lass. It's hard work is this, and it'll take me until nightfall to mow this meadow.' Tom Oversby wiped his brow free of sweat, after taking a long gulp of the fiery brew. 'I'll have to ask you or your mother to milk the cows tonight. I want to crack on and get this done.' He looked at his daughter, who seemed to feel no love for the farm that would be hers one day.

'I suppose I could do the milking, as long as that awkward old Buttercup doesn't stand on my foot. I'm sure she does it on purpose every time I fasten her up in her bink. I hate the creature.' Meg sighed, thinking of how much she had to do nearly every day and wishing her father wasn't too stubborn to hire a farmhand.

'You show her who's boss, she's nobbut a cow.' Tom leaned on the end of his scythe and looked around him. 'Did you see anybody, while you were over in t' other dale?'

'No, only Uncle Harry, and of course Mr Cockett was kind enough to give me a lift, as you know. Gunnerside was busy, but I didn't see anybody I know; and no, I didn't talk to any lead-miners. Mother has already lectured me about that.' Meg knew what was expected of her in the future. She was supposed to marry a steady lad from a good farming family, ensuring that her home of Beck Side was in safe hands after her parents' time.

'I never even mentioned that. But she'll be right in what she says. You want nowt by looking at one of them. We are only saving you from heartache – we want the best for you and the farm. I'm not putting all my sweat into it just for it to be frittered away after my day in the hands of some beer-swilling navvy miner.'

'Father, I only dance with them. You'd think I'd committed a mortal sin; it's not like I'm about to run away with one of them,' Meg said with her head bowed, remembering the lecture she had endured when her father had heard, through one of his farming friends, that two of the lead-mining lads had been at her side all night at the Spring Ball, and at previous dances.

'Aye, well, see on it keeps that way. Happen you shouldn't go with me when I next go over that way. You

7

are best staying at home.' Tom put down his drink and drew out the whetstone that he kept in his breeches pocket. The sandstone made the blade gleam in the sunlight, as it did the job of sharpening the scythe to cut the green grass that would be harvested later in the week for the farm animals to feed on through the winter. He then wiped his grey sweat-filled hair with his checked flat cap and placed it back on his head. He was as brown as a berry, his face weathered like the countryside around him and his body as wiry as the hawthorn tree he was taking shade under.

Meg said nothing. She knew that if she protested too much, her father would instantly know that her head had been turned by her dance partners. So instead she picked up the jug of ginger beer and walked to the edge of the field with it, placing it in the shade of the hedge before returning. 'I'll be away, then. Mother's baking and I've to collect the eggs, and then I'll milk the cows.'

'Aye, alright, get yourself a move-on.' Tom put down his whetstone and started slowly dragging the sharp edge of the scythe through the long meadow grass, in an age-old rhythm that he'd known since he was a lad. His father had mowed the same field, and his grandfather before him. What a pity he didn't have a son to carry it on, he thought, as he watched his headstrong lass walking down the mown swathes of grass.

Meg muttered to herself as she collected the eggs from the hen-house. The hut was full of flies, and the smell of the hen droppings meant she was glad when she had finished taking the eggs from the hay-filled nests and emerged into the bright, fresh sunlight. She left one egg behind, to deceive the hens into thinking it was safe for them to lay more in the same place. Now, to track down the one hen that knew otherwise.

She walked over to the cowshed and went to the huge clump of nettles that her mother had described. She thought twice about tackling them with her bare hands, so she put down the bucket of eggs and reached for the mucking-out fork to flatten the weeds. No sooner had she done so than she saw the beady-eyed old hen that had a mind of its own looking at her, with its brown feathers covering her eggs. Or was it eggs? Meg laughed and whispered, 'So that's what is so precious to you, is it?' as a small, fluffy chick's head peered from under its mother's wing. 'You're alright, I'll not harm your babies. I'll leave you be, but we'll have to put you in your own pen tonight, else a fox or the farmyard cat will get them.' She lifted the flattened nettles back into place and smiled; it would be good to have some chicks about the place, even though it meant more work.

'Did you find a nest?' Agnes lifted her head and looked at her daughter as she put the eggs into an enamel dish, ready to wash.

'I found where she had laid them, but they are not eggs any longer. She's got a brood underneath her wings. Another day and they'd have made themselves known to all of us. I don't know how we have not spotted her before, with her being right next to the cowshed door,' Meg laughed.

'Is your father alright? I bet he's jiggered. Why he'll not take on any help, I do not know, the stubborn devil.' Agnes wiped her hands on her apron and dusted her apple pie with a coating of sugar.

'Aye, he's alright; browner than ever, with being out in the sun again all day. He's asked if one of us will do the milking, as he's going to be late in for his supper. I'll do it, despite Buttercup being an awkward old devil.' Meg wiped each one of the eggs with a damp cloth and put the collection in the coolness of the slate-shelved pantry. 'I'll have a sup of tea, and then I'll move them chickens into that little coop that Father made last year. It'll hold them until they get older.'

'I don't know what he'd do without you, our Meg. You might not have been the lad he wanted, but you are just as good as any sons that I could have had. He wants to think himself lucky.' Agnes sighed and held back a tear. Her heart had been broken after having Meg and losing her twin brother at birth. It had been even worse when the doctor had told her she would not be able to carry any more babies, but it had been Tom who had felt it more. He'd always set his heart on a son – one to take over the farm, after his day.

'Aye, well, that's how it is. He can't trade me in for a lad. And I can't make him see that I can farm as well as one. So the stubborn old devil will have to sweat out in the fields till his supper.' Meg lifted the iron kettle from the Yorkshire range and poured her mother and herself a cup of tea.

'Meg, don't forget he is your father: show him some respect.' Agnes pulled her daughter up short.

'I will do, when he recognizes me for what I am, and doesn't try to keep me at home at his beck and call. But I'm always a disappointment to him, no matter what I do.' Meg supped her tea as she looked out of the kitchen window, thinking of the things she would really like to do, instead of being her father's farm lad. She loved her home, the farm, with its drystone-walled fields and the long whitewashed house that was cold in summer, but warm in winter. She knew it was centuries old and had always been in her family, but sometimes she yearned to escape.

'You will never be a disappointment to us, Megan, so I'll not have you say that.' Agnes put her arm around her daughter and kissed her on her cheek. 'He'll realize that one day, when he's got grandbairns around his feet and a son-in-law who is as big a farmer as he is. That will be all he wants, when the time's right.'

Meg looked at her mother. Her hair, which was once as black as her own, was starting to turn grey, and her figure, once slim and petite, was now broadening out, like most women of her age. 'You see, you are just as bad. I'm expected to marry and be happy with a farmer, and do as I'm told. What if I don't want to farm? What if I want to leave this dale and see more of the world? There must be more than sheep, cows and hen-muck.' Meg scowled at her mother as she sipped her tea and thought about the places and other countries she had been taught about in school. How she wanted to see more of the world and escape a life of drudgery, like her mother's.

'Quiet now, Meg; you be thankful for what you've

11

got. There's many a lass in those northern mill towns would swap places with you any day. You know nothing yet.' Agnes sat down and looked across at her dissatisfied daughter. She remembered how, when she was young, she had had similar dreams herself, but then Tom had come along and she'd settled down to running the farm with him, investing for a good life in the future for the un-grateful Meg and themselves, by putting every waking hour into their farm. The farm that fed them well and protected them from some of the harsh realities of the world outside the dale. One day her headstrong daughter would realize just how lucky she was with her lot.

Meg pushed her chair back from the table. 'I'll go and move those chickens, and then I'll milk the cows. After all, what else have I got to do?' She fought back the tears; she actually didn't know what she wanted from life, but she knew that what she had now wasn't enough.

She placed the fluffy yellow chicks in her apron, after battering the stinging nettles down with a brush, and encouraged the old hen to follow her brood into the netted coop, with the aid of grains of corn and the chirp-ing of her chicks. Meg watched as the old bird clucked around her brood, making sure they were all there and accounted for. Usually she would have loved taking care of the new family, but she was battling with her desire to spread her own wings, and at this moment the old hen and her brood simply reminded her of what was expected of her.

Even the cows knew better than to try their luck and rebel as Meg switched the stick around them, urging them into the cowshed, where she tied them up and gave them something to eat. She pulled up the stool and placed her head on their flanks, as she gently pulled on their teats and started to fill the metal bucket with creamy fresh milk. She drew comfort from the smell of the hay and cows, a smell that she had grown up with. She rested her head on the old roan-coloured shorthorn and started to cry as she watched her bucket fill. She knew she was lucky; she knew she was loved, especially by her mother. But she wanted more than to spend her life milking cows on the farm. Her tears fell down her face and she wiped them away with the back of her hand as she breathed in deeply, concentrating on the job in hand. She would do more than simply stay at home and be happy with her lot, of that she was sure; she'd make her way in the world and leave the farm behind.

2

'Here, you've forgotten your bait.' Betty Alderson passed her eldest son, Jack, his lunch box and stood at the small cottage door, as he took it from her hands and then made his way up the stony track, following in his brother Sam's footsteps to work at the lead-mines. She stood leaning against the doorframe and watched as both her sons disappeared up the brant hillside, to where she could hear work had already started. The sound of iron against stone echoed around the dale, as the ore from the earth was hammered and melted down, ready to be transported down the dale to its final destination.

She sighed heavily as she looked around her at the grand view along Swaledale and the promise of another fine day; it was a shame that every day was swathed in a cloud of worry. It was like the cloud of dirt that hung about the smelting mill where Sam worked, along with tens of others along the fellsides, filtering in and out of her thoughts all day, finding her forever worrying whether she would see both lads home safely; or would she have a neighbour rushing to tell her news of one of them being maimed or, even worse, dead? Every day she went through the same ritual of worrying as she watched her lads go to work – the same work that had taken her Bill away from her and had left her a widow, with two young lads to bring up on her own.

She'd never forget the day she'd watched her husband being carried down the fellside on a stretcher, his body broken, his clothes torn and his face so black she hadn't been able to recognize him. She remembered the scream she had let out, as the miners – some of them close friends – placed Bill on the kitchen table, and the look on her two sons' faces as they realized they no longer had a father. She never would forget the look in those innocent blue eyes of Jack and Sam as they cried and tried to make sense of why their father had left them. Why, of all the men down that pit in Arkendale, had Bill to be the one to check why the charge had not exploded, when he knew that he had a wife and two sons waiting for him at home? Still, that had been her man: always ready to help others and support folk, never thinking of himself or, on this occasion, his family.

Robert Jacques, one of the owners of the CB mine that Bill had worked for, who lived in his grand house nearby, had not even given her the time of day when she had pleaded with him to let them stay in their cottage, but had seen her and her boys homeless after the funeral. If it had not been for the fact that her two boys had secured jobs with the Owd Gang – one looking after the pit ponies, and the other turning the 'windy king' – they would have had no money; and no home, if they had not initially been given a dwelling that had been left abandoned for something better by its last inhabitants. Betty would always remember looking around at the wattle-and-daub walls and at the ling thatch that acted as a roof, and wondering just how low she would get before giving in and asking for places in the poorhouse. But she was a proud woman and, one way or another, she had made her way in the world, taking in washing and even helping to sift through the spoil heaps that covered the fellsides for any lost ore to sell, no matter what the weather. With that, along with the ninepence a day that both boys brought home, they had survived.

With both boys now men, and with them all settled in a decent house once more, life was starting to look better, as long as the mine kept going; and God forbid that there were no accidents within it. Both her boys were handsome young men, full of life, and she knew her Bill would be proud of them being in reasonable jobs, especially Jack at the smelting mill. They had always been there for her, teasing her and cheering her along when they could see she was down, and making sure that if there was nothing to eat in the house, then a fish or rabbit would appear. They were her lads and always would be, if she had her way, Betty thought, as she started to make the bread for the day.

'Here, tomorrow's Sunday, our Jack. We could make a bob or two helping locals with the hay, seeing as we

16

won't be at the mine. The farmers are always busy and looking out for somebody. And I don't know about you, but I could do with an extra bit of brass. It'll be Reeth Bartle Fair before long, and I wouldn't mind going.' Sam walked backwards up the incline of the fell, looking at his brother and waiting for a reply.

'Just think about what you've said, numpty! It's Sunday: nobody works on a farm around here on a Sunday. They go to church or chapel and pray to the Lord to keep the weather fine until the following day. Sometimes you worry me; if you had brains, you'd be lethal.' Jack strode past his younger brother and laughed to himself. Sam was always conjuring up some plan in that empty head of his, and they always came to nothing.

'I know, but there must be one of 'em that isn't bothered whether he goes to hell or not, for the sake of getting his hay in dry. We've to find that one. Or I know, why don't we borrow a pit pony and go over to the next dale and try our luck at asking Meg Oversby's father if he wants a hand? You know you are dying to see her as much as I am, and it would be an excuse to see Meg, even if he did tell us where to go.' Sam pulled on Jack's jacket, stopping him in his tracks just before they reached the entrance to the mine, which was abuzz with miners, ponies, tubs of ore and folk shouting at the tops of their voices as the day's work began. Hammers driven by water-wheels clanged up and down, breaking stones in search of the ore, and the noise echoed around the fell-sides.

'I'll see. Now, you get to work, and mind yourself

17

with them explosives.' Jack knew that his brother thought nothing of carrying the alarming combination of matches, candles, gunpowder and tobacco for his clay pipe in his pocket – a combination that he warned Sam about every morning, and every morning he ignored his concerns. 'Keep safe and I'll give some thought to what you say.' Jack watched as his brother made his way over the tramlines along which the tubs, full or empty, ran into the mine's dark mouth.

'Ah, I got you, with the mention of Megan. I know your answer already. But it's me she loves, not you. You'll have to fight me for her,' Sam shouted back, and grinned as he saw the look on his brother's face.

'The trouble with you is that you are all gob. Get below in the dark place where you belong,' Jack yelled back.

'Better than burning in the fires, like you will today at that furnace of yours, dear brother.'

'You'll both have nowt to grin about, if I put a boot up both your arses.' Albert Calvert, the blacksmith from Gunnerside, who had left his son in charge of his business in the village and was now building a new water-wheel to drive something called a compressor, shouted at them both. 'You lads are not worth a penny in wages, and I'll tell Sir George Denys, when next I see him.'

'Bollocks! Tell him what you want; he never shows his face here, and wouldn't ken us from Adam.' Sam smiled as he entered the darkness of the mine, lighting the partly melted candle on his wide-brimmed felt hat to give him some illumination. Sir George Denys might own the mines, but he'd not know any of his workers if he fell over them – and that included the gob-shite of a blacksmith, with his fancy water-wheel to be housed in its own little engine house. It would never do the work of men, ever, Sam thought, even though Sir George had great faith in the new invention. He'd told the men gathered around his plan that it was a compressor driven by air and powered by water from the fellside, which would soon obliterate the main pit face, making it faster to get to the precious ore and doing the same work of at least six men with picks and shovels. Sam would believe it when he saw it, but until then he'd no time for the cocky blacksmith who thought he knew everything, when really he knew nowt.

Sam made his way down the length of the mine, his candle flickering as it hit pockets of dank air. He listened to the constant drip of running water coming through the centuries-old rock and felt the wetness as he gazed into the darkness, or stepped to one side as a tub full of waste or ore was driven past him. Down here he knew every piece of stone, every rock; he'd been down this tunnel since he was ten years old. And now he was starting on the new Sir Francis level with his fellow workmate, working in six-hourly shifts five days a week, mining nearly two hundred feet deep to get to the galena that would lead to a better life for everyone.

He passed the young lad who was operating the windy king; he was sitting in the darkness all by himself, giving the miners ventilation at the end of the mine. That had been Sam's first job and he remembered how frightened he had been, sitting in the pitch-black peering into the darkness and hoping for the fleeting illumination of a miner's candle to come and shed light just for a second or two, when his candle had burned down and he hadn't been able to afford another one from the tool shop. The tool shop that he still had to buy his candles from, and have use of its picks and spades, both of which were weighed monthly, to be charged for the amount of steel lost through constant usage. Sir George definitely knew how to make money out of his miners.

'Alright, lad?' Sam patted the ten-year-old on his head and then went on his way when the lad looked up at him with a black face and nodded. Poor little bugger, Sam thought, he should be out in the sunshine; you were six foot under soon enough, especially in this work.

The tunnel inclined upwards to enable drainage, and so that the pit ponies had to make less effort with full tubs from the pit face, and Sam made his way to the face of the mine, where he could hear his partner already picking and drilling at the rock, with a pit pony and tub waiting patiently for the removed ore.

'Now then, Sam, so you've decided to join me. I thought you might have run off with some fair-game floozy and given this up for a living.' Robert Winn laughed and then carried on drilling at the rock that was falling around his feet. He'd heard Sam brag that many times about how many women and young girls he'd either slept with or made do as he wished, over the years they had worked together.

'Oh, aye, and you'll have been dining with Sir George himself, I suppose, this weekend? You've only come back because you've missed me, haven't you?' Sam picked up his shovel and started to fill the tub with the loose stone.

'If that's what tha wants to think, then you think it. But I'd rather be in bed with my old lass than looking at your ugly face.' Robert exchanged his drill for a pick, then swung it at the pit face, making a fresh fall of rock around his feet. 'I tell you what: I think it's going to be a bloody long while before we hit this new seam. The old bugger might need his newfangled machine.'

'Na, not with thee and me on the job; we are all he needs – me and thee and old Ned here, who never buckles, no matter what his load.' Sam tousled the mane and ears of the fell-bred pit pony as he carried on loading the tub. He wished he was looking at the face of Meg Oversby, instead of Robert's face and the pony's backside. But beggars could not be choosers, and he needed the money if he was to get on in life.

'Well, we'll see. This new seam that he thinks is here is taking some finding, and what's going out now is not worth our pay, let alone anyone else's.' Robert wiped the sweat from his brow. 'I just hope he's right and that this new seam is a big one when we hit it, else it's going to be a hard winter for all us poor buggers.'

Sam said nothing and kept loading the tub. If he could think of another way of making a living, he would; but at this moment there was nowhere else to go, and he had his mother to support. Tomorrow was Sunday; he'd think of that and try to brighten his gloom, and perhaps, with a bit of luck, he might catch a glimpse of Meg; and, even better, persuade her to meet him alone.

Jack walked across the fellside to where the smelting house stood, nodding and touching his cap as he passed the men called the dressers – the poor souls who worked outside, exposed to the elements in all weathers as they hand-processed the ore from the stone, large pieces of ore going direct to be smelted, while rock was washed and pounded by the bouse-teams into small pieces until any lead was exposed. This was back-breaking work and Jack was thankful that although he fried in summer at the smelting house, at least he was not sodden and frozen all winter. His main problem was the foul, heavy fumes that stuck to his lungs and made him short of breath of a morning, when he climbed up the fell to work.

The black smoke from the furnace was already drifting along the hillside, and the air was filled with the acrid smell of molten metal as he stopped to look around him. Swaledale and Arkendale had been taken over by industry, and water-wheels, mines and the tall chimneys of the smelting houses covered the fellsides, together with the criss-cross pattern of tramlines for the lead-tubs to run along. But most telling was where the fell and hillsides had been washed away by what all miners knew as a 'hush'. This was where water had been dammed up and held back, then suddenly released down the fellside to expose any lead-veins near the surface. This had been done in both dales and had left considerable scarring on the high fellsides. No doubt nature would reclaim it and regrow the spoilt topsoil, but at present the surrounding fells looked raped of their beauty – and all because of the lead that lay beneath them.

Lead-mining was a way of life on the fellsides now, but down in the lush green valley lay the farms with their fields full of golden buttercups, ready to be mown. That was where Jack longed to be: a holder of his own farm, nurturing the land, not ravaging it for what he could get out of it. But land cost money and he had even bigger dreams, which involved sailing to America, where land was nearly given away by the government. So every penny he earned had been saved for his trip, and the smelting house was his life for now and he'd have to be content with that. He sighed as he put a brick of peat into the wheelbarrow that was standing empty, next to a stack of dark, earthy peat from the moor to keep the smelting-house fires burning. He could dream, but for now he had ore to melt and ingots known as 'pieces' to be made, if he wanted there to be bread on the table for the three of them tonight.

One day he would have his own farm; he didn't know how, but he would.

3

'I only hope this weather holds.' Tom Oversby looked up to the heavens and thought about his two hay fields with their grass mown, smelling sweet and dry and ready to be taken into the barn the following day. 'There's a wind getting up. Perhaps I should harness Blossom and get the hay in before it changes. But my father never worked on a Sunday and I have always vowed it to be day of rest, just like him.' He turned from standing in the porch of Beck Side and sat down at the dinner table.

'I don't know why you stand on ceremony on a Sunday; it isn't as if you ever go to church,' Agnes exclaimed, with a tea towel in both hands holding a tray of Yorkshire puddings, as she placed the scalding-hot tin on the table, before putting a pudding on each of the dinner plates that were already filled with roast beef, potatoes and fresh peas straight from the garden. 'I never get a day off, and you'd soon be moaning if Meg and I decided not to cook dinner.'

'I find my God up the fell, woman, as well you know. And you women were put on this earth to look after us men, and well you know that, too – Sunday or no Sunday.' Tom stabbed his Yorkshire pudding and looked across at Meg, who couldn't repress a sound of contempt for her father's views on womenfolk. 'Aye, and you can hold your noise. I'll have none of your lip while I'm eating my dinner.'

'I never said owt, Father. If you want a hand getting the hay in, I'll help you after dinner. It would be better got in than lying out wet, if it does rain.' Meg looked at her brooding father.

'We'll see. With a bit of luck, it will keep fine. Folk would only talk if they saw me leading in on a Sunday. And you'd be worth nowt anyway.' Tom put his head down and set about eating his dinner.

Meg looked across at her mother and said nothing, but inside she was seething. She never would be worth anything in her father's eyes, so his bloody hay could get wet, for all she cared. Trouble was, it would be at a cost to the farm and the farm animals, and that would affect every one of them come winter, when the only source of feed for the livestock was some fusty, bad hay. 'The meat's good, Mother. I think there will be just enough for another boiling of peas on the plants outside in the garden, and then we will have to wait for the second row that I planted.'

'You and that garden – you've definitely inherited your grandfather's green fingers. He'd be proud of you, if he could see what you've done with his little plot. Have you looked at it lately, Tom? We'll want for nothing, this back-end. She's planted cabbage, turnips, beetroot and cauliflowers and the onions are already huge, and there's no better taste than these newly dug potatoes.' Agnes smiled at her daughter; she deserved some praise, because when she wasn't helping out around the farm, she was spending time in the square of garden that her grand-father had always planted behind the house. It was there, as soon as Meg had been able to walk, that she had helped him nurture plants and grow vegetables for the house.

'It's the soil, it's nowt to do with how good she gar-dens. Anybody could grow anything in that soil.' Tom scraped the gravy from his plate with the edge of his knife and licked it off, before pushing his plate to one side.

'Pudding? I've made a rice pudding, I've just to stir some sugar into it.' Agnes put her knife and fork down and left her half-eaten dinner in order to serve her hus-band. She picked up his plate and placed it in the stone-ware sink, before opening the range's oven door to retrieve the golden-skinned rice pudding from the oven.

'Here, Mum, you sit down and finish your dinner. I'll serve my father.' Meg drew her chair back and picked up her half-empty plate.

'But you haven't finished, either, love.' Agnes turned round and smiled at her daughter.

'I've had enough. I might go for a walk, if my father doesn't want me,' Meg said. 'Sit down and enjoy your dinner – I'll see to the pudding. I'll put mine to one side. I prefer it when it is cold, especially if it has sultanas and nutmeg in it, like I saw you adding.' Meg reached for the sugar pot and stirred two good tablespoons into the golden-skinned pudding and smiled as her mother sat back down to finish her meal.

'Give me the skin – it's the best bit of the pudding,' her father growled as he watched her fold it to one side.

'You can have it for me. I don't like it.' Meg spooned out her father a portion of pudding and placed it in front of him, before taking her mother's clean plate away and placing a dish of rice pudding in front of her. 'I'll put the kettle on to boil, and then I'll go and get my shawl from my bedroom. As you say, Father, there is a sneaky wind today and it does look a little cloudy.'

Meg left her mother and father at the dinner table and hurried upstairs. She hated Sunday afternoons, as her mother would knit or sew while her father sat and read the newspaper, or simply sat and said nothing. Usually she would read herself or write letters or, as today, go for a walk, just to get away from the stifling silence, apart from the constant ticking of the grandfather clock in the hallway. She grabbed her shawl from behind her bedroom door and stopped for a second to look at herself in the mirror. As she did so, she thought of her father's words and how he demeaned her very existence. She did love her father, but sometimes his words could cut through her like a knife.

She stopped for a second as she heard a knock on the front door, and her father muttering about callers coming at dinner time on a Sunday. She listened as her mother answered the door.

27

'Yes, what do you want?' Meg heard her mother ask.

Then, as she heard a voice she recognized instantly, she listened harder, with her stomach churning, hoping her father wouldn't realize who was standing on his doorstep.

'We just wondered, missus, have you any haytime jobs we can help you with? The weather's on the change, and we can see you've two fields full of hay to get into your barn.' It was Sam, the more confident of the two brothers, who did the asking, as Meg tiptoed to the top of the stairs to listen to the reply.

'Stay there, I'll ask my husband, but we don't usually work on a Sunday. And you lads should know that you are probably wasting your time anyway.' Agnes turned and asked Tom, even though he'd heard the conversation clearly enough himself.

Tom got up from his seat and looked at the two grinning young men on his doorstep. 'And what brings you to my doorstep then? By the looks of you both, you are a long way from home. It's mining that you are both good at. You are not from this dale – that I do know – so bugger off and don't be bothering me or mine again. I can do without your sort of help.' He grunted and then closed the porch door in their faces; he'd no time for the likes of them, and besides, it was Sunday and they should know better.

Meg waited for a second, listening to her mother chastising her father for not making use of both boys, and at Tom raising his voice in anger at being questioned for his reply. Then she raced to her bedroom window and looked out of it. She watched as Sam and Jack decided on their next course of action. Then, resolving that she would take charge, Meg quickly wrote a note, wrapped it around her bedside candle, securing it with one of her hair ribbons, and opened her bedroom window, making both boys look up at her at the sound of the sash window moving. She placed a finger to her lips to tell them to be quiet and then threw her message to them both.

She watched as Jack ran for the message as it landed inside the garden wall, right in the centre of some white asters. She held her breath as Jack retrieved it and untied the ribbon to read the contents. Both boys scanned it quickly and then glanced up at her, not saying a word, but putting up their thumbs to acknowledge the message that had been written to them.

'Megan, are you still upstairs? Get your arse down here and help your mother wash up. There's some chancers from over t' dale hanging about. I'll not have you wandering just yet,' her father bellowed up the stairs, as Meg quietly closed her window and watched as Jack and Sam made their way down the farm track.

'Yes, Father, I'll come down and help Mother. Is that who was knocking on the door?' Meg tried to sound surprised.

'Aye, good-for-nothings,' her father ranted.

'Good-for-nothings that would have got your hay in by nightfall,' Agnes muttered.

'You hold your tongue, woman. I can do it without the likes of them.' Tom went and sat down next to the empty fireside, got out his pipe and unfolded his paper. 'It'll wait until I can do it myself. It'll not rain today, so you just whisht.'

Agnes gave a glance to Meg as she picked up the tea towel and started to dry the plates and dishes, both of them saying nothing as they looked out of the window of the kitchen. Meg could make out the forms of Jack and Sam walking over the bridge down in the hamlet of Appersett. She had to get away, if she was to meet them at Hardraw Force, as she had suggested in her scribbled note to them.

She bided her time and tidied around the sink as her mother finished the washing-up, then went to sit across from her husband and knit. Not a word was said between any of them, and Meg felt her heart racing as she prayed for her father or mother to let her go and do what she wanted, as she looked out into the midsummer day. She went and sat down at the kitchen table and pretended to read her mother's magazine, watching her father as he folded his newspaper down by his side and then closed his eyes for his Sunday-afternoon nap.

'Mum, Mum, can I go out now?' Meg whispered, not wanting her father to hear her as she put the magazine away.

'Aye, go on – those two young men will be long gone. They were only after a bit of work, the poor devils. They could have had it and all, if it were up to me. Be back in good time, else your father will only worry,' Agnes whispered as she watched Meg rush to the door. Her daughter was only young; she should enjoy the summer's day and not be penned up like a caged animal longing for its freedom.

Meg ran along the track leading down the front field, her long skirts impeding her way as she opened the gate that led on to the road between Hawes and Garsdale. She caught her breath and looked to her right, at the small hamlet of Appersett. The few houses that were made of local stone and slate looked quiet, as usual on a Sunday, apart from old Mrs Baines sitting outside her house on a bench, knitting and admiring her garden full of cottage flowers.

She closed the gate behind her and made her way over the narrow bridge that spanned the River Ure, which flowed the full length of Wensleydale, getting larger as it joined the great River Ouse and then flowed to the sea. Usually she would have stood at the top of the bridge and admired the view of the village and the river, but today she had to make her way fast to the waterfall at Hardraw, where hopefully Jack and Sam would be waiting for her.

Meg felt her heart pounding as she ran along the roadway to Hardraw, ignoring the fields full of summer flowers and the wild dog rose that was flowering abundantly in the hedgerows. She'd no time for nature today; her head was set on reaching the Green Dragon at Hardraw and then following the stream that ran by its side, up to the most spectacular waterfall in the district – a distance of a good mile and a half, just far enough to feel away from neighbours' prying eyes. She caught her breath as she walked over the bridge to the Green Dragon Inn and then through the doorway that led to the inn's bar and stables, ignoring any men who looked at her as they sat and drank their gill.

The waterfall was well known to locals, and plenty of people were strolling along the river's bank, admiring the wildness of it and the spectacular falls at the end of the deep, dark gorge, which fell nearly one hundred feet, making it an amazing sight. Meg glanced around her; she recognized nobody, and was thankful that the people strolling on a Sunday afternoon did not know her, as she spotted Jack and Sam sitting on the circular wall of the bandstand, which was halfway to the falls.

'I thought you weren't going to make it.' Sam stood up and smiled at Meg as she ran towards them both.

'Aye, your father gave us short shrift. He's a man of few words, isn't he?' Jack stood up and joined his brother.

Meg stopped in her tracks and caught her breath. 'I had to wait until he was asleep. He said I'd to stay at home until you good-for-nothings had made yourselves scarce.' She grinned as she recovered herself and looked at both lads.

'Cheeky bugger, he doesn't even know us,' Sam exclaimed. 'Anyway, you've made it now and we can at least have an hour together, so it was worth the trail over.'

'I'm so glad you have. I was hoping I'd see you both again. Even though I've had lecture after lecture from both my mother and my father about the ways of you miners, and that I should set my sights higher.' Meg linked her arms through those of the boys, as they walked up the narrow path that led to the waterfall. 'I'll see who I want, and they won't stop me. Anyway, my mother was grumbling that my father had turned down your offer of help with the hay, as she'd have let you help us. It's just my father, really; nobody but a wealthy farmer will be good enough for me, in his eyes.' Meg dropped her arms when the path narrowed and the roar of water could be heard, as they made their way up the tree-lined glen.

'It would serve him right if it rained, the moaning old bugger,' Sam shouted above the surging river water. 'It's been dry for the last weeks, so I'm amazed there's plenty of water in the beck,' he went on, as he balanced on the well-trodden track.

'Yes, there is.' Meg trod carefully between both boys, hanging onto the small sprigs of hazel and sycamore that were growing along the steep sides of the ravine, to keep her balance. Then, as they rounded a corner, the waterfall came into view: a raging torrent of water coming over the lip of the fell above, and splashing down into a deep, dark pool that ebbed and flowed down into the beck that ran through Hardraw.

'God, that's amazing!' Jack gasped as they all stood in the glade among the wet, dark boulders at the side of the waterfall. The spray hit their faces, and the summer

33

sun, when it could make its way through the surrounding foliage, shone and sparkled on the gushing water. 'We've plenty of falls up Swaledale, but nothing like this.'

'I knew you two would like it here. Look, if you follow the path around, you can stand right under the waterfall. There's a small cave behind the fall, and you can stand and look behind it, if the rocks aren't too slippery.'

'Come on, we'll hold on to one another and go there.' Sam reached for Meg's hand and Jack took the other as they gingerly stepped along the path and under the waterfall. 'This is so special,' said Sam, as he laughed and whooped in excitement when they all stood in the middle of the falls.

'Look at the rainbow that the sun is making on the droplets. It's like magic.' Meg held her breath and squeezed both brothers' hands.

'It's wonderful, and made better by having you with us, Meg.' Jack looked at her and smiled.

'Ah, you soft old lump. Don't let him win you over with his words. He's not half as clever as I am.' Sam squeezed Meg's hand harder and glared at his brother.

'Ah, shut up, you are only jealous because you can't flatter like I do. You've not got a romantic bone in your body.' Jack leaned in front of Meg and pushed his brother softly.

'Now don't you start falling out over me, you two, and spoil the day. We are just friends for now – and that's how I like it. I don't know about you two, but I'm getting quite wet with the spray, and cold. I'm going to walk

34

onto the path and back out of the glade and into the sunshine.' Meg ran her hand down her skirts, feeling the damp on them, and looked at Sam to move.

'Before we do, give me a kiss, Meg – a magic kiss behind the waterfall.' Sam grinned and waited, looking at the disbelief on his brother's face at the cheek of his request.

Meg hesitated for a moment. 'I'll give you both a kiss, because I think the same of both of you.' She leaned forward and kissed Sam on his cheek, then turned sideways and kissed Jack on his cheek, making him blush. She looked at them both and smiled. 'There, I don't think any of us will forget this day, it's so magical.' Meg gazed around her at the marvellous colours made by the waterfall, at the moss-filled glade and the beautifully clear water; it truly was a marvellous place.

'I expected a bit more than that,' Sam said cheekily, bringing her back to her senses.

Jack glared at his brother: how dare he! He'd been the first to spot Meg at the Christmas dance; he was going to have to state his case in no uncertain manner on the ride home, and make sure Sam knew that he had set his sights on Meg Oversby.

'Well, that's all you are getting, so move.' Meg pushed Sam gently and was relieved when he walked carefully back along the ledge and onto the river bank. For a minute she had felt a slight panic when she realized that she was on her own and nobody knew where she was, with two young men she hardly knew. Her parents' warnings about the brothers were ringing in her ears as she walked back along the path and into the wider glade beyond the waterfall. 'I'd better not stop much longer. By the time I've walked back home it will be at least five, and time for milking. Even though it's Sunday, the two cows we have won't wait and don't know what day it is.'

'Do you do the milking?' Jack asked.

'Sometimes, but I usually help my father, and I've various other jobs to do before evening.' Meg hesitated for a moment. 'I'll be coming to Gunnerside on Thursday, as my mother supplies the shop there with our butter. Can we meet? Or will you both be too busy? I was going to climb up to the mines to find you anyway, even if you hadn't shown your faces today.'

'I'll not be able to leave the smelting mill; once it is up and fired, I can't leave my job.' Jack's face dropped a mile.

'Hard luck, brother. I can make it, Meg. They won't miss me at the pit face for an hour. Where are we to meet? Just up the gill from Gunnerside there's a huge sycamore tree; it's the last big tree before you reach the open fell. We both pass it every day on our way to the mine. Do you think you could meet me there, and I'll bring my bait to eat while we talk?' Sam waited for an answer and smiled at the look of disappointment on his brother's face.

'I think I know where you mean, and I'll manage to find it anyway. Is one o'clock alright? If I'm not there, don't worry; it'll be because my father has changed his mind about me joining him. It'll depend on his mood that day.' Meg sighed, for it seemed everything was determined

36

by her father's mood. 'I'm sorry you'll not be there, Jack. I hope we can meet again soon.'

She looked up at the sky; it was beginning to cloud over, and the rain that had threatened all day was on its way, she feared.

'I'm going to have to go, the day's worsening.' Meg looked at the two brothers.

'Aye, we will have to get home. It's a long trek back to Gunnerside, and we will have to take our pit pony back to its stable before it's missed. But it's been worth it, just to see you again.' Sam held out his hand for Meg's, but she didn't take it.

'I'm going. I'll see you on Thursday, hopefully, Sam. And Jack, you take care of yourself.' Meg picked up her skirts and ran back down the riverside track as she felt the first raindrops fall. She hadn't time to look back at the brothers, for she had to get home before she was found missing, and before her father lost his temper over the hay that was about to be ruined.

'Where the hell is she?' Tom Oversby swore and scowled at his wife. Both of them were soaked to the skin, with rain pouring down their faces, as they tried to salvage as much of their hay as they could.

'It's no good blaming our Meg. You've had all day to get the hay in yourself, and them two lads knocked on the door after dinner – it could have been in dry, and we would be right with the world. Sometimes it doesn't do to follow your neighbours and abide by the Good Book, especially if you are so stubborn as not to get help; and

37

it doesn't make sense at all, seeing as you never attend chapel nor church.' Agnes forked the hay from the laden hay-sled into the square, stone-built barn and looked out on the field, which was still half-full of haycocks getting wetter by the minute.

'If she'd have been here, we'd have had it in on time. Why you let her out of your sight, I don't know.' Tom grabbed the horse's reins and led the horse and the now-empty sled back into the field. 'I'll get the hay that's in the lee of the land; it's not that wet, but the rest will have to be left. Bloody weather – it could have held off until tomorrow.' The rain dripped off the crown of Tom's cap, and his waistcoat and shirt clung to him as he stepped out with a hesitant horse to the bottom of the hay field, where the haystacks were sheltered from the summer storm by a group of trees along the beck's edge.

Agnes sighed. It was always Meg's fault, never his, and yet he was the one who always turned help down from neighbours, and who hadn't made the most of the good days that the Lord had sent him. Tom was a difficult man to live with, and sometimes she wished herself a different life – somewhere she and Meg were appreciated, and not treated like second-class citizens and cursed at and blamed when things went wrong.

She picked up her pitchfork and stabbed the partly dry hay, throwing it up into the hayloft, frightening a roosting barn owl as she did so. It flew out of the barn like a silent ghost and was chased by a flock of crows, until it made its escape into the woods that followed the beck side. She watched as the owl swooped and dived and ducked the onslaught, birds of the day attacking a night creature that was in their territory. Men, she thought, were not too dissimilar: anything that seemed to be weak was often shunned and derided by them. But sometimes they were wrong, and the weaker ones were perhaps the stronger, just not in that place or time. After all, the barn owl could spot the slightest movement in the dark night, when the crow would fly blindly and would have to be content to roost until the morning. Tom was like the crow: blind to Meg growing up; and one day she would retaliate and he would not like what she would say to him.

Agnes had noticed how Meg had bitten her tongue of late, and how she was beginning to lose respect for her father and his harsh words. If he wasn't careful, Meg would leave them one day; she was old enough now, with a good head on her shoulders, and bonny with it. Agnes stopped for a second and looked out of the barn doorway. Thank God: Meg had turned up; through the pouring rain she could see her, bedraggled and sodden, helping her father load the sled before driving the horse up the steep meadow towards the barn. She heard the coarse, harsh words that Tom was yelling at his daughter, as tears ran down Meg's face and mixed with the rain.

Tom Oversby was a bastard and she should never have married him; she should have listened to her parents when they warned her and begged her not to wed him. But instead she had been smitten with him and, despite her parents' pleas, they had married within six months. Six months later she was regretting that wedding day. Tom never hit her, but the constant verbal abuse and belittling of her ground her down; and now he was doing the same to Meg. Agnes breathed in and stepped out into the rain, grabbing the horse's harness as it, too, dropped its head and looked worn down by the harsh words.

'She's bloody back. She's been trailing down into Appersett, visiting that Baines lass, or so she tells me. The gormless bitch hadn't noticed it was raining,' Tom snarled as he started to unload the cart. 'Look at it – this is worth nowt!' He forked the hay down from the cart, and Meg and her mother both stood with their heads down, knowing that it was no good saying anything when he was in such a mood.

'It's brightening up. Look, it's only been a good hard shower.' Agnes lifted her head and looked down the valley towards Wensleydale. 'The rest will soon dry out in the morning – all's not lost, Tom,' she said as the rain began to ease.

'You know nowt, you stupid woman. Take this stupid bitch home with you, and get me some dry clothes. I don't want to see either of your ugly faces again today, if I can help it,' Tom snorted, and stabbed forkfuls of the damp hay into the barn. 'We'll be bloody lucky if the barn doesn't combust, with this damp stuff inside it. If it does, it's you two's fault,' he shouted at Agnes and Meg as they walked away together.

'I hope it does go up in flames – and him with it,' Meg whispered to her mother.

'Shush now, he will hear you,' Agnes muttered.

'Good, because I hate him – father or no father.' Meg turned her head and watched him on top of the hay-filled sled, forking the hay off. 'I hope he falls off the sled and breaks his neck.'

'Quiet, child. Stop it with your wicked thoughts – you don't mean them.' Agnes put her arm around her daughter and concentrated on her walk home, along with worrying about just how long Meg could live under the same roof as her father without coming to real blows.

Meg looked at her reflection in the wardrobe mirror as she sat on the edge of her bed. Supper had been spent in silence, her father not talking to her or her mother. So as soon as it was dark and all her jobs were done, she had decided to retreat to the privacy of her bedroom and leave her mother to sit alone with her bad-tempered father. How her mother put up with his ways, she did not know; but unless she wanted to cause a family scandal, she had no choice, Meg presumed. She knew one thing: she herself was not prepared to take much more of it. He was a bully, but he was not always going to dictate her life – of that she was sure. However, if she wanted a lift over to Gunnerside with him on Thursday, she would have to act like the perfect daughter and do whatever he bade, to gain his trust.

She looked out at the moonlit night as her candle flickered in her small bedroom over the porch, and prayed for a fine day tomorrow, to help him in with the dried hay and get back in his good books. She had to go and meet Sam, although it was a shame that Jack would not be there. In truth, she liked Jack slightly more than

Sam. He was quiet and not as sure of himself, and she had caught him a time or two giving her a secretive glance when he thought she was not looking. But it was Sam she was to meet on Thursday, so that was that.

She blew out the candle, pulled the counterpane around her chin and gazed up at the ceiling. Please, please let the sun be shining and her father in a good mood in the morning, else life would not be worth living.

4

The swallows and swifts screeched and dived above Meg's head as she climbed up beside her father on the small donkey cart as it stood in the farmyard, loaded with butter and spare produce from the small garden that was Meg's pride and joy.

'Make sure you ask how Mary is. I know she's not been so good of late.' Agnes looked up at her daughter, who looked exceptionally beautiful in the early-morning sunshine. Her long, dark hair was tied back neatly with a blue ribbon, and her plain blue dress matched her eyes, while the small binding of lace softened the look around her neck and cuffs.

'I will, and I'll make sure I get a good price for the lettuce and cabbage.' Meg smiled down at her mother, wishing that her father would get a move on in stirring the horse and cart out of the yard, before her mother picked up on her feeling of excitement. Her father she barely needed to speak to, but her mother knew her all too well, and Meg was frightened that at the slightest indication of the happiness and butterflies flitting about in her stomach, her mother would start to question why.

'Take care on that road, and I'll look forward to seeing you back later in the day.' Agnes stood back and watched as her husband and daughter trotted out of the yard and down the farm path, stopping at the gate at the bottom of the field for Meg to climb down and open it, as her father drove the horse and cart out onto the main road. She watched as they carried on their way, and hoped that both would be wary of their words to one another on their trip. It had been a hard week since that rain-drenched Sunday, but at least the pressure had been taken off them with the new week bringing good weather, enabling the remaining hay to be gathered, and Tom to simmer down and not take his wrath out upon Meg. A day over in Swaledale together might bring them a little closer. Neither had an agenda, except to go there and come back, once the butter and vegetables had been delivered. Tom's spirits were always a bit higher after a gill or two and a catch-up with one or two locals in the King's Head each week. It also gave her a chance to have a day to herself, without having to worry about the friction that seemed to be building between father and daughter. It was beginning to wear her down, and it was good to have time to sit and enjoy the day without any concerns.

Meg and her father sat silently as the horse trotted along the road past the Green Dragon Inn, which brought back memories of the stolen afternoon with Sam and Jack; and then onwards, passing the magnificent Simonstone Hall, before climbing steeply up the moorland road with its sweeping bends and rises that tapered along the fell edge, gradually bringing the stunning scene of rich pastureland and the glittering River Swale into view, down in the bottom of the valley. Meanwhile, the fell tops were busy and filled with the noise of the lead-miners at work.

'Look at the buggers, they are ruining the fellsides with their hunt for lead,' Tom growled as they dropped down to the valley floor, following the River Swale's banks through shaded glades and yellow, buttercup-filled hay meadows. 'They'll not stop until there is nothing left of these fell tops. And what for? To line some rich man's pockets down in London, or the like.'

'But there has always been lead-mining here. I remember my mother telling me when I was small that the Vikings were the first to find it, when they invaded our lands,' Meg answered back.

'They might have done, but they didn't make a mess like this lot have done lately. It's all in the name of greed,' Tom moaned as he flicked the reins over the back of his horse, urging it on through the small village of Muker. 'There wasn't half these houses when I was a lad. Now they are built with stones from the beck bottom, and crammed to the rafters with miners and their families, living any end up. There's more miners than farmers here – this new industrial age has a lot to answer for.'

They drove on in silence.

'Get out my way!' Tom shouted at a drove of ten

Galloway packhorses with lead-ingots strapped to the side of them, and the drover dawdling as the poor animals dealt with the weight. 'If they are not knackered now, they will be by the time they get to Richmond. I bet they will be thankful for the newfangled railway line that's been built there, else they would still be hauling lead to the mouth of the River Tees at Stockton. On their return journey they will get no rest, either, as they will be made to carry stores or coal back to the mines, after going up to the Tan Hill coal-mines perhaps, poor buggers.' Tom looked ahead of him as he passed the packhorses; the lead horse had a bell that tinkled loudly, making his own horse toss its head and shy. 'Get on, you soft ha'p'orth. It's only a bell,' he swore at his old horse, as she jolted the cart and took offence at the noise she was unfamiliar with.

'Don't be frightened, Blossom. They've a lot harder life than you, old girl,' Meg shouted down at the only horse they had on the farm.

'Aye, it's no life over here. This dale is usually cut off in winter from our end of the dale, as well you know. You've got to be hardy to survive here,' Tom said. 'This 'un wouldn't last five minutes with twenty stones of lead across her back every day.'

Meg looked around her and couldn't help but think that although, far above her in the fells, was an industry that dealt in filth and grime, down below the valley floor was a beautiful place. The meadows were lush and the ancient stone walls ran up and down the valley sides, with many a well-to-do house set back out of sight behind strategically planted trees. No wonder the Vikings had made their way up the River Ouse and then up the Swale tributary, to the valley that bore their long-forgotten names right along its length – Muker meaning 'the narrow acre' in Norse, and Gunnerside being named after the Viking king, Gunner, and his summer pasture. They must have settled in the summer months when all was pleasant, Meg thought, because in winter it was like her father said: the dale was a grim place to be, cut off from the rest of civilization, sometimes for months on end. She looked up as they crossed the bridge into Gunnerside, passing the blacksmith's and the forge, her father bringing Blossom to a halt in the narrow street between the King's Head and the shop owned by Mary and Harry Battersby, whom she had always known as a surrogate aunt and uncle.

'I'll give you a hand unloading the cart, and then I'll take Blossom to the forge for young Calvert to look at her; she's needing reshoeing, so he can measure her up and then next week we'll get them put on her. I shouldn't be long, as he'll know from our past visits what I need. Then I'll go for a gill and a bite to eat at the King's. You stay at Harry and Mary's, or wait outside the door of the King's Head. I don't want to see your face in there, though. It's no place for a young woman.' Tom watched as his daughter climbed down from the trap and picked up one of the baskets that were filled with butter. He then followed close behind her, with a sack of vegetables and the other basket of butter.

'Now then, Tom, Meg, I thought it was about time for you two to be showing your faces. The old lass 'as just

47

shouted down from upstairs and asked if you'd been or not.' Harry Battersby took the laden basket out of Meg's hands and patted her on the back. 'Well, it's like you said last week: your mother's been busy and sent us plenty; and by the looks of your father, he's been busy in the garden and all.' Harry glanced into the hessian sack and grinned at Tom, who didn't contradict him from thinking the vegetables were all his hard work.

'How is Mary, Harry? Is she improving any?' Tom asked, as Meg unpacked her basket and placed the warm, almost melting butter on the marble slabs in the cool pantry of the little village shop.

'Nay, she's not so good. In fact, she's going downhill fast. I dare say I'll not have her much longer, and then I don't know what I'll do.' Harry looked down at his feet, holding back his emotions in front of the man he had known the best part of his life. 'She says she'd like to see your Agnes – will you be good enough to bring her over with you next week? They've always been close, haven't they? Maybe she wants to have one last talk to her?' Harry lifted his head and looked at Tom; the man was a different breed from himself, for Tom was hard and didn't show his emotions, so as he spoke he tried to hold back with his own.

'I'll bring her over, Harry. But now I've got to take my horse to the Calvert lad, as she needs reshoeing; and go for a bite to eat and drink before she takes us home. Meg here has brought her own bread and cheese with her and is going to stay with you or wait outside until I'm ready. Either way, tell her not to get in your way; or she'll help, if you want something doing.'

48

Tom made for the doorway of the shop, which was stocked with almost anything anybody could want. He wasn't going to stay and listen to Harry Battersby's woes, as he had enough of his own. Besides, it was a warm day and he'd looked forward to a long, cool drink of the King's Head's finest porter. He patted his friend on the back; although they were both the same age, Harry's hair was still dark and he had a ruddy complexion, making him look younger than he was. The years of serving behind a shop counter had not weathered his skin, like they had Tom's. But in his eyes there was a sadness, for Harry knew all too well that his wife was dying.

'Right you are. Meg, do you want to pop your head round the door and spend a minute with Mary, as she'd appreciate seeing a new face?' Harry Battersby smiled at Meg as she put the empty baskets down and started to unpack her father's sack of fresh vegetables, placing them on the wooden table outside the shop window, following in her father's footsteps out of the shop.

'I can, Uncle Harry, and if there is anything else you want of me, just ask.' Meg felt that she couldn't do anything other than give the heartbroken man her support, even though she was counting the minutes until she could go and meet Sam. She made her way through the shop, taking in the smell of paraffin, soap and a mixture of scents that assailed her senses. The shop was full of everything the farmers and miners in the dale needed, from packets of seeds to candles, tea and tins on shelves that reached to the ceiling, and fresh food on the counter, not to mention what lay in the dairy behind the shop: flitches of bacon, butter, eggs and milk were kept cool in the spotless whitewashed room between the shop and the stairs that led to the couple's living quarters.

'Aye, just go up the stairs. She'll have heard your voice.' Harry went into the dairy to check how much butter had been delivered to him, and to send the money owing back with Meg, leaving her to climb the wooden stairs to the bedroom where Mary Battersby lay.

'Is that you, Megan? I thought I could hear your voice.' Mrs Battersby raised herself on her pillows and smiled at the young woman in front of her.

'How are you feeling, Aunt Mary? You look a little improved today,' Meg lied as she looked at the skeletal form of Mary and remembered her when she was such a beautiful woman.

'Do I? I don't feel it. I think these old bones are about done, lass.' Mary reached over for the glass of water on her bedside table, but couldn't quite manage to reach it.

'Here, let me help you.' Meg reached for the glass of water and stood over her as Mary took a delicate sip, before passing it to Meg and placing her head back down onto the pillows, then closing her eyes. Meg couldn't help but notice the stench of ailing flesh as Mary moved; her breast cancer was eating her alive, and there was nothing anybody could do about it. 'It's a lovely day out there, Aunt Mary, the meadows are full of buttercups and all the farmers are waiting to start their haytime. We've just finished, so my father's glad to have got it in for another year.'

'Aye, Swaledale is always a couple of weeks behind Wensleydale in starting its harvest; it always has been that way. How I wish I could see them buttercups and meadows – you make the most of those sights while you are young. Life's too short, and is gone before you know it. Don't you waste your time with me, lass, go and enjoy the day.' Mary fought for her breath and tried to smile at the young woman looking worried in front of her. 'Tell your uncle I'm going to have a sleep now, and for him not to worry.'

'I'll tell him, Aunt Mary.' Meg turned round and left the dying woman behind her. It was a terrible thing to happen to one of the nicest women she had ever known, and she felt sorry for the couple, whom she had known to work hard all their lives.

'I know, she's seen enough of you and wants to sleep. It's all she does nowadays. Thank you for giving her a minute or two, though; she will have appreciated seeing you. Now, here's your money for your mother and father – it's all there. And if you can ask your mother if she'll come and see Mary next week, we'd both appreciate it; Mary keeps asking for her.' Harry passed Meg the money and bit his lip, trying to control himself.

'I will, Uncle Harry. Would you like me to do anything else while I'm here?' Meg held her breath; she had to ask him, but what she really wanted was to escape and make her way to Sam.

'Nay, you are alright, lass. Go and enjoy your dinner in the sunshine, as this is no place for you to be at the moment.' Harry glanced up the stairs as he heard a low moan from the bedroom above. 'Here, take a barley-sugar twist, it can be your pudding.' He passed a heavy jar filled with golden-orange barley-sugar twists over to her and opened the lid for Meg to help herself.

'Thank you.' Meg took one of them and then picked up her empty baskets and made for the door. 'I'll not forget to tell my mother. I hope Aunt Mary improves.'

'She'll not be doing that, lass, I only wish she would,' Harry Battersby replied, as Meg stepped out into the summer sun.

'Are you done at the Battersbys' already?' Tom turned and looked at his daughter as she put the empty baskets into the donkey cart and walked over to him, while he held his horse for the blacksmith as he examined its feet.

'Yes, Mary's in a lot of pain. She was glad to see me, but I don't think they wanted me to stay today.' Meg reached for her dinner of bread and cheese, wrapped in a piece of plain paper, from under the seat of the cart.

'Aye, well, I've nearly done here and then I'll just have an odd 'un in the King's. What are you going to do?' Tom looked at his lass and wished she'd been longer in the shop.

'I'll go and have my dinner up at the gill edge and enjoy the day, like Aunt Mary said I should. Do you want me back for two, or a bit earlier?' Meg asked, knowing the answer before she heard the reply.

'Nay, two will do. I've a bit of business to do, so there's no great rush. But don't you go trailing – and behave yourself,' Tom growled as he watched Meg make her way up the path between the forge and the gillside, to where there was a well-known beauty spot and seat to

52

enjoy the view. He'd have to sup up and catch up on the gossip quickly today, else she'd be moaning or up to no good, he thought, as he left his horse with the blacksmith's lad.

Meg picked up her skirts and ran along the gillside; she felt bad about lying to her father, but technically she wasn't lying, just not telling the whole truth. She *was* going to have her lunch by the side of the gill and admire the view – albeit the view of Sam Alderson, and not simply down into the dale. She climbed up the rocky stream's side, slipping occasionally in her rush to walk the half-mile out of the village towards the tree line, before the wild moorland opened up and gave way to the fells. She could see the last large tree and, underneath it, she could just make out the form of Sam sitting there. He looked to be eating his dinner, dappled by the sunlight shining through the fresh green leaves of the sycamore.

'I thought you weren't going to show.' Sam looked up from his seat at the base of the tree, as Meg caught her breath and stood with her hands on her hips, looking down at him.

'I couldn't get away. I had to go and see Mrs Battersby and give her a few minutes. The poor woman, I think she's dying.' Meg sat down by the side of Sam and looked at him. 'You are as black as the back of our chimney! How can you eat your sandwiches with hands as mucky as that?' She noted the big black thumb marks on his white bread, which contained beef dripping, and pulled a face.

'You get used to it. I can't come out of the earth all clean and pristine, else I wouldn't be a miner. A bit of muck never hurt anyone.' Sam finished off his sandwich as Meg looked at his soiled black face.

'I can't stay long. My father thinks I'm only just outside the village, not half a mile up this gill. He's in the King's Head, but once he's caught up on the gossip and had a drink or two, he'll want to get back home.' Meg unfolded the brown paper from around her bread and cheese and started to eat it. 'Is Jack alright? I take it he definitely couldn't make it, then?' she said between mouthfuls.

'Now what do you want him for, when you've got me? But aye, he's alright; he thinks of work and nowt else. He's got this notion of buying himself some land. He'll have to work a bloody long time for these bastards, to be able to do that.' Sam pointed his thumb up the fell to where the main mines were.

'So, he thinks himself a farmer, does he?' Meg grinned, thinking of Jack and his quiet ways. 'And what about you: do you not want to do more in life?'

'I make enough from mining, and when the Sir Francis level is properly opened, I'll make my fortune. It's better than working with thick-headed sheep; they are ignorant animals. I'm the better prospect, you know – you don't want to be looking at our Jack. He will never make nothing of himself.' Sam leaned back against the tree, pulled his clay pipe out of his pocket and lit it with a Vesta from his case. 'You look bonny today in that

54

dress. Did you wear it specially for me?' He gazed at Meg while she sat upright next to him.

'I might have done, but then again it was the first thing I came across this morning,' Meg lied, for she had taken at least half an hour pondering what to wear in order to look her best, but not raise suspicion from her parents.

'Well, tha does look a bonny lass in it. I might be in need of a kiss before you leave me, because tha does look such a picture. Besides, I didn't walk this mile down the fellside just to pass the time of day. I want to court you, Meg Oversby, and I aim to get one over on my brother, because he's got designs on you, too.' Sam sat up and dampened the tobacco in his pipe with his finger, before putting it back in his pocket. 'Oh, bugger!' he said quickly and fished his pipe back out of his pocket. 'Wrong pocket! Left for a light, and right for a fright! I nearly blew us both up then, by putting my pipe in with the gunpowder, which I always keep in my right pocket. We'd have a lot to answer for then. But, you see, that's what you do to me. I lose my head when I look at you.' Sam ran his fingers through his hair and stared down at the young lass under the tree. He meant to bed her, if he had his way; and he'd made a bet with Robert Winn when he had told him of his liaison, saying that Meg would be his by the time summer ended, if not sooner.

'Gunpowder! You could have blown us both to kingdom come, you idiot. I think you'll just have to see me a bit more often, won't you? And then you can get used to me, and me to you. Let's make this our meeting place once a week, on a Thursday, when I usually come over with my father. Do you think Jack would be able to join us sometimes as well? Father would probably kill us both if you called at the farm again, so we've got to keep it a secret.' Meg stood up and looked at Sam; she knew he was smitten with her, but she didn't feel quite as strongly about him. Although he was good-looking, he was a bit cocky for her, and she knew what he was really after.

'Aye, alright. But never mind Jack, you want nothing with him. I'd better be heading back – it's a fair walk up to the mine. Any chance of a kiss to make my day?' Sam puckered his lips and squinted, as he closed his eyes in hope.

'It'd be like kissing Old Nick himself, with that mucky face. Next week you can perhaps chance your luck, Sam Alderson, when you've a clean face and know me a little better.' Meg started to walk away; she wasn't going to give herself that easily.

'Nay, be damned.' Sam grabbed Meg by the arm and pulled her back, holding her in his arms, and kissed her long and hard as she pretended to protest. 'Now you are as black as Old Nick's wife.' He laughed as he let her go, looking at the hand-marks on her arms and the dirt on her face.

'Sam Alderson, I don't know if I want to see you again next week after that,' Meg protested and laughed, then washed the dirt off herself in the river, before starting to walk down the fellside. She stopped to turn and shout at him, 'Remember me to Jack. And next week have a wash before you meet me.'

'You want nowt with him. It's me that you need, and always will be,' Sam shouted after her, before starting on the long walk back to work.

5

'Thank heavens you are both back. I've been counting the minutes, because I just don't know what to do.' Agnes met Meg and Tom, looking distressed and carrying a letter in her hand that the postman had delivered that morning. 'It's from your sister, Anne. I'm afraid it is bad news, but I don't know what we can do to help.' She brushed back a tear and looked at her husband as he took the letter from her hand, before seeing to the horse's needs. 'It's cholera, Tom. We can't go, we can't bring it back to the dale, no matter how much Anne is begging you to go.'

Tom stood in the bright sunshine and read, with trembling hands, the letter that had brought dark clouds to his day:

Dulcie Street
Liverpool

Dear Tom and Agnes,
I'm writing to tell you that I have lost my Bob,

last week to cholera. I, too, have the most terrible stomach cramps and have never been off the privy for the last day or two. I fear that I will be following my dear Bob shortly, unless the good Lord intervenes, as I am writing this on what I believe to be my deathbed. I'm begging you to see to my burial and to save our son, who is so far unaffected. I know that you will do right by us all, my dear brother. Dan is, after all, your nephew and is your own flesh and blood. Come and save him, if no one else.

With my most grateful thanks, and with my love on earth and in eternity.

Your loving sister

Anne

Tom stood and looked at the letter, then scowled as he took in the news of his sister's predicament. 'She made her bed when she walked out on my father, when he needed her most. Leaving him here in his dotage, for me and you to look after. She should never have gone to that hellhole of Liverpool with that bloody Bob, who was worth nowt and has never done a day's work in his life. What does she expect me to do? I'm not trailing to that godforsaken place, so don't you be fretting.'

'But she needs you, Tom! She's your sister – do right by her and see that she gets a proper funeral. And there is her lad, he'll be almost sixteen now. I know there's not much between our Meg and him, although none of us have ever clapped eyes on him, so we've no idea what he looks like or what he does. She's begging you to take care of him. Surely you are not that heartless?' Agnes looked at her husband, who had never forgiven his sister for following her heart instead of staying on the family farm; he'd not spoken to her since she'd moved to the hellhole of Dulcie Street, with its terraced slums and open sewers. He was unable to understand how she could leave behind a life of reasonable wealth and comfort for the back streets and slums of Liverpool and a useless, ale-swilling dock worker.

Tom turned his back on his Agnes. 'I'll see to the horse and then I'll be in for my supper after I've milked the cows. I don't want her name mentioned again to me. She'll get buried by the authorities anyway, if she's got cholera; and the lad's old enough to look after himself. They are both nowt to me.' Tom screwed up the letter in his hand and threw it down to the ground. 'You can stop your wailing and all; Anne never did owt for you when you were run off your feet and carrying our bairns. So stop looking at me with those eyes, and don't think you'll change my mind.'

Meg watched as her father led the horse and cart off towards the stable, before she walked to her mum's side, picking up the discarded letter from the farmyard and passing it to her. 'Don't fret, Mum. He'll do something. Father's not that heartless. Let him go and mull things over while he's milking. You know what he's like.' Meg put her arm through her mum's and walked with her back into the house. She'd never met her Aunty Anne, and now it sounded as if she never would. She'd barely ever been mentioned, and she had no idea she had a cousin called Dan. Would he die of the terrible disease of cholera as well, so that all the family would be wiped out by the creeping death that stalked the slums and streets of the city, or would he survive?

'He's a hard man, your father, and he never forgives. He used to be so close to Anne, we both were; we used to go everywhere together. And then that Bob turned up, with his fancy words and posh suits, and it all changed. Everyone tried to tell Anne that he was worth nothing, but she wouldn't listen and ran off with him to Liverpool, just when her father needed her most. Your father never understood that her heart led her there, as he's always that hard-headed.' Agnes wiped her nose with her handkerchief and pulled the kettle onto the hearth to boil. 'Now, how was Mary? It seems all my old friends are dying around me,' she sobbed.

'She's really ill, Mum, and I don't think she will be with us much longer. She's asked you to go and see her next week. I think she wants to settle things before she leaves us all,' Meg said as she spooned leaf tea into a teapot.

'I'll go and see Mary next week, God bless her. At least she has had a good life, married to Harry, but I don't know what he'll do without her. That shop of his takes some running.' Agnes filled the teapot with the boiling water and stirred the tea leaves before letting it stand, while she mulled over Anne's request. 'Your Aunty Anne will need to settle things with your father; that's why she will want to see him. I don't want him to go, but I know that he should, perhaps just to see her for five minutes; he'd not catch anything if he was only there that long. He could at least see that Dan will be alright and will have a roof over his head. He's not seen him since he was a baby. I don't know . . . it doesn't seem five minutes since we were all footloose and fancy free, and now two of us are going to meet our Maker. I suppose I should be thankful for my lot.' She sat down and poured herself a cup of tea.

'Try not to worry, Mum. Is it bacon and eggs for supper?' Meg pulled the stool out from under the table and stood on it to reach the rolled flitch of bacon that hung in the driest corner of the kitchen, on a bacon hook hammered into the low oak beams. She struggled with the weight of the flitch as her mum nodded her head and walked over to help her.

'Aye, that'll do tonight. It's as good as anything, and it'll be more than poor Anne and Mary will be having, God bless their souls. I'll speak to your father tonight, when he's had time to think. He can't do anything about them in Liverpool. Don't you get involved, else he'll dig his heels in even more. I'll talk to him when we are in bed tonight.'

Meg got the sharp knife used for carving any meat that the family ate and started to slice the flitch into rashers, placed on the kitchen table. 'I don't know 'em, so I can't say anything, can I? But if it was my sister, I'd be supporting her.'

'Aye, well, that'll never happen. But that's another tale.' Agnes sighed; life was a challenge, of that she was sure.

*

Meg lay in her bed and listened to her parents talking in mumbled voices through the wall. They'd been chatting for over an hour now, and surely her mum must be winning, with her concern for her sister-in-law and her son. They'd be 'townies', as her father had heard them being called; a different breed from northern dales folk, and he had no time for them. The morning would reveal whether her mum had won the argument or not, and her father would either be as black as a thundercloud in mood or would be making himself scarce to keep out of everybody's way. Either way, it was good for her, as she was no longer the centre of their world and had not been asked who she had seen on the visit to Gunnerside.

She smiled, remembering her meeting with Sam. He was full of cheek – perhaps a little too confident, she thought, as she remembered him asking for a kiss. Jack was perhaps the better of the two and certainly earned more than Sam; working in the smelting works was a science, as they watched the ore melting at exactly the right temperature. But it wasn't about the money – it was about who was the better man of the two, she reminded herself. Jack was deeper in mood than Sam and slightly more handsome. She blushed at the thought of the two men as she pulled the covers up around her and remembered the meeting under the sycamore tree. Next Thursday could not come quickly enough. She'd be counting the hours, let alone the days, and she might be willing next time for a kiss from either brother.

*

63

'You needn't do your usual jobs this morning, Megan. Instead, put on your boots and walk into Hawes and catch the Penny Post with this letter.' Agnes took the hand-written letter down from the mantelpiece and placed it next to Meg's bowl of porridge. 'The sooner it goes, the better.'

'The sooner it goes, the sooner I say goodbye to my hard-earned brass. Because I'll never see any of that again,' Tom growled and pushed his chair back, after finishing his breakfast. 'I'm off up to the top pasture – there's some thistles to get rid of.'

Agnes said nothing in reply as she watched him leave the farmhouse and make his way up to the pastures that led to the fellside. 'That's the best place for him, prickly old bugger,' she whispered to Meg.

'So, he's let you write to Aunty Anne?' Meg picked up the letter and looked at the envelope, addressed to both her aunt and Dan.

'Aye, I've got him to do that, and send them some money. At best it will give Anne something to pay a doctor with; and at worst it will give her a decent burial, and happen enough money to keep the roof over Dan's head for a while. At least he's old enough to make his own way, unless he's like his useless father. It's the best we can do for them at this time.'

'Well, at least it will ease my father's conscience. He'd only have had regrets if he'd done nothing.' Meg bent down and fastened the buttons on her boots with the button-hook, then placed the letter in her long white apron's pocket. 'I'll not be long.' She smiled; she was glad to have an hour to herself, and she would enjoy the mile walk into Hawes for a change.

She walked along the dusty road, singing to herself and admiring the summer's day. The summer would soon be gone, and there would be plenty of days when it was too cold and wet to enjoy the walk into the market town of Hawes. Then it was a bind to go and get provisions and post letters, but she was happy to do so today and glad that her father had shown pity on his family in Liverpool.

Hawes was bustling, and the narrow street that ran the length of the small town was busy with traders. She stopped and watched as some young geese were sold to a local farmer. He'd be fattening them up for Christmas, the poor things; they were only going to be on the earth for a short time, in order for him to make a profit and to keep him fed.

She passed the squawking gaggle and made her way to the postbox, walking down the cobbled street and over the river bridge, where she stopped for a while to watch the water-wheel turning the stones that ground the corn inside the mill. The waters of the fosse were low, but they still made a spectacular sight as she urged herself on with the task in hand.

She stopped outside the post office and looked at the letter, before placing it in the postbox. Would it be arriving at a house of death, and would her cousin Dan succumb to the terrible sickness? Perhaps her father's money would never be needed, or would be spent by someone who was left to open the letter on the death of her aunt and Dan, if it arrived too late for any good to come of it? Anyway, she had done her bit, she thought, as she listened to it slip into the metal basket, for collection from the hexagonal green box marked with Queen Victoria's head. It was truly a marvel that a letter posted in Hawes would be read by somebody in Liverpool in a few days' time. She only hoped it would not arrive too late.

The smell of fresh bread at the baker's made her linger and press her nose up against the glass window of the shop. Inside she could see newly baked bread, scones, cakes and biscuits, and although she was still full from her normal breakfast of porridge, her mouth watered at the temptation of a treat. A treat she couldn't have, as she was penniless. She looked up as the shop's bell tinkled and a middle-aged woman, reasonably dressed but not in too fine clothes, exited, only to stop in her tracks as the shop girl called her back. She heard the conversation from within as they both talked.

'Hey, our Jack and Sam would never talk to me again if they knew I'd been over to Hawes and had forgotten their favourite. In fact, Jack asked for it especially, before I left the house and got in the trap with Mrs Pratt. What two long faces I'd have, when they returned from the mine this evening. Thank you, pet, for reminding me.'

Meg's ears tuned into the conversation, wondering how likely it was for somebody else to have two sons called Jack and Sam. She watched as the tall, grey-haired woman with a kind face put in her basket the brown bag filled with some treats.

'No problem, Mrs Alderson. We look forward to seeing you next week, perhaps?' The shop girl smiled.

'Aye, while the weather's good I'll be over this way. My two can eat me out of house and home most days, so a bit of fresh baking that I haven't had to do myself is a real treat. Goodbye for now, pet.'

Meg watched the woman she now knew to be Sam and Jack's mother walk past her and trundle up to the marketplace. She seemed a goodly woman; one who loved her sons – as long as she knew when to let go of them, Meg mused, as she made her way home. The trip into Hawes had been worth her while, if only to catch a glimpse of Mrs Alderson, she thought to herself as she reached the farm gate. At least now she knew that they both came from a good, loving home and were who they said they were. The brothers couldn't be that bad, despite her parents' warnings.

The following Thursday could not come soon enough, but she only wished Jack would be meeting her as well as Sam. Jack was the quiet one of the pair and she liked him for that, whereas she knew that Sam was already sweet on her. He didn't hold back with his attentions, and she found herself thinking of him more and more instead of the placid Jack.

6

'I'm only taking the trap today, so there will be no room for you, if I'm to take your mother. Besides, I need you to stay at home. I don't like to leave the farm without anybody about it.' Tom looked at his scowling daughter as he strapped the horse into the lighter trap, which was not as heavy as the donkey cart and easier for his horse to pull up the steep climb into Swaledale in the hot summer sun.

'But I've got to come, Uncle Harry will be expecting me. I always go with the butter.' Meg tried to hide her disappointment and the tears that were starting to build.

'Your mother's going in your place, so she'll explain. Besides, the deathbed of a woman with cancer is no place for a young lass, and your mother and Mary will want time together. Now whisht – go and tell your mother I'm ready.' Tom hadn't time for Meg's protesting; he'd noticed that she never moaned about not going into Swaledale when the weather was bad, but on a fine summer's day she couldn't wait to go.

Meg walked out of the farmyard and into the cool-ness of the farmhouse kitchen. 'Father says he's ready,' she muttered to her mum with a surly face.

'You know, if the wind changes, your face will stay like that, and then no one will look at the side you are on, with such a sullen face.' Her mum placed her cotton milk-cap on her head and tied the bow under her chin, as she glanced at her unhappy daughter.

'I wanted to go today, but he says there isn't the room for me.' Meg sat down at the table and hid her head in her folded arms.

'Now, how old are you? Nine or nineteen? Don't you be doing this on me, my girl. I'm going to see Mary, and you are staying at home. So I don't want to hear another word. Haven't your father and I got enough worries, what with not knowing who's alive or dead in Liverpool, and Mary so ill she can barely speak? You moping about is just not good enough, especially when it's over some-thing and nothing! You can go next week.' Agnes picked up her basket of butter and sighed. 'Pass the day in the garden. Besides, we won't be long. Your father will not be calling in the King's Head today; he's getting Blossom shoed while I sit with Mary, and then we will be straight home.'

'But I wanted to come,' Meg wailed.

'I haven't time for this. Hold your noise and stop being so selfish, else you are not too old to get your father's belt around you,' Agnes threatened. She'd made the same threat for nineteen years and never once had it come to pass. Tom would never raise his hand to his

69

daughter, let alone belt her. 'Right, we'll be back later in the day. Make yourself busy. The Devil makes work for idle hands, as your father always says. Next week will soon come round. I didn't realize the trip into Swaledale meant that much to you, as you've never bothered about it in the past.'

Agnes stood in the porch and looked back at her daughter. She wasn't going to exchange places with her, as she knew that her oldest friend, Mary, was in need of her comfort.

'That lass of ours is enough to make you swear sometimes,' Agnes said to Tom as she climbed up in the light gig and balanced the basket on her knee.

'It's because you've spoilt her, with her being the only one,' Tom growled as he gently whipped Blossom into action.

'That's it, blame me. It always is my fault, no matter what,' Agnes moaned as she held onto the narrow seat of the gig while they made their way down the rough field track.

Meg watched her parents for as long as she could, seeing them eventually going out of sight as they crossed the river bridge. She wiped the tears from her eyes and went out of the dark, cool farmhouse into the sunshine, sitting down on the branch of a fallen damson tree in the orchard, at the side of the farmhouse that adjoined her patch of garden. She looked at her rows of weeded potatoes, cabbages, beetroots, radishes, carrots and Brussels sprouts, along with other vegetables that she usually enjoyed tending. Her heart wasn't in it today, as she thought about Sam waiting for her under the sycamore tree in Swaledale, with no explanation as to why she was not there. Would he realize that she'd had no choice; that if she could fly like the robin that was picking through the garden grubs she would have been there by his side, no matter what the weather or the distance? She put her head in her hands and sobbed. She'd never felt like this before. The feelings that were stirring in her were new to her; all she knew was that she needed to see Sam again as soon as possible.

'Hello, is there anybody there? Hello?'

Meg lifted her head and wiped her eyes and running nose with the back of her hand as she heard an unfamiliar voice echo round the farmhouse.

'Yes. Hello, I'm here, can I help?' She stood up and breathed in, making herself respectable for her unknown visitor, as she walked round the front of the house to where the voice was coming from.

'This is Beck Side, isn't it? Tom and Agnes Oversby do live here, don't they?' A mucky-faced lad stood in front of Meg, his clothes as dirty as his face and looking worn and too small for his lean, wiry body. His trousers were halfway up his leg and held up by a piece of rope.

'They do, but what do you want with them? We've no need of a farm lad, and we don't encourage beggars or hawkers,' Meg added quickly when she noticed the hessian sack by his side.

'It's a good job, then, that I'm neither of them.' The lad grinned and pulled his flat cap off his head. 'Am I

71

bloody glad to be here! I didn't think I'd ever manage it. If it hadn't been for the wagoner giving me a lift from Lancaster, I'd still be tramping the roads. You must be Meg – my mother said Uncle Tom had a lass.' He held a hand out to be shaken and looked across at Meg, who was gawping at him.

'Are you Dan? What are you doing here? Does your mother know you are here?' Meg ignored the out-stretched hand and looked at the scruff of a lad who stood in front of her, not quite believing that this could be her cousin from Liverpool.

'Aye, that's me: Dan Ryan. And don't you be fretting about my mother – she died on Sunday, but told me to find you all, as she lay dying on her deathbed, and gave me the money your father sent her, to help me on my way. Look, I still have a bob or two in my pocket. I was lucky because, as I said, a wagoner helped me most of the journey. He took pity on me, although he wouldn't have done if I'd told him I'd lost both my mother and father to cholera. Everybody seems to think you can catch it, but I heard them that came to take my mother's body away that it's the water that's been killing everybody. The water pump at the end of our street has something in it. That's why I'm alright. I've been spending my time in Toxteth and haven't been drinking from the same pump.' Dan put his grimy hand in his pocket, then revealed the change from the money sent to his mother. 'Your father can have it back, now I'm here, because my mother said he'd look after me once I got here.'

Meg stared at the strangely spoken lad and didn't

know what to say. He seemed to have taken the death of both his parents in his stride. He also seemed to think that now he was with her at Beck Side, he had a new home and everything would be alright.

'Any chance of something to eat? I'm starving, and my belly thinks my throat's been cut. I've walked on my own from Ingleton and never stopped until I was here.' Dan looked around him. 'Big spot this, innit? It must be worth a bob or two.'

'Sorry, I just can't believe you are standing in front of me and talking about your parents' deaths without any tears. I'd be broken-hearted. I dare not even think about losing my dear mother. You poor thing, you must have been through hell.' Meg started to walk towards the kitchen door, with Dan following her.

'It's life, innit? One day you are here, and the next day you can be gone. There's ten folk died on our street. The authorities never left the street alone, with their hessian sacks and sprinkling of McDougall's powder over the bodies. They've all been buried in one grave at St Mary's, so at least my ma and pa are together.' The young man walked behind her with his hands in his pockets.

'McDougall's powder? What's that?' Meg stopped in her tracks and looked at the hard-headed lad who was standing in front of her.

'It's a powder they cover the dead with before they put them in a hessian sack, and then they place them in a coffin and cover that with the powder and all, before they are buried. It's a disinfectant, if that's what it's called? I'm not right good with big words.' Dan shrugged his shoulders. 'Anyway, all I know is that I've no home; they cleared the house out and burned all the furniture, even though they said it was the water that made my mother and father badly.' He breathed in deeply as he looked around the oak-beamed kitchen of Beck Side. 'Bloody hell, I was right. I thought I'd want for nothing if I made myself known here. Just look at this kitchen: you've bacon and ham, and look at the bread that's on the table. Cut us a slice, Meg, and put some butter on it. A pot of tea would go down well and all.' His eyes took in everything as he glanced around the kitchen and made himself at home in Tom's chair.

'That's my father's chair – you'll have to shift when he comes back.' Meg placed the kettle on the fire and sliced and buttered two pieces of bread, placing them on a plate along with some cheese and boiled ham that she brought out of the dairy.

'He's not here yet, so he's not to know, is he? A bit of a stickler, is he? I heard he was a miserable old sod, but that your mother would keep him straight, when it came to me.' Dan filled his mouth with bread, cheese and ham and looked at Meg as she poured the tea.

'He can be, but he works hard and looks after us all.' Meg sat down opposite her cousin and wondered if she should have asked him into the house. After all, he could be contagious, but she hadn't had much choice in the matter. 'Where's Toxteth? You said you'd been there.'

'Aye, I have. I've been cow-keeping with old Fawcett – he's got ten cows that he keeps in the house next door to the one he lives in. Toxteth is a part of Liverpool; it's got a big park, and Fawcett's allowed to let his cows graze there, as it keeps the grass down. He feeds them brewery grains and molasses from the factories down by the docks, in winter. I deliver the milk to folk in a trap some days, for the old bugger, and some days I help with his packhorses, but to be honest I've had enough of it all. Especially now that I can see what a life I could have here. I bet you want for nowt.' Dan belched as he made himself comfortable in his uncle's chair.

'Cows living in houses – I've heard it all now.' Meg shook her head in disbelief.

'It's right, I tell you. He's converted the terraced house downstairs to hold his ten cows and he has a dairy to keep the milk cold, and outside in the yard he's got a stable and hayloft, with a midden in one corner. It's a farm in the middle of the city. There's a lot of cow-keepers getting to be in Liverpool, as city folk need their milk just like you lot do.' Dan yawned. He was tired, as the journey here had been hard, and in truth he hadn't slept for a good few days.

'You look tired. Why don't you have a sleep, and then my mum and father will be back by the time you wake.' Meg cleared his empty plate and watched Dan close his eyes and stretch out his legs.

'Aye, I might do that,' he mumbled as he made himself more comfortable in Tom's chair. 'I'm right glad I'm here. I know I'll be alright now, as my mother said Uncle Tom would do right by me, because he owes us.' He closed his eyes and hoped that his mother's words would come true.

Meg glanced behind her, at Dan asleep in her father's chair. She was fretting that perhaps she should not have let him into the house, and that her parents would not be happy with her decision to do so. But what else could she have done? She made her way round the side of the house to her garden and picked up a hoe, deciding to weed her newly planted rows of lettuce. They would be the last batch until after the winter, she thought, as she raked away thistles and dandelions from around the small plants. She couldn't concentrate on the task in hand as she kept thinking about Dan, already making it sound as if Beck Side was automatically going to be his new home; and about the fact that Sam would think he had been forgotten by her. How long would he have waited for her under the sycamore, she wondered, and would he ever want to see her again?

'What are you wittering on about, our Meg? For heaven's sake, calm down.' As Agnes climbed down out of the trap, she felt in no mood for Meg and her hysterics. She'd just left the bedside of her best friend, who was dying, and had little patience for her daughter's selfishness.

'He's here, Mum. Dan is here! He walked into my garden, as bold as brass, and he's asleep in the kitchen.' Meg pulled on her mother's arm, as her father climbed down from the trap and led the newly shod Blossom into the stable.

'Oh, my Lord, you let him into the house! We will all be to bury; we will all catch cholera and be blamed for bringing it into the dale.' Agnes herself was hysterical as

76

Tom, hearing all the fuss, joined them before stabling Blossom.

'It can't be our Anne's lad – how's he got here? Why's he not with his mother?' Tom looked at Meg.

'He says his mum is dead and that she told him to come here, and that you'd look after him. He's really cheeky, doesn't stop to think what he's saying, and I don't think he cares,' Meg said as she watched her father's face cloud over with the thought that his sister was dead, and that she had sent her son to be his ward. 'But Dan does sound as if he's been through hell. I think he's been on the road for at least four days. A carter brought him from Lancaster to here, else he'd still be walking.'

'So, our Anne is dead – that's me on my own then.' Tom breathed in and then lifted his head. 'Especially now that her lad sounds just like his bloody father,' he growled and walked up through the farmhouse porch and into Beck Side's kitchen, where he stopped in his tracks as he saw the scruff of a lad asleep in his wooden Windsor chair.

'We can't have him in here. Look at him, Tom, he's nothing more than a vagabond. How do we know he is who he says he is? He could be any Tom, Dick or Harry!' Agnes gasped as she looked at how mucky and scrawny the lad in front of them was.

'No, Mum, he's definitely who he says he is. He's got the change from the money Father sent to Liverpool. The reason he hasn't got cholera is because he's been helping somebody who keeps cows, and Dan hasn't been drinking the same water as his parents. That's how they've both caught it, he says,' Meg whispered as all three of them looked down upon him.

'Here, you, wake up!' Tom shook the urchin by his shoulder and then harder still, when he did not stir.

'Sorry, sir, I didn't mean to fall asleep. Don't hit me, sir, please don't hit me!' The lad jumped up, still half-asleep, and looked at the three pairs of staring eyes as he came to his senses. 'Sorry, I thought it was my old boss and I'd fallen asleep on the job; he didn't half used to give me a thrashing when I did.' He looked at the surprise on their three faces and wiped his eyes. 'You must be my Uncle Tom and Aunty Agnes – nice to meet you.' He held out his hand to be shaken, but nobody took him up on it. 'It's alright, you'll not catch owt. I'd be six foot under by now if I had anything.' Dan dropped his hand, knowing exactly why he was not being welcomed with open arms.

'So, you are Dan? Our Meg tells me that your mother's died and that's why you are here. Well, I'm sorry for your loss, but I don't know what our lass thought I was going to do with you. We are just holding our own, without having another mouth to feed.' Tom looked at his nephew and searched for any likeness to his sister, but he also heard the voice and accent of the man who had got Anne pregnant and had split the family apart.

'Meg has fed me more this morning than I've had for over a week. You've no idea how we have been living – it's nothing like here, isn't Liverpool. My mother said that you'd look after me, as you are all I've got. I'm a good worker, honest, Uncle Tom. I'll sleep in the barn

78

and you'll not even know I'm here. Please let me stay.' Dan's eyes filled with tears, and he started to bawl and carry on.

'Tom, the lad's your flesh and blood and is in need of our help. You loved your sister, Anne, and you need to do right by her. She's obviously entrusted you to look after him, even though he's old enough to stand on his own two feet. He'll be no bother. I'll make him a bed up in the barn, until we know that he's not contagious. And then he can have the spare bedroom, once we know he's clear of cholera.' Agnes looked at the lost soul in front of her and thought that if Megan had lost both her parents, she'd want someone to look after her until she got back on her feet again.

'Thanks, missus – I mean, Aunty Agnes – you'll not regret it. I'll work for my keep, I'm not idle.' Dan smiled and wiped the tears away from his cheek.

Tom breathed in deeply. 'I don't know. I wasn't expecting this, but you are our Anne's lad, so you are blood, and I can't turn you away.' He looked at the lad in front of him and saw himself at the same age and his heart softened. 'Make him up a bed in the hayloft and then if he's still with us next week, he can move into the house,' he grunted at Agnes and Meg. 'Now don't you be thinking you will have a soft life here, as we work long hours and I'll expect you to do the same, helping out around the farm,' he said to Dan as he watched a smile light up the boy's face. 'Get him some of my old clothes and all, then burn the ones he's in, after he's had a swill in the horse-trough. Happen then he'll look a bit more

79

like a worker,' Tom growled as he walked out of the farmhouse to see to the still-unstabled horse.

'Thank you, I'm so grateful. Here, I've the change from what you sent my mother.' Dan fumbled in his pocket.

'Keep it, lad, you might need it, if I throw you back out down the road,' Tom shouted back.

'He doesn't mean it, Dan. Now go and wash in the horse-trough out in the yard, and Meg will bring you some fresh clothes, blankets and pillows. Next week, if all's still well, you can have the back bedroom. Your uncle's not as bad as he makes out, but he can be a stickler, so don't push your luck too much.' Agnes looked at the scrawny lad as he walked out into the yard; her heart bled for him, and she could not see him being turned away from his own family. Perhaps this was the lad that Tom had always wanted, if he did but know it, but only time would tell.

7

'Tom, Tom, wake up. The cows are out, they are going past our garden gate.'

Agnes shook her husband, who was still asleep and had not been disturbed by the sound of his milk-cows making their way across the farmyard, unlike her. She pulled back the bedroom curtains, still in her nightdress and with her hair in rags, and squinted at the two cows wandering back into their pasture, with Dan walking behind them with a switch.

'It's alright. Dan's putting them back where they belong – he must have heard them as well.' Agnes breathed a sigh of relief as she started to get dressed for the day ahead.

'They've never done that before, and I'm sure I closed the gate last night. Happen it's a good job he slept out there last night, else they'd have been in Hawes by now. What time is it, anyway? It must only be dawn, by the looks of it outside. Get back into bed, woman, for a bit longer.' Tom yawned and stretched.

'It's six, the hall clock's just struck. I might as well get up, now I'm awake. Besides, Dan's up and going, so I'll make him some breakfast.' Agnes looked down at her husband, who was still in bed.

'Now, don't you go pampering him because you feel sorry for him. He'll have to rough it, like the rest of us. We don't even know if he *is* our Anne's lad – we've only his word for it.' Tom sat up on the edge of the bed and relieved himself in the chamber pot.

'You've got to be blind not to see that he's your nephew. He has a look of his mother, Anne. Poor little bugger, he's got nobody but us.' Agnes put on her apron over the top of her long skirt and blouse and sighed. 'Anyway, he's proved he's of worth already, making sure the cows weren't halfway down the road. So hold your noise.'

'I will not; we know nowt about him, and he might be a right wrong 'un, especially if he takes after his father.' Tom pulled his breeches on and went over to the jug and bowl filled with cold water for a wash.

'I thought you were going to lie in,' Agnes said as she stood next to the bedroom door.

'Nay, I'm up now, I might as well do the milking. Besides, we have Jim Pratt from Sedbergh coming today to kill the pig. It's best that I'm up and going, as the shed will need all scrubbing out and making clean before he kills it in there.' Tom pulled his braces over his shirt and looked out of the window. 'Well, I'll be buggered, look at this!' He stood and watched, as Agnes joined him by his side. 'The little bugger's done the milking for me. Look, the milk kit is full; he's just rolled it into the dairy, and he's bringing a bucket of milk for the house across the yard. I didn't expect him to do that.'

'Looks like you've got a farm lad, Tom. So stop complaining and look after him, as he's kith and kin after all.' Agnes smiled. 'Now, I'll make some breakfast and you can thank Dan for doing your job without being asked. I'll give our Meg a shout. She's a busy day ahead of her, helping me once the pig is butchered.'

'Aye, our Dan's done something she's never done without being asked. She'll need to pull her socks up now.' Tom pulled on his jacket and grinned.

'Oh, it's "our Dan" now, is it? Now that you know he's a worker.' Agnes laughed as she shouted into the bedroom next door. 'Meg, stir your shanks. Jim Pratt will be here in another hour or so, and we've to make all ready in the kitchen.' She stood for a second and heard a faint reply from under the bed sheets. Little did Meg know, but it would seem that she had a rival for her father's attentions now, Agnes thought, as she went down the creaking stairs and into the farmhouse kitchen. She opened the door to let in the late-summer sun and smiled as she found the bucket of milk on the step, along with Dan's cap full of freshly picked field mushrooms. Well, he'd sorted breakfast out, that was for certain, she thought as she picked both up.

'Morning, Aunty Agnes. I thought I'd make myself useful,' Dan shouted across the yard.

'Thank you, lad, we weren't expecting that. Meg will bring you some breakfast across in a little while. Another week and you can live with us. It's just that we don't know if you are carrying—'

'Aye, I know, better safe than sorry.' Dan stopped her in her tracks. 'I slept like a baby anyway, so don't you worry.' He watched as his aunt went back into the house, before going and sitting in the early-morning sunshine outside the barn. He hadn't slept well really; he'd tossed and turned and had thought about his life, and wondered how long he would be able to stay with his new family. He was grateful to get out of Liverpool, especially now, as he sat and looked around him at the beautiful scenery, but it was not far enough away to feel totally safe. His life had been nothing but hardship and trying to make ends meet, and all the time people like this wanted for nothing. He was going to make the best of it for as long as he could, that was for sure.

The smell of frying bacon made his mouth water as it drifted across the yard: bacon for breakfast, now what a bloody good treat that would be. If he were back home in Liverpool, he'd be lucky to have anything to eat at all until dinner time, and then it would only be bread and dripping if he was lucky. No, he didn't miss the hellhole or the folk within it. He would make sure this was his home from now on. He'd have to impress Tom to ensure that he won him round, because he was a cantankerous old devil. He'd have to make himself irreplaceable; that's why he'd milked the cows and taken them back to the field, to make himself look good. He yawned and stretched his limbs as Meg walked out of the porchway towards him.

'Morning, Cousin,' Dan yelled. 'Beautiful day.'

'It is, if you are not a pig,' Meg said as she placed a plate of bacon, eggs and mushrooms in front of him, along with a mug of tea. 'The poor old sow's hours are numbered, as the butcher's coming up from Sedbergh today to kill her.'

'Oh, the poor bloody thing, but it'll mean we've plenty to eat over this winter, so I'm not going to complain.' Dan looked at the crispy bacon, then picked up the knife and fork that lay next to the plate and tucked in.

'I am. I hate today. I hate the sound of the pig squealing for its life as the butcher slits its throat, and the fact that I always have to stir the bucket of its blood, so that it doesn't clot, before we make it into black pudding. But most of all I hate the smell of the pig's head boiling in the copper, which I'm having to fill with water in a minute. It all turns my stomach.'

'You really know how to put someone off his breakfast, don't you?' Dan looked at his bacon and decided to tackle the eggs first. 'What did your father think, when I milked the cows? Has he said anything?'

'Aye, he said he could get used to someone else doing his job for him, but that the poor old lasses will have wondered what was going on, as they aren't milked as a rule before eight in the morning. What made you milk them so early? It must still have been dark when you brought them in from the field.' Meg sat a distance away from Dan and watched as he cleaned the egg yolk off his plate with his crust of bread.

'We always start milking at four in Liverpool. Folk expect the milk on their steps before they go to work. It was no hardship to me. I'm used to it.' He started to eat his bacon as Meg watched.

'Is Liverpool really huge? Furthest I've ever been is Gunnerside and Sedbergh. I've never been to a city or even a big town.' Meg waited until Dan had finished chewing the rind from the bacon and then listened to what he said.

'Liverpool's full of folk. All different colours, from all over the world. It's one of the main ports, so there's ships coming in with different cargoes every day. The docks are always busy. I used to go there with my father and watch all the fancy stuff being unloaded and loaded: oranges, spices, fancy cloth and the like. A day would soon pass as you watched the different ships come and go. Then the folk there live in all sorts of ways: some are really well-to-do in their fancy town houses, and there's the merchants who buy and sell and move house every so often, when their deals have either gone badly or well. But there's plenty of poor on them streets and all, just like we were. At least we had a roof over our heads; a lot of the poor buggers live on the streets, begging, or sleep in doss-houses, where all you get is a straw sack to sleep on, and some fleas and lice to call your own. There's never any quiet, and you've to watch your back all the time and learn to look after yourself, else you'd never survive, if you are the likes of us. I can't say I'm going to miss it, not now, when I know what this place is like.'

Dan pushed his plate back and looked across at Meg.

'Are you not walking out with a young man yet? The lasses at Liverpool are nine times out of ten nearly married by your age – either that or they have a bun in the oven!' He grinned.

86

'Bun in the oven?' Meg looked at her cousin, wondering what he meant.

'Aye, you know, having a baby! But most times they don't know who the father is. There's many born into the world like that.' Dan laughed.

'Oh, I see.' Meg blushed. 'No, I'm not courting, and I'm certainly not with child.' She scowled at her cousin; things like that were never talked about in her family, and she found it quite shocking that he was so forthright. 'I'd like to see a bit more of the world before I settle down. I know, as you say, that I am lucky to live here, but there must be more to life? I want to see the sea and to visit other lands, perhaps. I don't just want to marry a farmer and stay here all my life.' Meg sighed and thought of Sam: would she ever get the chance to see him again, especially now that Dan sounded as if he aimed to make Beck Side his home? Perhaps it would be Dan her father took into Swaledale every week instead of her, if he was to stay, and then she'd never get to visit Sam again.

'So that's what you think, is it, my lass? We are not good enough for you?' Tom Oversby had overheard the two of them talking as he had walked across the farmyard and was not impressed by the words he'd heard from his daughter.

Meg turned to face her father and immediately regretted the words she had said. 'No, Father, it's not like that. I simply know there is more to life than this small dale, and I'd like – given the chance – to see more of the world.'

'Aye, well, you go and get your arse into the kitchen with your mum. She needs you this morning,' Tom growled as he watched Meg quickly disappear with Dan's dirty plate. 'Now, what are we to do with you? It seems you've already milked the cows for me, so you might as well clean the cowshed to earn your keep, while I clean the pig-hull out, ready for the butcher to come later this morning.'

'Meg said it was going to be butchered today. Can I help? She said she hated stirring the blood. Well, I could do that. I've never watched a pig being killed before.' Dan jumped to his feet.

'I don't know. I don't want any of us catching anything that you might be ailing with. It's better that you keep your distance from folk at the moment. Now, you'll find a shovel and fork in the cowshed, and when you've finished that, come and see me and you can whitewash the pig-hull out, ready for our next pig.' Tom looked at his nephew; if he thought he was going to have an easy life away from Liverpool, he could think again. He'd have to earn his keep like anybody else.

'I'd not get too close to Dan, Meg. Just until we know he's healthy and not carrying cholera.' Agnes looked across at her daughter as she filled the copper boiler with cold water from the pump outside the back door.

'I've no intention to. Besides, I don't think I'll get a chance, as my father is lining him up with jobs already, from what I can see. Neither of them is going to smell very pleasant tonight, especially my father, as he's cleaning the old sow's hull out, while she has her last few breaths of fresh air and freedom in the orchard. The poor thing!' Meg wiped her brow and smiled at her mum. 'How was Mary Battersby? With Dan arriving on the scene, I never got a chance to ask you yesterday.'

'She's not good. I don't think she will see the week out. Poor Harry doesn't know what to do; he's even talking of selling the shop after she's gone, because he doesn't think he'll be able to manage on his own.' Agnes held back the tears while she greased the baking tins that the black pudding was going to be cooked in.

'I'm sorry, Mum. I know you are close. If there's anything I can do, you've only got to ask.' Meg stopped for a second and looked at her mum, who was heartbroken about her friend being so ill. And she, like a spoilt brat, had thought only of herself yesterday, when she had behaved so selfishly.

'You are a good girl, Meg. These things happen, and you've got to grin and bear it. Now what do you think of Dan? I haven't had much to do with him, and I hope you are keeping your distance from him, just until we know if he's contagious or not.' Agnes lifted her head and waited for a reply.

'He's alright, Mum. He's had a hard life, not at all like ours. He's been telling me about his life in Liverpool and the people there. My father heard me say that I wish I could travel, like Dan, and thought I was being disloyal. But I wasn't. I was simply envious of what Dan has seen.' Meg sighed. 'I love my home, and it seems that Dan thinks he's here to stay – his mum must have told him so.'

'Aye, dear, your father is always finding fault with folk.

89

I don't know if Dan will fit in or not; we will have to wait and see. However, he did make an impression on him when he got up so early and had done the milking and, by the sound of it, he doesn't shrug off work. He'll happen make our lives easier, Meg. Besides, your father always did want a son. Well, now he's got a nephew instead. His poor mother did right in sending him here; it's where he belongs.'

Agnes went into the larder to get the pearl barley and sage that were to be used for the black pudding, and left Meg wondering if Dan might not do her any favours, if he won her father over. After all, this was her home, not his, and perhaps he'd have been better staying in Liverpool.

The squeal of the pig as it was caught by the butcher and her father made Meg's eyes fill with tears. She hated the fact that its life had to be taken, for them to have something to eat.

'Go on, it's gone quiet now – they've done the worst. Go and get the bucket and stick and come back with the blood,' her mum prompted Meg as she stood in the porchway. Tell your father all's ready, and that I've made Jim Pratt a bite to eat.' Agnes watched as Meg ran across to where the dirty deed had taken place, knowing full well that her daughter hated her allotted task.

'About time.' Tom looked up from the bucket of blood that he was stirring below the pig's cut throat. Its body had been stretched upside-down from the pig-hull's beams, and the butcher was just securing its feet tightly, before shaving the animal free of its bristles and then removing its head and innards. 'Here, take this and keep stirring until it's cool, else it's no good to no man, if it starts to clot. Dan, go across to the house and wait outside until your Aunt Agnes gives you some boiling water. Jim will need it to scald the bristles off.'

'Yes, Uncle.' Dan grinned at Meg as she nearly retched at the smell of death all around her, then took the bucket from her father and started walking back to the farmhouse with him by her side. 'I've never seen a pig-killing before. The bloody thing didn't half scream.'

'You'd scream if you had your throat slashed open. The poor creature.' Meg concentrated on keeping the bucket of blood level, and paid no attention to Dan's cold-blooded comments on the pig's demise.

'Your father said I did well to watch, and that I'd know what to do next time,' Dan said as they reached the kitchen.

'You might not be here next time. We only kill a pig once a year. That's a long time away – things might have changed.' Meg put the bucket of cooling blood down and sat on the porch shelf, stirring her abhorrent mixture.

'Oh, I'll be here, I mean to stay. Besides, give it a few months and your father won't know how he's done without me,' Dan smirked as blood splattered onto Meg's face.

'Mum, Dan needs some of that boiling water for the butcher,' Meg yelled as she stared at her new rival.

'You needn't do that job next year. I'll be doing it, along with anything else that your father sees fit to give me to do. He's a grand fella, is your father, I respect him already.' Dan smirked as his aunt brought him a bucket of boiling water. 'Thank you, Aunt Agnes, and can I say how much I enjoyed my breakfast this morning, and thank you again for the loan of these clothes. I look quite the young gent.' Dan winked at them both. He was already planning to stay longer than he had intended with the Oversbys.

'That's no problem, Dan; after all, you are Anne's son, and it is the least we can do, under the circumstances.' Agnes looked at her nephew and then glanced at Meg, who appeared anything but happy as he walked away with the steaming bucket of water. 'Well, I'll give him this: at least he has manners, that lad. Now, you keep stirring that for another few minutes and then come in and help me. Leave the men to it this year. After all, there's now three of them, and I could do with you in the kitchen.'

Meg bit her tongue. She could see that she was going to have to stand her ground when it came to Dan, else her place in the family was at risk. Why had the bloody lad turned up, and when was she ever going to get to Swaledale again to see Sam? And would he still want to see her, after her non-appearance?

8

The pantry at Beck Side was full to the brim, after a busy week of cooking by Agnes and Megan. Both of the pig flitches were curing in a zinc bath full of brine, and the black pudding was baked, along with the brawn made from the pig's head. Tasty patties called 'savoury ducks', made of the pig's liver, pork and herbs, had been enjoyed at teatime, and everybody was full and content as they sat outside on the garden wall, looking down the dale as the sun slowly faded below Stagg's Fell.

'Well, lad, it looks as if you are not going down with anything, else it would have shown by now.' Tom puffed on his pipe and sat back. 'Mother, tomorrow you'll have to make up the spare room for him. Dan can come and live with us properly, now we know that he's fit.'

'I was thinking that myself. It's partly done already. I'll just put some clean sheets on the bed and then you can call it your own.' Agnes smiled as she concentrated on her knitting, which she had brought outside with her.

'This is coming on nicely.' She lifted the stitchwork up for everyone to see. 'It's a pullover for you this winter, Dan. You brought nothing with you when you came, and we can't have you freezing.'

'You all look after me far too well. I can't thank you enough. My mother was right when she said my true family was here. I only wish she was here, too.' Dan dropped his head and then looked up at Meg secretly, with a slight smile on his face.

'It's funny how she never came to visit us – your mother. That is, if she loved it here so much,' Meg commented casually, aware that Dan was playing on her father's feelings.

'It would be his father that stopped Anne. He was the one who split us up in the first place. He never did like me,' Tom spat.

'That's right, my father didn't like country ways. It's a good job I take after my mother, isn't it? That I appreciate all this around me, and the kindness shown to me.' Dan looked bashfully at his uncle and then sneered at Megan.

'I'm going for a quick walk up the fell before it's dark. Clear my head.' Meg stood up; she was sick and tired of listening to the perfect Dan and of his love for his new family. How long would he be prepared to keep his false face on? Because she was sure it was a false side of Dan they were seeing. She remembered all too well Dan arriving on the Sunday she was alone with him, and watching him as he realized that he had landed on his feet. Now he was even trying to hide his terrible, grating accent, which she found so annoying, so that he fitted in with the three

94

of them. And as for making himself useful, well, wherever her father went, so did Dan. It was ridiculous!

She drew breath as she climbed the steep pasture that opened out on to the heather-clad moorland. There she stopped and sat on a limestone boulder that had been left there since the Ice Age; it was a place she often went to when she was worried or needing peace. She looked around her: the oil lamps and candles in the dale's houses were just starting to be lit, and she watched as one by one, like stars, they twinkled down in the valley below.

Tomorrow she was to go into Swaledale; at least Dan hadn't taken her place when it came to taking the cheese and butter over there, although she was surprised that he had never offered to go in her place, or that her father had not told him to do so. It was probably only because her father liked a drink at the King's Head with his cronies to catch up with the gossip, away from his home life. No doubt Dan would be talked about and would be introduced to them soon enough. She knew it was only a matter of time before he replaced her on the weekly trip. However, tomorrow she was going. And come hell or high water, she would make her way to the sycamore tree halfway up the fell, in the hope that Sam would be waiting for her there, even though she was a week late.

A shiver went down Meg's spine as the night suddenly decided to close in. Autumn was on its way, she thought, as she looked up at the stars starting to appear, and soon it would be too cold to wander and get lost in her own thoughts. Instead she would have to share the warmth of the kitchen with the cuckoo in the nest: Dan. Although he was always pleasant to her, she had really grown to dislike the lad in the last week. Perhaps it was jealousy, as her parents were making a fuss of him; but no, she knew it was more than that. Dan was sneaky and was play-acting for attention – of that she was sure. No doubt he would show his true colours eventually, she thought, as she hastily picked a bunch of the newly flowering purple heather for her mum, before wrapping her shawl around herself and making her way back down to the farmhouse.

'Things don't look good, lass. That's the doctor's gig outside the shop. He must be visiting Mary. I'm amazed that she's still on this good earth – I thought she was about to leave us last week, when your mother visited her.' Tom urged his horse to stand next to the doctor's black horse and gig, to let Meg climb down with her basket. Then, noticing that the bedroom curtains were pulled, he stayed in the gig and looked down at his daughter. 'Stay there. I'll stable the horse at the King's Head and then I'll join you.'

Meg nodded her head and caught her breath. She'd never seen a dead person before, and was thankful that her father was going to come into the shop with her. With her basket of butter on her arm, she leaned against the small wall that surrounded the shop's entrance and waited.

The shop's bell rang as the door was opened and she watched as the doctor, along with Harry Battersby, came out of the door. She smiled at them both, but said nothing as the doctor spoke to Harry.

96

'You did all that you could for her, Harry. She couldn't have wanted better care. Now you've got to look after yourself – she'd want you to do that.' Meg watched as the doctor patted Harry on the back, before climbing up into his gig. Harry, who was usually a strong man, looked crippled with grief as he wiped away tears and thanked the doctor for doing his best. Meg felt her legs go weak and her eyes fill with tears of her own as she realized that Mary Battersby, her adopted Aunt Mary, had died.

She watched as the doctor drove his horse and gig away and then walked over to Harry. She spoke softly and put her hand on the distraught man as he turned to her. 'I'm sorry. I overheard the doctor. Aunt Mary's passed, then? Perhaps it was for the best, as she was in a lot of pain.'

'I don't know what I'm going to do. I lived for her. I'm nothing without her.' Harry cried and wiped his eyes with his handkerchief. 'I'm sorry, Meg, you shouldn't see me like this.' He blew his nose and tried to smile at the young girl he'd known since she was born. 'You've brought the butter, I see. Are your father and mother here?'

'My father is. We saw the doctor's gig and thought something had happened to Aunt Mary, so he's just stabling the horses and then he'll be here.' Meg linked her arm through Harry's and walked with him into the shop. 'Here, I'll put the kettle on while you sit down and gather yourself. Do you want me to put the "Closed" sign up at the shop window and pull the blinds?' she asked, as she walked through to the back living quarters.

'If you could, lass. I feel all of a dodder. I knew Mary

was dying, but I didn't expect her to go so fast, when it did come. She seemed to be a bit better yesterday, and then this morning she was in agony. I didn't know what to do for her.' Harry broke down once again as he sat in his chair, next to the dwindling fire that Meg was adding logs to, as she placed the kettle above it. 'She was screaming for mercy, and there was nothing I could do.'

'Well, she's at peace now. And she knew how much you loved her, so you must not feel any guilt.' Meg got three cups from the china cupboard and placed them on the table, before walking through into the shop. She pulled the blinds down on both windows and was turning the sign in the shop's doorway to 'Closed' when her father walked in.

'She's gone then? How's Harry? He's going to miss her.' Tom patted his daughter's shoulder as he saw tears in her eyes.

Meg sniffed and wiped her cheeks. 'Yes, she's gone, and Uncle Harry's heartbroken,' she replied as she smiled wanly at her father.

'It's for the best. I wouldn't have put a dog through what she's been through these last few weeks. Now we've got to look after the living.' Tom looked at the basket of butter that Meg had put on the shop counter. 'Put that in the pantry, Meg, and give Harry and me a minute or two together. He'll need to talk.'

Meg nodded her head. She understood; the two men would not want her as they shared their feelings together, and she was grateful to be busy while they probably said their goodbyes to the dead woman upstairs. She just hoped that she wouldn't be asked to do the same.

She placed the butter in the pantry, along with the cheese that had been left on the shop's counter from the previous day. She looked around her for other jobs to do, as she heard the floorboards above creak and the muffled voices of her father and Harry talking as they looked down on the departed Mary. The shop was in a state – goods were partly unpacked, and what baking there was on the counter was not fit to eat. Harry had obviously not been coping, with his wife being ill and with running the shop on his own, she thought, as she tidied around her. It had always been a good business, and Harry and Mary had been happy with their lives there. As a child, she had stopped the odd night with them and had loved playing shopkeeper with her 'Aunt Mary', weighing sweets out and helping to serve the customers, with Mary's help.

The memories came flooding back as Meg stocked the shelves and swept the floor. She'd enjoyed her time there; the smell of paraffin and carbolic soap always reminded her of the shop, as it was those smells that had hit her in the morning when she made her way down the cold stone steps into the Battersbys' back living quarters, to sit in front of the blazing fire in her nightdress, a luxury she was never allowed at home. They had been good times, and now they were gone, because Harry would never run the shop without Mary; that was obvious to everyone.

She stood with the brush in her hand and looked round the shop, then glanced at the clock on the wall: half-past one, the hands told her. She realized that even if she left now, she'd not be in time to meet Sam, even if he had been there waiting for her. That was two weeks on the trot that she hadn't made it to meet him. He'd definitely think she was not interested in him, which could not be further from the truth.

The sound of her father and Harry coming down the stairs made Meg regain her thoughts on what she was about, as she finished sweeping the wooden floor.

'Meg, do you want to go up and say goodbye to Mary?' Her father walked into the shop. 'She looks peaceful – you've nothing to fear.' Tom looked grey and sombre.

Meg shook her head. 'No, I prefer to remember her as she was.'

'Right, I understand. Come through and make us that drink you were on with. The kettle's boiled – I've just put it to one side.' Tom turned and walked back into the living space in which Mary and Harry had lived quite happily, all their married life.

Meg was relieved that she had not been made to go and see Mary. She was frightened of the dead and had dreaded having to show her respect.

'You are not going to see her then, Meg?' Harry looked up, his eyes red with tears.

'No, I hope you don't mind.' Meg waited for the kettle to reboil and looked at the crestfallen man.

'No, it's happen best that you don't. She isn't laid out yet. Old Mrs Stavely will be coming to do that for me, and your father's going to call on his way back home to tell her. She lives in the last cottage, going out of the village.

I don't know what I'd have done if you two hadn't come when you did. I'd probably have broken down and done nothing. I can't think straight, let alone put my mind to doing anything.' Harry shook his head and then placed it in his hands as Meg poured the tea.

'Do you want something to eat, Harry? Meg here will make you something.' Tom looked at his old friend. Harry was in such a state that he didn't know what to do.

'No, that's the last thing I want. I just need my Mary back. I can't face life without her, and she's always been there for me,' Harry sobbed.

Meg looked at her father as she sat down. She didn't know what to do.

Tom nodded his head in the direction of the door, signalling for her to make herself scarce while he comforted his friend. She needed no further prompting, as she understood what he meant and gladly left the grieving house behind her, walking out into the small village of Gunnerside and the afternoon sun. She walked past the King's Head and past a row of small miners' cottages until she came to the bridge that crossed the Gunnerside Gill and looked up towards the head of the beck, thinking of Sam and hoping that he had not thought she had forsaken him.

High above her, she could hear the sound of the men at work in the lead-mines. The fell was being burrowed into by an army of lead-miners; like ants, they were. And Sam and Jack were two of them, Meg thought, as she listened and leaned back on the bridge, looking round at the small village green and the cottages that surrounded

101

it. Where did their mother live, she wondered, and what was she like? She obviously spoilt her boys, judging by the conversation she had heard in Hawes on her earlier visit.

Meg decided to walk up the path she had taken to meet Sam, passing the blacksmith's and the newly built Literary Institute, which was not yet open and which would shortly be used to widen the knowledge of the miners and their families of an evening. Then she walked up to the last cottage at the side of the gill. There she could just see the leaves of the sycamore tree under which she should have met Sam, between the dip of the fells. At the last cottage she stopped for a moment and held back her tears. She'd been full of hope when she had set off this morning. Although she had known that Mary had been ill, the thought of seeing Sam had gladdened her ride into Gunnerside. But now it seemed that she had lost both loves.

'Are you alright, lass? Nowt the matter, I hope?' A voice came from the garden next to the cottage.

Meg turned to see the woman whom she knew to be Sam and Jack's mother looking at her worriedly.

'There's not been an accident up there, 'as there? I've not heard owt.' Betty Alderson came to the garden gate and looked at the obviously upset young lass, who was shedding tears on the path outside her house.

'No, no, there's been no accident. I've just come from the grocery shop to get some fresh air. Mrs Battersby passed away this morning. My father's comforting her husband.' Meg sniffed and fought back the tears, which were shed both for Mary and in self-pity.

'Aye, dear, she's been bad for a long time, 'as the poor woman. A right martyr she was; you could see her getting worse by the day. I don't know what Harry will do with himself now. The shop's already gone down this last week or two, as his heart's not been in it. Are you related to them, then?' Betty quizzed.

'No, she was my mum's best friend, but I always called her "Aunt Mary" because she was more of an aunt than my real one.' Meg smiled.

'That's families. I'm sorry for your loss, lass. Do you know when the funeral will be? I'll have to go.' Betty stopped at her gate.

'No, not yet. I expect it will be sometime next week.' Meg paused. She wanted to ask about Sam and Jack, but knew it was a bit flippant, after the conversation she had just had. Then her heart got the better of her. 'How's Jack and Sam?'

Betty grinned at her. 'You know my lads, then? Where did you meet them, because you aren't from this neck of the woods, else I'd have seen you before?'

'I met them at a dance in Hawes. Can you tell them both I've been asking about them? The name's Meg, and I'm from Appersett.' She looked at the woman and could see a twinkle in her eye.

'Aye, I'll tell them. You won't be the first, mind. They are popular, are my lads. But they are both mother's boys at heart, although wild as mountain hares. It'll be a fine lass that pins one of them two down.' Betty turned and went back into her garden.

'Thank you,' Meg shouted after her, smiling as she

walked back down by the gill edge. At least both Sam and Jack would know that she had been asking after them. All was not lost after all, she thought, as she leaned against the bridge and waited for her father to appear from the gloom of the shop; and she thought about Sam and Jack as she looked round her at the village they lived in.

Tom said very little on the first few miles of the drive back home, and Meg did the same as they sat together, thinking about the death of Mary.

'I wondered whether to offer for you to stay the night with Harry, but then his neighbour came round and said she'd keep an eye on him.' Tom looked across at his daughter as she sat quietly next to him. 'He was impressed with the tidy-up you had given him in the shop. He said his heart hadn't been in it lately.'

'No, I could tell that. Aunt Mary always had the shop spotless when she was alive and well,' Meg said quietly.

'It's been a bit of a month, with us losing the folk we love. I can't get it into my head that I've lost my sister Anne. We were never really close, but she was my sister. I suppose you cannot remember her? She left the dale when you were just a baby. And now her lad's with us; he's not a bad soul, but he's a townie, no matter what he does and says. He's half his father, that's his problem; and Bob was worth nowt to no man.'

'I thought you were getting on with Dan, Father? He seems to follow your every move, and he's always talking with you.' Meg was surprised that her father was broaching the subject of Dan and his mother. She wondered whether to say honestly what she thought of Dan, but held her thoughts back.

'I have to, lass – we are all Dan's got, I owe it to his mother, and half of our home should really have been hers, if she hadn't run off with that idiot husband of hers. But he'll never replace you, so don't you fret. You are our daughter, and although you are not the lad I'd set my heart on, you are our lass and will always be more precious than any cocky nephew from Liverpool.'

Tom smiled at his daughter. He'd noticed Dan pushing his way into the family and it had made him realize how lucky he was to have a daughter who knew what to do around the farm. Besides, Harry had asked him something that he didn't know how to handle, until he'd asked Agnes that evening when they were by themselves. However, he didn't know how both women in his life would take it, as it would mean changes in their lives and he didn't want to bring heartache and upset to his relatively happy home.

Agnes lay in bed next to Tom, who was gazing up at the crack running along the bedroom ceiling. 'Aye, I'm going to miss Mary. She's always been there for me, and I hope I was for her. I don't know how Harry will cope without her.' Agnes sighed. 'There'll be another death yet, they always come in threes.'

'Don't say that, lass; we've had enough, don't you think?

105

Harry is a broken man. I nearly left Megan with him tonight to keep him company, he was in such a state.' Tom turned his head and looked at Agnes.

'You should have done. She'd have been alright for one night. We could have picked her up in the morning. I wouldn't like to think of him on his own.' Agnes looked at her husband, imagining what it would be like not to have anyone to talk to, if anything terrible happened to Tom.

'Nay, his neighbour came and she said she'd keep an eye on him.' Tom hesitated for a second. 'But Harry did wonder if we could spare Meg to go and live with him, just for the next month or two until he gets back on his feet. He knows she would be a good help to him, as well as company of an evening. She'd have her own bedroom and time to herself, and you'd see her once a week when we take the butter over to him.' Tom waited for Agnes's reply, but knew it wasn't going to be favourable.

'It's that bloody nephew of yours – you always have wanted a lad, and now that you've got one, you are turning your back on our Meg. I know Harry will be lonely, but he'll have to cope. An odd night or two with Meg for company I wouldn't have minded, but months is another matter. Once winter sets in, nine times out of ten we can't get over the Buttertubs pass, and then she'd be on her own,' Agnes retorted.

'It's nowt to do with us having Dan stopping here. I'm worried about Harry; he's taken Mary's death badly and he's exhausted. I'm not keen on leaving Meg there – how many times have we lectured her about not mixing with the lead-miners over there? But Harry needs her, to keep his sanity. He'd look after her; Harry's a good man and he'd make sure she was kept safe and fed and warm.' Tom knew what the response from his wife would be; that's why he'd waited till everyone was in bed – including Dan, in his new bedroom at the other end of the long farmhouse; he didn't want Dan to think he was king of the farmyard, cocky little devil.

'No, Tom, she's not going. I need Meg. Besides, folk would start talking – a nineteen-year-old lass living with a widower. No, it's not going to happen!' Agnes put her foot down.

'It's Harry we are talking about, not any old man. Besides, Mary told him to ask us, just before she died; she knew Harry wouldn't cope on his own.' Tom waited; the mention of Mary's last wish might sway Agnes, but he also knew it would hurt his wife to lose Meg, albeit only for a month or two, until his old friend got back on his own two feet.

'I'm off to sleep. We will talk about this in the morning. I'm not happy with this, Tom Oversby, not happy at all. Our Meg is still young, and I know the lad can't help it, but I think since Dan walked into our lives, your head is on looking after him, not your own daughter!' Agnes turned her back on her husband and pounded her pillow, trying to make herself comfortable to quell the worries he had presented to her.

Tom looked up at the ceiling again. No matter what

he said, he probably wouldn't win the argument tonight. Best to let Agnes sleep on it; she was upset and couldn't see that he was only looking after their dearest friend in his loss.

9

Agnes looked across at Meg and wondered whether to mention what Tom had told her before he went to sleep. She'd not slept for thinking about it, her thoughts flitting between being loyal to her best friend's dying wishes and to her own wish to keep her daughter at home. She'd be lost without Meg; besides being a help to her, Meg was female company, as she was growing up quickly and they both had a lot in common.

Agnes had sworn under her breath at Tom. If his nephew hadn't turned up out of the blue, he'd never have thought of Meg leaving the family home, because he needed her to help him with the jobs around the farm. After all, it was Tom who had recently put his foot down about Meg seeing the lads from Swaledale that she had been dancing with, and now there he was, expecting her to go and live over there. Harry was a good man, but Agnes was still of a mind that her daughter should not be seen to be living with him alone. The more she thought about it, the more she was opposed to giving the idea the time of day.

'Are you alright, Mum? You seem quiet this morning, and you look as if you haven't slept.' Meg looked up from the brass candlesticks that she was cleaning with Brasso and a soft cloth, her hands already black with dirt. 'I expect you are feeling sad over losing Aunt Mary. I would be, if I'd lost my best friend.'

'Aye, I'm broken-hearted over Mary's death. We were, as you say, good friends – like you and Hattie Baines, although I don't hear you mention her of late. You've not fallen out with one another, have you?' Agnes looked across at her daughter and thought how bonny she was, even when wearing one of her old pinnies to protect her from the dirty job she was doing.

'No, we've not fallen out with one another. It's just that Hattie is courting John Thwaite from Burtersett and she's got a job in the dairy, so she hasn't time for me. Besides, I don't want to play the gooseberry and sit between them both and know they don't want me there.' Meg rubbed the candlestick hard and looked at the shine she had brought to it, before she moved on to the next one.

'I'm surprised her mother is letting her court some-body a lot older than her. I remember Hattie being born. It was a really hot August that year and we hardly had any water; the well had dried up and I was worried that we were all going to die of thirst. And then it poured down and never stopped until Christmas. It's funny how you remember things. It doesn't seem five minutes ago really.'

110

'Well, there's talk of her getting married next year, it's that serious.' Meg didn't look up at her mum.

'Your father was right, telling you not to go with either of them lads from Swaledale. There's plenty of time for courting.' Agnes looked across at Meg and smiled. 'I suppose we will all have to attend the funeral next week. I can't say I'm looking forward to that.' She decided to mention the fact that Harry had asked for Meg to stay with him, and see her daughter's reaction to his request. 'Your father said Harry was in a bit of a state; he even asked if you could go and stay with him for a while, until he sorts himself out. I think he appreciated your help in tidying the shop.' Agnes looked at Meg and noticed that she didn't even bother to stop cleaning the brass as she listened to her.

'Oh, I'm not interested in any lads. And, like my father says, the lead-miners over there are worth nowt. It is better that I wait for the right one to come along – a farmer, perhaps. That would suit my father, and give clever Dan something to think about.' Meg tried to keep her heart from beating fast. She had to conceal any hint of affection for Swaledale and its inhabitants, else her mum would never let her out of her sight.

'Dan is a clever devil, on that you are right. He tries too hard to impress your father and, like a fool, I think Tom falls for it.' Agnes grinned. 'Would you be happy going and helping Harry out? I don't want you to go, but I think Mary suggested it to him before she died.' She waited for an answer from Meg.

'I don't know, Mum. I've never been away from home

before, and although I know Uncle Harry well, it would feel strange living there on my own with him. How long would he want me to be there? I'd want to be home for Christmas.' Meg put on a worried face as she pretended to be unsure of her decision.

'I don't know – until he feels more like running the shop, I presume. I'll be honest with you, Meg, I don't want you to go, but I rather think your father got pressurized into saying you would stay. He felt obliged, because of Mary dying. He'd never even have dreamed of agreeing to it once upon a time.' Agnes sighed.

'But he would now – now that he's got Dan staying with us, to give him a hand with all the jobs. Let's face it, I'm surplus to requirements when it comes to the farm.' Meg looked across at her mum and tried to hide the excitement that was building inside her at the thought of going to live in Swaledale and being near the Alderson brothers.

'No, it's not like that. You'd just be giving a close family friend comfort when he needs it most. You'd be back before you knew it.' Agnes hung her head and held back the tears. She didn't want Meg to feel unloved, and she would much rather keep her at home.

'Then if Aunt Mary asked it of me, I really should go. We've got to respect her last wishes, after all. Can I have a few days to think about it? I'll let you know before the funeral, and then perhaps you can leave me with Harry, if I decide to stay?' Meg smiled at her mum, hoping she could not read her true feelings.

'Of course you can. You don't have to go if you don't

want to. If you go, I'll be lost without you.' Agnes looked across at her daughter and realized how Meg had grown up in the last few months; she was no longer the young girl she had protected all her life. Perhaps it would be good for Meg to spread her wings, and a month or two away from the family nest might make her realize that home comforts were the best.

Meg didn't reply. She loved her mum, but the thought of perhaps being able to see Sam every day made her heart skip with excitement, and it offered an escape from Dan and his ways.

'Well, that's Mary buried.' Tom stood back from the graveside and put his arm round Agnes as she sobbed into her handkerchief. Meg looked around the small graveyard on the outskirts of Gunnerside. She could hear the water rushing and gurgling in the nearby beck and looked up at the high fells above her. It was a remote place but beautiful, with the square-built Methodist chapel in its grounds. If a soul was to be buried anywhere, this was as good as you could wish for.

'I'll miss her. We'd been friends for a long time, and she was more like a sister than a friend,' Agnes sobbed, and then looked at Meg. 'You sure you want to stay over here, Meg? You can always come back with us. Harry would understand.' Her tears were not only for Mary, but also for the temporary loss of her beloved daughter, although she was trying hard for Meg not to see them.

'No, I can't do that. Look at him, he's absolutely heartbroken; he needs me. Besides, it's only for a few weeks, until he gets back on his feet.' Meg looked across at Harry, who was beside himself with grief as he thanked the minister for giving his wife a good send-off.

'She'll be alright, Agnes. You'll see her once a week when we come over with the butter. She's not going hundreds of miles away; and she's with Harry, he'll keep a good eye on her.' Tom smiled at his wife; he knew it was a big step for her, as well as him, letting their daughter be independent for the first time in her life.

'I don't know if he will. I think it's going to be the other way round. Harry hasn't even bothered to organize a funeral tea for poor Mary, he's in such a state.' Agnes glanced across at Harry and went quiet, as she saw him finish his thanks to the minister and walk towards them.

Harry looked at his closest friends and wiped away the tears that kept falling. 'You don't know how grateful I am that Meg here is going to come home with me, and keep me company and the shop running. I couldn't have walked back into my home by myself.'

'You've no need to do that, Harry. We will come back home with you and settle our Meg into her new temporary home. And Agnes will make sure you have a cup of tea and something to eat before we return home.' Tom patted his old mate on the back. 'Didn't you think of putting on a funeral tea? Folk usually expect something to eat, and a chance to give their condolences to you.' Tom looked round at the mourners standing in groups, left with nothing to do other than talk between themselves before making their way home.

'I didn't want anything afterwards. I couldn't face folk

and their sympathies. Best we get home, like you say.' Harry lowered his head and started to walk down the path of the churchyard.

Agnes looked round the living quarters of the shop and shook her head. 'What have you been doing, Harry? There's not a clean spot in the house, and you've not had a tidy-up since she died, by the look of things. No wonder Mary asked for our Meg to come and keep you straight.'

'I can't be bothered. What's the point? Mary was everything to me.' Harry sat next to the fire and held his head in his hands. 'We should have had some bairns; they'd be here now to look after me, instead of your lass. But we were never blessed. Meg's room is tidy. Mary made me get it ready before she died, in case you did agree to Meg staying with me, so you needn't worry on that score.'

'That's just as well, because I'll be honest, I'm in two minds about leaving her here with you. You are going to have to learn to deal with Mary's loss. Look to the future, and run that shop well, like you used to do. It must have made you a pretty penny or two over the years, and Mary was so proud of it.' Agnes started to pick up the clutter that had mounted over the last few days, as Harry had wallowed in self-pity.

'Give him a chance, Agnes. You can see he's in no way to be lectured by you. Meg will soon get him straight, won't you, lass?' Tom looked across at Meg as she watched the sorrowful man she was going to have to live with and finally realized that this was her home for the next few months; and that perhaps living in the same village as Sam and Jack was not going to be recompense enough for what she would have to endure.

'Yes, yes, I'll soon get everything straight, and tidy the shop. It won't take long. Do you mind if I take a look at my bedroom, Uncle Harry? Mum, do you want to come too, and then you know where I'm living?' Meg picked up her carpet bag, filled with the clothes and other necessary items for a short stay, and made for the staircase.

'Aye, make yourself at home. You can do what you want and go anywhere you wish, just as long as I have you to keep me tidy and fed; and a bit of your company of an evening would be welcome.'

Harry looked up at the young lass, whom he had promised Tom to look after while she was with him. He had been in two minds about carrying out Mary's wishes, but now he realized that, after coping with her illness for so long, he was exhausted and at a loss with himself. But would Meg be able to keep his secret, which he had tried to keep to himself for so long? However, right now he needed some care, in order to get back on his feet.

'Your room's right at the top, under the rafters. I thought you'd prefer a floor to yourself, and Mary thought it best. She said you'd appreciate your privacy.'

Meg turned and looked at her mum as she went up the stairs. 'He's in a bit of a state. What do I do if he gets any worse?' she whispered as they climbed the second lot of stairs to the attic bedroom.

'You send for us. Hopefully Harry will cheer up a bit, after today. Have patience with him; he's just broken-hearted.'

116

Meg opened the heavy oak door that led into the attic bedroom that was to be her home. She looked around her, at the iron bedstead made up ready for her to sleep in, with a patchwork quilt on it and clean pillows. There was a dressing table and a stool, and a water jug and dish on a marble washstand; and on the opposite side of the room were two windows that looked out on to the village green.

'Well, at least your bedroom is tidy and you've got everything you need.' Agnes lifted the bedcovers and checked that there was a chamber pot for her daughter's use. 'There's a bolt on your bedroom door and all. I'm glad to see that; at least I know that you are safe of a night, once it's bolted. You never know, with living above a shop – somebody might break in and threaten you both. These lead-miners are not to be trusted; they never have any money.'

'Mum, surely they are not as bad as that! I'll be fine. It's a nice room and I'll make myself busy through the day, and keep an eye on Harry until he gets over his grief, and then I'll come home. So stop your worrying.' Meg hugged her mum and kissed her. 'Now, let's go and make him that cup of tea, and then you and Father can get back home and see what Dan has been up to while you were both away. I bet he's been asleep in front of the fire, taking advantage of you two not being about. I don't trust him an inch.'

'Now who's the doubting Thomas! You'll take care, won't you? You'll not get up to anything you'd be ashamed to tell me about, will you?' Agnes looked sternly at Meg.

117

'Oh, Mum! I'll behave, you know I will.' Meg sighed as both of them made their way back down to the living quarters, past the bedroom of Harry and Mary, which brought back sad memories of the much-loved woman they had just buried in the graveyard, without any celebration of her life with friends afterwards. Mary wouldn't have wished for that, Agnes thought, as she entered the small living room where Tom and Harry were sitting in silence.

'The bedroom's lovely, Harry. Meg will be fine in there. Now, we'll have a brew and then we'll get back home before it's dark. You'll promise to look after my lass, won't you? See that she's right. And you'll send word if she needs anything, so that we can bring it over on a Thursday when we come with the butter and anything else?' Agnes stood next to the kettle and waited for it to boil.

'Aye, don't fret, she'll be fine. I'm just grateful for her company and her help. I don't think I could face life on my own, and Mary knew that, God bless her soul. I'll look after Meg.' Harry lifted up his face towards Meg's. 'We'll be alright, won't we, lass? We'll rub along like two old shoes.'

'I'm sure we will, Uncle Harry. I'll open the shop up again tomorrow, once I've tidied up, and I'll make sure you get fed.' Meg smiled at the old man. She felt sorry for him; he'd lost the one he loved, and she could understand his pain. Even if her bedroom had been in a terrible state, she would have stayed, because this was going to give her the freedom she craved; and she was now near the two lads who had taken her eye – and because of that, she was going to take full advantage of her stay. What her parents didn't see they wouldn't worry about, and that was how she wanted it.

10

Meg placed scrambled eggs on toast in front of Harry and poured his tea, as he sat at the table next to the window that overlooked the shop's yard and outhouse. The evening following her parents' departure had been a little awkward, with Harry not having a lot to say as he smoked his pipe and sat next to the fire.

'I hope scrambled eggs are alright? I didn't know what you usually eat for breakfast.' Meg watched Harry's face as he looked at the plate of food she had put in front of him.

'Aye, they look grand, but I don't know if I fancy them. I haven't been eating much of late. Did you find everything you needed, and did you sleep alright? I never heard you get up. I slept pretty hard last night. I think I was grateful the funeral was over. It had been the hardest week of my life last week, and I needed to catch up with my beauty sleep.' Harry smiled at the young lass, who looked a bit lost in her new surroundings.

'I was fine, thank you, Uncle Harry. I got up early because I thought I could tidy up in here properly, rather than disturb you when you were about today. I know Mum had a quick pick-up, but I've dusted and shaken the rug and swept the floor. So you can sit by the fire and take it easy, while I mind the shop.' Meg waited for Harry to reply as he ate a mouthful of eggs.

'Aye, the shop – I've neglected it all this week. Stuff will be old and stale, and everything will want a good tidy. I don't know . . . I was alright when my Mary was alive, but things have got on top of me lately. She did right to tell me to ask your father if you'd come and take pity on me for a while. If I don't get myself together in the next week or two, just kick my arse, Meg, because that's what Mary would have done. I can see her now, standing with her hands on her hips, giving me a lecture and saying, "Get on with it", because she'd no time for shirkers.' Harry smiled and put his knife and fork down by the side of his plate, before starting to sob again.

'Uncle Harry, don't be so upset – life goes on. Look at the lovely day outside. Why don't you, after you've eaten, go for a walk round the village? It'll do you good. It's what I always do when I've something on my mind.' Meg wanted to comfort him more and would have done, if it had been her father in the same situation, but Uncle Harry was different; he wasn't quite family, and she felt it was inappropriate to be too close to a man who wasn't her blood relative.

'I might just do that; a breath of fresh air might do me good. Can you manage on your own? I know you've helped in the past, so you know where everything is.' Harry wiped his eyes and picked up his knife and fork as he started to tackle his breakfast again.

'Good, that sounds about right for the day. Now, I'll go into the shop and open for business, as usual. You can't let the villagers down, else they'll start to go elsewhere. And as you say, there is a lot to catch up on.' Meg watched as Harry made short work of his breakfast, then put on his cap and jacket, before reaching for his walking stick.

'Do as you think fit in the shop. I'll have a wander and be back for my dinner. Frank Metcalfe will be bringing you an order of bread and suchlike shortly; the money to pay him is in the till. Mind you take no notice of what he says to you. He's given to romance a lot, when he talks of folk.'

Harry put his walking stick under his arm and quickly made his way out of the back door and down the paved back yard, before Meg could even say goodbye or clear the table. She watched him go and sighed. This was not what she had envisaged. Her Uncle Harry was not concerned with the running of his business, like he used to be when he and her Aunt Mary had worked together. In fact, she was sure that if she didn't open the shop doors, he wouldn't even notice or care. He seemed to be in a world of his own and must still be grieving for Mary, although sometimes it didn't look that way. Anyway, it was his loss. In the meantime she'd get the chance to know Sam and Jack better, once they knew where she was; and she knew that would soon reach their ears, in the close-knit community of Gunnerside.

Meg turned the sign on the shop's door and opened the door wide to let the late-summer sun into the dusty room. Its rays showed how neglected the shop had become since Mary's death, and Meg suspected even before then, by the look of the cobwebs that coated the oil lamps, and by the smell of rotting cabbage from the shelves, where she had previously placed the fresh vegetables brought from her own garden. It was going to take some time to get the shop back on its feet, but at least her days would pass quickly. And she would have Sundays to do whatever she wanted. Meg smiled as she thought of strolling arm-in-arm with Sam. There was no one to stop her, and as long as they kept away from the landlord at the King's Head across the road, nobody would tell her father, when he visited for his weekly gill.

She held her fingers to her nose and picked up the pile of rotting cabbage, walking out of the shop and down to the riverside, where she threw it onto the bank; it would hurt nobody there, and the ducks on the beck might even enjoy it. When she returned, the shop instantly smelt sweeter, as she opened the window to let more air in and picked up her brush to sweep the floor and get rid of the offending cobwebs.

'Now then, has old Harry got himself a shop girl? It's about bloody time! Since Mary took bad, the place has gone to the dogs.' Frank Metcalfe placed his wooden tray full of freshly made bread and buns, and a varied assortment of cakes, on the large wooden counter and looked across at Meg. 'I've seen you before. You've sometimes been here on a Thursday with your parents, when I've been running late. You bring the old bastard his butter, or part of it, don't you?'

'Yes, I'm Meg Oversby. My parents and Mary and Harry have been friends nearly all their lives. We live in Appersett and, as you say, supply him with some of his butter and other things – eggs or vegetables, if he's short, or if we have too much for ourselves to eat.' Meg looked at the tall, red-faced man who was still wearing his apron, as she emptied the wooden tray and opened the till to pay him, when he gave her a slip stating how much he was owed. But she fell silent as the till drawer opened to reveal hardly any money inside it, let alone enough to pay for the goods that had just been delivered.

Her face must have told Frank Metcalfe of her plight, as he coughed politely. 'Has he not enough in there, the old bugger?' He looked at the dismay on Meg's face.

'No, he's got next to nothing in here, but he said there was enough to pay you.' Meg blushed; she felt awkward and didn't know what to do.

'Tell you what, lass, pay me in the morning. Harry's had his mind on other things, what with losing poor Mary and having other business to think about. Hopefully he'll come to his senses, now he's got you to help out in the shop.' Frank picked up his wooden tray and looked back at Meg. 'See you tomorrow – and you watch that old Harry. He's a bit of a ladies' man on the quiet, but I'm sure you will soon find that out, if you are staying here with him.' Frank winked at Meg as he turned and left the shop.

Uncle Harry, a ladies' man? What could he mean? The Harry she knew was never like that. He'd been devoted to her Aunt Mary, and they'd been inseparable for as long as she had known them. Then she remembered that Harry had said Frank Metcalfe was always full of mischief and was 'given to romance a lot'. Meg decided to dismiss his words as she placed the bread on display and waited for her first customer, then tidied the shelves and dusted the many jars and tins on them. All the while she was thinking of Sam and Jack as she hummed to herself, hoping that any minute they might come through the door and smile at her, even though she knew both men would be at work. She smiled to herself as she thought of their cheeky grins that had bewitched her, then carried on with her dusting.

The morning went quickly, with customers coming and going, all of them welcoming Meg's presence in the shop and showing gratitude that one of the mainstays of the community was back up and running. On the whole the customers expressed their sympathy and showed their concern for Harry, asking where he was and how he was, while they bought the supplies they needed.

Meg looked down into the till as she neared dinner time, checking that there would be enough money to pay Frank Metcalfe the following morning. His bread and baked goods sold well, so it was best that he was kept straight and wasn't owed anything. She was about to turn the sign in the shop's window to 'Closed' when she noticed Mrs Alderson, Sam and Jack's mother, coming over to the doorway. She looked in a hurry, and Meg rushed back to the counter to serve her.

'Oh, it's you that's here, is it? Folk are saying that old

Harry's got a young lass working for him, but they didn't say who you were.' Betty fumbled in her small leather purse for some change as she looked at Meg. 'I'll have two ounces of suet, please – that is, if you have any.'

Meg smiled at the straight-talking woman. 'Yes, I'm here for a few weeks, just until Mr Battersby gets back on his feet. And yes, we have some fresh suet; it's in the back, in the pantry.' She left Betty standing in the shop as she went and got her some suet.

'You've got your work cut out, looking after this place. Harry will be no good to you, that I can tell you. Poor Mary, she always had to keep him right. No wonder she was that ill – it would be the worry of having Harry as her husband, the useless bugger,' Betty yelled through to Meg, as she came back with the suet and weighed it out.

'Uncle Harry's not that bad; he worshipped Aunt Mary.' Meg looked up at Betty Alderson and felt aggrieved that she saw Harry in such a bad light.

'Oh, I'm sorry. I keep forgetting he's your uncle. Forget what I said. I'd got it into my head that he'd just taken you on to help him.' Betty reached for her small bag of suet and fell quiet.

'He's not really my uncle. I just call him that, because he's always been a part of my family. It was Mary who asked for me to come and take care of the shop, until he gets over her death.' Meg held her hand out for the money.

'That's probably because she knew that at the first chance he got, Harry would be going down to Reeth, to his fancy woman that runs the boarding house there. The poor woman; there she was on her deathbed, and him

126

carrying on with that floozy. There was him pretending to be so broken-hearted, looking so upset – but more guilty, if you ask me, as he didn't even give poor Mary a decent send-off. Her friends expected a tea at Mrs Price's tea room, if nothing else. I suspect folk know what he's up to, but are too decent to say anything. Well, now he's free to do as he likes. You'll not see much of him, lass. He hates this shop and it was beginning to go to the dogs; nothing was ever fresh. Take my advice, lass, and don't stay here, as you'll not have a roof over your head for long. Give him a month or two and he'll be moving in with his trollop.' Betty leaned on the counter and watched Meg taking in the gossip she had told her.

'No, it can't be right. Harry's not like that! He loved Aunt Mary!' Meg exclaimed.

'Where is he now? I bet he left first thing and it'll be nightfall before he returns. Folk used to come and knock on the shop's door and he'd be busy down the dale, doing his thing with her, while poor Mary was either dying in her bed or trying to serve people behind this counter. She deserved better, did the poor woman. Sorry, lass, but that's how it's been this last month or two. I just hope that you keep this place open for us locals. It would be missed if it closed, and Mary knew that. I presume that is why you are here.' Betty looked around her. 'I'll have a dozen candles and all, while we are about it. It will save my lads buying them from the company; the thieving bastards charge twice the amount you do.'

Meg climbed up the small stepladder and counted out twelve tallow candles from a wooden box, then climbed back down, placing them in a bag for Betty. She looked up at her. 'Are Sam and Jack keeping well?' She held her breath, not wanting her true feelings to show, as her heart fluttered when thinking about them both, while she put to the back of her mind the shocking news about Harry being unfaithful.

'Aye, they are grand. They are good lads; they look after their mother. Do you know them well? They've never mentioned you, and both simply looked at one another the last time I spoke of you,' Betty quizzed Meg and looked at her hard.

'I met them both at a dance in Hawes. We are just friends.' Meg blushed.

'Aye, well, I'll tell them you are here. You'll need somebody to talk to, if you are to work with Harry – or should I say "without Harry", because he'll never be here, except on a Saturday, when he usually goes to the King's Head for a gill or two and a game of dominoes. Now, what do I owe you?' Betty waited and watched Meg as she totted up the total.

'Ninepence, please.' Meg looked as Betty put the goods in her basket and passed her the change.

'Now, you take care, lass. If you want to know anything, or need anything, you come and see me. My door's always open, and I bet you've caught our Sam's eye already, because he's a devil for a bonny lass. Our Jack is a bit less forward; he's the deep thinker of the two. They'll both be visiting you, but not necessarily buying owt, I bet.' Betty grinned as she walked to the door, leaving Meg thinking of both brothers, but also of how badly wrong her mother and father had got the marriage of Mary and Harry. It would seem that all love had died between them a long time ago, and now it would probably only be a matter of time before Harry sold the shop. And then she would be back home and would have to endure Dan once more. Meg didn't want that to happen, not yet; she was going to enjoy her independence in Swaledale, running the shop and being part of the community. She was needed and appreciated for the first time in her life, and she didn't want that to stop. And besides, she had some courting to do, with one or other of the Alderson brothers.

It was supper time at the Aldersons'. Betty had been busy cooking a steak-and-kidney pie in the small but spotless kitchen most of the day, and was serving it with potatoes freshly dug from the kitchen garden. Although the cottage the three lived in was only small, it suited them well and was always kept clean and tidy. The brasses shone and the pots were washed, and Betty demanded that both her boys cleaned themselves up in the water butt outside the back door before they entered the low-beamed cottage. She dished her steak-and-kidney pie out to both hungry sons, then sat down to join them over supper at the kitchen table.

'Well, what's fresh at the mine – anything or nothing? Is everybody behaving themselves?' Betty watched as both sons ate their dinner and hardly spoke, tired after their hard day's work at the mine-face and at the smelting mill.

'No, nowt's fresh, Mother, apart from we've no money

for going to Reeth Bartle Fair this next weekend, because I've been charged for my shovel weighing light – the robbing bastards.' Sam tucked into his supper and didn't even lift his head.

'No, there's nowt fresh, Mother, it's just the same as ever.' Jack smiled. Sam had been in a mood for days now, and it was all because he thought he'd been dumped by the lass from over at Appersett. Perhaps she had heard about Sam's wicked ways with women and had thought better than to let him string her along, like he had the others.

'Well, I've a bit of news. The shop's back open, now poor Mary Battersby's been buried. I went there for some candles for you two today, and good job that I did, seeing as neither of you have any brass. The lass there seems to know you both. She asked about you both last time, if you remember.'

Betty sat back and watched as both her sons raised their heads.

'Her name's Meg. I told her straight about Harry. When I said she'd not get any help from him, as he was too busy getting his leg over the woman that runs that boarding house for what that haughty minister of ours calls "colluvies", she seemed shocked. I think that she thought Harry was as white as snow. She was even more shocked when I explained that "colluvies" is another word for the scum of the earth, according to the minister. She thought that he had no right saying suchlike.'

Sam stopped eating his dinner. 'You didn't say anything to upset her, did you? Did you watch your language?'

'Why, is she something special? She's nobbut a shop

130

lass. I said you two would probably be calling on her, once you knew she was here. I knew, once I saw her, that she was too bonny for you two to ignore.' Betty watched as Sam pushed his chair back, leaving half his supper behind on his plate.

'Here, don't you leave your supper! Where are you going?' she shouted after Sam, as he walked quickly across the kitchen floor and slammed the door behind him. 'Well, it seems he knows her better than she was letting on!' Betty scraped what was left on his plate on-to Jack's. Here, you have his leftovers – it's too good to waste.' She looked at Jack, his face telling her every-thing.

'All I ever get are Sam's bloody leftovers. Why haven't I got the gift of the gab, Mother? He's always one step ahead of me, because of his mouth and his charm. He makes me sick.' Jack put his head down and finished his extra portion. Better to have a full belly to help soothe his aching heart, he thought, as he gazed out of the window.

'So, she's taken your eye and all, 'as she? Well, lad, faint heart never won a fair maiden. But don't you hurt your brother, and don't let her part you both, else she'll not be welcome in this house. I didn't know our Sam knew her that well. We'll have to see where it goes. Nowhere, I hope. You are my two lads, and I don't want to part with you yet.' Betty sighed. 'Find yourself a different woman at the Reeth Bartle Fair. I'll give you both some money out of the savings box. It'll do you both good, but no arguing over that flibbertigibbet in the shop. She'll not be worth the pain.' Betty ruffled Jack's dark hair. 'There's a lass out there for you somewhere, lad, she just hasn't met you yet. But as I say, your mother still needs you, so there's no hurry in finding her.'

'But I know where she is, and she shouldn't be with our Sam – he'll break her heart. He loves and leaves each one and doesn't care. But this one's different, Mother, she's kind and she doesn't deserve to be treated badly.' Jack hung his head.

'Well, happen your brother will change with this one. Happen this time he's serious.' Betty kissed her eldest son on his brow and went to the stone sink with the dirty plates. How she wished the bonny lass in the shop had not come to Swaledale. She could see that her lads were smitten with her, by the look on Jack's face, and there were bound to be tears and words between them before, hopefully, she went back to her true home.

11

'Meg, there's somebody hammering on the shop door. Go and tell them we are closed, and that they'll have to come back tomorrow,' Harry yelled as he ate the bacon-and-egg pie that Meg had taken out of the oven and served him, on his return from his long 'walk', which had strangely kept him away from home all day.

'Yes, Uncle Harry.' She quickly came out of the pantry and walked through the shop, unbolting the door as it rattled to another round of blows. 'I'm coming, but we are closed. Can you not read?' Meg drew back the bolt and opened the door, stopping short in her tracks when there in front of her stood Sam, leaning with one hand on the door lintel and the warmest smile on his face she had ever seen.

'So, my mother was right: it is you working here. I didn't dare believe it. I thought she must have got it wrong.' Sam stepped forward and almost entered the shop.

Meg pushed him gently back onto the street and closed the shop door behind her. 'I can't let you in. Harry's in the back, having his supper, and he'll tell my mum and dad that you've been calling, when they come to check up on me and deliver the butter on Thursday.' She smiled at Sam and started to laugh, as she noticed that his braces were hanging loose at the sides of his trousers. 'Haven't you had time to dress to come and see me?'

'Oh, my mother told me over the supper table that you were here. And I'd just had a wash and I always leave the braces hanging, before putting them on for the rest of the evening. I'd forgotten, I was in such a rush to see you.' Sam ran his fingers through his curly black hair and then pulled his braces over his shoulders, tucking his white shirt into his corduroy breeches. 'I had to see if it was true, check that Mother wasn't seeing things, and know why you didn't come and meet me the other week.' He propped his hand against the doorway and looked down on the girl who had taken his fancy – the one he hoped to have his way with.

'I couldn't. Aunt Mary had died and then there was the funeral. But I'm working here every day now for the next month or so, until Uncle Harry gets back on his feet.' Meg looked up into Sam's blue eyes and longed to kiss him. It was true: absence did make the heart grow fonder, and she'd wished for this moment.

'Meg! Who is it? Tell them to bugger off. We are open long enough. If they can't get what they want in the hours we are open, then they needn't come knocking on my door,' Harry yelled from within.

'I'll have to go! Meet me down at the turn-off for Crackpot, next to the big bridge over the River Swale, about seven tomorrow evening.' Meg turned to go and opened the shop door, hoping that Harry had not heard the conversation.

'Aye, I'll be counting the minutes – nay, even the seconds, come to that.' Sam grinned and then shouted, 'Thanks for the gripe-water. If that baby doesn't stop crying, I'll chuck it and the missus out onto the street.' He blew Meg a kiss and ran back home along the street.

Meg watched him and then locked the door behind her.

'Who was that, then?' Harry grunted.

'Some miner, by the looks of him. His wife had sent him for something for colic, so I gave him a bottle of gripe-water from the top shelf. Poor devil, he looked fraught.' Meg put the plates away, hoping their lie would not be detected.

'He should have made it cinder tea. Drop a red-hot cinder into some warm water – that's the best cure. Still, if he wants to spend his brass with me, who am I to complain?' Harry stretched out and looked at his young assistant. 'You look as if you've been busy today, and the shop takings are good. Perhaps they prefer to see a bonny face behind the counter, instead of this miserable 'un.'

'I think everyone was just glad you were open again.

They'd missed the convenience,' Meg said as she tidied the supper things away.

'Aye, well, I enjoyed my day of freedom, so I might do it again tomorrow. I feel a lot better for it. But I'll have to be about when your mother and father come on Thursday. Otherwise, I think the shop's in good hands with you running it. And my belly certainly appreciated your cooking this evening. Mary was right, God rest her soul. She knew that you'd look after me.' Harry sighed and then went to sit next to the fire.

'Would you mind if I went for a walk myself of an evening, to get a breath of fresh air and clear my head before bedtime? I'll be back before twilight,' Meg asked Harry coyly, paving the way for her meeting with Sam the next evening.

'As long as you've done what there is to do, the time's your own. But you take care, walking around on your own at dusk. The miners over here come from all walks of life, and some wouldn't think twice of taking advantage of a young thing like you. There's more bairns born out of wedlock than in, over in this dale. But perhaps I've said too much; it's up to your parents to keep you straight over suchlike.' Harry reached for his pipe and newspaper and left Meg washing the dishes.

She smiled to herself as she thought about her rendezvous with Sam. The hours could not pass quickly enough for her to get back to her lead-miner. He was different from the rest; he wouldn't take advantage of her or lead her astray. Yes, he was confident, but surely that was a good thing. Her parents were definitely wrong when it came to Sam. Anyway, he'd found her, so that was nothing but good, in her eyes. As for Harry and his daily 'walk', well, that was good too, for she was her own boss and she quite liked being a shop girl and housekeeper for him.

Customers came and went all day. Frank Metcalfe delivered his baking and smirked when Meg told him she was in charge once again. A delivery of chandlery goods was made, which Mary had placed before she died, and Meg found herself raiding whatever money she had earnt to pay for the goods, leaving her short of change for the next customers. She would have to say something to Harry that evening. She was balancing the books purely with the money that came in through the till. Surely he had extra funds, for goods ordered? Along with that, no money or wage had ever been mentioned to her, but now Meg was beginning to think that perhaps she was being used as slave labour while Harry wandered with his love, if the gossip was true.

Her heart fluttered as she finally turned the notice on the door to 'Closed'. Another hour and she would be meeting Sam, down by the banks of the Swale. She was glad the weather had held; the clouds had threatened rain all day, but now, as evening approached, the sun had broken through and it was warm and inviting outside. Meg heard the latch of the kitchen door being lifted. She'd give Harry his due: he timed his return spot-on, and by six o'clock on both evenings he had appeared like magic, just as the day's work in the shop had ended.

137

'That you, Uncle Harry?' Meg shouted through to the kitchen as she discarded her shop apron behind the counter, before stepping into the kitchen. The smell of mutton stew cooking in the side-oven filled the room as she made her way through the doorway.

'It's me, Megan. I did knock, but you didn't hear me, so I tried the door.' Jack stood in front of her, looking down at his shoes, aware that he'd not officially been invited into the living quarters of the village shop.

'Jack, what are you doing here? Is Sam alright? Has he sent you to tell me he can't join me later?' Meg looked worriedly at the quiet man.

'No, but I'm here to warn you not to meet him. Sam's a good man, but when it comes to women, he breaks their hearts and doesn't care. Don't you give your heart to him, Megan, you deserve better.' Jack bowed his head, knowing that to say such things about his brother was not showing any family loyalty.

'You mean perhaps I deserve you? Could this be jealousy between brothers? I'm meeting Sam, and you can't stop me. If he is like you say, I'll find out in my own time,' Meg snapped. She'd expected better of Jack, as she thought both brothers were close.

'I just wanted to warn you. I don't mean to upset you. I'll be on my way. But take care, that's all I'm saying. Sam sometimes shows no respect to his women. He'll use you, Meg, like he has so many other young women. Please don't be fooled by his charming ways.'

Jack walked slowly out of the kitchen door, leaving Meg wondering what his confession about his brother was all about. She breathed in and got on with laying the supper table, thinking all the time of the words said by Jack. Surely it was jealousy; she'd seen how the quieter of the two had looked at her. But it was Jack's loss – he should have been more forward, like his brother. His warning only served to make her more determined to court Sam, and convinced that Jack should mind his own business.

'Now then, lass! Was that Jack Alderson I saw, coming away from here? He's not been bothering you, has he? Him and his brother are a bit wild. That Sam is a bugger with the women, so I understand; broken many a lass's heart. So you keep them two at arm's length, else your father will have something to say to both of us, I expect.' Harry threw his cap onto his fireside chair and sat down at the table. 'Timed that well, haven't I? Supper smells good.'

'No, nobody's been here, apart from the usual customers in the shop. I don't know the Alderson lads, and I'll keep away from them if they are that bad.' Meg placed the dish of red-hot mutton stew on the table and started to spoon it out onto plates, ready for eating.

'Aye, it's as well you do. I promised both your mother and your father I'd look after you, and we will have no trailing tomcats calling, when you are under my roof. Now how did the shop do today? I forgot to tell you: if you get a delivery, the brass is in the desk in the other room. Just make sure you lock the desk and leave me a receipt of what you've paid for.' Harry smiled across at her.

'I paid for some chandlery goods that were delivered

from Richmond out of the till's takings, but I do have a receipt.' Meg looked across at Harry as they both ate their meal.

'You must have made some money today, then, if you were able to do that? I'll fill your till up and check the stock while you go on your walk. You deserve a bit of time to yourself. And I'll wash the pots. Else the day will be nearly done by the time you get out.' Harry tucked into his mutton stew and said nothing more as they both ate.

'I'll be away, then.' Meg wrapped her shawl around her and made for the back door.

'Aye, be back by nine, else it'll be pulling in dark. The dinner plates will be washed by the time you come back.' Harry yawned as he watched Meg close the door behind her, and thought he'd rest his eyes for five minutes before tackling his one chore of the day.

Once out on the street, Meg started to run down the road, passing over the bridge that spanned Gunnerside Gill and past the market cross surrounded by well-weathered stone cottages, then down the road, which was still bordered on either side with late-flowering cow parsley and buttercups, until she reached the wide river bridge that spanned the mighty River Swale. There she could see Sam, waiting for her on the arch of the bridge. He was looking down into the deep waters, concentrating on something that had caught his eye. She had mulled over the words of warning said by Jack about his brother, and those of her Uncle Harry, but had decided to dismiss them. One lot had been made through jealousy and the

140

other because her parents had lectured Harry about keeping her virtuous.

'Sorry I'm late. Uncle Harry has only just finished his supper, and I didn't close the shop until gone six.' Meg stood breathlessly next to Sam. She looked at him and felt her stomach churning. She'd never felt like this before, almost light-headed and stuck for words, as she felt a flush come to her cheeks and urges that she had never previously experienced.

'No matter, you are here now. Besides, I've been admiring tomorrow night's supper. Look at the big bugger – it's the largest salmon I've seen up here for a long time. I'll come back later and catch it.' Sam gazed down into a still part of the river, where the salmon was floating gently in the shelter of the shade of the bank. 'I hope it stops where it is. I can lie down on the side of the bank and tickle it. Anyway, never mind the fish – you are here, and that's all that matters.' Sam turned round and grabbed Meg's hand. 'Come on, we'll go and sit under the bridge and then nobody can see us.' He showed Meg the smile that had captivated her. He pulled on her arm and led her down by the riverside, to a sandy and pebble-strewn river bank, where he took off his jacket for them both to sit on. 'There, my lady, just for you.' He sat down and held out his hand for Meg to join him.

'Why thank you, sir, you are so kind.' Meg held Sam's hand and pulled her long skirt around her legs, to join him beside the river.

'So, how was your day? I still can't believe you are here in Swaledale, after all those lectures your parents gave

141

you. And then they let you come and stay.' Sam looked at Meg as she threw a stone in the river, scaring his fish. 'Hey, don't disturb my salmon!'

'Oh, sorry, I forgot. No, I can't quite believe it, either. Although Uncle Harry is watching me; he gave me a small lecture before I came out – not as bad as my mother and father, though. Anyway, he can't say anything. I think he's got a woman in Reeth he visits every day, and I've hardly seen him since I came to live with him. As long as his breakfast and supper are on the table, and the shop is looked after, I don't think he'd say a word to anyone. He just needs an easy life.' Meg looked at Sam.

'Aye, that will be her that has the boarding house on the green. Everybody knows he's been going with her, even though Mary was so ill. I suppose he had to get his oats somewhere, the old devil.' Sam chuckled. 'There's no fool like an old fool, so my mother says. But perhaps he's not such a fool – a kiss and a cuddle make life go round.' Sam placed his hand round Meg's waist and pulled her towards him. 'Give me a kiss, Meg, just one. You know you want to.' Sam squeezed her tightly and put his other arm round her.

'I don't know if I should, Sam. Please don't hold me so tight.' Meg pushed him away slightly.

'Go on, Meg, don't be such a prude – you don't know what you are missing.' Sam squeezed her tightly again and closed his eyes, then kissed her passionately, while Meg protested at first and then, enjoying the first real act of love ever shown to her, relaxed and let him kiss her again. Both of them lay back on the shingle beside the stream. Sam decided he'd try his luck a little further and ran his hand up the outside of her skirts, only for Meg to smack his hand and sit up straight.

'I'm not having any of that, Sam Alderson. I don't mind kissing, but that's where it ends. I'm not one of your common mine-lasses,' she exclaimed, feeling her cheeks go red with shame.

'And who says I go with common mine-lasses? Because they are lying. I only have eyes for you, and always will have. In fact, I've got it in my head to marry you, Meg Oversby. I knew from the moment we met that you were the girl for me.' Sam sat back from her and looked shocked at the suggestion of him going with the mine-lasses who helped clear the rubble from the mine and wash it, to find any remaining ore. They acted and swore more like men, and even though he didn't find them one bit beguiling, he'd had one or two of them all the same, but now he'd enough of them. They'd been easy game. His sights were now set higher, much higher.

'Now that is codswallop, Sam Alderson. You've not known me for more than five minutes. Don't think you can win me over by coming out with such rubbish. Nearly everyone I've spoken to tells me that you are a ladies' man, and that I've to watch you!' Meg laughed at the face Sam was pulling.

'Aye, that's because they are jealous. Nobody can kiss as well as me – you should pay me for my services!' Sam joined Meg in laughter, then leaned across and kissed her again. 'Now, didn't you enjoy that?' He held her close

143

and looked into her eyes. 'Aye, you are a bonny one, Meg Oversby. I think you'll break my heart with your big blue eyes, if you don't learn to love me.'

'I don't think that will be too hard, Sam Alderson. I'm halfway there already,' Meg whispered as she lay back in his arms and let him kiss her again, while she pushed his hand away from wandering over her body again. She did enjoy his advances, but no – a kiss was as far as she would go, for now. 'Now keep your bloody hands to yourself, else I'll be hitting you where it hurts,' she said, looking sternly at her overexcited lover.

12

'Aye, it will be good to see our Meg, I haven't half missed her.' Agnes bundled what she thought Meg might need for the coming weeks in the back of the cart, as Tom and Dan filled the rest of the cart with butter and cheese, and some freshly pulled beetroot from Meg's garden that had been neglected since her departure.

'She's nobbut been gone a week and, by the sounds of you and what you are loading onto this cart of hers, you'd think she'd gone to the other side of the world,' Tom growled. 'I've not missed her. Some days she had a right face on her. Besides, Harry will have taken care of her. I bet she's enjoyed running that shop, it'll have kept her out of mischief and given her a purpose. That's what was wrong with her most of the time: too much time on her hands.'

'Nay, she never had that; she was always busy. You've just to look at the state of the garden to see where she's being missed.' Agnes sighed. 'Are you coming with us,

Dan, or are you staying? It's up to you.' She looked down at her nephew as she climbed into the cart. She hoped he would say no, as she needed some time away from him and his lippy ways; he'd never replace Meg, in her eyes.

'I told Uncle Tom I'd stay at home this time. It'll give you more time with Meg, because you won't have to hurry home for milking.' On the quiet, Dan was looking forward to an hour or two on his own and was not wanting to go into Swaledale. Tom had kept him busy since his arrival, and life on an upland farm was not always a bed of roses, especially when he was expected to run here, scurry there, acting almost as the second sheepdog while his uncle cursed him if a sheep escaped from them both. 'Tell Meg I asked after her.' He smiled angelically, not really missing her one jot.

'Yes, I will.' Agnes pulled her skirts around her and looked ahead of her as Tom urged the horse forward.

'So what do you make of Dan, now he's been with us for a while?' Agnes asked as the horse and cart started to plod up the winding road past the Buttertubs.

'He's like his father – all gob! But he's a good worker, and sometimes I look at him and see a lot of our Anne in him. He could be worse, seeing as he was brought up in Liverpool. He made me laugh when I took him to mend that wall at the fell bottom. He was soon moaning; his hands were too soft for handling the limestone and he doesn't like bending his back. Another six months and I'll have made something of him.' Tom grinned at Agnes.

'You make sure you've time for our Meg, when she comes home. I bet she feels pushed out anyway, having

146

to go and live with Harry. I can understand him wanting company, but surely he'd be better off keeping himself busy running the shop on his own. It isn't that big, after all.' Agnes was still not happy that her daughter was away from home and she'd noticed that Tom was taking time to teach Dan jobs he would never have taught Meg.

'Well, I don't know. All I know is that Mary asked for Meg to look after Harry. She always did think a lot of our lass. It's a shame they never had any family of their own.' Tom pulled the horse up sharply as they came out of the track between the fells, which opened up to reveal a full-length view of Swaledale.

'I know I was born and bred in Appersett, but I don't think there is a bonnier view than this anywhere in the world,' Tom said to his wife as he gazed around him. There was a bluish haze surrounding the fells, and the green fields of the valley were divided by the sparkling River Swale, which meandered its way the whole length of the dale. The fellsides were dotted with whitewashed farm-houses, and limestone walls showed the farms' boundaries while the skylarks sung and bobbed above their heads.

'Aye, it's a good 'un. It's just a pity they are scarring the land up there on the fells in search of lead. You aren't looking at that.' Agnes brought him back to reality.

'Those bloody lead-miners! I hope our Meg has kept clear of them, else I'll bloody kill her.' Tom flicked the reins over Blossom's haunches and started the precarious descent down the fellside into Swaledale.

'Harry will be keeping her straight, don't worry. He promised. It'll be strange visiting the shop and not seeing

Mary behind the counter. She's always been there, even when she was young. Her mother and father kept it immaculate when she was growing up. Her mother even did all the baking they sold there; she must have been run off her feet, when I think about it.' Agnes pulled her shawl around her as a sharp breeze blew at her when they dropped into the valley bottom.

'That's why she asked for our Megan to go and help him. She knew Harry's not a worker. It doesn't take much to turn his head, and he's always been the same. Likes the money, but doesn't want to work for it,' Tom said.

'Well, I hope he isn't asking too much of our lass! She's over here away from us, with no friends, and I bet he hardly gives her anything to spend, because although he likes his money, he's tight with it and all. He'll think she's getting free board and lodging, so I bet he's not putting his hand in his pocket. I've brought her a few pence anyway, just in case. I thought she might need it,' Agnes confessed as they made their way nearer to the small but busy village of Gunnerside.

Tom pulled his horse and cart up outside the shop's doorway and looked up at the sign over it. 'Battersby's for everything that you need', it read in black writing on a peeling green board. He turned and said to Agnes, 'I think his sign is a bit out of date. He didn't have much stock last time we visited,' as he tied the horse to the similarly green-painted railings that ran around the entrance to the shop.

'That's only because he'd taken his eye off the business

while Mary was ill. Look, there's plenty of customers at the counter, and I can see our Meg serving them.' Agnes smiled and picked up the basket full of butter from the cart. 'You bring the rest of the stuff in. I can't wait to catch up with our Meg.' She lifted her skirts and put the basket over her arm, the shop bell tinkling as she entered the crowded store.

'Agnes, aye, it's grand to see you.' Harry came down the stepladder he had been balancing on, arranging some jars of jam, and beamed across at Agnes, before shouting to Meg, who was busy serving a customer, that her mother was here. 'I know a lass that will be glad to see you.' He winked at Meg as she served and took payment from her customer before moving on to the next one, who was only in need of a loaf of bread, so was quickly dealt with and was soon making her way out of the shop's doorway.

'Mum, it's lovely to see you.' Meg came out from behind the wooden counter and gave her mum a hug.

'Aye, you've not given me many of them in the past. Are you alright?' Agnes put the heavy basket down and took her hat off as she smiled at her daughter.

'I'm fine. Uncle Harry and me are getting along just grand.' Meg smiled across at Harry, who had put in more hours at the shop that morning than he had done all the time she had been there.

'I'll put this butter away and make right with the money I owe you. Go into the back room and make yourself comfortable, Agnes. I take it Tom is coming not far behind you?' Harry picked up the basket and peered through the window, to see Tom unloading the cart with some of Meg's things in his arms. 'I'll stay in here with Tom and then you two can talk – catch up on things without me listening in. I know how you women like to talk. Us fellas will share a pipe or two, and catch up with the important things in life.' Harry grinned as Tom came into the shop with one arm full of Meg's skirts, and in the other a bucket of beetroot.

'Don't you get them skirts mucky, Tom. Here, give them to me. Meg will be wanting those, if she's happy staying here longer.' Agnes grabbed the skirts and other items belonging to Meg from Tom's hands and then passed them to her daughter. 'Here, I thought you might be needing these, now you are settled in and staying. I presume you are staying a while longer?'

'Thank you, Mum, of course I am! I'm really enjoying looking after the shop for Uncle Harry, and the people are so friendly. Just give me a minute. I'll take these up to my room and then I'll join you in the back room.' Meg grabbed her belongings and quickly ran upstairs with them, abandoning them on her bed in her haste to talk to her mum.

'So, you are alright? Harry's being right with you?' Agnes quizzed as Meg put the kettle on.

'He's been more than right with me. I'm enjoying every minute. He lets me do what I want, as long as I'm polite with the customers. And I think he's quite happy with me, as he says we have a few more coming in through the door, now that's there's a new face behind the counter.' Meg sat across from her mum and saw that she looked sad and a bit dejected. 'How's things at home? I suppose Dan is still with you both?'

150

'Oh, him – he's still with us. He's not like you, though, our Meg. I mean he's alright, but he's got a few funny ways with him, and he knows nowt about the countryside. Your father takes him out with him most days, trying to teach him our ways, but he'll always be a townie, I think. Although he's a good hand with the cows, so that's something, I suppose.' Agnes looked at her daughter. Life over in Swaledale seemed to be doing her good; there was a sparkle in her eyes, and her cheeks were glowing. 'Have you had time to make any friends yet?'

'No, not really. By the time I've finished in the shop and made supper, it is nearly bedtime. I spend some of the time up in my room, or go for a walk if it is still light, but I can't honestly say I've made any new friends.' Meg smiled as she poured the tea. After all, she wasn't lying to her mum. Sam wasn't a new friend.

'And you are behaving yourself – no flirting with the men of the village? Your father was saying that he hoped you'd behaved yourself when it came to the miners, as they are such a rum breed.'

'No, Mum. I haven't the time or the inclination. Besides, Uncle Harry would be the first one to tell you, if any young man was calling for me. All we get are folk needing the shop and nothing else,' Meg exclaimed.

'Well, I had to ask. Your father worries, you know.' Agnes sipped her tea.

'He needn't worry, I'm fine. Besides, I'm not a child. I can take care of myself,' Meg retorted.

'I've brought you a bit of money. I thought you might

151

need some. I didn't know if Harry was supposed to be paying you or not. I don't think him and your father ever got as far as sorting that out.' Agnes opened the drawstring bag that was on her wrist and took a few pence out for Meg and passed them to her. 'I thought that you might need it for something.'

'Thank you. Harry lets me have what I want from the shop, but this will come in useful, as there's a fair in Reeth next weekend and I thought I might go, if he lets me have the time off. I could do with some new ribbons.' Meg looked at the pennies in her hand; at least now she had some spending money, albeit just under sixpence, by the look of it.

'That will be the Bartle Fair. I don't know if you should be going, really. It gets a bit rough, I've heard. The miners get drunk and there's brawling in the streets, and it isn't a place I'd want you to go to, Meg. It will be full of riff-raff. I'll have a word with Harry before we leave and tell him I'm not happy for you to go.' Agnes looked across at her daughter's now surly face.

'So I can stay here with a man by myself, but I can't go to the fair, like most young folk of my age. What do you think I'm going to do? Run away with some raggle-taggle gypsy? I'd just walk around on my own and be back by dusk, long before any fighting or drinking can take place.'

'It's the miners, Megan, not the locals – they are a law unto themselves. They'll be drunk before noon, and fighting and womanizing. I'll not have you going near it, do you hear?' Agnes stood her ground. Meg had no idea how rough the Bartle Fair was; it was notorious for getting out of hand, and many a fight had to be broken up by the local peelers.

'It's always the miners: they are to blame for everything, aren't they? Or at least they are in yours and Father's eyes. They are not so dissimilar to us – they work long hours and try to make the best of what they've got, from what I can see.' Meg stood with her hands on her hips.

'I didn't come all this way to argue with you, my lass. You will not go to the Bartle Fair. And I'll give Harry the same instructions, which he will follow, else you can go and get your belongings from your room and come back with us this minute.' Agnes scowled at her headstrong daughter.

'Oh, I can't believe you!' Meg folded her arms and stood looking out of the window down the yard, as she tried to compose herself and not act like a spoilt child. 'Alright, I'll not go. I'll not even ask Uncle Harry for the day off, so you needn't say anything to him.' Meg turned and looked at her mum and smiled, trying to ease the tension in the room.

'Good, but I'll still tell Harry you are not to go.' Agnes sipped her tea and watched Meg's thunderous face. 'I know you all too well, miss, so never forget that. I haven't brought you up all these years not to know how your mind ticks. You'd only regret it if something unsavoury happened to you, so listen to your old mother for once.' Agnes kissed Meg on her brow and wiped a tear that was beginning to fall from her cheek. 'You are my baby, and always will be, and I want to protect you for as long as possible from the hardships of life.'

'I was just looking forward to going, Mum. It was something new,' Meg sobbed.

'New it might be, but no decent lass would attend on her own. Now, how long do you think Harry will want you for? I need you back well before the middle of November, although in truth I could do with you now, as your garden plot is already starting to look a bit unloved. Dan might be many things in your father's eyes, but he's not a gardener.' Agnes patted her daughter's arm lovingly and then sat back down.

'I miss my garden. Uncle Harry's only got a back yard. As for when he will send me home, I don't know, although he's not as maudlin over Aunt Mary as he was when I first came here. In fact, he rarely mentions her.' Meg sat down next to her mum and breathed in. 'As long as he needs me, I'll stay. He's good to work for, and I quite like keeping house for him and serving in the shop.' Meg realized that if her mum thought she wasn't needed, she would say she had to return sooner rather than later.

'Aye, he'll be alright with you. But you belong in your own home, and he can't keep you forever.' Agnes lifted her head as Tom and Harry entered the room and looked at the two women deep in conversation.

'Women's talk, is it? If we are not wanted, we can always go to the King's Head for a quick gill.' Tom winked at Harry.

'No, we've said what we had to say.' Agnes glanced

across at Meg. 'I've told this 'un here, Harry, that she's not to go to the Bartle Fair. It's not a fit place for her to go on her own. Now, you'll make sure my wishes are adhered to, won't you?' Meg looked hard at Harry and then at Tom, wanting his backing on the matter.

'If you say so, Agnes, but all the young 'uns from roundabout go, and I'd make sure she'd not go on her own. The Bartle Fair's not as bad as folk make out. But if she's not to go, she might as well look after the shop, as I was thinking of closing it for the day. There's never anybody in Gunnerside on fair-day, but we might get the odd customer.' Harry looked in sympathy at Megan, who quickly wiped a tear from her eye as her father looked sternly at her.

'Aye, Agnes is right. Meg doesn't want to be mixing with the ruffians that go there – no good will come of it. Now make sure she doesn't go, Harry, else we can take her back with us right now.' Tom looked at his friend and watched him wanting to fight the corner for Meg attending the fair and then thinking better of it.

'I promise that I'll do right by you and listen to your wishes. It is, as you say, nothing special. And everybody does get a bit worse for drink, and then they make fools of themselves. So don't fret now, she'll be safe with me.' Harry slapped his old friend on the back and grinned at Agnes. 'Now, are you stopping for some dinner or are you away back, to see what young Dan has been up to in your absence? He sounds like a fair case, from what Tom has been telling me. You might go back to find half your house missing, if he takes after his father. I always thought he was a light-fingered bugger. Mary and I always blamed Bob when the candlesticks went missing from Hawes church. Happen it was just coincidence it was the same day that he and your Anne left for Liverpool.'

'I think we'd better get back. Have you two women finished saying what you've got to say to one another? You can catch up again next week. It isn't as if we are a million miles away, and you seem to have settled, Meg, so Harry tells me.' Tom looked at his wife, who didn't want to leave Meg yet, but at the same time a worm of doubt was starting to creep into her mind about the wisdom of leaving a near stranger in their family home, alone and safe in the knowledge that they would not be returning for some time.

'Yes, we've done. Meg tells me she's enjoying life over here and that she's well looked after. Don't you, Meg?' Agnes stood up and leaned over and kissed her daughter softly on her cheek. 'Now, you behave yourself and earn your keep.'

Meg kissed her mum back and looked at her father as he put his flat cap back on his head.

'We'll be away, then. Behave yourselves, the pair of you, until next week.' Tom patted his friend on the back, but made no move to say goodbye to Meg.

'Aye, and don't worry: she'll take no hurt while I'm looking after her.' Harry stood in the shop's doorway next to Meg, as her father and mother climbed up into the cart for the journey home.

Meg also stood in the doorway, watching them head down the winding street of Gunnerside until they were out of sight. Then she turned into the sanctuary of the shop, where she sobbed into her handkerchief.

'Aye, lass, what's up? Did you want to go home with them?' Harry asked gently.

'No, I wanted to go to the Bartle Fair in Reeth, and now I'm not allowed to. I'm sick of being treated like a child. Some women are married and have families at my age,' Meg wailed.

'Is that what all this is about? Well, that's soon remedied. I might have promised your mother and father that you wouldn't go, especially on your own. But I said nowt about you coming with me, or with the other lads and lasses out of the village. There will be cartloads of them going, and they all look after one another. Your father and mother have never been; they've only heard the bad news that comes out of it all. Now, your mother's brought you a change of clothes. You put on your Sunday best and get yourself off to the fair next weekend, either with me or with a cartload out of the village. What the eye doesn't see, the heart doesn't grieve about. And as long as you promise to behave yourself, I'll not let on you've ever been near it.' Harry grinned.

Meg raised her head and smiled. 'Thank you. Thank you so much. I've never been to the Bartle Fair before and I really wanted to go.' She couldn't believe her ears.

'Aye, well, we all have our secrets. You look after me, and I'll look after you. That's the way to do it, Megan Oversby. But don't you be doing anything you would be ashamed of your mother and father finding out about, then we will be alright.' Harry ran his fingers through his

157

greying hair. 'Right, you look after the shop. I'm away for my walk, now they've gone. I'll be back in time for supper.'

Meg couldn't stop grinning. She was going to the Bartle Fair, and no one was going to stop her. She'd tell Sam when she met him for a brief moment together that night. He'd be sure to be pleased.

13

Meg was taken aback by Sam's attitude when she told him she was going to attend the Bartle Fair.

'What do you want to go to that for? Your parents were right – it's no place for you,' he said in a surly voice.

'I thought you'd be pleased that I was going. That I could be on your arm for most of the day.' Meg smiled and pecked him on the cheek as they both sat on the gravel at the side of the river, in their agreed meeting place.

'It's a day for us miners to get drunk and enjoy ourselves. Your parents are right when they say there's fighting and the like. There's many a dispute on the green in Reeth settled on fair-day.' Sam sighed and threw a pebble into the swirling waters of the river.

'Well, I'll not go then. But I wanted to have a look round the stalls. I know all the traders come from miles around, and it would make a change to be able to buy myself some new ribbons and hankies.' Meg bowed her head and felt like arguing with Sam, but she valued his friendship too much.

'If you must go, I'll tell Peggy Dobson that you are to join us. She'll look after you, when I can't. That way, we can both do what we want, without being in one another's pockets. You'll need a friend if you are to stay over here, and Peggy is a grand lass; she'll see you right. She'll enjoy having your company going round the stalls, and she's sweet on our Jack, so she'll be all too happy to make up a foursome with us.'

Sam's mood lifted slightly as he thought of Meg being taken under Peggy's wing as well as his own. He didn't want to be tied to Meg's apron strings all day. He'd set his head on having a gill or two too many, and even taking a chance on thumping the boxer who usually appeared with a promoter from down south. The pot that was being boasted about was worth getting a bashing for – five guineas – and would set him up well for the coming year. Plus there was another reason for him not wanting Meg to go, for he was frightened she would meet one, if not several, of his conquests, all of whom he'd abandoned once he'd had his way with them.

'Peggy Dobson? I don't think I've met her.' Meg looked in surprise at Sam.

'No, you won't have. She works at Scar House for Reverend Gilpin, over in Arkengarthdale.' Sam stood up and held out his hand for Meg to grasp. 'Come on, get your arse up. It's nearly dusk, and your uncle will begin to worry about you. Besides, these midges are bloody well biting me.' Sam pulled Meg to her feet, then went on to swat a couple of midges that were taking bites out of him.

'You must be bad meat – they aren't bothering me.' Meg tidied down her skirts.

'Aye, that's me, bad meat. That's what my mother would say about me.' Sam smiled.

'I don't think so. She worships the ground you walk on. She's always saying "my Sam" and "my Jack" when she comes into the shop. You are both all she thinks about.'

'My mother talks to you about me?' Sam looked surprised.

'Yes, but don't worry, she doesn't know about our meetings. She keeps telling me that you are her boys and that although you take the eye of many a lass, you will always be hers first.' Meg smirked and held Sam's hand tightly.

'Aye, she'd say that alright. She'd keep the both of us at home forever, if she had her way.' Sam released Meg's hand as they climbed up the river bank onto the road. 'There's usually a cartload of us going from out of Gunnerside on Saturday. Do you want us to pick you up, or will you be walking in with old Harry?' Sam asked as they walked side by side in the twilight.

'You can pick me up, if you like. Uncle Harry will be relieved that he's on his own and that I won't be a party to meeting his lover, if I was to walk into Reeth with him. Besides, it'll be nice to mix with some people of my own age, and I'll look forward to meeting Peggy. I'm sure we will get on fine. She can tell me all about you both – all

161

your dirty little secrets that you will never ever tell me.' Meg giggled.

'What do you mean? I haven't any secrets. Besides, don't go poking your nose into my business, because there's nowt to find out.' Sam looked darkly at her. 'We'll pick you up about eleven, then. You'll probably hear us coming, as we are all usually in good voice.' Sam turned quickly and held Meg tightly and kissed her, before moving to leave her. 'Behave yourself, and I'll see you Saturday,' he whispered, before turning on his heel and leaving her standing on the outskirts of the village.

Meg stood in the twilight and looked around her, as a blackbird made a noise in the nearby hedge, its warning call echoing around the village as candles and oil lamps were lit with the oncoming evening. Perhaps she should heed its noisy song. Sam Alderson had caught her heart, but he had secrets, she was sure of it, judging by what he had said when she joked about speaking to Peggy. No doubt, in time, she would find out what they were, but on Saturday she would enjoy herself.

'Now, you'll behave yourself, won't you? I can trust you?' Harry looked at Meg, all dressed up in her Sunday finery. Her lilac dress and straw hat with violets and primroses around the brim made her look the perfect picture, and Harry thought to himself that if he'd have been thirty years younger, he'd have been proud to have her on his arm.

'Yes, Uncle Harry. I promise at the first sign of trouble I'll make my way home, and I'll not let any lad touch me where he shouldn't.' Meg blushed; it wasn't the sort of conversation she had envisaged with her uncle.

'Aye, well, that's all I can ask of you. My mind's a bit more settled, now that I know you are going with Peggy Dobson. She's a good lass and she'll look after you.' Harry went to the till and took a shilling out of it. 'Here, have a good day on me. You've helped me a lot since you came, and you've never asked for a penny.'

'No, I can't take all that! Besides, my mum has already given me some spending money,' Meg protested as Harry thrust the coin into her hand and she tried to give it back.

'You can never have enough money, lass. If you don't spend it, keep it. It'll come in handy sometime. Now listen, I can hear the rowdy buggers coming. They do it every year, and every year they roll back into the village in various states of distress and no work gets done at the mines for a day or two, because of thumping headaches or cuts and bruises. And that's just the women!' Harry joked. 'Now don't let me down, but go and enjoy yourself.' He opened the shop door as the sound of 'Widecombe Fair' being sung echoed round the small village, and a cart full of local lads and lasses pulled up for Meg to join them.

The big, heavy wooden cart pulled by two roan horses drew up, the tailgate was dropped and everyone squeezed up tightly together, to make room for another passenger.

'Come on, come on, we haven't time for farewells. There's drinking to be done and stalls to look at. Pull up your skirts and climb in.' A young man held his hand and

163

arm out and helped Meg climb into the cart, then squeezed her in next to a blonde-haired lass, who smiled at Meg as she sat down next to her on the wooden planks that ran down either side of the cart.

The young man stood up and nearly fell backwards as the horse jolted the cart and it trundled on its way. 'One, two, three, four.' He conducted the cartload of young people in another chorus of 'Widecombe Fair', with the cart creaking and groaning as it crawled along the road:

Tom Pearce, Tom Pearce, lend me your grey mare.
All along, down along, out along lee.
For I want to go to Widecombe Fair
Wi' Bill Brewer, Jan Stewer, Peter Gurney,
Peter Davy, Dan'l Whiddon, Harry Hawke,
Old Uncle Tom Cobley and all,
Old Uncle Tom Cobley and all.

And when shall I see again my grey mare?
All along, down along, out along lee.
By Friday soon or Saturday noon.

Meg caught her breath as the repeating chorus was sung and the young lass sitting next to her made herself known.

'God, isn't it noisy? And this is without a drop of drink within them. I'll not be making my way back with this bunch, that's for sure. I'm Peggy; you must be Meg. Sam said you were a bonny lass, and he's right. He always has an eye for a looker.' Peggy smiled at Meg and looked her up and down.

'It's good to meet you, Peggy.' Meg looked at the young woman dressed in a plain blue dress with a straw bonnet in her hands, with forget-me-nots around the brim. 'I hope you don't mind me joining you today. I mean, if you want to be with Jack, that's alright with me.' Meg didn't want Peggy to think that she would spoil her day. Besides, she wanted to spend most of her time with Sam, rather than with a lass she hardly knew.

'Oh Lord, no! You leave the lads to it – they'll not be fit to know by the end of the day. Especially the Alderson brothers; speaking of whom, here they are, the ugly mugs.' The cart pulled up and Jack and Sam climbed in, both grinning as they hauled the cart's tailgate down and perched on top of it, with their legs dangling over the edge.

'Peggy, Meg, you've met one another then? Are you both alright?' Sam looked round and winked at Meg, while Jack just smiled at both women as the cart jolted and another song started up.

'Yes, we are going to become the best of friends – of that I'm sure – and look after one another today, as I bet you two will have plenty in mind as to what you will be doing.' Peggy cheeked Sam and put her arm through Meg's.

'Nay, we'll hang around with you for a while. But then there might be one or two things that might not interest you ladies, eh, Jack?' Sam nudged his brother.

'Aye, you won't want to be with us both when we

take on folk in the boxing ring. It'll not be a pleasant sight when one of us two has burst our opponent's lip, broken his nose and he's flat-out begging for mercy from either me or Sam.' Jack winked at his brother.

'But we'll take you both for a gin and a wander around the stalls,' Sam said quickly, when Meg showed her displeasure at perhaps not seeing him as much as she had planned.

'A gin – I've never drunk gin,' Meg exclaimed for everyone to hear, which made the rest of the cart laugh out loud.

'Well, you are the only one of us that hasn't. A drop of gin is good for the spirits. It makes you forget your worries.' Sam grinned.

'"Mother's ruin" it's called, Meg. Don't you listen to Sam. He'd love it if you got drunk on the stuff, it's been many a poor girl's downfall. We'll stick to tea, or happen sarsaparilla, if there's a stall selling that, Sam Alderson. So don't you go leading this lass on with your wicked ways.' Peggy shuffled her bum further back onto her seat and gripped Meg's arm tighter, as the cart bounced and swayed with all its passengers along the rough road between Gunnerside and Reeth. The singing and laughing continued until they reached the slight hill that dropped down into the village of Reeth.

The village stood on a hillside, with the village green in the centre, surrounded by houses and public inns. It wasn't as large as Hawes, but the views from it were spectacular, spreading out in front of the cartload of revellers.

'Just look at all these folk!' Peggy gasped.

Meg looked around her. They had passed many folk making their way on the road, but now, as they reached Reeth's outlying cottages, the road was filled with eager fair-goers. 'I can't wait. This fair looks ten times larger than the one they hold at Hawes,' she said excitedly.

'Aye, and ten times rowdier. Look at that fella there – he can hardly stand up already, and it's only eleven in the morning.' Peggy gawped at the inebriated miner coming out of the Black Bull as he swayed unsteadily in front of the horse and cart.

'Silly bugger nearly got run over,' Sam shouted and then jumped down from the tailgate, along with Jack. 'Come on, lasses, let's be having you. We've not got all day and there's a lot to see before supper time tonight.' He held his hand out for Meg to take and then decided to lift her down instead, holding her tight round her waist and almost kissing her as he held her against him once she was out of the wagon.

'Now then, you two, we'll have none of that.' Peggy giggled. 'Not yet, anyway.' She hooked her arm through Jack's, once she was out of the wagon, and grinned at Meg.

If Jack was going to be courting Peggy, then she would latch on to Sam, Meg thought, whether he liked it or not. She was not going to play gooseberry all afternoon.

'Now, what do we do first? There's so much to see.'

Meg wished Peggy would shut up, as she wanted to be alone with Sam, but it seemed that Peggy thought they

167

were a foursome, as they pushed their way through the crowds.

'Look, look, there's a dancing bear. And look, there's also a monkey, it's going round collecting money in its hat from the crowd. Look, Jack, isn't it sweet? Just look at the little thing in its waistcoat.' Peggy pulled on Jack's arm, dragging him to the centre of the crowd that had gathered to watch the performing animals.

'Does she never shut up?' Meg whispered to Sam and smiled as they followed in Jack and Peggy's tracks.

'No, she makes up for our Jack. He's hardly said two words all day.'

'That's because he can't fit any in,' Meg whispered back. 'Look at that monkey – it reminds me of someone quite close to me, so cheeky that you can't help but like them.' Meg smiled as the monkey chittered and ran from person to person with its cap, which was getting ever heavier from the money placed in it.

'Are you likening me to a monkey, Meg Oversby?' Sam pulled Meg towards him and gazed into her eyes.

'If the cap fits,' Meg laughed.

'For that, you'll have to pay with a kiss,' Sam said as he held her close.

'Not now, in front of everybody,' Meg gasped, but it was too late. Sam quickly kissed her on the lips, with the squeals of Peggy's disapproval ringing in her ears.

'Now, you two, behave! Jack and I will not be so forward, will we, Jack? It gives a girl a bad name.' Peggy looked at Jack and then gave a stern glance to Meg.

'I might be, if I got the chance, but I can't say I'll be

in luck today. Not if you're making so much racket over a peck like that,' Jack grunted.

'It starts with a peck and then you men get carried away. I know that's how a girl gets in bother.' Peggy unfolded her arm out of Jack's and stood by herself, watching the bear, which was tethered through the nose by a chain connected to a stake in the village green. Its owner was whipping the poor creature, as it stood up on its back legs and danced for people's amusement.

'Please let us move on. I can't stand to see that poor creature being hurt. It should be the owner that's getting whipped, for being so cruel.' Meg averted her eyes and pulled on Sam's arm, weaving their way through the crowds with Jack and Peggy following them.

'You soft ha'p'orth. You'd better not stay around this afternoon, when Jack and I take on the big bugger from Ireland; that will be in the boxing ring over there.' Sam nodded to the far side of the village green, where a boxing ring was in the process of being erected. 'There will be some blood flowing, if Jack and I get our way, because we aim to win that pot of five guineas today, come hell or high water.'

Meg looked across to a tent and the canvas boxing ring, which had signs all around it announcing: 'The Giant from Kildare. Keep standing for ten rounds or knock the man out, for five guineas.'

'You can't take him on – you'll be killed, both of you,' she gasped as she saw a huge man, at least six foot six, come out of the tent in a pair of green trunks held up with an orange sash.

'The bigger they come, the harder they fall. Hey, Peggy?' Jack laughed as the girls on their arms breathed in, looking at the boxer, whose face appeared battered and scarred from many a bout.

'Aye, he hasn't met up with the Alderson lads yet. He doesn't know how hungry we are for that pot of money.' Jack laughed as they walked on through the crowds.

'Meg, look over there! There's stalls with ribbons and purses on them. And look, next door there's one with lace and cottons, and see those bonny handkerchiefs on that stall.' Peggy bounded forward, pulling Jack behind her.

'Now, ladies, if you are about to be buying the fancy things of life that we know you like so much, Jack and I will go and have a quick gill. Catch up with the lads from the Owd Gang; we said we'd meet up and have a gill or two in the Buck or the Black Bull, or whichever one we find them in.' Sam felt that the time was right to abandon the loves of their lives in search of a bit of refreshment, before the girls sent him and Jack round the bend with their talk of frills and fancies.

Meg looked at Sam. She didn't want him to leave her. 'You won't be long, will you?'

'No, we'll meet up with you under the market cross in about an hour, I promise, and then we will have a bite to eat.' He smiled at Meg.

'Let them be off, for the Lord's sake. We'll shop better on our own, and all they'll want to do is have a drink. They'll both bloody need one, if they are to take on that big Paddy in the boxing ring.' Peggy put her arm through

Meg's and walked away from Jack and Sam, intent on looking at all the stalls.

'I don't think I've seen anywhere so busy,' Meg said as they walked around the edge of the village green, past women in their Sunday best, men in suits and children playing with whips and tops and hula hoops.

'It's always like this – and those two are always like that. Don't expect to see them again today, unless you want to pull them out of one of the public houses or from under a barrel of beer on one of those carts over there. Just enjoy yourself. Buy what you want, enjoy the cheek that you get from the fellas full of drink, and then we will wander back home before it gets too rowdy.' Peggy pushed her way to the front of the stall that sold ribbons and passed Meg a piece of blue ribbon. 'Here, what do you think of this? It's blue velvet, isn't it bonny? It'll really suit you.'

'Oh, it is bonny! How much is it?' Meg ran the ribbon through her fingers.

'It's a penny-ha'penny, but you can buy six lengths of ribbon for sixpence. Get yourself in here next to me.' Peggy made space next to her so that Meg could get to the stall herself and pick out her own ribbon. 'See, there's every colour of the rainbow, and for sixpence you can't go wrong – you can wear a different colour every day.'

Peggy held her hand out with six ribbons in it and a silver sixpence in payment, and watched as Meg did the same.

'Let's look at the next stall. It seems to have some posy-bags and purses. I bought this one there last year, so his stuff lasts.' Peggy showed Meg her small bag of velvet material and lace, which was gathered together with blue ribbon and which she held on her wrist, containing her handkerchief and her money.

Meg looked at the blue posy-bag decorated with flowers and frilly lace, and decided that if there was one similar, she'd buy herself one, too. However, she had to watch how much she was spending, as there was dinner to be had yet. The stall's table was covered with the prettiest collection of purses and bags that Meg had ever seen, and all too soon she spotted a posy-bag that she knew to be just right for her.

'How much is this one?' She picked up a red-and-green taffeta bag with embroidered roses on it and waited for an answer from the stallholder.

'Ninepence, miss. It's one of the more expensive ones, seeing as it's made from silk.' The stallholder saw a look of disappointment on Meg's face and knew she was probably not going to buy it.

'Oh, I didn't want to pay that much for it really.' Meg sighed and then looked up as a young man shouted to the stallholder, 'Sell it to her for sixpence and I'll give you the rest – that is, if she'll give me a kiss in return.' The blond-haired man with an elegant moustache smiled down at Meg as she blushed in embarrassment. Peggy giggled and dug her in the ribs, urging Meg to take on the challenge.

'Go on, it's only a kiss – and then you'll get your bag,' she whispered into Meg's ear. 'Besides, he's ever so handsome. I'll not tell Sam, so there will be no harm done.'

172

'No, no, I can't.' Meg hung her head and then looked again at the bag she coveted so much.

'Go on, and then we will leg it, once you've kissed him,' Peggy whispered as she looked at Meg, still holding the bag, undecided.

'Just a kiss!' Meg looked up at her handsome bene-factor and smiled.

'Just a kiss! That would be enough, from your sweet, innocent lips.' The blond man grinned down at her.

Meg gave the stallholder her sixpence and watched as her suitor gave him the remaining threepence, as she hung her new posy-bag on her arm.

'Come on, leg it – you needn't even kiss him, if you are quick about it.' Peggy pulled on Meg's arm.

'Nay, not so quick, my bonny lass. A deal is a deal.' The blond-haired man, who was a little worse for drink, grabbed hold of Meg's waist and held her tightly. 'Now, my payment, if you please.' He bent his head down and nearly lifted Meg off her feet as he forced a passionate kiss on her.

Meg wriggled out of his grasp and wiped her mouth with the back of her hand, then looked at him in fear. His breath stank of ale and his moustache prickled her delicate skin.

'Nay, lass, come back to me. I haven't finished yet.' He lurched forward and pulled Meg tightly to him again, only to let go of her suddenly, as Jack pushed his way through the crowd, coming to a halt in front of the man, with a thunderous look upon his face.

'Let her go, Ben Armistead – she's our Sam's girl. He'll

bloody well thrash you if he knows you've been taking advantage of her.'

'Nay, the boot's on the other foot. We had a deal: a kiss for threepence. Ask her who partly paid for that fancy bag of hers, when she could have had any ordinary one and no advances from me.' Ben stood still. 'But if it's a fight you are after, I can soon arrange that.' He spat on his hands and started to roll up his sleeves.

'Jack, he's right – we did have a deal. I was a fool. I wish I'd never agreed to it, for the sake of this stupid bag on my arm. Leave him be. He's had his fun, and now I've paid him. Let's be off,' Meg pleaded, feeling like a stupid fool and realizing how much trouble her innocent kiss had got her into. But at the same time she was relieved that Jack had come to her aid. Peggy looked on, saying nothing, knowing that if she hadn't encouraged Meg, none of it would have happened.

'It's a good job I'm not Sam, or you'd have been flat out on that floor by now.' Jack swore at Ben. 'Come on, you two, follow me and try to keep out of trouble.' He pushed his way through the crowds, with Meg and Peggy following him.

'I've never had a man fight over me – that could have been exciting,' Peggy whispered to Meg as they tried to put some distance between themselves and Ben Armistead.

'Believe me, I don't think I'd call it exciting. I'm just glad Jack came to my rescue,' Meg turned round and said to the romanticizing Peggy.

'Aye, well, now you know what can happen if you don't keep your wits about you. It's a good job I spotted him and knew that's how he picks up a lass every fair-day,' Jack said as they reached the market cross and sat down on the steps below it.

'He was handsome, though,' Peggy tittered.

'And I'm not, Peggy Dobson? Just you mind, else you might have to make yourself known to Ben Armistead.' Jack looked at Meg, who was staring across the green, out towards the distant fells.

'It's lovely here – look at the view. You can see for miles. I've never been to Reeth before,' Meg exclaimed as she looked along the length of Swaledale.

'Aye, it is a bonny part of the world.' Jack stood next to her and gazed at the view with her.

'It isn't in winter. It's blinking starvation; the north wind cuts right along this village, and you wouldn't be standing here for long if it were January,' Peggy added, watching Meg as she looked down towards the bottom of the green, where she had spotted Sam.

'Who's that with Sam? She's carrying a baby in her arms.' Meg turned and looked at Jack.

'I don't know. It could be anybody.' Jack put his head down and went quiet.

'I know who she is. It's Margaret Parrington. She must just have had that baby, by the look of it, but I've not heard of her getting wed. Wasn't she courting your Sam for a while, a bit back?' Peggy squinted at the couple and then, realizing what she had said, tried to deny any connection between the two events. 'He wasn't serious about her, though. She must have gone on and found another fella.'

Meg watched as Margaret Parrington, clutching the baby in one hand, pulled on Sam's jacket when he tried to leave her grip. She said nothing as she watched the poor woman begging for some sympathy from her ex-lover, as he made his way towards them.

'Was that Margaret Parrington we saw you with, and has she had a baby?' Peggy asked tactlessly, as Sam joined them, looking flustered.

'It was. She was pissed on gin and the baby was wailing. She was begging for money, as her father and mother have disowned her,' Sam growled.

'She was such a bonny lass when you were with her last year. She must have got herself in bother and fallen on hard times,' Peggy said as she watched the poor woman and child wandering through the crowds, begging.

Meg looked at Sam and then at Jack. Jack's face said it all, for he was not as hard as his brother.

'Aye, well, she's nowt to do with me now. And you'd do well to mind your own business,' Sam snapped. 'Let's be away, Jack, for a proper gill or two. I'm in need of one before the fight.' He slapped his brother on the back and said nothing to Meg.

'I think I'll just have a look at the pot stall and then go home. I've seen what I want to see,' Meg said quietly.

'I'll come with you. We can both get a portion of hot black peas and eat them next to the beck on our way home. It'll only get more rowdy as the day goes on, and I've seen enough. Besides, I don't want to see these two getting thumped to a pulp in the boxing ring,' Peggy said, linking her arm through Meg's.

'Will you be alright? I'll see you Monday night at our usual place?' Sam said quietly to Meg.

'Yes, you take care – both of you, that is. Don't get your blocks knocked off.' Meg smiled at both brothers as they walked away, leaving her and Peggy to wander home on their own.

'You know, Sam is a grand lad, but Jack is the nicer of the two,' Peggy confessed as she linked arms with Meg and they both viewed the many cups, plates and other items of china on the pot stall. 'Sam can be a bit dark in his moods and is sometimes a bit cocky, whereas Jack is quiet and will always be loyal to those he loves.' She picked up a set of Staffordshire pottery dogs, looked at the faces painted on them and smiled. 'And they've both got as much brain between them as these two ornaments.'

Meg smiled. 'They won't have that much, once the boxer finishes with them later in the day. Especially if they have been drinking all afternoon.'

'What I'm trying to tell you is: don't give your heart to Sam Alderson. He's a charmer and he knows it.' Peggy put the pot dog down and reached out and squeezed Meg's hand.

'I know, although I do think a great deal of him. But I'm not stupid. Do you think that baby is his, and that he will not have anything to do with it or the mother?' Meg thought back to the poor woman, nearly begging on her knees to Sam.

'I don't know. But don't let him take advantage of you in the same way.' Peggy smiled. 'Sam's a devil when it comes to knowing how to charm a woman into his way

177

of thinking. Never mind, let's go and get something to eat and then we will away home and leave the idiots to it. I'm spent up anyway, and I've got to be back at Scar House by eight, else I'll be for it.'

'I am nearly spent up, too, and I'll be glad to be back home in Gunnerside, in truth.' Meg smiled to herself as she called Gunnerside her home. After all, it wasn't her true home, but it was beginning to feel like it more and more.

Jack swayed forward, unsteady on his feet after the pummelling he had received in the boxing ring and the amount of beer that he and Sam had drunk. 'I'm away, our lad, I've had enough. Are you coming with me?'

'I'll just have another and then I'll be with you.' Sam looked up, both eyes swollen, as he sat and realized he had spent nearly every last penny and had nothing to show for it but bruises and a bad head.

'You want to get your arse back with me. We are back at work on Monday, and Mother will not sleep until you are home.' Jack winced, feeling his ribs hurting as he made for the pub's doorway.

'Well, you'll not be going, the state you are in, so stop bloody lecturing,' Sam growled and summoned the weary barman for another gill.

'Well, mind what you are doing when you go home – you don't know who's out on these roads at this time of night.' Jack didn't feel like arguing; he was in pain and needed his bed.

'Get yourself bloody gone. I'll not be far behind you.'

Sam watched as his brother closed the door behind him and stumbled into the night. He should have gone back home with Jack, but he needed to drown his sorrows. Losing his money was the least of his problems. Margaret Parrington was going to name him as the father of her child, when she looked to the parish for relief, and he could well do without that. The gossips would soon get to hear, and that would put a stop to his courting of Meg Oversby.

'That's the last gill you'll get tonight,' the bleary-eyed barman said as he placed the tankard in front of Sam and blew out the candles on the bar, leaving him nearly in the dark.

'I'm bloody well going anyway.' Sam stood up and swigged back as much as he could from the pewter tankard, then threw what change he had onto the table before making tracks home in the darkness of the night.

Margaret Parrington and her baby hid in the shadows on the pathway near the small bridge at Gunnerside Gill. She'd waited there, knowing that Sam would have to pass it on his way back from the fair at Reeth. However, when Jack passed her on his own, she was about to leave and find shelter in a nearby barn, when Sam appeared, stumbling and swearing as he wandered down the road home.

'I thought I'd catch you here, and I also knew you'd be the last one home from the fair.' Margaret held her baby to her and latched it onto her breast to stop it from crying, as she tied her shawl tightly around them both.

'What do you bloody well want of me now? Isn't it enough that you are going to slander me throughout the dale, because of the brat that's at your breast?' Sam stood next to Margaret and looked down at the baby suckling.

'I wouldn't have to, if you had married me. I love you, Sam, you know I do. Let's walk down to the big bridge one more time, and then perhaps you'll remember how you used to love me and will come to your senses over this baby, which you know is yours.' Margaret pulled on his arm and led Sam like a drunken donkey, as he argued and cursed at her, stopping at the archway of the bridge that straddled the Swale.

'I'm not going a bloody step further, you stupid bitch. I never loved you. You were just another girl that I'd had my way with, and one I could easily forget.' Sam lashed out at Margaret and hit her across the face. 'Now leave me be and do what you must. I don't care, because I'll bugger off and you won't be able to find me. Go to hell – and your baby with you,' he shouted as he turned and stumbled homewards up the road, leaving Margaret in tears and heartbroken, clutching her baby. It was Sam Alderson's baby and he knew it; she'd not slept with any other man than Sam. She looked down at the child lying contentedly asleep and felt her cheek, where Sam had hit her. She had nothing to live for. Nobody loved her and nobody cared.

14

'Just look at the state of you two! Whatever possessed you to take him on?' Betty Alderson chastised both her sons as they sat at the kitchen table, battered and bruised.

'Don't moan, Mother, we are in no fit state to be lectured.' Sam hugged his cup of warm tea and glanced across at his brother, who was not well enough to go to work, with two of his ribs cracked and bandaged. He himself was sporting two black eyes, along with a thumping headache, brought on mainly by the amount of alcohol he had consumed when they were enjoying themselves at the fair.

'I thought, at the age you both are, you'd have more sense by now. But no, you are still as daft as brushes and not as useful, either.' Betty stood with her hands on her hips and glared at both of them. 'You'd better tell the boss man, Sam, that Jack will not be fit to work this week. What we will do for brass, I don't know. I presume you are going to work, once you've got yourself sorted?'

Betty looked as Sam picked up his jacket and put it on, then pulled his cap down over his eyes. She'd lectured them both all day Sunday, after hearing them roll home the worse for wear. And now Jack was definitely not fit for work, and Sam didn't sound as if he'd be worth much as a worker for the Owd Gang, this wet Monday morning.

'Well, one of us will have to work, and I suppose our Jack will not be the only one not turning up this morning,' Sam growled, then put his pipe and Vesta case in his pocket, before going out of the back door.

'That lad gets worse. But don't you think I've any sympathies for you, either. Broken ribs or no broken ribs, you can make yourself useful around the house. I really don't know what I've done to deserve you two.' Betty took Jack's half-eaten dish of porridge away from under his nose and stood washing up at the sink.

'Well, if I'd won that fight, you wouldn't have had me to worry about. I'd have booked myself a passage to America with the winnings. They are calling out for miners and railway engineers over there. They are even giving you your own piece of land, if you help them on the railroads.' Jack looked up and moved gingerly from the kitchen chair to the one next to the fire.

'You wouldn't leave your poor mother, would you, our Jack? This is your home, and it always will be.' Betty turned and looked at her eldest son. She had had no idea that was what he'd been thinking.

'I know, Mother, but things are changing. There's not always going to be lead in these fells and, if there is, folk will be able to buy it cheaper than we can mine it for. Besides, I'm fed up with always being in Sam's shadow. He's got the looks and the gob on him, he gets whatever he wants and I never get anything.' Jack reached for his clay pipe and winced when he strained the muscles around his ribs as he took it from above the fireplace.

'You mean he's got the lass that had taken your eye and all? The bonny slip of a thing that works in the shop? He might have her now, but he'll not keep her! Women and our Sam are like sand in your hand – there one minute and gone the next. Just be patient. You mark my words, something will go wrong and that will be the end of that fling.' Betty sighed as she scrubbed out the porridge pan.

'Aye, well, if she's any sense about her, she'd see how callous our Sam can be. That lass he went out with, about this time last year, found him at the fair. She was carrying a baby in her arms, but Sam was having nothing to do with her, even though she was nearly on her knees, begging him for help. And Meg saw it all going on. I bet she'll be having second thoughts this morning about having anything to do with Sam.' Jack drew on his pipe and sat back and thought about the scene that all three of them had witnessed.

'The baby's not his, is it? He'd better not have got a lass into trouble, else he'll be answerable to me.' Betty stopped her scrubbing and turned round, looking red in the face and angry.

'Nay, I don't know – but it could be. She was a bit forward with her affections with quite a few folk. Sam's never said anything about her anyway, but he was in a bad mood for the rest of the fair. That's why he went on the lash. My God, he'll be suffering in that mine, but like he says, he'll not be on his own. To make matters worse, look at the weather. It's pissing down; he'll be sodden before he gets to work this morning.' Jack grinned.

Betty shook her head. 'You'd think you hated one another, to hear you talk. It's a good job I know better. Aye, the weather's bad. Before you know it, we'll have snow as well as rain, and then you'll be dragging your feet up that fellside to work.' She went back to her pots.

'Another reason to go to America – it would be a whole lot warmer than this hole,' Jack said quietly.

'I'll have no more talk of going to America, do you hear? Not while you are living under my roof,' Betty shouted.

'Aye, I hear,' Jack mumbled. But his mind was set. He'd been keeping some of his wages in a box under his bed, without his mother knowing, and another six months should see him right. Then he'd book a passage and free himself of his mother and brother, and make a life for himself doing what he wanted to do.

Meg leaned on the shop counter, her face cupped in her hands and her feet tapping to a tune she had heard being played by the fiddler at the fair, which was going round and round in her head. She looked out of the window and watched as the rain came down in torrents. There wouldn't be many customers in the shop today, she thought, as she looked round the dark, low-beamed shop. The weather had even stopped Harry from taking his daily walk – the first time since her arrival that he had missed his visit to Reeth. However, he didn't seem to have any incentive to help her in the shop, staying by the fire with his pipe and paper and catnapping, once he was on his own.

Meg yawned; she'd not slept well since the fair. The picture of Sam rejecting the woman and her baby kept replaying in her mind, and the niggling question of whether the baby was his had still to be answered. That, along with Jack's warning about his brother's wanton ways, was beginning to play on her mind. Perhaps she should not be taken in by Sam's winning grin and dashing good looks. Perhaps he was as shallow as Peggy Dobson had hinted. Or was she just jealous, like Jack was?

But Meg had only to think of the words that Sam said to her, and the way he touched and held her, and her heart fluttered like the trapped late-summer butterfly that was trying to find an escape to freedom through the shop's glass windows. He'd won her heart and soul, if he did but know it, and every minute away from him seemed a minute too long. Even though the rain was pouring down, she would make her way to the bridge, their secret meeting place, that evening. The river wouldn't be that swollen yet. She could shelter and wait for him under the spanning arch, and yell at him when she heard him call her name. He was bound to come to her – he'd promised –

and a drop of rain would not quench the desire to hold one another, of that she was sure.

Lost in her dreams, Meg was suddenly woken from them as the shop door flew open, the bell above it nearly breaking away from its coil, as Frank Metcalfe burst into the shop without his usual batch of baking.

'Where's Harry? I need Harry!' Frank yelled. 'For God's sake, fetch him. I was minding my own business, urging my old nag on, when I happened to look over the top of the bridge into the rising waters below. It was then that I spotted her: a body, just lying there. She must have gone and thrown herself in! The poor lass, she's dead for sure; she's half in the water and half out. Tell Harry I need his help to get her out, and I'll go and knock on a few more doors for the men of the village, before she gets washed downstream when the waters rise. Harry, bloody well move yourself, you lazy old bugger. I know you are at home; it's too wet to be going to get your leg over in Reeth. Move, and come and give me a hand!'

Frank yelled through to the back room once more, then flew out of the door, leaving his horse and cart outside the shop while he knocked on the door of anybody who lived nearby, telling them the same tale and asking for help.

'What's he yelling, that bloody mad fool?' Harry came in from the back room where he'd been catching up on his sleep, and listened while Meg told him what had been said. 'Give us that lump of rope, lass, from up on that shelf. We might need it. And go and get a blanket from your bedroom, then bring it down to the river bridge. She might not be dead, if we are lucky. Whoever she is, she must have been bloody desperate, as there is not enough water in that beck yet to drown yourself in.' He grabbed his oilskin coat from behind the back-room door, slung the rope over his shoulder and ran out of the shop, leaving the door wide open.

Meg ran upstairs and grabbed the blanket from the bottom of her bed, then went to the back room, placing the fireguard around the fire. She quickly put her shawl round her shoulders and then abandoned the shop, to join the crowd that was gathering at the base of the bridge that spanned the River Swale. She couldn't get there fast enough, and the breath in her throat hurt as she ran the last few yards, before peering down into the ebbing waters of the mighty river.

She watched as Harry and Frank and two other men pulled the body of a woman out of the river onto the bank. The crowd gasped as the body revealed its secret, once she was rolled onto her back. When the shawl tied tightly around her was undone, it revealed a baby underneath the woman's loose blouse, its feet tucked into her skirts and bound by the tightness of the shawl that had been wrapped around them both.

'God rest their souls.' A woman wailed and crossed herself, as both mother and child lay dead on the bank.

'Does anyone here know who she is?' Harry looked round the crowd and up to the archway of the bridge, and watched as Meg made her way through the crowd. 'Don't come near, lass, it's not a pleasant sight.'

'But I know her, Uncle Harry. I saw her at the fair on Saturday. I think she's called Margaret Parrington, and that's her baby.' Meg's eyes filled with tears as she bent down and looked at the once-beautiful Margaret, her long wet hair straggled along the shingle and the dead baby lying on top of her, as if suckling on her breast. The memory of her and Sam arguing crossed Meg's mind, and she felt angry and frustrated at the thought that Sam might have had something to do with this.

'She'll be the youngest of the Parringtons from Fell End. I heard her father and mother had thrown her out,' Frank said, as even he – tough as he was – brushed a tear away from his cheek.

'It's a sad do. There's too many lasses getting in the family way, with no man to stand by and wed them. It's alright sowing a few wild oats when you are young, but you should be a man and stand up to your commitments when needed.' Harry looked down at the dead pair.

'Here, Uncle Harry, cover her with my shawl and stop everybody gawping at her.' Meg took off her shawl and passed it to Harry, who covered most of Margaret's body with it, while Meg stood getting soaked to the skin in the pouring rain.

Harry looked up at the crowd. 'Somebody fetch the preacher and bring the handcart from the chapel. We'll put her in there until her parents come for her, if the preacher gives us permission. Surely her parents will show her some mercy now,' Harry whispered to Frank as they both looked at the bodies lying under the shawl. 'Will you go and tell her folks? You ken them and I don't. Or should we leave it to the preacher? But he'll only give hellfire and brimstone to them, and that's the last thing they'll want to hear.'

'I'll go. I'll drop your baking off and then go back down the valley to tell them. Meg, you come with me, this is no place for a young woman. Then you can take receipt of the baking. It's a good job you are the last shop on my rounds, else I'd not have been able to go.' Frank shook his head and left Harry and the other men from the village with the bodies, as he and Meg climbed up from the river bank and followed the road into the village and back to the shop.

'I know what I'd like to do to the lad who got her that way,' Frank growled. 'But her parents should have taken pity on her. She isn't the first to have got into that state, and she won't be the last. These things happen. I should know, I ended up having to get wed pretty fast myself.'

Meg said nothing, but all the time she couldn't help but think about Sam dismissing the poor, begging woman, and the mood he had been in afterwards.

'Now, will you be alright until Harry gets himself back?' Frank lifted the tray of baking from the canopied cart and put it down on the shop's counter. 'It wasn't the prettiest thing to see, and you are nobbut young. Harry will need a change of clothes, as you do, by the looks of you. It's raining harder than it seems, and your hair is sodden. Go and get changed before you catch your death – we can't be losing you. Old Harry would be lost without you, as the shop had gone to the dogs before you

189

came along.' Frank smiled at the crestfallen lass. 'Chin up. That, I hope, will never happen to you. Remember not to get your head turned by any fancy words that a lad says to you, and to keep your legs together – although it's not my place to tell you such. Right, I'll be away. I'm not looking forward to telling her parents the news, but somebody has to do it.'

Frank stopped for a second in the shop's doorway as he saw the preacher running down the road, following the cart from the chapel that was used for funerals.

'Aye, it's a sad day. I wish I'd never seen her. Why she had to choose that bridge to end it on beats me, when she was from Reeth. She must have walked five miles to get here.' He shook his head and closed the door behind him, leaving Meg cold and shivering in the gloom of the shop.

Her thoughts were as dark as the day as she turned over the 'Closed' sign for a few minutes, while she went upstairs to change out of her wet clothes and towel her hair slightly drier. Why had Margaret Parrington thrown herself off that bridge? The river wasn't as deep as further down the dale, or as fast-flowing. Could it be that the bridge held a certain meaning for her? Meg couldn't help but wonder if Margaret had met Sam, just like she did, beneath its arches, and that that was the reason for her choice. As it was, there would be no meeting with Sam Alderson there tonight – or any other night, come to that. Not now, for the dead woman and her child would be there to haunt them. But she did need to speak to Sam and find out the truth. Was the baby his or not? And if it was, what was she going to do about it?

She changed quickly into a dry blouse and warm skirt and went to the shop door to turn the sign back round to 'Open'. Her hair was still wet as she started to put the baking onto the shop's shelves, when the doorbell sounded again.

'Bloody hell, it's wet out there. It's a good job it isn't the Bartle Fair today, else it would have been up to nowt.' Jack entered the shop quickly, with his jacket over his head, and winced in pain as he pulled it back onto his shoulders. 'It might be bloody wet, but there seems to be a lot of folk about the village. What's going on, do you know?' He grinned at Meg as she turned and looked at him.

'There's been an accident. Well, when I say "accident", it's more like a death, down at the bridge. That's what all the commotion is about. The preacher is down there now. They should be bringing the bodies back up, to be put in the chapel.' Meg glanced at Jack, and didn't really want to tell him the news.

'Bodies! You mean there's more than one? What the hell has been going on down there?' He stared at Meg.

'It's Margaret Parrington, she's thrown herself into the Swale – both herself and her baby. She's drowned herself. The poor woman's drowned herself out of desperation.' Meg broke down and cried in front of Jack. Until then she'd been strong, but when she had said the words and seen a flashback of the scene that she had just left, emotion got the better of her.

'Oh my God! Margaret was at the fair on Saturday – we all saw her talking to Sam. I thought then she

191

looked terrible. But come here, you. You look upset, and you didn't even know her.' Jack held his arms out for Meg as she sobbed and cried in them, wincing in pain as he did so.

'No, I'm alright. It was just the sight of them both, and the little baby still in her arms. It was all blue and lifeless; it didn't deserve a death like that, nor did she.' Meg blew her nose with her handkerchief and looked up at Jack. 'I'm crying for selfish reasons, because I've been wondering if Sam was the father. His mood seemed to change after he had seen her, and Margaret seemed to be begging him for something. He doesn't deserve anyone's love, if he can be that callous not to look after his own.' Meg held back her sobs and waited for what seemed an age before Jack replied.

'If it was Sam's baby, he's said nothing about it to me. He was sweet on her for a while last year, but I don't think he went that far with her. You needn't worry your head about it. He'd have been sure to have told me if he thought it was his, so stop worrying.' Jack tried to put his arm round Meg to comfort her, but she stood a little away from him.

'But why did she throw herself from *this* bridge? It's the same bridge that Sam and I meet under – and it was he who suggested it. Did he meet Margaret there, too? I'm beginning to think he's exactly what my parents warned me of: a low-life miner.' Meg breathed in deeply and wiped her swollen red eyes again.

'It's just coincidence. Nothing more. You are reading too much into things.' Jack hated himself for slighting

Margaret, as he went on to clear his brother's name. 'Everyone knew Margaret Parrington – half the men in the dale will have been with her, she was that popular. Although I shouldn't talk ill of the dead.' He bowed his head and then raised it to look at Meg. 'There's nothing that can be done. But stop your worrying that Sam had anything to do with it, because he hadn't, I promise you. He'd have told me; he tells me everything.'

'Alright, I'll believe you. But I can't get the picture of Margaret and the baby out of my head. It was so shocking,' Meg whispered. 'Can you tell Sam I'll not meet him tonight, that it's best if we play it by ear for a day or two? There were some angry people down at the bridge, after seeing poor Margaret. They will have it in for you miners, I expect.' Meg smiled wanly at Jack. She didn't know whether to believe him or not, but Sam would have to answer a few questions when she did see him.

'That's nowt fresh. It's always us miners who have done everything that happens over here.' Jack leaned on the counter. 'Oh, my bloody ribs – they don't half hurt! And our Sam isn't much better.'

'Why, what's wrong with you both?' Meg asked, suddenly concerned for the brothers' welfare.

'We got a pasting by that bloody big Mick. He's broken my ribs, so I'm not at work. And our Sam is black and blue all over. You wouldn't want to see him anyway, as he's not a pretty sight,' Jack said.

'But he's alright, isn't he? He's not broken anything?' Meg quizzed.

'Happen his nose. It is hard to tell, as everything's that

193

swollen. But he's gone to work, which is more than I have. That's why I'm here, wanting half an ounce of Kendal Twist. And my mother wants her usual, whatever that is.' Jack stood upright and noticed Harry about to come into the shop, as he looked through the window in the door. 'And you can give me a quarter of humbugs, please, Miss Oversby.' He winked at Meg as Harry entered.

'You not at work? I suppose you and your useless brother are still recovering from the fair, like all you miners,' Harry growled. 'Well, you needn't hang about here. Get your shopping and bugger off!'

Meg put her head down and said nothing, as Jack picked up his mother's white bloomer loaf, along with his sweets and tobacco, and handed over the money for them.

'Now, that's no way to talk to your customers. Especially when you rely on us miners so much.' Jack looked at Harry.

'If it were up to me, I'd shoot the bloody lot of you. Now get gone, before I get my gun. There's a lass and her bairn dead in that chapel because of the likes of you, and I'll not have you hanging around this shop. So clear off.' Harry went and stood behind the counter next to Meg and watched as Jack left the shop. 'He's a wrong 'un, is that 'un. Both them Alderson lads are – and the rest of the buggers they mix with. They want to be hounded out of the dale.' He looked at Meg. 'Are you alright now? You did well to say who she was. It wasn't a pleasant sight for a young lass to see.'

194

'I'm alright, Uncle Harry. Just sorry that Margaret felt she had to end her life, and her baby's, in such a way. Whoever the father is needs to be brought to justice for her death.' She held back the tears again.

'Aye, well, what's done is done, and there's no fetching them back now. I bet her parents are regretting not looking after Margaret now. Be thankful you've got a good home and that your parents would never turn their backs on you. It means a lot, does that, when it comes down to it.'

15

Sam and Jack lay in the darkness of their bedroom, both unable to sleep because of the day's events.

'Well, was the baby yours? Everybody saw Margaret talking to you at the fair. She looked so upset, and she must have said something to you,' Jack whispered across to his brother, who was lying on the other side of the room from him.

'She never said whose it was, so I don't know why you should think that,' Sam whispered back.

'I saw the look of desperation on her face when she talked to you. She told you, didn't she, that you were its father? That's why you were in such a mood all day, and why she threw herself into the river where she did. You used to spend many an hour down by that river bank with her last summer – just like you are doing now with young Meg from the shop. You've got yourself to blame for her and the baby's death,' Jack said with contempt.

'Hold your noise, else our mother will hear you. It

was nowt to do with me, I tell you. Besides, her parents are as much to blame. They should have looked after her. How could they turn their backs on their own? At least our mother would never do that, as she worships the ground we both walk on.'

Sam hugged his pillow and thought about Margaret Parrington and the hours they had spent together that summer, which seemed to last forever as they made love and laughed together, unknowing of the fate that was to befall her. Then he thought of the words he had said to her in his cups, and how he had left Margaret and the baby there on the bridge top in the early hours of the morning. He was to blame for the baby's death and for Margaret's, but he wasn't about to tell anybody that.

'Aye, well, she and the baby are dead now, and God help you if you are the father, because you'll be hounded out of the dale, if the locals get to know. Your life won't be worth living.' Jack rolled over, turning his back to his brother and wincing with pain, as his cracked ribs made lying down uncomfortable. The baby was Sam's, of that he was sure. Before he went to sleep he whispered, 'I saved your skin with Meg. I lied and told her that Margaret had been with most of the lads of the dale, else you would have broken her heart, too. I couldn't tell her that my brother was really an uncaring bastard.'

'I'm not its father, do you hear? At least Margaret never said I were. She didn't know whose it was. I swear that's what she told me on Bartle Fair day.' Sam looked up at the ceiling, not hearing any response from his

197

brother. He sighed and closed his eyes, but the thoughts rushing through his mind would not let him sleep.

He knew Meg had witnessed his meeting with Margaret. Thank God that Jack had made excuses for him. But to make things worse, he daren't be seen with her yet, not until the scandal had blown over. Jack was right; there would be hell to pay throughout the dale. The minister at Reeth had already been giving services and lectures stigmatizing the miners as 'colluvies' – a term that he used for collections of filth and foul matter, which he thought the miners had brought to the dale. Locals were getting fed up with the ways of the miners, with illegitimate babies being born frequently and marriages postponed, because of the women being unsure who to call the father to the child they were already carrying; and husbands-to-be realizing that the woman they were about to marry had been unfaithful to them.

To make things worse, Meg would be upset, Sam knew, and for once he had fallen in love good and proper. But now, because of Margaret Parrington's suicide, he might lose her. He was taking their courtship seriously. His former lies, when he had flippantly said he wanted to marry her, had now become the truth. But they might as well be a dream, because all hope of marrying Meg would never come to anything.

Meg kept her head down all week, listening to the gossips who came into the shop talking about the death of Margaret and her baby, and naming names of who the wretch of a father was who hadn't stood by her. Nearly every young miner's name had been mentioned, including that of Sam and Jack, as the women stood with their baskets waiting to be served.

'They needn't start blaming my two lads,' Betty Alderson stormed, as two local women brushed past her without so much as a by your leave, nearly knocking her over as they left the shop. 'Neither of mine would leave a lass in that way, I'd make sure of that,' she said loudly as the door closed behind them.

Betty looked at Meg. 'Besides, our Sam is sweet on you at the moment, from what I've heard and seen, although he never lets on to his old mother. But mothers have a way of knowing what their bairns are up to, without being told.' She smiled as Meg threw a worried look to the back room, where Harry was doing his accounts. 'I'll not say owt else. But do you want me to take him a message?' she whispered.

Meg's face lit up. 'Can you – would you, please? I can't meet him down here at the moment, as the village is full of talk of revenge for Margaret's death, and if I was seen walking out with him, I think the local lads would set upon him.' Meg glanced at Betty as she got her shopping together. 'Can you tell Sam I will meet him under our tree on Sunday? Nobody will see us there.'

'I will, lass. Sunday, what time?' Betty grinned.

'Tell him eleven. Everybody will be at church or chapel by then.' Meg changed the subject as Harry came into the shop. 'I'm sorry, Mrs Alderson, but no, I can't do that.'

'I hope you aren't asking for tick. We aren't giving any at the moment, especially to you mining families,' Harry growled, putting his new policy into action, knowing it would hit the miners hard.

'I've never asked for tick, and I'm not about to now.' Betty reached into her purse and got out the change for her shopping, passing it to Meg. 'Thank you, young lady. Enjoy the rest of the day. I'm told that the weekend looks good, weather-wise, especially Sunday.' She smiled as she left the shop.

'She thinks she can foretell the weather now, the old bugger. She should be concentrating on her lads, the wild pair,' Harry growled. 'I'm away to stretch my legs, but I'm not going far, nobbut to the end of the village to show my respects to the Parrington family. They are taking their lass and her baby back home to be buried. Although I've heard that she's not allowed to be buried in the churchyard – suicide, you see, they'll not let her.' He put his cap on and headed for the door, shaking his head in despair.

Harry watched as the coffin containing Margaret and her baby was loaded onto the back of the undertaker's cart. The narrow road through the village was lined with local mourners who didn't even know the dead woman and baby, but felt they had to show their respects to her and her family. 'What's that poor woman going to feel like, seeing her daughter and her baby dead and knowing she could have done something about it?' Harry whispered to the blacksmith's wife who stood next to him as they watched the distressed family walk slowly past them, following the cart out of the village.

'It takes two to make a baby. I'd like to know who the father is. I'd cut his balls off, if I could get hold of him, the bastard.' The blacksmith's wife spat on the road and stared at the heartbroken family.

'It'll come out in the wash. Somebody will know who he was and, when it is made public, God help his soul. He'll not last long in this dale. His life won't be worth living.'

Harry placed his cap back on his head and wandered over to his wife's grave in the chapel's graveyard, once the family and bodies had passed him by, the locals all returning to their homes.

'Aye, lass, it's a rum do. It's a good job you are not around to see all that's going on. You wouldn't be suited to present events.' Harry bent down over Mary's grave and talked to her. 'I suppose, when you are looking down at me, you can see what I'm up to. I'm sorry, my old lass, but I can't live without a woman in my life. And I know I should have waited until you were cold in the ground, but Lizzie Bannister at the boarding house and I just clicked. She'd been recently widowed, and you were so ill that I broke down one day when she was in the shop. That was how it started: me being broken-hearted over you, and her needing a shoulder to cry on and all. They say there's no fool like an old fool. Well, I hope you can forgive this old fool. He loved you when you were alive, and I hope I was a good husband to you.'

Harry rubbed his eyes with his handkerchief. 'I'll always love you, old lass, but I can't live on my own. But you already knew that when you asked Tom to send his slip of

201

a lass over for a while. She's a good worker, but she'll have to return home before winter sets in and then I'll be back on my own. Unless I do as Lizzie is begging me to do, and move to Reeth and marry her. But it's too early yet, lass. I've got to show some respect to your memory.'

He stood up and looked around him. 'I'll bide my time, old lass. There's no need to marry in a hurry at our age – unlike half the buggers round here, who can't keep what they've got in their pockets. That's the trouble with them.' Harry smiled as he walked away; he felt better for saying what he had to his late wife. Whether she had heard him or not, it had lightened his load, getting his confession off his chest.

'I can't believe it's been a week since your mother and father were here. Time goes so fast, since you came along.' Harry looked across at Meg as they ate breakfast together.

'Yes, it does seem to go fast – too fast. The summer's nearly gone and, before you know it, I'll have to be going home.' Meg sighed.

'You like being here, don't you? I've seen how you like running that shop of mine, and talking to the customers. I'll miss you when you do go home.' Harry smiled. 'You are no bother whatsoever to have living here, and I'll tell your mother and father that. Speaking of which, that sounds like your father now, but he's early today.'

Harry shouted through to the shop as he heard Tom's low voice calling for him, 'In here, we haven't even finished our breakfast yet. Have you pissed the bed, to make you be here this early?' he joked, as Tom and Dan entered the room. 'Oh, I thought you'd have Agnes with you, but this must be Dan, I take it?' He stared at the young lad beside Tom and decided there and then that he wasn't keen on him, as he had a shifty look about him.

Meg cleared the breakfast table and smiled at her father and Dan as they sat down in the two spare chairs. Dan sat at the back of the room, skulking and looking nervously around him. He hadn't really wanted to visit Swaledale, but he'd not been able to get out of it without it looking suspicious.

'I've a cow thinking of calving, so Agnes has stopped at home to keep an eye on it. And I thought Dan here could do with knowing where you are at.' Tom leaned back in his chair and thanked Meg as she poured both him and Dan a cup of tea. 'How's things over here? You both look well. I think life over in Swaledale is suiting you, our Meg.'

'Not as much as my new life with you, Uncle Tom. Every day I wake up and think how lucky I am,' Dan piped up, not giving Meg the chance to reply.

'Well, you'd nowhere else to go, and you belonged with us. Your mother was right to send you back to her home,' Tom said quickly. 'I hear there's been a bit of a to-do over here – a lass and her baby found dead in the river. The poor bugger!'

'Aye, it has been terribly sad. If it hadn't been for your Meg, we wouldn't have known who she was. It was her who recognized her, from when she went to the fair last

203

weekend,' Harry said innocently, forgetting his own and Meg's promise that she wouldn't attend.

'Bloody hell, Harry, you promised me you'd not let Meg go. And as for you, young lady, it's no good looking all innocent. You well knew we both forbade you to go. I've a good mind to take my belt to you.' Tom's face was like thunder, while Dan sniggered at a shamefaced Meg.

'No harm came of it, Tom. She went with a good lass from up Arkengarthdale and a few others from out of the village, and she was back well before supper time. Before all the drunken idiots emerged. Besides, she's not a baby any more; she's a grown woman. She's the best help I've ever had, and I'm glad that she's here.' Harry stuck up for Meg, knowing how hard her father could be.

'She still shouldn't have bloody gone. What else are you two up to, behind my back? Perhaps you are as well to come back with me and Dan – it's obvious I can't trust you both,' Tom growled.

'Father, I behaved myself. And I like being here with Uncle Harry. I enjoy working in the shop, and the folk over here are so good to me. I know I haven't been here long, but I feel like I really have settled in. And now that you have Dan, you don't need me like you used to do,' Meg said indignantly.

'What, settled with all the miners, who are nowt but rubbish? Have some pride, lass,' Tom stormed.

'Tom, think of what you are saying. I know I call them a rough bunch, but some are decent souls that are just making a living. Besides, as things stand, the young fellas are going to get it rough around here until it's clear who fathered the baby that was drowned alongside its mother. So Meg's as well over here as back home with you at Appersett,' Harry said curtly.

'You've not the sense you were born with, letting her go to the fair in the first place. And you are only saying that because you need Meg to stay with you and do your work.' Tom looked across at Dan. 'What are you grinning at? You can get your arse outside with our Meg, and bring the butter and whatever else Agnes sent over out of the cart and into the shop while I speak to Harry.'

'Yes, Uncle.' Dan stopped laughing and looked across at Meg, who was all too ready to get out of her father's way.

'You are in a bother now. I bet you have to come back with us, once your father's finished with Harry,' Dan smirked as he lifted the basket of butter down from the cart and passed it to Meg.

'No, Uncle Harry will stick up for me. He can't run the shop without me – or not as well – on his own.' Meg grabbed the basket and watched as Dan picked up a sack of apples from the farm's orchard.

'Well, I'm set for life, because since you've gone, your father's taught me all there is to learn about farming. He says I learn better than any lass and that, come spring, I can have some lambs of my own. We let the ram out yesterday, so he's busy with all his girls. A bit like the miners over here, from what your father says.' He gave a sly smile.

'You wash your mouth out, Dan Ryan. You and my father know nothing about how folk live over here.' Meg glared at him. Not only had Dan wormed his way into her home, but now he was talking just like her father.

'I'll say what I want, and you won't stop me. Your father thinks more of me than he does of you, because I'm a lad and his nephew. And you will soon have your head turned by a fella, and then you'll have no time for him or your mother. I bet that's why she didn't come with us today. The cow that's supposedly calving isn't due for another week yet.' Dan leaned back against the cart and smirked. He was enjoying watching Meg get upset, as he'd set his heart on owning Beck Side one day, if he could get Meg out of the picture.

'You are lying. My father wouldn't leave my mum at home if there wasn't a reason. I wish you'd bugger off back to Liverpool, you sneaky rat.' Meg picked up the basket and her skirts and stormed back into the shop, turning her back on the grinning Dan.

'Harry says you hardly stop working, and that he knows you are behaving yourself. Happen I was a bit hard on you, but your mum and I are only trying to protect you.' Tom stood in the doorway between the shop and the living quarters and watched as Meg placed the newly made butter on the counter.

'I'm alright, Father. I'm not daft, and I can look after myself.' Meg looked over at him. 'Is Mum alright?' she asked.

'Aye, she sends her love and says she will try and get over to see you next time.' Tom smiled and watched as

Dan placed the sack of apples on the counter. 'We've let the ram out. Dan, here, has been helping me.'

'He's been telling me,' Meg said curtly, while Dan said nothing.

'Aye, well, you look grand and Harry enjoys your company, so you can stay a bit longer, until the weather turns. But then you must come back, no matter what Harry says.' Tom made his way to the shop's doorway. 'Owt to tell your mother?'

Meg looked up. 'No, just tell her that I love her and I'll see her next time.' She held back the tears. Dan's words had cut deep, and she couldn't help but think there might be some truth in them.

'Right then, we'll be away. Dan, you drive us back, and try not to take us off the edge of the road.' Tom looked back at his daughter as Dan left the shop and got into the cart. 'You alright?'

'Yes, Father, I'm fine.' Meg breathed in and looked on as her father climbed up into the cart. She watched as he and the sneaky Dan made their way along the road home, until the cart and its occupants were nearly out of sight.

She was fine, but her heart was being torn between her parents and her love for Sam, along with that for her new life.

Sunday morning came and Meg, dressed in her best clothes, looked at her uncle as he glanced at his pocket-watch; she hoped he wasn't thinking of going to chapel. He wasn't a religious man, so she had taken advantage of that and had told him she was to attend chapel that morning, to cover her assignation with Sam.

'Ten forty-five, Meg. You'd better get yourself away, if your soul needs saving. Although why you need to go, I don't know. Singing a load of hymns, and listening to the preacher bleat on about the sins of the world, is enough to put anybody off ever going again. A walk's far better for you. I find my God on a hillside or down by the river, not under a roof and four brick walls.' Harry watched as she reached for her bonnet from the peg next to the door.

'I just thought I'd go and pray for the poor lass that drowned herself,' Meg lied.

'Aye, you do that, lass. Perhaps I should be ashamed of myself for not going. But I'll go for a walk out and think of her instead. I'll be back for my supper. Especially now I can smell the bit of brisket you've got slow-cooking in the oven. I'm fair looking forward to it. Now get yourself gone, you've not left yourself much time. You'll have to nearly fight for a pew, as it is.'

Harry sat back and drew on his pipe, watching Meg as she closed the door and ran out of the back yard. He was off to seek solace with Lizzie Bannister, which, in his eyes, was more comforting than any chapel meeting.

Meg lifted her skirts and held onto her bonnet with the other hand, as a sharp wind blew in off the fells when she walked up the gillside to the tree that was to be her meeting place with Sam. Her stomach churned as she saw him, waiting on the grass bank at the side of the tree, throwing stones into the gill as he waited for her.

'I thought you weren't going to show.' Sam looked up at Meg as she caught her breath, before sitting down next to him.

'I had to leave it to the last minute. I told Uncle Harry that I was going to the chapel. I thought that way it could be my excuse every Sunday, and I wouldn't have to keep making up a different lie. I feel bad enough about it, because he is so good to me.' Meg untied the ribbons of her bonnet and placed it by her side. 'Look at the sight of you, with two lovely black eyes. You and Jack are idiots for taking on that boxer.'

'Never mind me, I'll soon mend. Your Uncle Harry's not that caring. My mother says he's not doing right by us miners, by not giving us credit. Not that we need it, but many a poor bugger does, especially with winter coming. There will be some days when there will just not be any work upon these fells, because of the cold.' Sam leaned back and put his hands above his head on the rough fell grass. 'Anyway, enough of your Uncle Harry. Come and lie down next to me. We are out of the wind on this fellside and you can look up through the tree's leaves and watch the sky. They are on the turn now, though – another month and it'll be bare.' He pulled on Meg's arm and urged her to lie next to him on the dry, tufted fell grass.

'I don't know if I should, especially with all this talk and gossip. It's been bothering me all week. Ever since I saw you talking to poor Margaret Parrington at the fair and she looked as if she was in tears. I can't help but think it was more than money that she was after from you.' Meg's stomach churned as she broached the subject that had made her feel quite ill, thinking about it all week. 'And now she and the baby are dead because nobody would stand by her when needed. It wasn't yours, was it? You should be ashamed of yourself, if it was.'

Sam sat back up and turned to look at Meg. 'That baby wasn't mine. I swear to you, Meg, the child was not mine. I did court Margaret, but so did half the lads in the dale. It's just that everyone in Gunnerside saw us walking out together. We used to meet at the bridge and then sit on the seat near the cross nearly all last summer, and then she stopped seeing me. Then she went with a lad from near Leyburn – it'll be his baby, if anybody's.' Sam gripped her arm tightly and looked into her blue eyes. 'Honestly, it's nowt to do with me. I swear on my father's grave, if you are thinking that it was.'

'I hear that she'd been a bit of a floozy. The baby could be anybody's, and if you swear it is not you to blame, then I'll believe you. I didn't think you could be so uncaring, anyway, but I wanted to hear it from your own lips. Surely you understand how I feel about it all. And then the villagers are full of gossip, and it is you mining lads that are getting the blame.' Meg blushed as Sam held her close to him.

'I'd never lie to you, Meg. I know we've not known one another that long, but I've never felt like this about a lass before.' Sam smiled and kissed her gently.

Meg breathed in deeply and whispered, 'I've never been with a lad before I met you. I don't know how I'm supposed to feel, but I can't stop thinking about you, either. I feel sick and my heart pounds whenever I hear your name, let alone when I'm with you, like now. Nothing seems to matter or make sense any more.' She gazed into Sam's eyes. She felt dejected by her parents' treatment of her at home, but with Sam by her side she felt loved again, especially when she lay in his arms. 'I'll not listen to a bad word anybody says about you, because they don't know you and they will just be making it up.'

'That's what they do about most things over here. Especially come winter, when nobody can go far and they all visit one another's houses with their knitting sticks, and sit around one another's fires and gossip. Their tongues clack as much as their needles and sticks, picking everybody's lives to pieces, without looking at their own.' Sam sighed. 'I think our Jack's right. He has plans to get away from it all and make himself a new life in America. But if he left, that would mean I would have to stay at home, looking after my mother. And I've no intention of doing that in a hurry.'

'Why? Your mother seems a good soul, and if it hadn't been for her, we'd not be seeing one another now.' Meg lay back in Sam's arms and they both gazed up at the scurrying clouds above their heads while the skylark's song trilled to them on the wind.

'Aye, she's been a good mother, but I want a life of my own – perhaps rent my own farm or at least have a bit of land, marry and have some children to call my own. I don't want to be tied to my mother's apron strings all my life, no matter what she thinks.' Sam turned his head and kissed Meg again as she smiled at him, and hoped she would be the one who would be his wife one day.

'I'm content with my lot at the shop at the moment. I don't want to go home, especially now, when I've to share my home with Dan. He's nothing but a bloody liar and a worm. I hate him.' Meg wrinkled up her nose at the thought of her cousin, and her face darkened.

Sam ran his finger along Meg's nose and leaned down and kissed her again. 'You are so cute when your nose wrinkles. Don't worry about bloody Dan – he's nothing. He'll blot his copybook one day. He's nothing to worry about. Our worry is how we are going to keep on meeting. I daren't walk out with you and court you officially. Your uncle would send you back as soon as look at me, and it's best I lie low until folk forget poor Margaret's death. So we will have to keep to your plan of seeing the good minister on a Sunday. I can give you all the guidance you'll ever need anyway, so you'll not be lying, in a way.' Sam laughed and winked as Meg blushed.

'I think you'll be leading me astray, Sam Alderson, not showing me the path of righteousness.' Meg bowed her head and then looked coyly at him.

'Aye, that I might, but you'll enjoy every minute,' Sam whispered as he held her tightly and felt her curves underneath her tight dress. 'I know I will.'

'I'm sure we both will, but God help us if our secret is ever found out. My life would not be worth living for sure, no matter how much I think of you, Sam Alderson.'

16

Meg had not been in bed long before she heard shouting and yelling, and all of a sudden the sound of breaking glass. She lit the candle that was next to her and sat up in bed, pulling her shawl around her nightgown, then went to open her bedroom door and walk along the dark corridor to the window, from where she could see straight down to the King's Head, from which all the noise seemed to be coming. She peered into the darkness, making out the forms of men fighting in the street, their shapes just visible in the dim gaslight of the pub and their voices echoing round the village in anger.

'So, they've woken you and all, have they?' Harry came along the passage and stood behind Meg, watching the affray. 'Somebody's getting a belting. It will be the local lads getting their own back on the miners for the death of that lass. It's been brewing all week. I thought it would have happened earlier than this, so I'm surprised it's taking place on a quiet Sunday night. Poor old Fred

Blackie will be shitting himself. Look at them – they've broken a window at least. Did you hear it smash? The bloody idiots! Fighting isn't going to bring the lass or her bairn back.'

'I hope nobody gets hurt. I can't bear to watch.' Meg closed one eye, but couldn't stop peeking, hoping that Sam and Jack weren't among the fighters.

'Hey up, the cavalry is here – listen! Old Fred must have sent for the peelers. I can hear them blowing their whistles. That'll scatter the buggers quick enough, as none of them will want to end up in the clink for the night.'

Harry and Meg watched as the shadowy figures dispersed quickly at the thought of arrest. The peelers' arrival scattered the crowds and made them slink away into the night.

'That soon sorted 'em out. I'll be away to my bed, now it's gone quiet. I'll go over and see old Fred first thing and make sure he's alright. He doesn't deserve all this upset at his age. He should be putting his feet up and being a man of leisure. But then again, so should I, and I'm just a slave to that shop.' Harry wandered down the passage with the candlestick in his hand, the light wafting in the draught and making shadows on the plastered walls.

Meg stared out into the darkness. She smiled at Harry saying he was a slave to the shop. How could he be a slave when he was never there? She was more of a slave than he was – without pay or a penny to her name. Then her thoughts returned to the fighting at the King's Head, as she made her way back to bed and lay there, thinking of Sam. It wouldn't be Jack who had got involved, of that she was sure, as his ribs were hurting him too much and he'd hardly ventured out of his home for more than a week. Sam, on the other hand, often went to the King's Head for a gill, and he was keen on raising his fists to defend himself. She closed her eyes and breathed in deeply, muttering to herself as she drifted off to sleep, 'Please don't let it be Sam mixed up in this. Please let him be safe.' Tomorrow, no doubt, the gossips would be out in force, and Harry would come back from the King's Head with some tale or other to tell.

'Well, they made a right good mess over there.' Harry flung his cap onto the peg next to the back door and looked across at Meg. 'Poor Fred – all hell broke loose when one of the Blades lads accused one of the Owd Gang miners of cheating at dominoes. Then it only took somebody else to say something about the death of that girl, and that it was one of their lot who was guilty, and the whole place erupted. I don't think he's got a chair left that isn't broken. And the bonny engraved-glass window that he put in when he first came here is smashed. He's an unhappy man this morning. I've told him to pack the place in, as we've both got to an age when we don't need the work any more, and he should have made his money by now.' Harry sighed.

'Was anybody hurt or arrested?' Meg asked in concern, thinking of Sam.

'No, but it had been a right carry-on and, as usual, the peelers came too late. They'd all scarpered by the time the peelers showed their faces. Fred said that the

Blades lads were accusing Sam Alderson of being the father of Margaret Parrington's baby, and all his mates were in and decided to defend Sam's corner. That's why it all started, seemingly – that and the dominoes. I always knew those Alderson lads were wrong 'uns.'

'Oh, was Sam himself not there then? I didn't think the Alderson brothers seemed so bad. They are always polite when they come into the shop. Sam always has a smile on his face. Why don't people pick on somebody else?' Meg felt her stomach churn, as she thought carefully about what to say in Sam's defence. It didn't surprise her that he was getting blamed for not standing by Margaret Parrington; after all, Sam had expected as much. But she wouldn't have his name blackened in such a way by her uncle.

'Pah – bloody smile! I'd give him a bloody smile if I saw him come through that doorway. You keep away from that lad, else I'll send you back home to your mother and father. Sam's a bad lot, always has been. He once came in here when he was a young lad and pinched some barley sugar off the counter. I gave him such a wallop. He's not to be trusted. He's a bad lot; goes with many a woman, married or single – he isn't bothered,' Harry moaned.

'Well, I take as I find. Anyway, he doesn't come in that often,' Meg said as she left Harry on hearing the shop bell ring.

'Aye, well, he's on borrowed time, if the local lads find him by himself one night,' Harry shouted through to the shop.

'What did Harry just shout about?' Mrs Woof, from the

neighbouring cottage, put her basket down and wanted to hear the latest gossip. 'Does he know what's been going on at the King's Head? What a mess this morning. Fred's out with his brush tidying up, and the poor man's nearly in tears.' She pulled her grey shawl around her scrawny figure and held her hand to her left ear to hear better.

'He says there's been a fight between the locals and the miners over dominoes,' Meg said as she saw to the order that Mrs Woof had thrust towards her over the counter, for her to put together.

'Aye, a right carry-on.' Harry came into the shop and leaned on the counter and talked to his neighbour. 'It wasn't just over dominoes, though. Our local lads took on the miners from the Owd Gang after they accused Sam Alderson of being responsible for not standing by the lass that killed herself with her baby. That's what it was all about.' Harry stood up and looked at his neighbour, as she pondered who Sam Alderson was.

'Well, what a to-do. I never did like the look of that lad, and his mother makes so much of her two boys – she's always bragging about them. They need hounding out of the village. We specially don't want his sort. Those miners act as if there will be no consequences to their grubby ways, and it's time they were taught different.' Mrs Woof folded her arms and shook her head. 'Wait until I tell Mabel. Her lads will sort the young bugger out – them and their mates.'

'But he may not be responsible, Mrs Woof. It's only hearsay. Nobody can take the law into their own hands. Perhaps Margaret Parrington was not in a fit state of

217

mind. And her parents had thrown her out, remember.' Meg tried to keep calm as she handed the gossiping old woman her basket filled with shopping.

'Well, if he's innocent, then I'm sorry, but perhaps he has to become an example, showing that us good God-fearing folk won't put up with wanton ways any more. Besides, you know nowt of what goes on over here. You've only just come out of Wensleydale, so you can't say owt.' Mrs Woof reached for her basket and passed Meg the money she owed. 'Anybody would think she's a bit sweet on the lad, Harry – you'd better watch her.'

'We'll not be having any of that, while she's under my roof.' Harry winked at Meg, who looked shocked.

'Aye, well, you are making up for her anyway with Lizzie Bannister. I hear you've been seen walking out to-gether in Reeth. Do you not think it's a bit early yet, with Mary not yet cold in her grave?' Mrs Woof gave Harry a knowing look.

'Whoever's been telling you that wants to get their facts right. It's a pity they haven't something more import-ant to talk about.' Harry went to the shop door and opened it for his nosy customer.

'Well, there's no fool like an old fool, and I should know. Sure didn't my old man go and leave me for a young slip of a lass, only to come back to me when she'd spent all his money. It was me who was the fool, for having him back. But I love him, so what should I have done? You make sure you are happy in your life, as the graveyard will be wanting us both too soon, I expect, for both our liking. Think of your Mary; she'd want you to be happy, I'm sure. Good morning to you both.' Mrs Woof sniggered at Harry as he closed the door behind her a tad hastily. The whole village knew what he was up to, but nobody dared say.

'Gossiping old devil. She never can mind her own business,' Harry growled as he looked across at Meg. 'I'd better have a word with you in the back. I'll bolt the shop door and put the "Closed" sign up for ten minutes until I've spoken to you.'

Meg followed Harry into the back of the shop, worried he'd guessed that she was, as Mrs Woof had said, a bit sweet on Sam Alderson.

'It's just about what gossiping Jenny Woof said.' Harry looked at Meg as she held her breath and waited to be chastised. 'It's true, I have been walking out with Lizzie Bannister, and it is where I go most days when I'm not in the shop. Trouble is, I don't want your father and mother to find out yet. They'd never forgive me. Mary and your mother have been friends all their lives, and your father – well, your father is a bit judgemental at the best of times.' Harry paused for breath and couldn't help but notice a look of relief on Meg's face. 'We are just good friends – company for one another. Lizzie's a widow and she understands what I was going through when Mary was dying.' He breathed in once more. 'But you know how it is: folk gossip around here, and read more into it than there is.'

'I'll not say a word to my mother or father, not until you want me to. And as long as you are happy, Uncle

Harry, it is of no consequence to me.' Meg couldn't help but smile at her rueful-looking uncle.

'Aye, that's grand. Mrs Woof is a terrible old gossip and reads things into stuff that other folk wouldn't even imagine. She was trying to tell me you were sweet on Sam Alderson, and you barely know the lad – silly old fool.' Harry sat down in his chair.

'Don't worry, Uncle Harry, you do what you want to do. I'm sure my Aunt Mary would have understood, and she'd want you to be happy. I'll go back into the shop now and you calm yourself. As you say, she's a gossip.' Meg was relieved that Harry was too busy worrying about his own love life to have witnessed the blush on her cheeks as Sam's name was mentioned. Now all she could think about was the safety of her Sam; with half the village against him, his life would not be worth living.

'Don't let them buggers get the better of you.' Jack stopped on the fellside, his ribs still hurting from the beating he had taken in the boxing ring. However, this morning his brother's safety on his walk to work was worth enduring a bit of pain for.

'You shouldn't be with us – you are in no fit state to walk up this gill edge to the mine, let alone pick up a shovel in the furnace.' Sam held his arm out for his brother to take, as Jack caught his breath and leaned backwards to take the pressure off his sore ribs.

'And have you battered and thumped to death by the local henchmen? I don't think so! You heard what Billie Collins said, when he hammered on our door in the early hours. The locals are out to get you. It doesn't matter if you were the father or not; they are out for revenge, and your face and your gob fit.' Jack placed his arm on his brother's shoulder as he caught his breath again and then looked solemnly at Sam. 'If I were you, I'd get myself away out of Swaledale for a while, until it all calms down. Something else will come along for them all to talk about and get worked up over, but I honestly fear for your life. You were seen so often with Margaret in and around the village last summer, they are bound to think the baby's yours.' Jack stood up and looked around him. 'It's not like this dale is owt special. And there are men forever wanted for the building of these new railways. I've even thought about leaving myself, but my head's really set on going further afield.'

'You mean bloody America – you are always dreaming of that place. I tell you what: there's only land, sky and water wherever you go. It's all just in different quantities, with different creatures on it and in it. I'm not going anywhere; they are not getting rid of me that easy. Besides, I'm not leaving Meg. Not now, when I think I've actually found the right girl for me – if there is such a thing – although I keep doubting myself. I'm a bit fickle when it comes to this love thing. Plus there's our mother. If you bugger off, she'll be on her own.'

'I'm only trying to help. Think about it. I'll help you out with some money – you know I've been saving without Mother knowing. You could pay me back when you've got a job. I'd rather not see your ugly mug for a month or two than have to bury it, when you've been battered to death

221

by those ignorant bloody farmers that are baying for your blood.' Jack bent double in pain as they nearly reached the top of the fell and the lead-mines.

'For God's sake, our lad, go back home. You are neither use nor ornament to anybody, the state you are in. Go back before anybody sees you. I've got to call in to Supplies for some gunpowder anyway, so get yourself home and we'll talk more tonight.' Sam patted his brother on the back. He was a good man and was only trying to protect him, in truth, but at this moment in time Jack hadn't the strength to blow out a candle, let alone take on somebody in a fight. Besides, it was *his* fight; nothing at all to do with his brother. And as far as anybody else was concerned, it was not his baby – not that anyone would believe him. He was being made a scapegoat for the locals' hatred; that had been obvious when the farmer who supplied the miners' cottages with milk had spat in his face that morning and had threatened to piss in their milk.

Perhaps Jack was right; perhaps he would be best getting away for a while. At least while he was at work at the mine he was with his own kind, he thought as he signed for his gunpowder and put it in his pocket, then entered the mine to many a slap on the back and a jape aimed at him. He was safe at work. But back down in the village was another matter. He'd have to lie low for a day or two, he thought, as he made his way into the dark bowels of the mountain and the relative safety of the place he knew best.

17

'I don't know. First it's a cow calving that stops me from seeing our Meg, and now it's a baby on its way. I'm sure Mrs Armstrong would have managed to bring Nellie Birbeck's baby into the world alone, but she's sent for me to help, so there must be complications and she won't be able to afford the doctor, the poor soul.' Agnes picked up her shawl and looked at Dan, who up till a few minutes ago was going to take her into Swaledale to see Meg, even though he'd moaned a bucketful about doing so. 'Here, take her this note and explain to Meg what's happened, and that her father's gone into Dent to look at some sheep. The poor lass will think we've forgotten her – especially me, I haven't seen her for nearly three weeks.'

Agnes scribbled a note quickly, giving her apologies to Meg and saying that she hoped she was well, and that she missed and loved her. 'Make sure you tell her I love her, and that both her father and I will be over shortly. Now I'll have to go. There isn't a minute to lose, if that baby is to be born alive.' Agnes thrust the note into Dan's hand and set off across the field in the direction of the Birbecks' house and the birthing mother.

Dan looked at the note in his hand – the note he had no intention of delivering to Meg. He screwed it up and placed it on the kitchen fire, then grinned to himself as he watched the flames engulf the words of love.

He was trying to win over Tom Oversby, playing on his misconception that women did not make good farmers, and placing himself in line to inherit Beck Side after his aunt and uncle's day. After all, half of the farm should rightly have been Tom's sister's, so he had as much right to it as Meg ever had. He'd go over to the shop and tell Meg that nobody could be bothered to come over and see her; that he'd only been sent because there was butter to be sold. That would really upset her and would make her feel unloved, the spoilt bitch. He couldn't have planned things better if he'd tried.

'What's up, Meg? You look a bit down this morning.' Harry looked across at his usually cheery guest and couldn't help but notice a gloom hanging over her.

'I'm alright. I thought my father or my mum would have come to see me yesterday. But Dan said they were both too busy, although he didn't know exactly what they were doing when I quizzed him.'

'Aye, lass, they'll have had their reasons. Your parents love you, and just because they haven't come to see you doesn't mean they aren't thinking about you.' Harry smiled at Meg. 'He's a bit of a chancer, is that Dan – takes after his father. I wouldn't listen to what he tells you, or at best would take it with a pinch of salt.'

'He seems to be popular with my father. He's teaching Dan everything to do with running the farm. At first I felt sorry for Dan, when he turned up at home after losing both his parents. But he's got this real cocky edge to him, and I sometimes think he goes out of his way to upset me.' Meg held back the tears. With Dan giving her cause to be concerned and Sam being bad-mouthed in the shop nearly every day by gossiping shoppers, life was not a bed of roses at present.

'Do you want to go home, lass? I can understand if you do. It'd mean I'd have to alter my ways, or perhaps put the shop up for sale. You've been like a breath of spring air to me. With you and Lizzie, I can see there is something else that life can give me.' Harry looked across at the young girl whom he had grown fond of, over the last few weeks. She was a good worker and housekeeper. And Mary, God rest her soul, had been right to ask for Meg to stay until he felt stronger.

'Oh no, I don't want to leave. I love it over here. It's just that I'm frightened that . . .' Meg paused, realizing what she was about to say made her sound jealous and petty.

'You are frightened that Dan is taking your place at home. That's what you were going to say, wasn't it? Well, I can tell you, he'll never do that. And I know the last few days in the village have been a bit unpleasant, but things will soon settle down. Some other scandal will come along, and folk will be talking about something else when they come into the shop. Who knows, it might even be good news next time.' Harry grinned. 'You see, I'm not as blind as you think I am. I've noticed you getting upset when folk have come in and done nothing but moan. That's part of running the shop; you've to be there to listen to other folk's problems, good or bad, and you've to take it in your stride.'

'I know, and you are right about Dan. I am jealous. But I know my father has always wanted a lad, and now he's got one and I feel he doesn't want me any more.' A tear fell down Meg's cheek.

'Now you are talking daft. Your mother and father idolize you, like I do. You are the daughter me and Mary never had. Now chin up, and stop feeling sorry for yourself. On Sunday go and see Peggy Dobson after going to chapel. You were with her at the Bartle Fair and she's a grand lass, although she's happen a tad too friendly with those Alderson lads.' Harry looked across at Meg. 'I hear they were with you, too.'

'Who told you that?' Meg looked surprised.

'Nay, that would be telling. I'm not as daft as I look, and I know you were with Jack and Sam Alderson, and the rest of the company they keep, for the main part of the day. I've only just heard, else I'd have been giving you a piece of my mind long before this. Keep those lads at arm's length, lass; you know my thoughts on them both. Your father and mother wouldn't like them, and they've caused enough scandal around here, without your name being dragged through it and all.' Harry had heard in the King's Head of Meg being seen with Peggy and the

Aldersons, but had kept it to himself until an opportune moment arose.

'They aren't as bad as everyone makes out, Uncle Harry, honestly.' Meg looked across at her uncle and couldn't help but wonder how much more he had seen and heard.

'Nay, they are a bad lot, Meg. You keep away, do you hear? Else I will be sending you back home, whether you like it or not. Go and see Peggy by all means – a lass needs a friend. But the less you have to do with the Aldersons, the better.'

Harry looked stern. He didn't like the way Meg had risen in defence of the two lads. Perhaps there was more going on than what he'd happened to hear in the pub, when talking to Fred, the landlord. 'I'm thinking of entertaining myself, on Sunday. I've asked Mrs Bannister for Sunday tea, and I thought later in the day you might like to meet her. She's heard a lot about you, and now that I've told you about her, I thought it was time you met. Some folk will be sure to be gossiping about me having another woman so soon after losing Mary, but life carries on and it's no good being miserable for the rest of your life.' Harry sat back and looked at Meg as he told her this.

'I'm glad you are finding happiness with Mrs Bannister. You deserve it, and people should mind their own business. That's the trouble with busybodies; they always think they know better, and nine times out of ten they know nothing,' Meg stated with fervour.

'Well then, that's settled. Lizzie will be welcomed here

for tea, come Sunday. And you go and see Peggy; she'll not see many folks, being a maid to Reverend Gilpin, and he can be a demanding old sod.' Harry added, 'Not like me.'

'I will go and see Peggy. I'll lay out tea before I go, though, and then everything is just right for you and Mrs Bannister. I'll make some tongue sandwiches and a trifle, and then you can help yourselves until I return.' Meg's mood lifted. She'd no intention of going to see Peggy, but she could spend the whole day with Sam and no one would ask where she had been. As for Lizzie Bannister visiting, she would not let Harry down when she made them both their teas. Harry could have chastised her a lot harder than he did, because someone had obviously told him that she had been seen with Sam. But Harry walking out with Lizzie, only weeks after the death of his wife, meant that he could not judge her own actions too harshly. However, she'd still play it safe and meet Sam away from the gaze of anyone from the village. And Sunday could not come soon enough.

'You look worried. Whatever is the matter?' Meg sat down next to Sam on the fellside and kissed him lovingly on the cheek.

'Nowt for you to bother about, really, but I do need to talk to you, to clear my head, because it's so full of rubbish. And I need someone to listen to me, and not judge me. My life is just hell at the moment; and not only mine, but the rest of my family's as well. My mother gets spat at as she walks around the village; my brother isn't showing his face outside our home, he's had that many names called at him, and he can't hold his own at the moment because of his ribs. And as for me, well, to the locals I'm the Devil himself, if you listen to them talking. The other night we had a stone with a message wrapped around it flung through our kitchen window. It could have killed my ma, if she'd been sitting in her usual chair.' Sam bowed his head and didn't dare look at Meg in case his worries got the better of him and he broke down in tears.

'What did the note say?' Meg put her arm around Sam and felt him shudder.

'"Piss off, you bastard – your sort are not wanted here".' Sam pulled at the tufts of grass between his legs and threw it into the river in handfuls. 'I never did anything to Margaret; the baby wasn't mine, and I didn't know she was going to top herself from off that bridge. I don't know what to do,' Sam lied. He knew that if Meg found out the truth, she would never be his. 'Our Jack has offered to lend me some money to leave home, just for a short while, but I don't want to leave you and my mother behind. I love living here in Gunnerside. I always thought it was going to be my home, especially when you came along.' Sam raged and lied through his teeth as he looked into the distance.

'I know you are having it hard. All the village seems to be blaming you. I hear them all when they come into the shop and start cursing and slandering you, saying that you should have stood by Margaret. And then I want to tell them that they know nothing, and to mind

229

their own business.' Meg reached for Sam's hand. 'Perhaps Jack is right; perhaps you should get away for a while. Till it all quietens down. It will be old news by this time next year.' She felt tears rising in her eyes as she looked at Sam and realized how fond she was of him; perhaps even in love with him, if she dared to admit it.

'No, I couldn't. I couldn't leave you.' Sam turned and kissed Meg gently on the lips. 'Unless . . . unless you'd come with me and we could make a new life together. We could get married and I'd get a job working for the railways – they keep advertising for miners and ex-canal men. We could be together forever then, and nobody need know who we both really are and why we are there.' Sam sounded excited suddenly. 'Mr and Mrs Sam Alderson: now that's got a nice ring to it – sounds like a name of distinction to me. We could go places together. You've got the looks and I've got the gab, so we were made for one another.'

Meg shook her head. 'No, Sam, I couldn't do that. I think too much of my mum and dad – I could never leave them. And I'm happy at the moment, helping Harry out at the shop. I know it's not forever, but I really do enjoy the shop and the customers.' She gazed into Sam's eyes and shook her head again, while her heart was being torn apart. She felt her heart race. She was being asked by the lad she loved to marry him and plan a new life with him, but her head was telling her no – she had to stay with the people who really loved and cared for her. Meg knew Sam was fickle; nearly everybody she had talked to recently had told her so. And no matter how much she

230

loved him, he might have his head turned next week by the latest girl to enter the dale. So no matter how much her heart said yes to his idea, her head said no.

'But I love you, and this would be our chance to be together. Jack has saved up a tidy sum. It would see us right for at least six months, and I know I'd be able to get a job working for the railway. We needn't go far; the train lines are coming to neighbouring dales, and I know I'd find work with them. Then we could rent a house and become a respectable couple. When we are settled, you could go back to your parents. They'd never disown you, as you are their precious only daughter and always will be, no matter what you think of them at this minute.' Sam held Meg tightly in his arms. 'Please, Meg; please say yes. I do love you – you know I do – and I need to get away, but not without you.'

'Oh, Sam, think of what you ask of me. I'd be turning my back on everything, and everybody I hold dear to me. You are asking a lot; too much, I fear, no matter how much I love you.' Meg bowed her head and breathed in heavily, as she didn't want to lose the man she loved.

Sam lay down by her side and pulled him towards her. 'I love you, Meg Oversby. I love every inch of you, and I can't live without you. But I have to leave, as the folk around here will never let me be, whether or not I'm innocent.' He looked down into Meg's eyes and kissed her, as his hands felt the curves of Meg's body and she did nothing to stop him. If he was going to leave, he'd be going on his own – no matter what he had told Meg. But before he left, he was going to have her: another conquest, one of many.

231

'We shouldn't, Sam – this is how we get into trouble,' Meg whispered as he kissed her neck and lifted her skirts on the warm grassy fellside.

'Shush, my Meg! Marry me and then there is no problem with what we are about to do,' Sam whispered. 'We have both felt this way for a while now. Well, if we leave together, it will make us stronger, knowing each other the way we do.'

Meg could feel tears welling up in her eyes as Sam unbuttoned his trousers and lay on top of her. 'Sam, we shouldn't. Please, I don't want to be the next Margaret Parrington. My family would disown me if I returned to them with child.' She gasped for breath as Sam kissed her more and more and finally entered her, making her wince.

'You'll not be doing that, I'll make sure of it. Besides, another few weeks and we could be married and away from here. Enjoy, my Meg; let's remember this moment as the first step in our life together,' Sam whispered as he took pleasure in Meg's inexperience of lovemaking.

'I do love you,' she sobbed as Sam lay to the side of her, smiling and spent. 'You promise I'll not get pregnant – that you took care?' Meg wiped a tear from her cheek.

'Stop worrying. You enjoyed it as much as me. I saw that, when you looked up at me and kissed me while I was busy on the job. It's what life is all about, as long as we are careful.' Sam turned his face up into the autumn sunshine and closed his eyes. 'You'll come with me? We could be out of here by next weekend.'

Meg composed herself and leaned on one arm, then looked down at the warm face of the man she loved. 'I've never noticed before that you have freckles,' she said as she traced the line of them over the bridge of his nose with a piece of mountain grass, before lying back down in his arms. 'You promise that we wouldn't move too far, and that we could go and see my mum and father, once we are settled?'

'Aye, they might not want to see me, though, seeing as I'll have pinched their little girl from under their noses.' Sam opened his eyes and leaned on his elbow, looking at Meg. 'We will be fine. I'll always be there to look after you. You'll never have any worries – I'll take care of them all. Come away with me. I can take on the world if I know you are by my side.' He stroked her long, dark hair and kissed her softly. He did feel something for Meg, but he hoped that she would not rise to the challenge of leaving everyone and everything she loved behind her. Yet at the same time he did not want to lose his latest lover. So he found himself uttering words that held no meaning. He would lead her on with his words until the very last minute, because saving his own skin was his priority.

'I'd be giving up everything. My home, my family – everything!' Meg sighed.

'You've said yourself that your father favours Dan over you. And your mother would always welcome you home, you know that. Especially if she ever gets to be a grandmother!' Sam grinned.

'Shush, Sam, don't joke. I'm worrying enough that we've gone too far this afternoon. After all, that's why you are in the mess you are now in. And I've been stupid enough to let you have your way with me.' Meg felt her

233

stomach churn as the heat of the moment cooled, like the sun that was quickly being hidden by dark, threatening rain clouds that had appeared on the horizon.

'You'll be alright – stop your worrying. And I'm not in any mess really, because it was not my baby! Now I'll talk to our Jack, get him to lend me some money. You sort out what you want to take with you and we'll meet as usual next Sunday, but then we will be away. Will you be telling your parents and Harry, or not? Are you strong enough to do that, or do you want me to be there with you?' Sam had to look as if he was planning his new life with Meg by his side, but knew she was still having doubts, and that these would win the day.

'No, I'm not going to say anything to anybody. I'll just leave a note to my mother and father, and to Harry. I couldn't bear to face them; they'd only go out of their way to make sure I'd change my mind. They regard you as a leper, as well you know. I'm going to cause them so much hurt, and I love them all so much.' Meg held back the tears yet again and looked at Sam, who was holding her hand tightly.

'Yes, but you'll have me to love you and look after you. And that I will, I swear. I love you, Meg Oversby, and we will be married and set up home, and will have a family once we are settled. That I promise you, with every bone of my body.' Sam kissed her. He'd said the same words to many a lass, but perhaps this one would be different, although he had no intention of letting Meg drag him down when he left the dale.

*

'Aye, lass, you are sodden. Have you walked all the way back down from Arkengarthdale? You look like a drowned rat!' Harry exclaimed when Meg came into the back room, dripping and cold.

'Yes, I got caught in the storm that brewed up out of nowhere. I didn't even have a coat.' Meg stood and looked at the pretty grey-haired woman who sat across from Harry, next to the fire.

'Go and get changed out of those damp clothes, before you are to bury.' The woman smiled as Meg looked her up and down. 'And then come and join us both for tea. Harry wasn't going to wait for you to return, but I made him when I saw the lovely spread that you had made for us both. There's far too much for us two old duffers.'

'This is Lizzie, Meg – Mrs Bannister. And as you may have gathered, she says what she thinks.' Harry smiled at Lizzie with a look of love.

'I always tell him there's nowt wrong with that. At least everybody knows where they stand with me. Not like half of the two-faced buggers around here. Now, go on: get changed and then join us.' Lizzie folded her arms and watched as Meg smiled at her.

'Nice to meet you, Mrs Bannister. Uncle Harry has told me all about you.' Meg smiled and looked at the couple. Lizzie was quite small with a perfect figure, her greying hair the only sign of how old she was, as there was not a wrinkle on her face. Meg could understand her attraction to Harry.

'It's "Lizzie"; we'll have none of this "Mrs Bannister"

larky. And I hope this old devil's not been telling you too much.' She giggled. 'You've not been telling her all our little secrets now, have you, Harry?'

Meg grinned as she noticed her Uncle Harry's face flush with embarrassment, then made her way upstairs to change out of her wet clothes and dry her hair with a towel. Lizzie was certainly different from her Aunt Mary, who had always been a woman of refinement and manners. Lizzie, on the other hand, seemed quite the opposite, with her glowing cheeks, perfect figure and open ways. Once in her room, Meg looked around her as she undressed out of her damp clothes and changed, to share tea with her uncle and his lover.

She looked at herself in the long wardrobe mirror and viewed herself critically. Her long, dark hair was sodden and her face, she thought, was not one of great beauty. Yet Sam Alderson had offered to elope with her and marry her. She ran her hands over her corseted figure, looking at her tight waist and small, pert breasts. She'd let Sam touch and fondle parts of her that no gentleman should ever have touched before marriage, and she closed her eyes, trying to blot out the sexual act they had both performed and enjoyed together. She should not have submitted to her feelings, she thought, as she stepped into her dry skirt and blouse. Is that what Sam had done with Margaret Parrington, only to leave her desperate and with child? Had he told Margaret that he loved her and wanted to marry her, only to discard her, as she had seen him do at the Bartle Fair? Now that she was away from Sam and his winning looks and smile, Meg had doubts about whether leaving everyone she loved behind her was the right thing to do. She was going to cause pain to her family. But she did love Sam, and a new life with him was more than tempting – a new life as Mrs Alderson, with a ring on her finger and a new home as well. That's what Sam had promised, after all. She quickly quelled her doubts and went downstairs to join Harry and his new-found love, Lizzie.

'Now aren't you a picture? Harry said you were a bonny lass. It's a wonder he isn't having to shoo all the lads in the district from his shop door.' Lizzie smiled at Meg and patted the cushion on the chair next to her, urging her to sit down.

Meg smiled and sat down next to Lizzie, feeling a bit uncomfortable at playing gooseberry between the two lovers. 'Have you enjoyed your day here, Mrs Bannister?' she asked politely.

'Now remember, it's "Lizzie"; you can even call me "Aunt Lizzie" if it makes it any easier.' Lizzie grinned. 'I have indeed. Harry has shown me his little empire. I'd never been upstairs before today, and they are good-sized bedrooms, I must say.'

'Aye, well, that's enough said about that.' Harry coughed and gave Lizzie a dark look. 'How about we have our tea, now that you are back? I take it Peggy was glad to see you. I bet she gets lonely, looking after the clergyman and his house.'

'She was glad to see me, and I've had a lovely day apart from the rain.' Meg got up from her seat and put the copper kettle on the hearth to boil, as she uncovered the tongue sandwiches that had lain below a dampened tea cloth, to keep them fresh, since the early morning when she had made them. She then went into the pantry and brought out the sherry trifle, which she had likewise made earlier in the day, along with a caraway-seed cake and rock buns. The tea table looked impressively full and, as Lizzie had pointed out, there was far more than they needed, as the three of them sat down together.

'I always say a little of what you fancy does you good,' Lizzie said. She reached for a sandwich and smiled at Harry as she bit into it.

'Aye, tuck in. I can't do with waste.' Harry winked at Lizzie as she reached for another sandwich, the first one being no sooner started than it was finished.

'Meg, you must think us both a bit forward, being friends like we are, so soon after Mary has died.' Lizzie looked across at Meg, her face now quite serious. 'It's just that we aren't getting any younger, and we both like one another's company. I've always believed that you've to follow your heart, regardless of what other folk think. Oh, they'll moan and call us all the names under the sun, but they'll get used to us eventually. I know I'm being forward when I say that I do think a great deal of Harry, and I'd like to think he does of me. So you might be seeing me as a regular visitor, if Harry agrees.' Lizzie held her hand out for Harry to grasp as she looked across at Meg.

'You know what I think, lass. I'd like our affairs all out in the open, as I don't like skulking about. Anyway, folk have seen us together, they know what we are about.' Harry looked across at her. 'You are fine with it, aren't you, Meg? You wish us well, don't you?'

'I do, Uncle Harry, as long as you are both happy.' Meg smiled at the old lovebirds.

'As long as we follow our hearts, we will always be happy, Meg. And you must always do the same in your life, and take no heed of what folk say.' Lizzie bent forward and kissed Harry on the cheek, making him turn bright pink.

'I'll remember that, Lizzie. I'll try and follow my heart at all times, no matter what,' Meg replied, thinking of her Sam, but also thinking: *If only it was that easy.*

18

The following week was one of the longest Meg had ever endured, with her head telling her to stay and be satisfied with her life, and her heart telling her to go with Sam and become his wife. By the time Thursday came and her parents were due to make their weekly visit, she felt guilty and unsure of herself, especially at the thought of lying to them and perhaps never seeing them again – or at least not for a month or two, until she and Sam had got settled.

'Tha looks white, lass. Are you feeling alright?' Harry glanced up from doing his books and looked at Meg, who had been strangely quiet all week.

'I'm fine, thank you, Uncle Harry. I've not been sleeping that well, these last few days. But there's no reason for it. I just can't seem to drop straight off, like I used to do.' Meg smiled as she felt her stomach churn at the thought of having to pretend until Sunday that her life was normal, so as not to give the game away about her forthcoming elopement.

'I'll have to give you more work to do – that'll make you sleep,' Harry laughed. 'You know, if you are pining for home, you can always go back with them today. I'll be alright now. But don't you say owt about Lizzie to them, not yet. She's a fine woman, but she'll never fill Mary's shoes, either in my eyes or your parents'. And they will never accept her, once they find out about her.'

'I won't say anything, Uncle Harry. And no, I'm not pining for home. I'm quite content to stay here for as long as you want me.' Meg hated lying to Harry, as he'd been good to her and he was a kind man. The more she thought about her pact with Sam, the more she knew it was wrong. She was throwing away everything because of her infatuation with a lad she barely knew. A lad that all the dale, with the exception of his closest family, hated; and a lad that she had let take her virginity, in a moment of weakness.

'Aye, well, as long as you are alright. And I thank you for not mentioning my private life to Tom and Agnes – not yet, anyway. Speak of the Devil, here they are, both your mother and your father, and they haven't got that Dan with them today, so they are both yours and you needn't listen to his blethering.' Harry watched through the shop window as Agnes was helped out of the cart by Tom, and both he and Meg smiled as the couple entered the shop.

'I don't know where the weeks go to, the days pass so fast.' Agnes took off her gloves and shawl and went straight over to Meg and hugged her. 'I'm sorry I've not seen you for a fortnight, but with calves and babies, I couldn't get away.'

241

Meg hugged her mum back and then exclaimed, 'Babies! What babies?'

'Nellie Birbeck's! Didn't Dan give you the note I sent you? I was coming over with him, until her young sister ran across the fields to say that Nellie was having bother birthing, and would I help. So I couldn't let her down. As it was, she had a lovely baby boy; he's a right grand 'un. Nearly ten pounds, that's why he took some getting out.'

'I'm glad for Nellie. But no, Dan never gave me your note, he just said you were both too busy.' Meg smiled at her mum; she should have known she wouldn't have let her down without a reason.

'Aye, that lad, he's not to be trusted with anything. The other day we found him looking at papers in the desk, and your father got mad with him.' Agnes sighed and kissed Meg on the cheek again. 'You must have thought we had deserted you.'

'No, I knew there would be a good reason for you not to be here.' Meg raised her head and nearly cried, realizing that Dan had been economical with the truth on purpose.

'Aye, I kicked his arse, Meg. And now I've put a lock on the desk, although we've never had to do that before. But you don't know what he's up to. Now Dan's got his feet under the table, he thinks he can do as he likes. Well, he's finding out that he couldn't be further from the truth, the cocky little bugger,' Tom growled.

'There, you see, my Meg, I told you there'd be a good reason they both hadn't appeared. She's had a face on her like a slapped arse, ever since Dan came on his own.

242

Neither Meg nor I think a lot of him. He must take after his father, I'd say.'

'Aye, you've got the better of the pair staying with you. Hasn't he, our lass?' Tom slapped Harry on the back.

'Goes without saying. Our Meg has always been the only one, in my eyes.' Agnes smiled at her daughter and noticed tears welling up in her eyes. 'Hey, what's this? What are these for? Are you wanting to come home?'

'You mean you don't like Dan, really? You realize he's not all that he seems.' Meg wiped away her tears; she'd felt unloved and jealous for nothing.

'No, he'll never replace you, and you are an idiot if you ever thought that. You are our lass. Now, how about you come home with us today, and put Dan back in his place as farm lad?' Tom smiled at his daughter, whom he had truly missed.

'No, I'm fine here. I just thought you hadn't time for me, now that Dan is with you, and he's that full of himself.' Meg blew her nose and grinned through the tears. 'He is all mouth – I should have known that.'

'Too right. He'll be out on his arse, if he carries on like he is doing much longer.' Tom put his arm around his daughter's shoulders and held her tight.

'Now then, let me put this butter away. You put the kettle on, Meg, and then we'll close the shop for an hour, and have a proper talk without bloody Dan!' Harry smiled at Meg and her parents. The colour had come back into Meg's cheeks already; she'd obviously been missing her mum.

243

'Aye, come on, Meg. Take us through to the back room and we'll have a catch-up. A cup of tea would be grand, before we get ourselves back home to see what damage Dan's done. He let next door's tup in with our ewes the other day. Lord only knows what's in lamb and what isn't, now. He's a bloody liability,' Tom swore as he sat down with Agnes and watched Meg, as she laid out the tea things and made them feel at home. 'No wonder Harry doesn't want you to leave. You are his house-keeper, shopkeeper – the lot.'

Meg smiled. It was the first time her father had rec-ognized her many skills. Perhaps Dan had blotted his copybook too many times, and at last her father had realized she was capable of doing anything a lad could do – and more. It was a pity he hadn't realized it before, as the thought of leaving with Sam would not even have entered her head if she had known she was that loved and wanted. As it was, she was torn now. Was she to go with Sam, or should she stay? Whatever path she chose, hearts were going to be broken.

Meg tossed and turned all night, unable to make up her mind which way to head with her life. One minute she was getting married and in a new life, with Sam working as a railway navvy; the next she was letting him leave without her, to remain with Harry until near Christmas and then return home – a home where she knew she was loved, now that she had got reassurance from both her parents. She sat on her bed, then pulled on her bloomers and skirt. She didn't know what to do, and she wished more than anything that she had not let Sam make love to her. The worry of perhaps getting pregnant was now beginning to play on her mind. If she went with Sam, at least he would look after her, come what may, whereas her family might well abandon her, just like poor Margaret Parrington's. It was simply one worry after another, she thought, as she went downstairs, lit the fire and opened the shop door for the early-morning customers.

'I'm off to see Lizzie this morn. Will you be alright in the shop on your own? It's Friday, and we are usually thronged with folk. I've heard the bell go a time or two already. I wouldn't go, but Lizzie's set her heart on a hat she's seen in a shop window in Leyburn, so I've promised her it for a treat.' Harry looked across at Meg while they had breakfast together. 'Tha looks red-eyed. Have you been crying?'

'No, no, I got something in one of my eyes and it's made it sore. I'm alright now. I think it was some coal dust from when I set the fire first thing.' Meg put on a brave face and smiled at Harry.

'As long as you are alright. I can stop around home, if you want me to?' Harry finished his plate of scrambled eggs and looked at Meg suspiciously. 'It was grand to hear what your mother and father really thought about that Dan. I think your father realizes now that he's got a cuckoo in the nest.'

'Yes, I think Dan's one for playing everyone along to his tune. Well, he'll get a shock with my father, as he'll only put up with Dan's ways for so long.' Meg cleared the breakfast plates into the stone sink and poured hot water from the kettle on them to wash them. She stopped as she heard the shop bell ring, drying her hands on her pinny.

'I'll be away then, Meg,' Harry said quickly as she went to serve the customer waiting in the shop. 'Don't make me anything to eat this evening. I may be late back.' He'd taken his chance to tell her this when she hadn't time to ask him why. Now he reached for his coat, cap and walking stick and made swiftly for the back door.

Meg sighed; it was going to be a long day on her own, and a busy one. But if Harry wasn't going to be back until late, she could sort out her belongings and see what she would be taking with her, if she eloped with Sam.

'Jack, what are you doing here?' Meg gasped, thankful to hear the back door closing behind Harry.

'I've come for some bread for my mother, but I've also come to bring you this from our Sam.' Jack hung his head and passed Meg the note in his hand. 'I've lent him two guineas. He promises he'll pay me back. I bloody hope so, else I'll never get to do what I want. As it is, my mother's going to kill me for lending him it, but he's better off getting out of this place. He'll never make anything of himself with this hatred hanging over him in the dale.' He looked at Meg.

'Thanks, Jack, I'll read it later.' Meg placed the note in her pinny's pocket and looked at Jack, who seemed crestfallen. 'He'll be alright, you know. Sam can look after himself.' She smiled at Jack.

'It isn't him I'm worried about. Sam says he's taking

you with him, or is he just winding me up? At the moment I don't believe a word that comes out of his mouth. If he is, then are you sure you're doing the right thing? Our Sam is an unknown quantity sometimes. He can be a moody bugger and he likes a drink – your life with him will not be a bed of roses,' Jack said, with concern in his voice. 'If he is taking you with him, I'd think twice.'

'I promised him, Jack. I must admit I keep having doubts, especially when my mother and father were here yesterday. But I think I do love Sam.' Meg smiled as she wrapped up a loaf of bread for Jack and passed it across the counter to him.

'"Think" isn't good enough – not for what Sam's asking you to do. You have to be deeply in love to leave all behind you and start out on a new life together.' Jack gazed across the counter at Meg. He knew what it was like to be in love, but he daren't tell the girl he was looking at how he really felt about her. She'd made it clear that it was Sam she preferred, and now he was going to lose Meg forever.

'Well then, I'm deeply in love with Sam and we will be happy.' Meg pushed the bread at Jack and didn't let on about the nagging doubt she was beginning to feel about her decision, or that she was starting to question if she did love him enough to run away with him. 'A penny, please.' She'd never forgotten the evening when Jack had said harsh words about his brother, and she wasn't prepared to listen to the same thing again.

'Aye, well, I wish you both luck, if your heads are set.

You go home, if Sam's not right with you.' Jack threw a penny onto the counter and picked up the loaf of bread. 'And I'll always be here, if you need me,' he added quickly.

Meg reached into her pocket for Sam's hastily written note. She unfolded the piece of paper and read it quickly, her hands shaking as she took in each scribbled word:

My dearest Meg,

Only another two days and then we will be together forever. Meet me at our usual place on Sunday morning. Travel light, and don't bring much with you. You can always return for your possessions once we are settled. I'm going to steal one of the ponies used at the mine; we will travel faster if we are on horseback. I love you, my Meg, and you'll not regret coming away with me when you are made my wife. Until Sunday, my love.

Sam

Meg breathed in deeply and closed her eyes, holding the letter in her hand. Should she go through with her escape to a new life? Was she really deeply in love with Sam, or was it simply that he was the first lad who had shown her any attention and she was besotted by his words and how he looked at her? Her mind raced with thoughts and words that had been said to her over the last few days. Even Jack sounded concerned that his brother was leading her astray. But no, he was just jealous; it hadn't gone unnoticed by her, the way Jack looked at her when he thought she wasn't looking. But it was

248

Sam she loved, and she would be leaving with him come Sunday, no matter what.

A chill wind blew along the fellside as Sam signed for a new amount of gunpowder from the supplies hut. He shoved it into his right pocket and turned up his coat collar against the cold as he walked the few last yards to the mine's entrance.

'You are late today, Alderson. The day's nearly over and you are only just beginning to stir,' the blacksmith yelled at him.

Sam shrugged his shoulders and didn't reply to his comment.

'Cat got your tongue? It's not that that the locals are wanting to cut off you, it's the other parts that you are just as free with using, from what I hear, and I don't blame them.' The scowling blacksmith spat in front of Sam and then went back to making the pump for the new shaft.

Sam trudged into the mine and lit the candle on his hat, then went to where Bob Winn was busy at work.

'Oh, so you've decided to show your face,' Bob said in the candlelight, stopping for a second from picking at the rock face to turn and look at Sam.

'Aye, I'm here, but not for long. I'm thinking of buggering off, Bob. I've had enough of everybody giving me a hard time over something I didn't do.'

Sam felt miserable and down, as he didn't want to leave his mother and his home. As for Meg, well, he was glad he had finally decided not to take her; after all, he seemed to be cursed with bad luck when it came to

249

women. She'd only drag him down, like all the other women had. She'd be over him in a couple of days, and he'd be free to do as he liked. He really never had any intention of Meg leaving with him; he didn't love her, so what was the point of having her with him? He only wished that he had not strung her along quite so much in the hope of getting his leg over her again.

'This will be my last day working with you. I've had enough.' Sam drew on his lit pipe, making the embers glow in the darkness of the tunnel.

'Don't let the buggers get you down. You'll be alright, lad. Somebody else will come along that they can pick on.' Bob slapped his mate on the back and looked at him by the light of their candles.

'I've just had enough, Bob, so I'm off. You can't change my mind. My bags are packed and I'm leaving home. I'm sick of being talked about, and spat at and slandered, so I'm off.' He sighed and damped down his pipe with his finger, then picked up his shovel and put his still-glowing pipe into his right pocket, forgetting his usual warning rhyme.

'Bloody hell – wrong pocket, Sam. Wrong pocket, you fool! Your pipe's in the wrong pocket!' Bob yelled, but it was too late, as Sam put his hand into his right pocket, panicking at what he had done and realizing the consequences. His rhyme was of no use to him now, as the smouldering embers of tobacco fell into the small linen bag of powder within his pocket.

There was no time for Sam or Bob to escape. The explosion was huge, with fire, dust and smoke filling the mine, and rubble and stones burying the two bodies – or what was left of them – deep within the mine's heart, along with the young boy who turned the windy king. Earth, dust and smoke billowed out of the mouth of the mine, as fellow miners yelled in despair for the workers trapped within. The miners knew that whoever was in there was surely dead, and would probably not be recognizable when brought out into the daylight; that is, if they were ever found. Gunpowder explosions were not unknown to the small mining group, and death and injuries were expected in their hard everyday lives.

The noise of the explosion echoed around the valley, heard clearly even down in the village below, and dark clouds of dust billowed over the valley from the mine shaft. Sam lay dead and battered, his body reclaimed by the mine that he had laboured in all his working life. The rhyme he had said so many times had not saved him this time, being forgotten amid his troubles and thoughts of escaping, and of abandoning Meg.

Meg looked up from the order she was putting together for Mrs Stanley. 'What on earth was that?' she exclaimed. 'I know we can sometimes hear them blasting, and that when they are hushing it makes a noise as the dammed water is released and the soil is being washed away from the land, but never as loud as that.'

'Nay, that was too loud. I think something might be wrong,' Mrs Stanley said. 'Somebody will be the worse for wear, I expect.'

'Oh, don't say that! I only hope nobody's hurt,' Meg gasped as she completed the order, more than a little worried in case the noise was coming from where Sam was. 'It could be that they are just excavating the new Sir Francis level. I heard a group of miners talking this morning, when they came in for their baccy and snap.' Meg smiled at her customer while she took the payment.

'Aye, that'll be what it is. No doubt we will know soon enough if owt's happened. It would be good riddance to some of them, anyway, if there has been an accident. They've no morals and no manners,' Mrs Stanley exclaimed, then put her basket on her arm. 'That young Alderson lad wants locking up and flogging! What a state that poor lass's mind was in, and all because of him. And for her to take the baby to its death with her and all, she must have been desperate. I bet her parents are regretting being so hard and all.'

'Nobody knows for certain that it was his child. It seems to me everyone is quick to judge. I know the family are having it hard, with people persecuting Sam for something he was perhaps not guilty of.' Meg rebuffed the woman, who was known to speak her mind.

'It'd be his. He was seen as regular as clockwork, courting her under the bridge. He's a bad lot.' Mrs Stanley dipped her head as she left the shop, to acknowledge that she was right in her assumptions. It left Meg biting her tongue and thinking that if only they would get to know her Sam, they would see what he was like and perhaps not be so harsh in their criticism.

Jack stood in the doorway of his home and looked up towards the mine above Gunnerside Gill on the far side

252

of Barney Beck, where he and his brother both worked. He'd heard the almighty explosion and had known instantly that something was wrong.

'I'm away up to the mine, Mother. I don't like the sound of what we've just heard.' He grabbed his jerkin and looked at his mother as she came to the doorstep when he closed the garden gate behind him.

'You think there's been an accident, don't you? I pray to God our Sam isn't in it. Haven't we had enough hardship this last week or two?' Betty wiped her hands on her apron and tried to hold back the tears. 'Go – go on! Take care, mind, as your ribs still aren't healed. Go and see if your brother is alright.'

Betty stood on her doorstep and watched as Jack crossed the gill and took the steps up towards the well-trodden path that led to the Owd Gang mines. She went back into the kitchen, but couldn't concentrate on the bread she had decided to make. She couldn't keep sending Jack for it; he'd be back at work soon enough. She'd had enough of the twitterings of the other women, and of the dark looks given to her as they accused her son of being the bastard that she knew he was not. The only one who had stood by Sam was the young lass behind the counter, and that was because she was sweet on him.

She sat down in her usual chair, then looked at the village through the window. She watched as people started to run up the hillside and shout at one another that there had been an almighty accident on the new Sir Francis level. The Sir Francis level was where Sam worked. She knew it! Jack needn't come to tell her the news he was about to deliver. When she had reached for the flour from the cupboard, a terrible feeling had come over her, as if a light in the world had gone out and part of her heart had been broken forever. She'd even turned and thought she had heard Sam calling her name, but softly and faintly, as if from some far-off world.

Jack needn't come and tell her the news he was dreading to say. Betty knew already that her youngest had been taken from her and that she'd never see him again.

19

'Meg! Meg, are you alright? Speak to me.' Harry stood beside Meg as she held onto the shop's counter for support. Her legs had turned to jelly and she felt sick and faint, after Harry had told her the news he'd heard on the way back from Reeth.

'Yes, I think I'm alright. I just feel faint . . . Oh my Lord, it can't be true!' Meg gasped and held out her hand for Harry to lead her into the back room, as he watched her turn white with shock.

'I didn't think you were that fond of Sam Alderson, even though he went to the Bartle Fair with you. Or was it Bob Winn you knew? The lad that turned the windy king was from Kisdon and he was nobbut ten, poor little bugger.' Harry watched as Meg shook and sobbed.

'It was Sam I knew best. He made me laugh when we all went to the fair, and I can't believe he's dead. Oh God, what am I going to do?' Meg couldn't control her grief and broke down in front of Harry.

'Perhaps you knew him better than you are letting on, eh, lass? I've heard and seen you stick up for Sam when other folk called him names. I was beginning to think that you'd your eye on him – and now this happens.' Harry sat down next to Meg. 'You know he was a wrong 'un. There'll not be many folk, bar his own family, grieving for him in this village. He's gone to meet his Maker, like the lass and baby that he washed his hands of. I know you'll not like me for saying this, but perhaps he's better off dead, then he can't ruin your life and all.' Harry didn't know what to do with the grief-stricken young lass, who was clearly heartbroken and beside herself over the death of Sam Alderson.

'He was going to marry me – Sam said so, soon after we met. He loved me, and now he's dead,' Meg sobbed, knowing that nothing could be done about her forbidden love, now that Sam had gone.

'Aye, well, I'll not speak ill of the dead, but I bet he's told many a lass that, if what I hear is true. By hell, if I'd have known you were involved with him, I'd have sent you packing back home.' Harry was torn between sorrow for his grieving lodger and anger that Meg had been seeing Sam behind his back. He sighed and shook his head. 'There, there. Now stop your crying – that's not going to bring him back. You'll just have to grin and bear it. Sometimes life can be a bastard, but in another few weeks somebody else will come along and Sam Alderson will be a distant memory.' He put his arm around the sobbing girl and breathed in deeply.

Meg lifted her head and looked at Harry. 'I'll never

forget him. What we had was special. You may have found somebody else in your life, but it'll never be like that for me,' she wailed, and ran up the stairs to the sanctuary of her bedroom. There she lay on her bed and cried until she felt sick with grief. The few possessions that she had put to one side for taking with her on their elopement stood, packed and ready, on the varnished oak floor and only added to her misery. They were a reminder of the new life they had planned together. Now there was no need for life, or possessions, or anything, Meg thought, as she lay sobbing on the patchwork counterpane that covered her bed.

It was late evening, and Harry had left Meg alone in her sorrow, not quite knowing what to do, other than be there when she needed him. He'd called up the stairs to offer her some supper, but she'd refused point-blank to eat anything and had said she wanted to be alone. Harry lit his pipe and went to bolt the back door, ready for nightfall, when he heard a knock.

Opening the door, he looked at the young man who stood in front of him.

'What do you want? Shouldn't you be at home with your mother? She'll need you, if what I hear is true.' Harry glared at Jack Alderson, withholding his condolences at the insolence of his late-night caller.

'I came to see if Meg has heard the news. But I can tell by your attitude towards me that she has. Is she alright?' Jack's face was black from the dirt that he had helped to clear from around the pitfall that had entombed

Sam and the two other workers. His eyes were red from crying and his spirit was broken, crushed by the death of his brother.

'Aye, she's alright – no thanks to the likes of you and your brother. I should offer my condolences to you and your mother, but your brother's caused that much hurt to folk, I can't bring myself to do it. Now jigger off, and don't come here again.' Harry looked at the lad, who hung his head in remorse.

'Uncle Harry, let Jack come in, please. I need to speak to him. Just for a minute, and you can stay with us both, if you want to.' Meg had heard Jack's voice as she lay in bed and wanted to speak to him, and for Jack to confirm the news. She hoped above hope that somehow Harry had heard wrong, but when she saw the pain in Jack's eyes, she knew it was true.

'Lass, are you sure? Haven't you had enough pain for one day, without bothering with this 'un?' Harry held the door open and looked first at Meg and then at Jack. 'You'd better do as she says and come in if she needs to talk to you, because I know nowt and I don't know how to help her.' Harry watched as Jack stepped into the back room and looked at Meg. 'Sit yourself down. I'll go and make myself scarce while you talk. No funny business, though, you behave yourself.'

Jack sat down in Harry's usual chair next to the fire and Meg sat across from him, her eyes filled with tears. 'It's right then – Sam's dead?' she sobbed.

'Aye, they think the silly bugger blew himself up. I bet that's what he did. I was always telling him not to put his pipe in his pocket. I knew that one day he'd put it in the same pocket as his gunpowder, and that's what he's done, I bet.' Jack tried to grin, but tears rolled down his cheeks as he looked at Meg. 'Are you alright? I take it old Harry knows, else he wouldn't even tolerate me sitting here with you.'

'He knows that I loved Sam, but he doesn't know we were planning to run away together,' Meg whispered. 'Oh, Jack, what am I going to do?'

'What we've all got to do: get on with life until it's our turn to kick the bucket. Sam wouldn't want to see you sad. He was a rum lad, but I think he really did love you.' Jack held out his hand for Meg to take and lied, to give her some comfort. 'I'm here, if you want to talk. Harry won't like it, but he knows you'll need somebody. After all, he's in no position to lecture; he found comfort with Lizzie Bannister when his wife was dying. And we all need someone to turn to when times are hard.' He smiled as Meg wiped away the tears.

'Thanks, Jack. Have they found Sam's body and the other two?' Meg tried to say without crying again.

'They have what's left of them. The Owd Gang stick together when there's trouble, and they've worked all day to get all three out. They are lying in the pumphouse up at the mine.' Jack swallowed down a sob.

'I need to see him. Sam can't lie there on his own without somebody who loves him by his side,' Meg cried.

'No, Meg, don't. Don't you go near. You wouldn't recognize what's there as human, let alone as Sam. Remember him like he was. Remember him like the last time you saw him. I've told my mother the same, and she's beside herself with grief. Sam was her favourite, although she would never admit it.' Jack hung his head and tried to block out the terrible sight of his brother's body – or what they thought was his body, when it had been reclaimed from the mine.

'Oh, please give my condolences to your mother. She must, as you say, be heartbroken.' She started to cry again and was shaking as she stood up to leave the room.

'Meg, I'm always here for you. I'll let you know when the funeral is. It'll be at the chapel. Even though Sam was planning to leave Gunnerside, he would only have regretted it, as he loved this village.' Jack stood up and watched as Meg, still crying, walked away from him and went up the stairs.

'You'd better go now, lad. Your mother will be wanting you.' On hearing Meg going up the stairs, Harry came into the room and looked across at Jack. 'I was a bit hard on you when you first knocked on my door. I should have shown more sympathy. Condolences to both you and your mother. It'll not have been good to see your brother in the state they found him. Sorry, but I listened in. I don't want that young lass to go through any more trauma, if I can help it. Aye, and I should practise what I preach, so I can't say to keep away from her, because Meg is going to need a friend in these coming days.' Harry stared at the dirt-encrusted miner.

'Thank you, Mr Battersby. I'll be there as a friend for as long as Meg needs me. And if you decide different, then just let me know. I'll be honest: I warned her about our Sam, but they were both too headstrong to listen to me. He wasn't – God rest his soul – the right man for her, and I knew it.'

'Aye, well, he's not with us any more. And now Meg's broken-hearted and I've to tell her parents why. They'll probably want to take her back home the next time they are here. So you'll probably not be seeing much more of her, lad.' Harry opened the back door and showed Jack out into the darkness of the night. He shook his head as he pulled the door's bolt across, to lock up for the night. He'd never expected all this upset when he got up this morning. God only knew what tomorrow would bring.

'I've shut the shop, just for today. I think you and I need to spend some time together. I've not been doing right by you, leaving you to run the shop while I go gallivanting about with Lizzie. That's how you got so involved with those Alderson lads. And now it's ended in tears and grief. You see, we never had children of our own, so I'm at a loss about what to do with you.' Harry looked across at the pale, drawn face of Meg. He'd got up early that morning and lit the fire himself and was now handing her a cup of tea, along with a slice of bread and marmalade for her breakfast.

Meg shook her head as he pushed the plate of buttered bread in her direction. She didn't feel like eating. She felt hollow and empty, but sickly at the same time, and all she wanted to do was lie on her bed and cry. 'It isn't your fault, Uncle Harry. I knew Sam and Jack even before I set foot in Swaledale. We first met at a dance in

261

Hawes, and my parents warned me even then not to set my cap at Sam or Jack, but I couldn't help myself.' She sipped her tea, her hands shaking as she confessed all to Harry. 'I've brought this on myself. They told me not to get involved with Sam, and now look what it's brought about. He's dead and I'm heartbroken.'

'Aye, well, these things happen. Now, what am I to do with you? I think you are best off going back home with your parents this coming Thursday. Get you out of this dale and back where you belong. I've enjoyed having you staying with me, but I've not got eyes in the back of my head to watch you all the time. And I doubt it will take long before Sam is forgotten and some other lad comes a-calling on you. Besides, we said that you'd be home for winter.'

'Please. Please don't send me away. Not before the funeral. And when it comes to seeing other men, I don't think I'll ever love anybody ever again. Please don't tell my parents; they'd only worry and insist that I did come home. My heart is here now, and always will be. Wherever Sam's body is, I've got to be near it,' Meg sobbed.

'Nay, I should tell your mother and father – they've a right to know. Besides, they'll hear about it and want to know what's gone on. And I can't see you being able to tell them without tears.' Harry rubbed his head and watched as the young lass in front of him broke down yet again. 'Aye, lass, I don't know what to do with you. Only time mends a broken heart, I should know that. Time and the love of good folk, and you've enough of

262

those around you, especially if you go home.' He sighed.

'I don't want to go home just yet. Please let me stay until after the funeral, and then you can tell them everything. I must see Sam buried,' Meg cried.

'We'll see, lass. I suspect he'll be buried before Thursday anyway, so you'll see Sam put into the ground. There will be a lot shedding tears this morning, especially the mother of that li'l lad; he'd not seen anything of life, poor devil.'

Harry got up and cleared the kitchen table while Meg stared into the fire, rocking herself gently to control her grief.

'The bloody weather isn't likely lifting anybody's spirits – look at it! It couldn't rain any harder if it tried. If it doesn't brighten up, I'm going to have to light an oil lamp to be able read my paper.'

'I don't care if it pours down forever. Sunshine is no friend of mine,' Meg said quietly, remembering Sam's smiling face as they lay together on the dry bank of the fellside, with the turning leaves of the tree above them.

'You'll not feel like that forever. Something or somebody will come along and, before you know it, you'll struggle even to remember his face.' Harry turned and looked at Meg. 'I loved my Mary, but she was in so much pain, I just wanted her life to end, so that she was free. And I know I shouldn't even have looked at Lizzie, but life has to go on and you've to grab happiness when it comes along. It's what Mary would have wanted, and it's what Sam would want for you. Think of the future, Meg.

263

You've all your life in front of you. It might look dark now, like those rain clouds outside, but even they will give way to sunshine sometime.'

'I don't think they ever will for me, Uncle Harry,' Meg whispered.

'They will, lass, they will.'

The rain poured down all weekend. It matched Meg's mood as she thought of the plans of eloping that she and Sam had hatched together, knowing now that they would never come to fruition, as she stared out of her bedroom window at the mist and rain hanging around the fell of Whitaside. It was still raining when Jack knocked on the back door of the shop on Monday. He was sodden to the skin, and the rain dripped off his hat as he spoke to Harry, before being invited into the back room.

'Meg's upstairs, lad. I'll call her. She's in a bit of a way with herself. I've looked after the shop, as she's been in no fit state to serve folk.'

'I've come to tell her the funeral's on Wednesday at eleven. I bloody hope the weather eases. They are starting to dig the grave now, and it's a worthless job in these conditions.' Jack took his hat from his head and shook it free of most of the rain, before standing next to the fire to dry out.

'Meg, Jack's here. Come down, lass, and hear what he's got to say,' Harry shouted up from the bottom of the stairs and then went back to Jack, shaking his head. 'I can make nowt of her. I've told her she'd be better off at home than moping around here. Anyway, her father and mother will be here on Thursday – they'll see to her.' Harry stopped talking as Meg came into the room.

'I'm here, so you can stop whispering about me. Now, did I hear you say the funeral's on Wednesday?' Meg looked up at Jack. Her face was ashen and her eyes were red and sore from crying.

'Aye, at eleven. They bury Bob and the young lad on the same day in the afternoon at Reeth.' Jack glanced at Meg. 'Are you alright? Will you be going to the funeral? I can call for you, if you like?' He stood awkwardly as Meg fought back the tears.

'I'll go with her, Jack. You look after your mother, as she'll be in need of your arm that day. Who would have thought, when they built that chapel a few years back, there would be so many we know in its yard already. No doubt I'll end up there eventually, alongside my Mary. Although I don't aim to be there quite yet – nor should you two, at the age you both are,' Harry said quietly as he watched Meg compose herself.

'Yes, I'll go with Uncle Harry. Your mother will need you, Jack. Besides, it looks better that way. And Wednesday will probably be my last day in Swaledale, as my parents will probably want to take me home, once Uncle Harry has spoken to them.' Meg sniffled and then held her head high. 'Is your mother alright? Is she coping?'

'Yes, she seems at peace with herself. She keeps saying that Sam shone too bright to be on this earth long, and in all honesty I think she may be right. He was always the one full of life, and I just tagged along.' Jack sniffed and looked down at his feet.

265

'And you, lad? Are you alright?' Harry asked, showing concern for the tall, dark, quiet lad who stood in front of them both.

'You have to be, haven't you? Bawling and crying isn't going to bring him back. But I tell you one thing: I don't think I can work at them mines again. I'm going to see what I can do with the money I've saved, and get away from here.' Jack looked at Meg.

'You wouldn't leave your mother behind, would you?' Meg gasped.

'No. I did have plans of making a new life in America, as they are crying out for young fellas like me, but now I'll settle for something a bit nearer and take my mother with me.' Jack watched Meg as she sighed and sniffed yet again.

'Aye, well, I don't blame you, lad. Those mines maim many a man; that is, if they don't take a life, like your poor brother's. You find something that's not as rough, although you'll probably have to leave this dale.' Harry looked at the lad, who was obviously not as hard as his brother had been, and felt sorry for him.

'Well, I'll away now. I don't like leaving my mother for too long, and the nights are beginning to draw in, especially in this weather.' Jack put on his hat and looked at Meg. 'I'll see you on Wednesday. I don't expect there will be many at the funeral – mainly lads from the Owd Gang. Sam wasn't exactly popular.'

Meg nodded her head and watched as Jack went out into the dusk of the evening.

'You alright?' Harry asked gently, as Meg sat down in the chair next to the fire.

'Yes. Like Jack says, I have to be. I'm not the first to lose someone they loved, and I'll not be the last.' Meg gazed into the fire; her heart ached, but she had to be strong.

The wet weather had not abated as Meg, Harry and their fellow mourners stood around Sam's grave in the chapel graveyard, their heads bowed in reverence as the preacher committed Sam to a life eternal and his coffin was lowered into the slightly waterlogged grave. The rain mixed with Meg's tears as she threw a handful of soil onto the coffin and gazed down at his last resting place. Sam's mother and brother stood, dressed in black and drenched to their skins, his mother sobbing as the last words were said over the body. She looked up and smiled wanly at Meg, knowing that she too must be grieving over Sam. But neither Jack nor Betty said anything as they turned away from the graveside, leaving Sam's workmates from the Owd Gang paying their respects.

'There now, lass, that's him gone now – let's hope to a better place.' Harry linked his arm through Meg's and walked her down the flagged pathway to the road. 'You've seen him off, and now we'll get back home. There's no funeral tea planned, but his mates will no doubt drink his health in the King's Head. It's their way of seeing him off.'

Meg said nothing, but shivered with the wet and the cold and wished she was dressed in black, instead of the darkest dress she could find that she had brought with her from home. Her heart ached and she wished she could join Sam in the grave beside him, as life would hold no meaning for her any longer.

'Let's get you home and both of us out of these wet things. Else we will be to bury and all.' Harry looked in front of him along the road and saw Jack and his mother making their way beside Gunnerside Gill back to their home, as they themselves walked over the small bridge past the King's Head and into the shop. It had been a sad funeral, and not the usual turnout. Folk had long memories when it came to locals being wronged, and nobody other than Sam's immediate family and Meg – and perhaps one or two members of the Owd Gang – was going to mourn the passing of Sam Alderson. What he was to do with Meg, and what to tell her parents in the morning, Harry did not know. Perhaps the Lord would give him guidance, he thought, as he opened the door of the back room and watched as Meg went upstairs to change out of her wet clothes.

She climbed the stairs and went into her bedroom, her stomach churning with pent-up anxiety, and tears ran down her cheeks as she stood at her bedroom window. She could just see the chapel yard from where she stood and she leaned against the window, her fingers touching the windowpane as she whispered, 'I'll not leave you, Sam. I'll always be here and I'll always love you.'

20

'Is this weather never going to change?' Harry stood in the shop's doorway and looked down the street. The houses were grey and sodden, and the fellside was alive with streams and tributaries gushing down towards a full River Swale. 'I don't think your lot will be coming today, lass, not if they have any sense.' Harry breathed in deeply. 'Even I'm housebound, as it's too wet to go and see Lizzie in Reeth. Anyway, I need to speak to your mother and father and see what we've to do with you, if they turn up.'

'There's no need to speak to them about me. I've realized that life goes on and that it's no good moping. Besides, everybody knew Sam was a bad lot, so happen it was meant to be.' Meg pulled a face, hiding her true feelings about Sam's death. She'd no intention of going home, just yet. In fact, she'd no intention of ever returning home while Sam's body lay in Gunnerside chapel's graveyard. She had to say what her uncle wanted to hear from her, to enable her to stay in Swaledale.

'By gum, thou's a fickle one. Yesterday you were bawling and crying at his graveside, and now it's as if he meant nothing to you. What's brought this on? Have you realized Sam was leading you on?' Harry walked over to the counter and looked at Meg as she leaned on her elbows, waiting for a customer to come in out of the rain.

'That's it – he was. I thought things over in my head last night, and Jack has been right all along about his brother. Sam cared for nobody, and I shouldn't have wasted my time on him.' Meg put her head down and pretended to be tidying the drawer under the counter, which held numerous items that made the shop work, all the while feeling guilty about lying.

'Well, I'm glad you've come to your senses. I never thought much of either lad, but Jack seems to be the sensible one, now that I've had something to do with him. I hope he gets his farm – it'll be better for him, and his mother, in the long run.' Harry looked around the dark shop; the weather outside did nothing for his spirits and he knew there would be worse to come, once winter set in. 'By God, I wish it was a bit brighter, I can't do with these dark days. These dales houses are set to keep the weather out, which is grand, but they don't let a lot of light in. And on a day like today, with the weather like it is and no customers, I could feel low myself. I'll need some company this winter if I've to keep sane, as I hate those long months.'

'Well, I don't have to go back home. My father's got a replacement for me in Dan, or at least that's what it sounds like, when Dan talks. Although I would like to go home to celebrate Christmas, as that is where I really need to be.' Meg perked up.

'Now, don't you get any ideas that you may be staying, just because I don't like being by myself. You stepped out of your traces before and didn't do as you were told, when it came to that Sam. How do I know you won't do it again?' Harry looked at her sternly.

'I won't, I promise. I've realized I was a fool,' Meg said humbly.

'Aye, well, we'll see. The lad's dead now. He won't be coming back, and you seem to have settled down this morning. But I'll be keeping a close eye on you, lady, don't you think I won't. But we've both got secrets, and perhaps they are best kept between ourselves for the time being. We'll see how I feel when your parents turn up.' Harry gave her a knowing look before he went into the back room.

Meg sighed. Thank heavens for the rain, as it had bought her more time to recover from her loss before confronting her parents. And with a bit of luck, Harry might not say anything to them, if he realized how much he needed her company.

Jack was scanning the local newspaper for advertisements announcing farms to let or sell.

'I don't know what you are looking at those for, as you are no farmer. Haven't I had enough heartache with losing Sam, without you going and leaving me?' Betty Alderson sobbed. The family home was not the usual pristine place, with washing-up now in the stone sink and clothes unironed, because of her grief.

'It's because we have lost Sam that I'm looking. You know my head was set on going to America, but now I'll have to stop in this country. You need me to look after you.' Jack scowled as he read the listings. 'If you think I'm going to go back and work at that mine after losing my brother there, you can think again. I can't face it. But I've still got to be able to support us both.'

'You know nowt about farming, apart from when you went to stay with your grandfather, and that was years ago. You needn't think I'm trailing to the other end of the country, leaving my boy not cold in his grave, and you with fanciful ideas in your head,' Betty moaned at her son.

'I'm not going the length of the country. In fact, I'll not be going more than five miles, if I get my way. Look, this would suit us both just right. It's on the outskirts of Muker, a big enough house and barns and twenty acres of land – that would keep you and me fed; it'd be ideal, especially if I could get a little bit of work as well.' Jack folded the newspaper and placed it under his mother's nose, pointing to an advert declaring that The Rash farm was up for tenancy. It was ideal, being only two miles away from Gunnerside.

'You can't afford that! Where are you going to get money like that from?' Betty stared at the figure of two guineas' rent and put the paper down, scoffing at her son's hare-brained idea.

'I've been saving up. I was going to lend it to Sam,

when he was thinking of eloping with Meg, but he'll not be needing it now. So it's time to give us two a bit of security and perhaps find a woman of my own, settle down and stop feeling like an outcast.' Jack looked at his mother. He knew the news of Sam having intended to leave the family home would shock her, but it was time she realized that he had not been the golden boy she'd thought.

'Sam was to leave with that flibbertigibbet from the shop! Don't be daft – he hardly knew her. And as for you having that sort of money, well, I just can't believe it. I don't know, these last few days have been like a living hell, and now you tell me this. It's as if I never knew my two sons, let alone loved them. I don't know what your father would say about it all, if he was still alive, I really don't,' Betty cried and shook her head.

'Well, I'll go and have a look around The Rash and, if I like it and think we can make a living there, we'll be moving. At least I won't have to put up with the gossips and dirty looks if we are out there on our own.' Jack stood his ground.

'Aye, and how am I to go about my business? Stuck up on a hillside, with no one for company,' Betty retorted.

'You'll be alright. I'll go in the morning and have a look around it, come rain or shine. The sooner we are away from this village, the better,' Jack said sharply.

Betty said nothing in reply. She knew his head was set on a new life, but she liked her little cottage by the side of the gill and the company of other mining families around her.

*

273

Jack stood back and looked at the long, low farmhouse and its stone-walled garden. It was set back on the hillside, with a twisting track up to it that his mother would not like. He breathed in and thought about his decision. The house needed a bit of work on it, and he probably could have done with another acre or two of land, but he could always find that once he was settled in. It would take all his savings, what with the rent and buying stock to put on it, but at least he'd be his own man and not answerable to anybody, as long as he paid his way.

'Well, what do you think? Are you interested? It's not a bad house; the boundaries of the fields could do with a bit of upkeep, but all in all it's a good enough farm for a small family.' Dick Turner, the owner, stood back and looked at the young lad whose money he was hoping to part from his pocket.

'Aye, you are right. It is a good enough spot.' Jack stood at the garden gate and looked across the valley to Beldi Hill and was reminded why he was set on farming instead of mining, as he looked up at the scars left behind by hushing and the constant search for lead. He couldn't go back to working in the mines. He needed to make more of his life, despite his mother's protests. Besides, now that Sam was no more, he was perhaps in with a chance of catching Meg Oversby's eye, once she had finished mourning Sam's death.

'Well, are you to rent it or not? I can have papers drawn up by the end of the week, providing you've got the brass.' Dick Turner looked at the young lad and wished he'd get a move on. Although it had stopped rain-

274

ing, there was a chill in the wind and he needed to get off the hillside and back down to the valley and warmth.

'Aye, we've a deal. And don't worry – I've the brass. I can pay you now, if you want, and then it is done with and I can't change my mind. Or, more to the point, my mother can't change my mind for me.' Jack held out his hand to be shaken by Dick Turner and smiled as the deal was struck. He had his own farm, albeit rented, but it was a start.

He was full of himself as he walked down the road, crossing the bridge back into Gunnerside. It had taken the death of his brother for him to realize that life was too short not to do what you wanted to do, and now he was going to put in place the next piece of his plan. He passed the chapel and its graveyard and thought about his brother lying in the cold earth, and vowed to himself once again to make the best of his life as he entered Gunnerside and decided to call in at the shop to tell Meg his good news.

Harry raised his head as he heard the shop bell go. 'Oh, it's you, is it? Are you still not back at work? Your mother will not be happy with that.' Harry looked up from slicing some bacon and acknowledged Jack.

'No, I'm not off back to the Owd Gang. I've had enough. And as for my mother, she can please herself. Is Meg around? I've something to tell her.' Jack smiled. Even though his heart was heavy with the loss of his brother, he could not quell his excitement.

'Now don't you be flirting with Meg. Don't you think your family has caused enough upset? But aye, I'll get her. She's in the back room, waiting for her father and mother to come, now that the weather's brightened up a bit.' Harry went towards the doorway.

'She's not leaving, is she? You're not sending her home?' Jack asked anxiously.

'That's for me to know, lad. Now, don't you go upsetting her.' Harry went to speak to Meg, who was dreading her parents' arrival, in case Harry told them all and she had to return home with them.

'There's Jack Alderson asking for you in the shop. Now don't you be leading him on. Remember that family are worth nowt,' Harry growled as Meg got up from her chair and went into the shop.

Meg looked at Jack and remembered the time he and Sam had stood under the waterfall at Hardraw together, earlier in the year, which seemed like a lifetime away now.

'Are you alright, Meg? You look not as pale this morning.' Jack smiled at her as she looked up at him.

'Yes, I'm as well as can be expected. How are you, and how's your mother?' Meg asked, aware that Harry was standing hidden in the doorway behind her.

'We are both coping. My mother is missing Sam, though, as they were always close.' Jack thought how beautiful Meg was. No wonder his brother had fallen for her.

'Yes, she will miss him greatly, I'm sure.' Meg nearly cried and then, knowing that her parents could enter the shop at any time, quickly controlled herself.

'I thought I would come and tell you my news: that perhaps some good has come out of Sam's death, and that I have decided to make a new life for myself.' Jack smiled.

Meg looked concerned. 'Are you leaving for America? Have you finally decided to go?'

He shook his head. 'Not America – not that far. I've just agreed to rent a small farm down near Muker. You are the first to know. I'm dreading telling my mother, as she'll not be at all suited. She told me so last night, but I need to live my life and not waste it.'

'I'm glad for you, I really am.' Meg stopped in her tracks and felt her stomach churn as she saw and heard her parents and Dan, with the horse and cart, drive up to the shop's doorway. 'My parents and my cousin Dan are here. Oh God, I don't want to go home. I need to stay here,' she whispered to Jack.

'Have courage – perhaps they will let you stay,' Jack whispered back, as the shop bell rang and in stepped Tom and Agnes, shortly followed by Dan, carrying the basket of butter.

'Thank you. Good luck with the new farm!' Meg smiled and wished Jack loudly, not wanting her parents to remember him calling at her home looking for work.

'Aye, thanks for that.' Jack turned and nodded at Agnes and Tom, then stared at the lad that Meg had called her cousin, noticing Dan pulling his cap down over his eyes so that Jack was hardly able to see his face. He glanced back again as he closed the door behind him. He knew that face, but where from?

'Now then, our lass, we didn't make it yesterday because the weather was so bad, but we are here now, so that's all that matters.' Tom looked over his shoulder as the door closed behind Jack. 'Who was that, then? Should I ken him, if he's a farmer? He looks familiar. I could swear I've seen him somewhere else before, but for the love of God I can't remember where.'

'That's Jack Alderson, but no, you'll not know him,' Meg said quietly.

'You look pale, Meg. Are you alright?' Agnes came over and kissed her daughter on the cheek.

'I'm quite alright, there's nothing wrong with me. Uncle Harry has been keeping me on my toes, busy with the shop and other things. Haven't you, Uncle Harry?' Meg turned to where Harry had been hiding, as he ventured out of the shadows, and she smiled at him.

'Aye, we are both alright, and that's more than can be said for the three that died in a mining accident at the end of last week. Terrible, it was.' Harry looked at Meg and noticed the worried look on her face. 'That's happen why Meg looks pale. Folk have been coming in with their grief all week, needing somebody to listen to their woes. It wears you down after a while. Anyway, it's good to see you all. I was getting a bit short of butter, so I'm glad you've made it over. Now then, Dan, give me your basket and we'll put it where it's cool. Not that we need to do so today, as winter will soon be knocking on our door and then we won't get to see a lot of you.'

Meg looked at Harry with relief. He was obviously not going to say anything about her and Sam, else he would have mentioned it already. 'Yes, it's been a bit of a week. Everyone has been in the doldrums, and the weather hasn't helped.'

'It's not been that bad with us. I've been helping your father with one thing or another,' Dan spoke up.

'It's not been good, lad. I don't know where you've been all week, but I've got piss-wet every time I've gone out.' Tom shook his head in disbelief at some of the stuff that came out of Dan's mouth. He had quickly come to realize that he had to take everything said by Dan with a pinch of salt. He seemed to have trouble telling the truth, a trait he put down to Dan's father.

'Never mind, you are here now. Go through into the back room and have a natter with Meg while I mind the shop. Dan, could you bring me some coal in from the coal-hole? I've a bad back, and I don't want Meg lifting it.' Harry patted Dan on the back and opened the shop door, taking Dan outside with him to the back of the building and giving Meg some time to talk to her parents and confess all, if she wanted to.

Agnes smiled at Meg. 'You are sure you're alright? You do look a little under the weather.'

'I'm fine, Mum, stop worrying. I'm as happy as I've ever been. Now, come and tell me what's new at home, and update me on any gossip.' Meg smiled and walked through to the back room. If she could manage to keep it together today, she could manage for the rest of her life, and her parents need never know of her heartache over Sam.

'That's alright then. As long as you are fine, that's all

279

we are bothered about.' Agnes smiled at her daughter. She didn't believe her for one minute – something was not quite right with her Meg. She didn't know what but, being her mother, she sensed something was wrong.

Meg and Harry waved their visitors goodbye, standing in the shop's doorway. Both were relieved to see the back of them.

'Thank you, Uncle Harry, for not saying anything about Sam Alderson,' Meg said quietly. 'They wouldn't have let me stay, you know.'

'Aye, well, least said, soonest mended. And you seem a bit brighter this morning.' Harry put his arm around the young lass that he knew to be secretly heartbroken, even though she denied it. 'Every day will get a bit better, lass. I know that, from my own loss.'

'I miss Sam, but life has got to go on, I realize that.' Meg looked up at Harry.

'Aye, well, we've all been there. Folk come and go, and there's nothing you can do about it. I tell you what: his brother's done well for himself, renting The Rash so soon after losing his brother. He's got a bit more sense than his brother had. But by, didn't he give that Dan a funny look. Jack must be like the rest of us and not be that keen on the little bastard. I know he's your cousin, but Dan takes the biscuit, telling his tall tales about nowt.' Harry laughed.

'I never noticed Jack's look,' Meg said, not really bothered.

'Aye, well, he did. It was if he had recognized Dan

from somewhere, but thought better of saying anything – unless it was my imagination.' Harry slumped down into his chair. 'I might go and see Lizzie tonight. Will you be alright on your own for an hour or two? You'll not do owt daft while I'm away?'

'I'll be fine, and I promise to behave myself.' Meg sighed with relief; an hour or two on her own was just what she needed – some peace, and some time to cry and remember Sam without anybody hearing her sobs.

21

'You've rented the place without even giving me the chance to look around it!' Betty exclaimed as Jack told his mother the news.

'I did – I had to, else somebody else would have taken it from under my nose. It's a grand spot, Mother. You climb up the field track to get to it, and it is just under the fellside, out of the way of the wind. The house looks right across at Beldi Hill – it's got such lovely views up and down the valley. There's a little over twenty acres, mostly fell, but there's two good meadows. And the house has got a garden and veg plot, so you can potter about in it.' Jack never stopped talking for a second, he was so happy with his deal for The Rash.

'What if I don't want to go? I'm happy here, so why should I follow you up to some godforsaken hillside? I've one or two friends down here in the village, and the shops are handy. I'll have to walk miles to get anything, or see anybody, up there,' Betty moaned.

'Oh, you'll get used to it. Besides, I'll buy myself a horse and cart and then you won't have to walk at all. Mentioning the shop, I'm going to go back there after I've had my dinner. I put my head around the shop door to tell Meg my news, when her parents and her so-called cousin came in. I need to ask her how she's related to Willie Fawcett's lad, Seth, who used to help him with the packhorses from Liverpool docks. I can't figure it out. Seth was from out of the workhouse in Liverpool – I'm sure that's what Willie told us, when he first took Seth on.'

'Never mind the bloody lad! You told that young Meg your news first, rather than me. Your brother's not even cold in his grave and you are looking at his lass. You were jealous of him when Sam was courting her. Well, now you are a bit quick in making your move. Show some respect, lad. Sam would have something to say to you, if he could.' Betty crossed her arms and glared at her son. 'Well, you've helped me make my mind up. I'm stopping where I'm at. If you must go, you can go and be a farmer on your own. I'll nobbut get in your way, especially if *she* gets to be about the place. But you'll have no luck if you've set your cap at that lass – she'll always be Sam's.'

'Don't be daft, Mum. We are just friends. I doubt old Harry Battersby will let Meg out of his sight now, let alone me court her. But I will ask her about that lad. I know it was Seth, because he used to be so cheeky to everyone when he brought supplies. But he's not been for a while now, and I never thought anything of it. As for

283

you stopping here, it's up to you, but I wouldn't want to see you on your own. And my belly would still need feeding, and you know I can't cook. You'd only miss me, you know you would. I could run you down in a horse and trap, when I get one bought. You could have a weekly visit into Hawes or Reeth market, like all the farmers' wives do. You'd soon be butchering your own pig and making butter along with the rest of them.' Jack grinned.

'I'm too long in the tooth for that, lad. You do need a woman of your own, but I'll think about it.' Betty shook her head as she saw to his dinner. She had no intention of leaving her cottage, if she could still manage to pay the rent. Jack would be doing this venture on his own, just this once.

Jack ate his dinner and, although excited about his rental of the farm, he was still thinking about seeing the lad he knew as Seth, from Liverpool docks. He cleared his plate and yelled his thanks to his mother, then made his way out of the cottage across the gill and down to the shop. It didn't add up: how could Seth be Meg's cousin? He'd seen Seth coming up to the mines in Swaledale since he was nine or ten; he'd even seen him break his leg when a mule kicked him, and Willie Fawcett had cursed at having to report the incident to the workhouse and being without Seth's help for a month or two. This couldn't be Meg's cousin!

Jack went round to the back door, instead of going to the shop, as he didn't want the local gossips to hear. He knocked loudly and waited for Meg or Harry to open the door to him.

'Hold your horses, I'm just having a shave,' Harry's voice shouted from within.

Jack waited for a second or two until the door opened.

'Oh, it's you, is it? What are you doing, skulking around here and not coming into the shop?' He wiped the lathered soap off his chin and looked at the lad whose family had caused so much bother over the past days, as he opened the door to the caller.

'Aye, I didn't come into the shop because I wanted to talk in private, either to you or Meg. I went away, after meeting her family, with a bit of a worry and I want one of you to say it is unfounded.' Jack hung his head; it seemed that he was always knocking on the back door with bad news.

'What is it this time? Let me guess: you want tick until you are up and running at the farm?' Harry threw the towel onto the chair behind him and scowled.

'No, it's nowt like that.' Jack breathed in. 'It's her cousin. How sure is Meg that he is her cousin, because I know him as somebody else,' he blurted out.

'Nay, lad, you must be wrong. Agnes and Tom wouldn't take him in if they didn't think he were kith and kin. Who do you know him as, then?' Harry looked at the concern on Jack's face.

'He's the lad that helps with the packhorses when they come over from Liverpool with stuff needed for the mines. He's even been known to help bring coal from Tan

Hill to here. I've known him for a fair while, and I'm sure he's the same lad.' Jack looked behind Harry, as Meg caught his last few words when she came into the back room from the shop, and stared at him in disbelief.

Harry turned to Meg. 'I told you that Jack gave Dan – or whatever he's called – a funny look as he went out. What do you make of it? Do you think he's your cousin, or could he be an impostor?'

'I don't know. He seemed to know everything about my aunt and uncle, and he talked plenty about Liverpool.' Meg thought back to her first meeting with Dan. 'He had the money that my father sent my aunt, and he knew all about us. Are you sure you know him, Jack? That you aren't getting Dan confused with another lad?'

'No, I'd swear blind that it's Seth. He knew I recognized him and all, because he pulled his cap down over his face. If it is him, he's got a scar halfway down his left leg, where a mule broke it and the bone came through the skin. It took weeks to mend. He did it the summer before last, and old Willie was going mad about it.' Jack stood his ground.

'Well, there's only one way to settle this, and that is to confront the lad,' said Harry. 'And we shouldn't waste any time in doing so. He could murder your parents in their beds and we'd not know about it. I'll close the shop in the morning and we will go over in the horse and trap. Jack, will you come with us, as you are the only one who knows him really, if what you say is true?' Harry looked worried as he thought about the lad, whom nobody had ever met until the day he turned up at Beck Side. He could truly be anybody. Everybody had been so eager to take him in as their blood relative.

'What the Devil!' Tom looked out of the kitchen window at Beck Side and spotted Harry, Meg and another passenger, as they opened the gate at the bottom of the field that led up to the farm. 'What's so important they've come this early in the morn? We've only just finished milking and had our breakfast.' He watched as they made their way up the farm path.

'I hope Meg's alright. She looked white the other day. I was bothered about her.' Agnes opened the kitchen door and stood in the porch, waiting for the visitors to arrive.

'I'll go and clean the cowshed, now I've done my breakfast. I'll get out of your way,' Dan said, wanting to make himself scarce. He suspected what the early-morning visit was all about, and had been waiting for his time posing as the Oversbys' nephew to come to an end, knowing full well that he had been recognized by one of the Owd Gang mine-workers. He'd packed some belongings, raided the cash box in Tom's desk and hidden it all under the hay in the barn, to make sure his departure was fast. He'd had a fair run at playing the part of the nephew he'd found, ill and dying of cholera, on the roadside outside Lancaster; bleeding him dry of information about his past and where he was travelling to, before stealing the money from his pockets, when he was too weak and helpless to fight him off; and eventually leaving him dead on the roadside, as he took on the boy's role as the orphaned nephew.

287

'Aye, all right, lad. It must be something important, to make Harry shut up shop and come over at this time of the day.' Tom watched as Dan looked down the farm track at the three visitors, then saw him go into the barn before he went to the cowshed; he thought nothing of it, as he tried to make out who the third person in the cart was.

'It's that lad that we saw in the shop with Meg yesterday – the one that had rented the farm. Now what's he doing with them both?' Agnes exclaimed, as she and Tom walked to the garden gate when the visitors arrived in the yard.

'Now then, Harry, what's made you visit us this early? If I didn't know any different, I'd say you must have pissed the bed.' Tom made light of his early-morning visitors, while Agnes scolded him.

Meg was the first to climb down from the cart, and she ran to her mum and hugged her. 'Thank heavens that you are both alright. I've worried about you all night, ever since Jack told me his news.' She stood back and turned to Jack as he climbed down from the cart and stood beside her.

'What news is this then, lad? I hope it's not the bad sort, else you can bugger off and take it back.' Tom looked at the tall, dark-haired lad who seemed to be friends with his daughter – perhaps a little too much so.

'Now, Tom, wait and see what he has to say. Where's Dan? He needs to be present when Jack tells you his tale.' Harry tethered the horse and looked at the couple, who had no idea what might be going to unfold.

288

'He's just gone into the barn – I'll shout for him. Dan! Dan! Get yourself here, you are needed,' Tom shouted across to the barn, but got no response. 'Meg, go and find him. He must have gone to clean out the cowshed.'

Tom looked stern as he walked in front of Agnes, Harry and Jack into the warmth of the kitchen.

'Now, what's this about, and why has Dan to be involved?' He sat back in his fireside chair while Agnes stood by the window, and Harry and Jack pulled up chairs around the yet-to-be-cleared breakfast table.

'Jack here says he recognizes Dan. He says he's a lad from Liverpool that comes with the packhorses. He recognized him yesterday, but didn't say anything until after you'd gone home.' Harry rubbed his hand on his brow and looked across at Agnes and Tom.

'Nay, that's not right – he's our Anne's lad. Dan was with her when she died; he knew all about us when he turned up on our doorstep. Anyway, he'll tell you himself, when he gets his arse in here.' Tom stared at Jack, wondering if there was an ulterior motive to his accusation.

'I swear, Mr Oversby, that lad's real name is Seth, and he's one of Willie Fawcett's lads. He gets them from the workhouse, so that they can't complain about the way he treats them. And in the case of Seth, he's one of the more cunning ones. I wouldn't trust him with anything I value.' Jack looked across at Tom Oversby and knew that he wasn't being believed. 'If it is Seth, ask him to show you his left leg, to prove I'm right. It'll have a scar on it, where a mule broke it when he was delivering supplies at Gunnerside.' Jack didn't mention the mine, or else he knew that being a miner would be held against him. 'All he does is go back and forth to Liverpool with supplies for Willie Fawcett – he'll have walked many a mile, if you ask him.'

'Aye, well, we'll see when Dan gets here. What do you think, Agnes? Do we have a cuckoo in the nest?' Tom looked at his wife, who appeared shocked at the news.

'I never have liked the lad. I couldn't take to him one bit, but that's not to say he isn't your Anne's. I just thought he took after his father – cocky and with that awful attitude they both seem to have. Here's Meg, anyway, but she's by herself.'

Meg burst in through the kitchen door. 'He's nowhere. I can't find him anywhere. I've looked in the barn and the cowshed. I've even looked in the pig-hull and dog-kennel. He's disappeared. I don't know where he is.' She caught her breath.

'I knew he recognized me yesterday. He'll have made a run for it, the little bugger, knowing that the game was up. You've nothing missing, have you? He hasn't robbed you of anything?' Jack asked with concern in his voice. 'If I were you, I'd call the peelers – not that they'll catch him. He'll be miles away by now, as he's built like a whippet.'

'Nay, we are not bothering them. Agnes, check Dan's room! I'll look in my desk. I found him rummaging in there on the odd occasion and thought nowt of it, and I told him to keep out. We've never had a need for locks in this house, and I wasn't about to start because of him, but then I thought better of it, as his father was that light-fingered.' Tom pushed his chair back and went storming off into the low-beamed room at the back of the house, where the newly locked desk stood with the cash box in it, while Agnes went up to inspect Dan's room.

'I can't tell if he's taken anything or not,' she shouted as she ran back down the stairs after checking Dan's bedroom. 'He'd nothing when he came and we haven't given him much, so it's hard to tell.'

'Well, he's been in the bloody cash box. He's broken the lock on the desk and I've the best part of five shillings missing from the cash box. And he'll have that money I said he could keep, when he first turned up with it in his hand. I will call into Hawes tomorrow and tell Sergeant Thompson to keep an eye out for the thieving little bugger. I wonder how he got that money he came with? He must have met our Dan somewhere on the way, for him to know all that he did about us.' Tom looked out of the window and gazed down the field. 'I've been a bloody fool, being taken in by a no-good vagabond. And what's become of my real nephew, I don't know, and probably never will.'

'You weren't to know. None of us did, and we never suspected a thing.' Agnes put her hand on her husband's shoulder.

'No, Father, don't blame yourself. It was me who let him in at first, if you remember. I should have known by the way he acted, when he walked in here, that he wasn't my cousin. But he knew everything, so he must, as you say, have met our Dan.' Meg sighed.

'Aye, well, it's easy knowing everything with hindsight. The lad's conned us all, and if it hadn't have been for Jack here, spotting him, he'd still be conning you. So it's a good job Jack had the mind to open his mouth and tell you of his suspicions. The little bugger; he'd know, as soon as he clapped eyes on Jack here, that the game was up. I bet he's never run so fast in his life as when he saw us coming up the field this morning.' Harry looked at Tom and his family and then at Jack. 'What do you think, lad? You are the only one who kens him.'

'I don't think he'll have done your nephew any harm. Seth's not a murderer, but he's obviously been with him, and he's definitely taken advantage of your nephew's predicament, as he has of yourselves.' Jack looked solemnly at the family that was in shock.

'Well, I can't thank you enough for coming to tell us, lad. And you, Harry, for bringing them both. He'd have been made welcome here all his life, if it hadn't been for you recognizing him. He must have thought we were idiots,' Tom growled.

'But what will have become of the real Dan? I can't help but worry. Although we never knew him, we should still be concerned about his whereabouts and whether he is still alive.' Agnes was nearly in tears.

Meg put her arm around her mum and kissed her on her cheek. 'We can't do anything about him. Let's just hope he is safe and that he's being looked after. I'm so glad that "Dan" has gone. I really hated him.'

'I miss you, Meg. You'll come home soon, won't you?'

Agnes looked at her daughter, whom she had missed so much over the last few months.

'Yes, I'll be home shortly. Give me a little longer with Uncle Harry, until the bad weather comes, and then I'll come home.' Meg looked at her mum and knew she needed her home, but at the same time part of her heart lay in Swaledale and she didn't want to leave.

'Meg tells me that you are renting a farm – The Rash, over near Muker.' Tom looked at Jack. 'If there's anything we can do, you let us know. I'll not forget you doing us this kindness, and letting us know about the bugger we have been keeping under our roof.' Tom patted Jack on the back; he'd taken to the young lad and felt he should repay him. He was still trying to remember where he had seen him before, but his memory was letting him down.

'Thank you. You really don't owe me anything. I was concerned for Meg, as I know she cares deeply for you both.' Jack looked across at Meg as she blushed and tried not to hold his gaze.

'Aye, well, we'd better be heading back. I've a living to make, and I can't do that if the shop's not open.' Harry walked to the doorway and was in haste to get back, now that he knew not much harm had been done.

'Aye, thank you again, Harry. You take care now, and you look after my lass,' Tom said as the three made their way to the waiting horse and cart.

'I will, you know I will – she's like a daughter to me.' Harry smiled as he held his hand out to help Meg up into the cart. 'Make sure you lock your doors tonight, in case the little bugger comes back.'

'We will. Now get yourselves home, and take care.' Tom and Agnes stood at the garden gate and watched as the horse and cart containing the three of them trundled down the farm track.

Agnes shed the tears that she had been withholding, as she entered the farmhouse.

'What's up, Mother? There's nowt to cry about now. The bugger's gone and it's a good job he has, else I'd not be responsible for what I'd have done to him.'

'It's not that. Did you not see how that lad looked at our Meg? She's not a little girl any more, and the way that he looked at her, he has his eye on her.' Agnes sniffed and tried to control her emotions. 'She's grown up. No wonder she doesn't want to come home, as she's her own woman over there, with Harry and his shop.'

'She'll be home soon. Harry can really do without her now. He's been able to all along. He never seemed heart-broken over losing Mary; in fact, I heard he's been seeing a woman in Reeth of late, so he's soon come out of mourning.' Tom put his arm around Agnes. 'She'll be back home before Christmas, and then you'll be happy.'

'I have a funny feeling she won't, Tom. That we have lost our daughter to another, but I don't quite know who,' Agnes whispered as she went to clear the breakfast table, which served as a reminder of the trust they had put in the lad they had taken in as their own.

22

Jack walked back up to his mother and his home, pausing to talk to an officious lady dressed in her Sunday best, who was giving out leaflets to those who would take them outside the newly built Literary Institute, which stood square and proud across the road from Calvert's, the blacksmith's. The good folk of Gunnerside had raised the money for the building to be erected, and now it stood in all its glory with the opening date carved on its side.

'Will you be joining us at our opening on Friday night, sir?' the woman said as she thrust a leaflet into his hand. 'Everyone's welcome. We want to be able to give learning to this village. Arithmetic and reading and writing are badly needed within our community. We also have lessons on geology, for miners who need to be aware of how to find new seams of lead, if that would be of interest.'

'Nay, I've had my fill of mining. I've recently lost my brother in an accident up at the Sir Francis level, and you'll not be getting me back there in a hurry.' Jack stopped to talk to her as he accepted her leaflet.

'I'm sorry to hear that. Was he one of the souls who died because of an incident with gunpowder? We have lessons on the use of that, along with dynamite, which is just as dangerous and needs careful handling. But we have an excellent library. Or perhaps you would benefit from learning accounting?' The woman was persistent in making known the virtues of the Literary Institute.

'Thank you, I'll think about it,' Jack said politely as he walked away, glancing quickly at the leaflet, but not giving it much thought. His thoughts were on his new venture into farming. He had stock to buy, and feed for the winter ahead, and the money he had saved would only just cover it. But most of all he could not stop thinking about Meg. She was not tied to his brother now and perhaps, given time, she would begin to realize how he felt about her – or at least he hoped she would.

'Oh, you are back then, from your wild-goose chase to Wensleydale? Well, was it their nephew, or were you right and it was the packhorse man's lad?' Betty stood with her hands on her hips and looked at her son.

'I was right. He'd made himself scarce by the time we got there. He'd seen us coming up the farm field and must have legged it, like a ferret out of a trap, knowing full well what would happen to him if he was caught.' Jack slumped down in his chair and threw the Literary Institute leaflet onto the table.

'Oh, aye, thinking of getting a bit of learning in your

old age? I bet it's that lass at the shop has put you up to that, and all. Why she can't leave my boys alone, I don't know. Since she's come along I've had no sense out of either of you. And I'll never get over losing my Sam in the way I did, but it's not as if you care. You'll be gone soon, leaving me to beg and scrimp. I'll have to ask the parish to give me some relief, and those pious bastards won't give me anything, when they know I've a son who should be supporting me,' Betty wailed.

'Oh, Mother, for once in your life, shut up. Sam is not coming back. Perhaps if he had listened to me, or gone to this new Literary Institute to learn more about things, he'd still be alive today. I must have told him a thousand times not to put his pipe in the same pocket as his gun-powder, but like the fool he was, he never listened. And as for you being abandoned, you are not. You can come with me: the choice is yours. And if you don't, then I will try to take care of you. I can always farm and work at the mine – not that I've a caring to do so, but I might have to,' Jack snapped at his mother, as he picked up the leaflet and looked at it with more care, following his mother's harsh words. Perhaps Meg would be interested; perhaps this was something he could ask her to attend with him?

'Sam would never have talked to me like that! I don't know what's got into your head lately, what with farms and not working at the mine – not to mention chasing after your brother's girl. Your father and Sam will be turning in their graves!' Betty sobbed.

'Aye, well, I've no intention of joining them just yet.

297

I've a life to live. I'm off out. I'll be back in time for supper, and I'll bring that back with me. I'll go and catch a salmon if I can, or at least a trout or two. The beck's in flood, from the rain that fell last night, so you don't have to worry about starving yet,' he said sarcastically as he headed to the kitchen door.

'Don't you get caught by the beck-watcher, or it'll be prison for you, and I've no money to bail you out with,' Betty yelled after him, as she watched Jack stamp angrily down the garden path with the Literary Institute leaflet in his hand. What had she done to deserve all this worry? she thought to herself, as she turned and looked around the two-bedroom cottage that she loved so dearly.

Meg looked up when the shop bell jingled as Jack entered.

'Are you back already? Although I'm glad, because I wanted to thank you for going to see my parents today, now that I'm on my own here.' She smiled at Jack and watched as he stood awkwardly in front of her with something in his hand.

'Your own? Mr Battersby's not about?' Jack asked quietly.

'No, he's gone to see his lady friend in Reeth, but I'm not supposed to say that.' Meg giggled a little. Her trip home with Jack had reminded her of how she had first been attracted to him, and perhaps it should have been Jack that she had fallen for.

'I just wondered . . . the new Institute is opening Friday night, and I wondered if you would like to go and have a look around it with me? I like to read, and the woman that gave me this leaflet told me there's going to be a library there.' Jack looked down at his feet and shuffled them, not really expecting Meg to say yes.

'Yes, that would be grand. I've kept wondering what it was going to be like inside, and now you've given me the chance to find out. A book to read of an evening is just what I will need, to pass the long, dark nights that we will soon be having.' Meg smiled.

'That's grand. I'll pick you up about seven?' Jack smiled back. He couldn't believe that she had accepted his offer.

'Yes, I'm sure Uncle Harry will not mind, as long as he knows who I'm with and where, and I'm not back too late.' Meg looked at Jack's face and noticed the delight upon it.

'I don't suppose you could get a day off and come into Reeth with me next weekend as well? I need to buy myself a milk-cow and a horse, if I can afford both.' Jack thought that while the going was good, he had nothing to lose by asking; and he could do with Meg's knowledge of both animals.

'I'll see what Harry says. I don't think he'll mind. I haven't had a day out of the shop since I arrived. So I can't see why not.' Meg grinned. 'Not that I'm the best judge of either, but I suppose I'm better than you are.'

'Aye, but I'll improve, once I'm up at The Rash. As long as I can be self-sufficient, I'll be alright. There's a good vegetable plot and a garden that just needs turning over before spring. And once I've a cow and a few hens,

I'll be right for butter, milk and eggs, and there's not much more that I'll want. My mother is being a stubborn old bugger and saying she's not coming with me, so I might still have to do a day or two up at the mine, to keep her roof over her head. I could have done without that, but then again there's a lot of farmers in the same position, so I shouldn't moan. Even though other farmers are not keen on the miners.' Jack looked serious.

'But you didn't want to go back to the mine. Especially not after losing Sam. Won't your mother live with you, and then you don't have to worry about her?' Meg asked.

'Nay, I'm happen better off without her. I'd like to take myself a wife, have a family of my own, and she'd not be happy for me to do that if she lived with me. She's over-protective, when it comes to her bairns. And now she's lost Sam, I don't think she wants me ever to leave her side, but I'm not falling for that.' Jack shook his head and glanced up at Meg. He wanted to say, 'I want you by my side', but knew the timing was wrong, and that she still mourned for Sam.

'I know. My parents still think I'm a girl, but in two months' time I'll be twenty, and my mum was that age when she married.' Meg sighed.

'I'll see you tomorrow night then. I'll pick you up. I'm on my way to catch some salmon for supper. It might take me some time, because I lie on the bank and tickle them. I know it sounds daft, but you lie down on the bank next to a pool that you know the salmon are in and, when they go under a stone near you, that's when

300

you put your hand carefully in the water, before placing it underneath them to stroke their belly gently. They like that, and they calm down enough for you to grab them out of the water and onto the bank, if you are lucky. My father taught me that before he died, God bless his soul.' Jack laughed. 'I'll bring you one, if you want – you and Harry.'

'No, you are fine, thanks. I don't like fish, and I've a stew cooking on the range for tonight, but I'll look forward to seeing you tomorrow night.' Meg smiled at Jack as he left the shop. She would look forward to choosing a book with him, and to a day out in Reeth with him. It would make a change, providing Harry agreed to both.

Harry pondered his stew, as Meg made both of her requests attentively while they ate supper together.

'I don't know if I should let you. I don't suppose there's any harm in you going to the Literary Institute together, but going into Reeth is a different matter. You'll be gone a full day with Jack. That gives you plenty of time for him to get up to no good with you.'

'Uncle Harry, we are friends. I'd never feel the same way about Jack as I did about Sam. And Jack is completely different; he's quite reserved and would never dream of doing anything against my will. Besides, I'm a long way from being over the death of Sam. I have no interest in such things.' Meg blushed; she'd not spoken so openly to her parents, let alone to a man who was not even related to her. However, she felt that between Harry and her there was a bond, and both had kept secrets about one another to themselves, so a special trust had formed.

'Well . . . Jack's got to promise to me that he'll behave himself, and then I suppose you can go. He'll have no idea what to look for in a cow, so he'll need your help. Why he's decided to farm is beyond me, but perhaps it'll suit him.' Harry pushed his empty plate to one side.

'His grandfather was a farmer, you know, down below Leyburn. They haven't always been miners.' Meg rose to Jack's defence.

'Aye, well, that makes no difference. You behave yourselves, else I'll have something to say to you both. I mean to send you back home in another month in the same condition you came to me in, if you understand my meaning.' Harry looked across at Meg and saw how embarrassed she looked.

'You'll have no problem with that,' she said quietly, with her head hung low. She was nearing tears as she said it, knowing full well that her monthly had not arrived on time and that she was starting to worry about the consequences. Never before had her monthly been late, and she feared the worst.

'Get yourselves gone then, I'll ask Lizzie up here to keep me company. She can help in the shop.' Harry smiled and watched as Meg tidied the supper table, thinking that she deserved a bit of joy in her life. After all, her head had been turned by the wrong lad and now that he'd gone, she would need a friend, albeit Sam's brother was not the best candidate. But Jack seemed to have more sense than the one that had just been buried.

302

'Thank you, Uncle Harry, and you needn't worry,' Meg said quietly, hoping that she was not lying and that all would be well when her monthly arrived. After all, she was only a day or two late.

'By, look at all these books – I've never seen as many. It's a grand thing they've set up here. It'll help many a miner become literate and will learn them more about their work. It's a bit like being back at school, mind, but that's not a bad thing, because some of the folk around here have never been to school and they regret it now.'

Jack walked through the Literary Institute, taking note of the lessons that were to be given of an evening to help promote education and welfare in the dale. The walls were stacked high with books and there were writing materials and paper, with desks to sit at and learn in every room.

'Our lad, if he was still alive, should have been coming here. Look, there's a geologist one evening a week, explaining how to find lead and how it is formed. That would have helped Sam, and he'd have been wanting my job and all, because the geologist's also talking about the proper way to go about smelting. I just did as I was taught. I know nowt about why I do it, in truth, and I should do.'

'Yes, it will help folk. And the library is a godsend. Folk can even take a book home with them, as long as they return it. I'm going to enjoy this one, it's about Dentdale and is called *Hope On, Hope Ever* and it should be good.' Meg looked at the book in her hand

and smiled. 'I'm glad Harry is letting me come with you on Saturday, I'm looking forward to it. You know I don't know that much about cows, but I can tell if they are going to be a good milker or not. As for horses, I know you look at their teeth to age them; other than that, you can count me out.'

'It'll be alright. I can only buy what I can afford anyway, and I've not that much brass to be flashing about. As long as the cow can supply the house with milk, and the horse gets me from one place to another, I'll be happy. I thought that if we had time I'd treat us both to a spot of something to eat in the Buck, if you fancy?' Jack stood in the doorway of the Institute and waited for an answer.

'Yes, if you like. I can't pay my way though. Harry doesn't seem to think I need paying for being over here and looking after him. Although I'm not complaining, because I have everything I need through the shop. And he treats me well, he's a good man.' Meg smiled.

'I don't think he's that keen on me. He gave me a right lecture when I picked you up. I didn't think he was going to let me come with you at first.' Jack shook his head.

'That's because of Sam. He knew I was a little heart-broken over him, and I'd sneaked about behind his back. That's why I asked him if it was alright if you accompanied me this evening and tomorrow. I don't want to deceive him again,' Meg said quietly.

'You *were* heartbroken – are you not still? You sound as if you have moved on with your life.' Jack quizzed her.

'I know it's early days since Sam's death, but I've had

time to think about things, and it would never have worked with me and Sam. I love my family too much. It would have broken their hearts if I had run away with him, and I think I was just infatuated by his attention to me. He was my first love, and I knew no different than to be obsessed by him. Sam made me feel special, but I think he did that with most girls, with hindsight. Death is all around us. My aunt and her husband have died, and Mary at the shop, but hardly any tears have been shed for them. You've got to get on with life, no matter how much you hurt.' Meg looked up at Jack. 'Don't think I'm hard-hearted. I was enchanted by Sam and I'll never, ever forget him, but I've done my crying now, especially if I have to go home in another few weeks. It's no good staying with Uncle Harry and moping, looking out at the graveyard every day, which is what I initially thought I was going to do. Besides, the so-called "Dan" has left now, so they'll need me back home. With winter coming, there will be a lot more to do on the farm. It's better to think of the living than the dead,' she whispered.

'I know, that's why I've rented a farm. Life's too short to be doing something you don't enjoy. The trouble is my mother: she's always got her own way, and she thinks I'm selfish. Believe me, I'm not. I just don't want to spend my days walking up that fellside, gasping for breath like all the old smelters do, when the dust from the ore has clogged up their lungs and they are dying a slow, painful death. You're right – death is all around us, and you have to embrace living and make the best of your life. Anyway, enough of this miserable talk. And speaking of my mother, I'd better get myself back to her, else she will be swearing at me. And Harry will be waiting for you. Do you want me to walk you home, or are you alright walking the short distance back?' He smiled at Meg.

'No, I'm fine. It's not as if it's a hundred miles away, just a short walk over the small bridge across the gill and then I'm home. I'll see you tomorrow. And something to eat there would be lovely. Thank you.' Meg watched as Jack made his way up the lane, past the smithy, following the gill edge to his mother's cottage at the end of the lane. There was more to Jack, she thought as she wandered home; he had ambition and he looked to the future. He'd always been in Sam's shadow, when she thought about it now. Perhaps Sam had shone too brightly in life to have lived to any great age.

Meg sighed. She'd lied to Jack, for there was a small piece of her heart that would always be Sam's. He had been her very first love – the love that no woman ever forgets – and part of him would always be with her, right to her death. However, with Sam now dead, she realized that Jack was perhaps the better of the two brothers, and she had no intention of hurting his feelings because of her puppy love for someone she was beginning to realize she had hardly known.

Reeth was busy. Market-goers had full baskets of fruit and vegetables, and women haggled at stalls, as the men of the family sold their livestock and discussed the politics of the day.

'That's the one you want.' Meg leaned over the hastily erected wooden pens that were in place on the sloping grassy marketplace in the centre of the village. 'That roan shorthorn, she'll give you plenty of milk and she doesn't look that old.' She pointed to a cow that looked bewildered as it stood penned up with the other animals that were for sale.

'You are sure? What about that one over there – she's a reasonable price, and the fella that is selling her has some sheep for sale and all, so perhaps I could do a deal?' Jack looked around him. He'd been to the market many a time, but not with this much brass in his pocket, and with so much at stake if he bought unwisely.

'No, she's no good. She's not got a good bag on her – she's no milk.' Meg pointed to her udders and then nodded at the cow she had recommended, as she yelled above the squawking of some geese in the next pen.

'Right, I'll see what he wants for her, and if he's willing to take her to Muker for me. Because I'm not paying a drover.' Jack fumbled in his pocket for his money and went over to the old man who was selling the bewildered animal.

Meg rushed to his side. 'We can walk her home, especially if you get yourself a horse. Speaking of which, there's a fell pony over there. She's not many hands tall, but she's sturdy and is just what you want, by the look of her. She's well-ridden, you can tell by her back – it's slightly dipped. And she seems good-natured enough.' Meg followed Jack as he went to negotiate his purchase of the

307

cow, all the time looking at what animals were for sale and hoping to spot a good buy.

'How much are you wanting for your shorthorn, sir?' Jack asked the gruff-looking old man in his workshirt.

'It'll be a half a guinea, and not a penny less. She's worth more than that, as she's a good milker and as calm as you like,' the old guy said.

'Will you take ten shillings? She'll have a good home and will be looked after well.' Jack held out his hand to be shaken.

'Nay, I promised my old lass that I wouldn't let her go for less than half a guinea. She's thought a lot of, is this old lass. The missus didn't want to part with her, but we need the money.' The old man rubbed his head and looked at the two young folk in front of him. 'Are you two starting out? I remember those days like yesterday, when me and my old lass were newly married and hadn't a penny to our names.'

Meg quickly said, 'Yes, we've just rented our first farm. Every penny counts.' She glanced at Jack, hoping that he would say nothing to the contrary.

'Because I like the look of your wife, and she looks that disappointed. Aye, you can take Daisy for what you are offering. Call me a soft old lump, and think of me when I get an earful of the old woman tonight.' He held his hand out to be shaken, after spitting on it for luck. 'Are you taking her now, or have you more business to be done? I'll be here until five or thereabout. I'm waiting on my lad; he's at the blacksmith's.'

'We'll be here for another hour. Can you hold onto

her until we return?' Jack passed the man the ten shillings and shook his hand, beaming at Meg as he realized that she had saved him money.

'Aye, I'll hold onto her. Go and get what else you want. Neither of us will be going far.' The old guy patted the cow's neck and looked at the loved beast; he was going to miss Daisy, for she was almost part of the family.

'Well, that's your cow bought. And the fell pony won't cost a lot. We'll have to try that again – looking like a newly married couple, folk have sympathy for us.' Meg giggled.

'Aye, it seemed to work.' Jack went quiet as he strode out in the quest for the dark-looking pony that Meg had spotted, but admired the dappled white horse next to it. 'I'd rather have the dapple, Meg. That pony looks as if it's been a pit pony, and its knees will not be in good shape.' He ran his hand along the dapple's withers and looked at its teeth. 'Aye, this one's for me, she's got a bit more spirit. Here, mate, how much will you take for the dapple?' Jack shouted at the horse dealer.

'More than you can afford, lad. She's a bonny horse, is that 'un.' The dealer came over and looked at Jack and Meg. 'She's a guinea. She's got to be that, because I paid a lot for her myself.'

'Oh God, that's nearly all of my brass spent, and I wanted to treat you to dinner and perhaps buy that cage of hens, and then we'd have eggs.' Jack rubbed his head and looked at Meg.

'Hens should come first, Jack. We couldn't live off a

horse.' Meg pretended to look down on the idea of being able to afford both.

'I'll knock a shilling off – that'll buy you your hens,' the dealer said, and rubbed his chin.

'Aye, that would help. What do you think, Meg, should we buy her?' Jack smiled at his accomplice in crime.

'Yes, let's, but I still like the little pony, and she'll be cheaper.' Meg ran her hand along the small black pony and smiled at the dealer.

'Two shillings. I'll knock you two shillings off my asking price, but that's my last offer,' he said and held out his hand to be shaken.

'Done – the bonny lass has a new home.' Jack shook the hand of the dealer and turned his dwindling money out of his pocket to pay him. 'We'll pick her up in a little while. She's got a halter, hasn't she?'

'Aye, and I suppose you'll want that in with the deal?' The dealer shook his head as he passed Jack his change.

'That would be grand.' Jack smiled and walked away with his arm through Meg's, towards a stall that was selling pies. 'I know I promised dinner in the Buck, but if you can make do with a mutton pie, I can actually buy that crate of hens. And then we can get back home. It's a fair walk from here to Muker, with a cow to herd.'

'That will do me fine. I'm just glad you have got what you wanted.' Meg smiled as Jack bought two mutton pies from a stall that was covered with home baking and passed her one to eat. 'Last time I was here, Sam was alive and I had such a good day with Peggy Dobson. It doesn't seem five minutes ago, and yet so much has happened since.' She looked down over the market and the village green, then above the houses of the small market town to the rolling dales in front of her. The leaves on the trees had now turned fully and the browns and oranges of autumn were starting to be shed onto the earth below.

'I know, it's been a tough year. But every year is a battle over here. You'll never be a millionaire, if you work in the mines or have a smallholding here, but as long as you survive, that's the main thing.' Jack wiped his mouth on his jacket sleeve and waited until Meg had finished her pie. 'Come on, cheer up. Let's get that crate of hens – they can go over Dapple's back and you can lead her while I drive Daisy.' He laughed.

'Dapple, that isn't much of a name for your horse! Surely you can do better than that?' Meg looked at Jack and smiled.

'You name her then. Make one up on our way home.' Jack turned and looked at Meg and wished, not for the first time, that his small farm could be home to Meg. But perhaps he was asking too much; he was just a friend, in her eyes, and he would never ever be able to compete with the ghost of his brother, Sam.

'I will – anything but Dapple!' Meg exclaimed. 'But I suppose we had better stick with Daisy, for the cow.' She grinned at Jack. For the first time in days she felt content; the hurt and pain were slowly subsiding and she was enjoying Jack's company. 'Come on, let's get these hens and then walk back. I'd like to see this farm that you've rented.'

'You'll be impressed, I'll tell you that. I know I was. I only hope I can make it pay.' Jack walked beside Meg and looked at her. He was going to enjoy showing her his new home and walking down the dale with her by his side. It might be autumn, with the leaves turning and a bite in the air, but in his heart it felt like spring, regardless of the recent death of his brother.

It had been a long walk from Reeth to where Jack's new home was, and Meg was thankful when they turned up the winding path that led to the long, whitewashed ancient farmhouse. It was low-set, with four windows upstairs and three downstairs, balanced in the middle by a slate-roofed porch to shelter callers from the wild weather.

'Oh, this is a lovely place, Jack. Just look at the view!' Meg stood at the garden gate of The Rash and looked down the length of Swaledale. 'It reminds me of home.' She breathed in and stood in awe of Jack's new property. 'The house will be lovely too, once it's been shown a bit of love and attention. Your mother will soon be able to do that, if she changes her mind. Anyway, I'm sure she will help you.'

'Nay, I don't think she will. She's a stubborn old bugger when she wants to be. What do you think of the garden? Look at the damson and apple trees, they are both covered with fruit. I'll turn the garden over this next spring and plant potatoes, cabbage and suchlike. I should want for nothing.' Jack looked over his kingdom and felt a sense of pride. Gone were all thoughts of America. He could hopefully make a good life for himself right here.

312

'It's grand, and it's the one thing I've missed while being over here – my garden. But I haven't had much spare time on my hands anyway, and I'll be returning home at the end of next month.' Meg lowered her head. She was ready for home, but part of her would always lie in Swaledale now.

'Come and have a look inside. It needs a lot doing to it. But I'll soon clean it up – a drop of whitewash on the walls, and some new cupboard doors and that.' Jack opened the front door and watched as Meg looked round the empty living room of the old farmhouse. 'I'll soon shift them crows that have nested down the chimney; they'll be needing fresh homes next spring.' He pointed at the mess of twigs and soot that had fallen into the hearth of the old fireside range. 'You know, I'll miss you when you return home. Do you think your parents would mind if I visited you?' he asked quietly.

'I'm sure – now that they think you farm, and because you saved them from life with an impostor – they would not mind in the least.' Meg smiled at Jack and was pleased to hear that he wanted to remain friends, once she returned home. 'But now I'm going to have to go. The nights are drawing in, and it will take me an hour to get back home.'

'It won't if I take you home on Dapple. I can show her to my mother.'

'I've been thinking about Dapple. Why don't you call her Rosie, because her muzzle is almost rose-pink and she is so beautiful? A ride home on her would save my legs, and I'd quite like that. Have you a saddle, or are we going bareback?' She blushed.

'Rosie, it is. And I'm afraid it is bareback – you'll have to hang onto me tight.' Jack looked at Meg; she'd made his day complete by accepting.

'Right then, let's go. And I hope Rosie doesn't mind two passengers on her back.'

As they trotted downhill among the golden leaves and branches of the autumn trees and followed the river into Gunnerside, they held one another close on Rosie's back. The setting sun shone and glistened on the flowing waters of the Swale, and there was a knowing silence between them that their friendship was growing, despite it being born of grief. Winter was on its way, but there was a warmth in both their hearts, although neither of them dared admit it to the other. It would be wrong, so soon after the death of someone they were both so close to.

'So you are back?' Harry met Meg in the shop's doorway. 'I'm glad you've made it back before nightfall, else I'd have been worrying.'

'It might have taken me that long, if Jack hadn't have brought me home on the back of his horse. We soon made it back into Gunnerside from his farm, and now he's showing his mother the horse. It's a grand place that he's got, Uncle Harry. I think he will do well.' Meg beamed as she took off her shawl and bonnet and made for the back room.

'Er . . . before you go in there, Megan, there's some-thing I need to tell you.' Harry caught her arm and looked serious.

Meg looked at him and feared more bad news. He never called her 'Megan' as a rule, so it must be something of importance that he had to announce. She felt slight panic and wondered if she had done something wrong or if someone was ill.

'Lizzie is still here. She's not going home this evening, so I thought it only fair to warn you. But the reason she's staying is that I've done the decent thing by her and asked her to marry me. I've proposed!' Harry looked at Meg with a face filled with happiness, but at the same time with concern.

'That's wonderful news. I'm so happy for you both.' Meg smiled and wondered whether to give the old man a kiss on the cheek, but thought better of it.

'Aye, well, folk have been talking. And I know there's no fool like an old fool, but you've to grab love when you find it. And the long winter nights on my own will be lonely, once you've gone back home.' Harry gave a soft, gentle smile and squeezed Meg's arm as they both walked into the back room, where Lizzie was sitting next to the fire, already part of the fixtures and fittings of the living quarters, with her knitting on the go.

'So, he's told you? He's worried all afternoon about telling you, and that I was to stay the night.' Lizzie glanced up from her knitting and looked at the young lass in front of her.

'Yes, he's told me, and I think it's wonderful. I'm glad that you've got one another. Congratulations! I hope you will both be happy.' Meg smiled at the red-faced Lizzie.

'Aye, it'll be strange. I'm going to sell my boarding

315

house in Reeth and move in with the old devil.' She pulled a face at Harry as he sat down next to her. 'Someone's got to keep him in line, once you've gone home, and he'll need something to keep him warm on a winter's night.' Lizzie chuckled, while Harry squirmed slightly in his chair.

'Yes, he'll need somebody to help him in the shop,' Meg said diplomatically as she made herself a cup of tea. 'I'll go up to my room and leave you two to it. I don't want to be in your way.'

'You'll not be in our way, lass. We are not exactly in the full bloom of youth, not like yourself. Now, I hope you had a good day with that Alderson lad. He behaved himself, did he?' Harry looked at Meg and saw her blush.

'Yes, he was the perfect gentleman. He bought a cow, a horse and six hens. And next week he's going to be looking for some furniture and then he will be moving in.' Meg stopped in the doorway that led upstairs.

'Well, he needn't look so far for furniture. I've no need for half of mine if he gives me a good enough price, and I'll sell him whatever he wants. I'll not be needing all that stuff at my boarding house, when I come to live here. After all, there's not enough room to swing a cat in this little back room, and the bedrooms are going towards getting full already.' Lizzie looked at Meg. 'You tell him that, next time you see him, and tell him to come down in the next week or two to take his pick. It'll be grand to think that it's going towards setting up a new home and helping somebody.' Lizzie put her head down and continued with her knitting.

'I will do. That's very kind of you. I'm sure Jack will appreciate it. I will go upstairs now, though. It's been a long day and I'm tired. Goodnight,' Meg said as she climbed the stairs slowly and went into the privacy of her bedroom, lighting the bedside light before lying down on her bed. She gazed up at the ceiling, and at the shadows made by the small paraffin light as it flickered in the evening's cold air. She hugged her pillow to her and stifled her crying, as she thought of Sam and of the day that she felt so guilty about enjoying with his brother, Jack.

But the tears were not only in remembrance of Sam; they were for the fact that Meg was beginning to realize that within her belly a new life was forming, and that her long-awaited monthly was not going to appear. The weeks had flown by since she had lain with Sam, and now she knew that she was carrying a dead man's child, and that she had no one to turn to for help and support.

23

'Now, tell me to mind my own business, but I couldn't help but hear you sobbing and crying last night. You know how it is, when you are in a new bed. I couldn't get comfortable and settle, and then I lay awake listening to you, with your heart breaking, if I heard right.' Lizzie looked at Meg as she dusted the shop's shelves, making use of the quiet Sunday morning. 'You are alright, aren't you? You look as pale as a ghost this morning. My Harry's been looking after you?' Lizzie held her arms out to the young frail lass and smiled.

'I'm fine. I'm fine, really. I'm sorry I kept you awake. I just felt a bit low in spirits.' Meg ignored Lizzie's outstretched arms. She knew that if she was to be shown any kindness, she would break down and cry again.

'Harry told me that you'd been courting the lad who died in the mining accident – behind his back, mind, which he wasn't that chuffed about. But it must be hard to hide your hurt and keep it to yourself. You are bound to miss him. And sharing the day yesterday with his brother must have been hard. However, Harry says he's not a bad lad; the better of the two, in his eyes. Perhaps it was meant to be.' Lizzie stood next to Meg as she tried to control the tears that were quickly overtaking her. 'Aye, lass, come here. Tell me your troubles while Harry's out on his walk – us women have to stick together. I know what it's like to have loved and lost, but you'll find true love again, if that's all your tears are for.' She wrapped her arms around Meg, who shrank into the tenderness of the older woman's embrace.

'I don't know what to do. I'm so frightened, and I've nobody to turn to,' Meg sobbed.

'Why, what's to do, my love?' Lizzie held Meg tightly, with her head on her shoulder, and stroked her long, dark hair. 'Soonest said, soonest mended. Nothing will shock me. I'm too long in the tooth for anything to upset me.'

Meg breathed in deeply, not raising her head off Lizzie's shoulder as she confessed her situation.

'I think I'm having Sam's baby! My monthly is late, and it's never late and I don't know what to do.' She buried her head in the older woman's shoulder and sobbed, not wanting to have eye contact with the woman she hardly knew but had confessed everything to. 'My mum and father will disown me, I know they will. And I can't help but think I'll end up like the woman who took both her life and her baby's, when she jumped from off the bridge at the end of the village.' Meg had thought about her predicament all night, and although she knew that she had blown things up out of all proportion in her own mind, she still thought there would be no love or sympathy for her at home.

'Now, it'll not come to that. I know your parents love you. Harry has said so many a time.' Lizzie held Meg straight out in front of her. 'Are you sure you are with child? Have you got your dates wrong, or is your monthly just late because of the upset you've had in your life recently?' Lizzie looked at Meg's paleness and knew what the answer was going to be as she shook her head.

'No, I'm having a baby. I know I am,' Meg sobbed.

'Well, you won't be the first, and you definitely won't be the last. The question is, what are we going to do about it?' Lizzie sighed and held Meg tightly against her. 'There's a woman over in Leyburn who would see you right; she'd get rid of it for you, but she might kill you in the process, the old witch. Or you'll just have to go home and face them with the truth. It'll be hard, but they'll have to cope with it. I know Harry will blame himself. He realizes he should have kept a better eye on you. That's why I've started to visit him now.'

'It's not Uncle Harry's fault. And I'm not getting rid of it.' Meg pulled away from Lizzie and wiped her eyes and nose on her sleeve. 'I'll go home and tell them everything. But it's not Uncle Harry's fault, it's all mine. I have been stupid and easily led.' Meg sighed. She realized now that she had not truly loved Sam, but that she had simply been infatuated with him.

'Aye, well, he was known for his way with women. You were easy prey, I dare say. His brother seems to have more sense, from what I hear.' Lizzie looked at Meg as she composed herself. 'Now, do we tell your Uncle Harry? I can keep it a secret if you want, but it will take some explaining, why you have decided to go home all of a sudden.'

'Tell me what? And why are you wanting to go home? Is it because Lizzie is going to be moving in?' Harry stood in the doorway, after quietly making his way in through the back door, and waited to be told what had been discussed in his absence.

Meg hung her head. 'I'm sorry. I'm really, really sorry. I've let you down so much, and all you have shown me is kindness. I wish I was dead – I've been such a fool,' she cried.

'Will one of you tell me what's going on, and why you two are nearly in tears?' Harry said, and looked at both Lizzie and Meg.

'She's having a baby, Harry. She's carrying that dead lad's baby and she's heartbroken, scared and not wanting to face her parents.' Lizzie put her arm around Meg and held her tightly. 'And she needs us both to support her, so don't you let her down.'

'Bloody hell – no wonder I'd no family of my own. They'd have sent me to my grave, if they had all been as headstrong as you, my lass. Your father will kill us all. It'll be my fault, and I promised I'd look after you,' Harry ranted.

'I'm sorry, I'm sorry. I regret it all now,' Meg cried.

'It's too bloody late now, lass. Of all the bloody lads, you'd to have your head turned by him. God help us!' Harry turned as the shop bell rang and glared at the customer who

321

entered. 'Talk of the bloody Devil! I suppose you have the same intentions as your bastard of a dead brother, trailing over here at all hours to see this 'un here!'

'What's going on? Meg, are you alright? What are you crying for?' Jack looked shocked at the temper Harry was in, and concerned for Meg as she stood crying in Lizzie's arms.

'No, she's not bloody alright, lad! She's carrying your bastard brother's bairn. He should have had his balls cut off at birth, that 'un. Then there wouldn't have been all this heartache in the dale. Now, bugger off and tell your mouthy mother that she can be proud of her favourite son, because he's just spoilt another young girl's life,' Harry raged and opened the shop door for Jack to leave.

Jack was taken aback. He didn't know what to say, and stood looking at the women sobbing and Harry raging. Meg was pregnant by his dead brother. What was he to do?

'I'm not leaving until I know Meg's alright. I'm not the same as our Sam, never have been. I warned you, didn't I, Meg? He never loved anybody; he used them for his pleasure. He may have been my brother, but he was a bastard when it came to women. And I'm sorry that he's left you in this state.' Jack hung his head. 'Please don't judge me by his standards. I think dearly of Meg, but I respect her too much to do as Sam did by her. I'd never do that outside marriage.' He looked across at Meg and tried to smile at the embarrassed lass, whom he thought so dearly of. He loved her, but she was not his to love any more, now she was carrying his brother's child.

'Aye, well, get your arse home. It'll be me and her parents that have to sort it.' Harry closed the shop door behind Jack as he left, and turned the sign round. 'Now, let's sit down and see what can be done about it. I've said my bit, and now I'll calm down. It's no good crying over spilt milk.' He looked at Lizzie and Meg as they comforted one another and cursed under his breath. He was going to be the one Tom and Agnes blamed for her state, and now he was wishing he'd never asked Meg to stay.

Betty Alderson had put up with her son's surly looks and mood all day and she'd had enough by supper time. 'What's brought about this long face on you tonight? Have you run out of brass, and come to your senses about leaving your poor old mother and a perfectly good home?' She looked across the supper table at her son as she ate her bacon and egg.

'There's nowt wrong with me. I've just got a lot on my mind. The sooner I get away from here, the better,' Jack spat back. 'I can never do right by you, no matter what I do. You can please yourself whether you come with me or not. Either way, I'll still support you, because I'll work a few days at the mine to make enough brass.' He wiped the yolk of his egg from his plate with his last bit of crust and looked at his mother.

'You said you'd never go back, after Sam died. That you couldn't face it! So there's no need to do that for me – the parish will see me right.' Betty cleared the table and turned her back on her son, as he pushed his chair back and grabbed for his coat, to face the wild, wet night that had set in around the dale. 'Where do you think you are going at this time of night?' she asked.

'It's best you don't know, Mother. But there's something I've to do, and I've got to do it before morning, else it will be too late – if indeed I'm not too late already.' Jack quickly put his coat on, turning up his collar against the wind and rain as he walked out with purpose.

He knocked heavily on the back door of the shop, in the hope that he was not too late with the proposal he had thought about all day.

'Bloody hell, you've got a nerve. I told you to piss off. We never want to see your family again,' Harry said as he opened the door, letting the dim lamplight from within fall on to Jack's sodden features.

'Please, give me a minute with Meg – if I'm not too late and she's not gone home already. Please, Mr Battersby. It's vital that she hears what I have to say.'

'She'll not want to see you, lad. She's upstairs packing, and tomorrow I'm taking her home.' Harry started to close the door on his unwelcome visitor, but Jack stopped him, wedging his foot in the doorway and pulling it back open.

'She can't go home until she's heard what I've got to say. And then, if she still wants you to take her home, you'll not see me again,' Jack pleaded.

'Let him in, Harry. After all, he's done Meg no harm; he'll just want to say his goodbyes,' Lizzie yelled, looking up from her knitting and listening to Jack's pleas, which filled her with sympathy.

'He'd better bloody well behave himself, else I'll have

him. It'll not only be his brother in the graveyard,' Harry growled as he let Jack into the warmth and shelter of the back room. 'I'll give Meg a shout. Whatever you've got to say to her, you can say in front of us all here, as I'll never trust one of your kind ever again.' He walked over to the bottom of the stairs and yelled for Meg and then, scowling, came back to his seat next to the fire.

'Sit yourself down at the table, lad. She won't be long.' Lizzie smiled and saw the worry on Jack's face. 'She'll be glad to see you – she needs a friend.'

'Phh!' Harry commented as he heard the stair-boards creak and Meg appeared.

'Are you alright, Meg? You look tired.' Jack looked across at the girl, who only the other day had been full of joy and happiness.

'I'm alright, thank you, Jack. Now, what do you want to see me about? I'm going home tomorrow; it will be for the best.' Meg hung her head and fought back the tears.

'I wanted to ask you this in private, but perhaps it is something everyone should hear anyway.' Jack breathed in and felt himself tremble inside, with fear and anticipation of the answer he was hoping to get from Meg. 'Will you marry me, Megan Oversby? I know I'm not our Sam, and I know I'm not the baby's father, but I'm the next best thing. And damn it, Meg, I love you – and have done since the first day I set eyes on you at Hawes Market Hall dance.'

Harry and Lizzie looked at Meg as tears filled her eyes. She shook her head. 'No, I can't let you do that. You are asking me out of sympathy. I think a great deal of you, but a few weeks ago I thought I was in love with your brother, and I can't burden you with his child's upbringing.'

'Meg, it will be no burden. I love you, and hopefully you will grow to love me. We have a home ready-made, which your child will make complete, when he or she comes along. I'll raise it as my own. And whether you tell your parents now that you are pregnant, or after we are wed, it makes no difference to me.' Jack reached for Meg's hand across the table. 'Marry me, Meg. You'll not regret it, I promise you.'

'Meg, think of what Jack is saying to you. He's asking you to marry him, offering to give the child a father and you both a home. There's many a man would turn his back on you, but he's willing to give you everything he has.' Harry looked at the lad who was offering her a new start in life and breathed in deeply.

'It's a good thing that you are doing, Jack Alderson. You must love the lass,' Lizzie whispered as she looked at Meg, who was sitting sobbing.

'I do. I love her with every breath that I take. I only wish she felt the same way about me, or could promise me that one day she might.' Jack looked up at Meg and smiled. 'I'm not asking out of sympathy. If anything, I'm being selfish, as I don't want anybody else to have you in their life.' Jack looked at Meg and smiled. 'Say yes, and try to grow to love me, and then I'll be the happiest man in the world. We could go and see your parents in the morning, just as you planned; ask your

326

father's permission to be wed and then arrange for the banns to be read and be married before Christmas. No one need ever know that you are with child, until the baby arrives early. Please say yes,' Jack pleaded.

Meg shook her head. 'I don't know. I do care for you. In fact, I've enjoyed our last few days together. But what if my father doesn't agree to our marriage – what then?'

'Then we will have to tell the truth to the minister; tell him that you are with child, so that he can apply for a licence for us, and you will have to say that you are of full age when you sign the register. Many a marriage is undertaken that way, when the circumstances demand it. But I'd rather have your parents' permission first.'

Meg raised her head and looked at Jack. 'Then I will marry you, Jack Alderson, and I will be forever in your debt. And I will grow to love you, of that I'm sure.' She smiled and then burst into another round of tears. She was a long way from being out of the trouble she was in, but at least she had a man standing by her now and a home, once wed.

'Aye, lad, you've no need to take this on your shoulders. It is your brother's doing,' Harry said as he went to shake Jack's hand.

'He was a fool. And besides, I do love Meg, she just never knew it. But she does now.' Jack smiled across at her and watched as she composed herself.

'I think it's lovely, and hopefully things will work out between you both and Meg's parents will agree to your plans. Everyone should have somebody to love them.' Lizzie cried into her handkerchief.

'Aye, well, tomorrow we'll have to face your parents, Meg, so let's hope they agree to our marriage and then all will be well.' Jack looked worried. It wasn't only Meg's parents they had to tell; it was his mother too, and she was sure to have something to say about it all.

'You are a bloody idiot, marrying that lass who you hardly know! I don't know what's got into your head of late – renting a farm, getting wed and going to the Literary Institute. Just look at all these books you brought back, putting rubbish into your head.' Betty gazed at the pile of books that Jack had been reading of an evening. 'What do you think you are, summat special? Tha's a miner, lad, and you should be proud of it,' she yelled at her son as he told her his news.

'I'm trying to better myself, Mother. And with Meg at my side, I'll prove that I can. Renting The Rash is only the start. I mean to work hard and buy more land and become someone.' Jack stood his ground.

'Well, you'll be doing it without me, because I think you've lost your senses and it's all down to that lass. I wish she'd never set foot in the dale,' Betty cried as she watched her eldest son storm out of the kitchen door. 'Don't bother coming back here. This is no longer your home – you've no respect for me, and our Sam was twice the man you are,' she shouted after Jack, collapsing in her usual chair and sobbing as she watched him disappear down the garden path.

24

'Tom, look – our Meg is coming up the field. She is on horseback behind that lad who came with her and Harry to tell us the lad was not Dan.'

Agnes rushed out into the porch, leaving Tom sitting by the fire. She waved at them both as they entered the yard and watched as they dismounted and tied up the horse next to the barn.

'Now, this is a surprise. What's brought this on? Were you missing home?' She kissed Meg on her cheek and smiled at Jack as he followed in her footsteps into the family home. 'Sit yourself down, Jack. You'll have a cup of tea and something to eat?' She fussed around her guests.

'So you've decided to visit us for a change, have you, lass? Now that Dan has buggered off. I still can't believe I was taken in by him.' Tom looked across at the young couple. 'It's a good job you knew him, else he'd have still been here.' He smiled at Jack and then looked at Meg, noticing that they both were quiet and seemed worried.

'I'd like to have a word with you, sir, if I may?' Jack fidgeted and felt awkward in front of Meg's parents. He realized they hardly knew him and he hardly knew them, so what he was about to ask would not be easy.

Meg could feel her stomach churning. She'd been dreading this moment and had hardly slept last night for going over it in her mind.

'Well, whatever it is you are wanting to say, you'd better get on with it. Else you are going to break that teacup you are holding, your hands are shaking that much,' Tom joked, noticing Jack's hand shivering with nerves as Agnes passed him a cup of tea.

'I wish to have your permission to marry your daughter, Meg.' Jack stopped in his tracks and watched Tom's face set like thunder and Agnes gasp in surprise. 'I know it's a shock, but I love her and I want to wed her. I have the means to see that she will want for nowt,' he carried on, and then fell silent as Tom spat in the fire and looked at him.

'Get yourself outside, Meg, with your mother. I need to talk to this lad alone. He's got ideas above his station and he'll not be marrying you, once I've finished with him.' Tom glared at all three, as Agnes pulled on Meg's arm to join her outside and not interfere with men's talk and her father's anger.

'But he does love me, Father, and we will marry,' Meg yelled.

'Shush, child! Come outside with me and let your father have his say.' Agnes pulled on Meg's arm and took her out into the garden, where she made her daughter sit

330

down beside her on the garden seat, as Meg put her head in her hands and cried.

'Whisht now, lass. You hardly know the lad, to be giving your heart away so easily. There will be more men yet to come in your life, and your father wished for so much more – and better – for you. As soon as you left the last time, once he'd calmed down over that Dan business, he remembered Jack's face from summer, when he and his brother knocked on our door looking for work. He's a miner, isn't he? Albeit he's just rented a small farm. You can do much better than that, lass.' Agnes put her arm around her daughter and felt her shaking.

'He is a miner, but he loves me and I need him,' Meg cried and looked at her mum.

'You need him – you don't say that you love him? Is there something else you should be telling me, our Meg? You're not carrying his child, are you? Is that what this is all about?' Agnes looked at her daughter and could see that she had hit the nail on the head. Her daughter was pregnant, and desperate. 'Eh, lass, I daren't tell your father – he'll go mad. God help us both, because it will be all our fault, and he'll kill that lad in there if he confesses to being the father.'

'It was a mistake, but he does love me, Mum, and he's a good man.' Meg looked with pleading eyes at her mother. She needed her help, but no sooner had she said the words than Jack came ranting out of the farmhouse.

'Meg! Meg, where are you? We are going home. I can get no sense from your bloody father – he's having none of it. He won't listen to a bloody word that I say.' Jack swore and went and untethered his horse, with Tom following close behind him.

'If you go with him, you need never come back here again, madam. I wash my hands of you, and don't think your mother and I will be trailing over to Swaledale to beg you to come back, either.' Tom watched as Meg pulled away from her mother and took Jack's hand to help her mount up behind him.

'Tom, think of what you are saying. History is repeating itself. Your father did this with your sister, and look at how that ended. This is your daughter – give them your blessing and let them wed properly.' Agnes pulled on Tom's arm, beseeching him not to be so hasty.

'Shut up, woman. He's no way near good enough for her, and he knows it. I tell you what: I'm washing my bloody hands of that Harry and all – he's to blame for this. I should never have let Meg go over there to him.' Tom cursed as Jack and Meg looked down on him from their seat on the dapple horse.

'We will be wed, with or without your permission, and I know Meg would like you both there. Perhaps you will have come to your senses by then and will join us.' Jack kicked the horse's sides and started to trot down the farm track, with Meg in tears, looking back at the home and the parents that she loved.

'Did you tell them you were expecting?' Jack asked Meg as they ambled quietly back down into Swaledale. She had been in tears for most of the journey, and Jack had been calming himself down after the cutting words that Tom had hurled at him.

'I told my mum. I couldn't help it. I think she had already guessed anyway. She'll probably choose her moment to tell my father, and then there will be hell to pay.'

'I didn't say anything about the baby. I thought it best not to do so. I'm sorry, I thought they'd be happy for us both, but this time he remembered my face from when we called on you in haytime, and he made short work of cutting me down. He was even accusing me of making it up about Dan, so that I could get my hands on his land, once I'd married you.' Jack lifted Meg down from the horse, once they reached the shop, and looked at her. 'I do love you.' He leaned forward and kissed her tenderly on the lips. 'Tomorrow we will see the minister and set a date and ask for a licence. It'll make no difference to him, as there's many a wedding without consent in this dale.'

'I know, but I wanted my parents to be there. I love them, especially my mum, and she will be heartbroken,' Meg whispered.

'Mothers! I've to face mine now, and she'll have all on to speak to me. She'd be different if she knew the truth,' Jack said quietly.

'Then tell her! She should be proud of you for covering for your brother,' Meg said.

'No, I'll raise the child you are carrying as my own, and no one except those who already know will ever know any different. It's our bairn.' Jack kissed Meg again and then bade her goodnight as he left her outside the shop's doorway, watching him cross the river bridge back to his home. He wished, for her sake, that her father had agreed to the wedding, but he was a stubborn old sod, just as Meg had warned him. In his eyes, Jack was not good enough for his daughter.

'Aye, I knew Tom wouldn't see sense. He's always had big plans for you, lass. Twenty acres, or just over, isn't enough for you to be happy with, in his eyes; he's always had you matched with one of the big landowners down Wensley-dale, in his head. And with Jack being a miner to boot, well, that would not suit him at all.' Harry listened to Meg and felt sympathy for both her and Jack. 'So what are you going to do now?'

'We are going to see the minister tomorrow. But can I still stay here? I've nowhere else to go until I'm married,' Meg whispered.

'Aye, you'll be alright here, lass. Who knows, your father might turn up for you yet, but I doubt it. Once he's set his head, that's it with him. I suppose he'll be cursing me fit to burn, and that will be the end of my butter delivery and whatever else your parents brought.' Harry sighed.

'Jack can supply you with butter. He's got the best milk-cow in Swaledale, and eggs, if you ask him. After all, we will need the money,' Meg said as she thought about how much she was going to miss seeing her mum.

'You can tell him he can supply me as soon as he can. Is he living up at the farm now?' Harry enquired.

'No, he goes back and forth, because his mother won't move, but he's talking about moving into The Rash next week, as they've fallen out over me,' Meg said.

'Tha's causing some bother, lass. Let's hope she doesn't go with him to his farm. Her face is fit to curdle any milk, and then where would we both be?' Harry grinned at Meg. 'Anyway, you don't want your mother-in-law living with you – it'd never work. Too many cooks, and all that.'

The minister looked at the young couple sitting in front of him. 'When are your sort ever going to remember that the horse comes before the cart, not vice versa? I'm getting a bit tired of quick weddings, and miners coming and telling me their woes. At least this child might have been conceived out of wedlock, but it is going to be born within it, and with God's blessing.' He looked over the top of his glasses as he filled out the form asking for permission from the Dean for the young couple to wed. 'Your age, madam?'

Meg looked at Jack before replying. 'I'm twenty today, sir.' She glanced at the dainty silver bracelet that Jack had given her and smiled. With everything else, she had forgotten her birthday and had woken up to find a necklace from Harry, and then Jack had surprised her with his gift.

'Oh, underage as well – and no parents' permission, I suppose. I'll have to put "of full age" and hope that no one questions it. You young women should learn not to lead young men on, as they can't control their manly

335

urges, while you women can,' the minister lectured Meg, making her blush as he continued filling out the form.

'Can we set a date, sir?' Jack asked and smiled at Meg.

'Erm . . . should we say Saturday the first of December at two p.m. Granted, of course, that you get permission.' The minister looked up and saw both of them smile at one another.

'Perfect – we wanted to be married before Christmas.' Jack grinned.

'You'll not be smiling when you are struggling to fill that baby's mouth and snow is on the land. I do wish you miners were more responsible. But then again, the farmers are just as bad. It's a good job the teachings of John Wesley are still guiding people in this dale, else it would be lost to hellfire and brimstone,' the minister said sharply. 'Now, good day. I'll let you know when I receive permission. You are both of this parish at present, so I can foresee no problems. However, perhaps a little more attendance at chapel would not go amiss in the meantime.' The minister dismissed the couple and watched as they left the recently built chapel. He shook his head and sighed as they kissed, before closing the chapel door behind them. 'Fools never learn,' he muttered as he saw to securing the licence.

November came to the dale with storms aplenty. The rain pelted down on the small village of Gunnerside and the becks and gullies overflowed, as the grey clouds hid the fell tops, making villagers stay in their homes and keep the fires lit.

Jack had moved away from his mother's and had started to realize what a hard life farming was. There was no money coming in, and his savings were going down rapidly. The only money he was making was by selling his few pounds of butter each week and, up to a few days ago, the eggs that the hens had been laying, but now even they had seemed to go on strike in protest at the inclement weather. He'd have liked to buy some sheep for the top pastures, but with making the house ready for Meg to move into and turning it into a fit home for a baby, those ideas had been put on hold. He realized now that they were going to struggle in winter, and so with a heavy heart he made his way back up through Gunnerside to the lead-mines and secured himself three days at the smelting works.

'You've not lasted long on your fancy farm then, lad?' his former boss said as Jack went about the job that he had vowed he would never return to. The heat and dust from the melting ore hit his lungs, and he felt the first sense of despair since his proposal to Meg.

'I'll not be working here, come the spring. I just need some work over the winter months.' Jack swore at the ferocity of the heat as he poured the molten ore out into ingots.

'Nay, now you are getting wed, you'll need every penny you can make – and more besides. You've hanged yourself good and proper.' His boss grinned, knowing that Jack would always be working there and that his grand plan of being self-sufficient on such a small acreage would never work.

'Don't matter. At least I'll have a home to go to on a night, and a wife to keep me warm.' Jack ignored his boss, who had always been single and always would be, because he never bothered with women.

'Aye, and probably in a few months a baby bawling. You are welcome to it, my lad, it's not for me.'

Jack stood up and looked around him. He could put up with this as long as Meg was by his side. Every time he saw her she looked bonnier, and they were both counting the days till their wedding day, now that they had been granted permission. His boss could say what he wanted. He was a happy man, and would be even happier, come the first of December.

'Now, don't you look lovely? Just look at her, Harry, isn't she beautiful? It's amazing how that old dress of mine has made such a pretty wedding dress. It's a good job you are even slimmer than me, so we had plenty of material to play with.' Lizzie stood back and admired her handiwork.

Meg stood before Harry and Lizzie and glanced at herself in the mirror, which had been brought down from Harry's bedroom.

'Pretty in pink. We couldn't really have you marrying in white, and that is a most delicate shade of pink – indeed, you can hardly tell it is pink.' Lizzie and Meg admired the dress, and the long sleeves and neckline that Lizzie had patiently sewn lace on, to pretty it up a little.

'You can't see my condition, can you?' Meg breathed

338

in and ran her hand over her stomach, conscious of the baby growing inside her.

'No, you are still as flat as a pancake. Besides, your bouquet will go there. I'm glad I rescued some chrysanthemums out of the garden; they would have been battered to death with all this rain.' Lizzie placed a small headband covered with fake roses around Meg's head and stood back. 'There now, pretty as any lass I've ever seen. That young Jack has done well for himself.'

Meg smiled at her reflection. 'Thank you, Lizzie and Harry, you have been wonderful. I don't know what I'd have done without you. I really don't. I just wish my mother and father had kept in touch. I miss them so much, and I would have loved them to be with me on my wedding day.' She sniffed and held back the tears that she knew were bubbling under the surface, as she looked at herself in the wedding dress that had been made with love.

'Aye, well, your father always was a stubborn old bugger. He was the same with your aunty – and look what happened there. You'd have thought he'd have learned his lesson by now. Your mother won't dare come without him, else her life wouldn't be worth living. I bet she's had it rough since you left.' Harry looked at Lizzie and then at Meg. 'If I could get them to your wedding, I would. Tom always wanted a son. Well, now he's as good as got one, and one who wants to farm if he has the chance. The awkward old bugger never looks to the future. He'll be cursing me up hill and down dale, and even more so when he learns that I'm to remarry this coming spring.'

'They might come, you never know. What's more important is that the weather improves for a week on Saturday – we can't have rain.' Lizzie went and tapped the barometer that hung next to the door. 'Hmm . . . Looks like there's a change on the way; perhaps the sun will shine.'

'I hope so. I know the chapel's only a short walking distance, but I'd look like a drenched rat if I went out in this, by the time I got to it.' Meg looked out into the dark grey skies; in fact, everything around her was grey and miserable, apart from the rose pink of her dress, which Lizzie insisted on calling a 'delicate shade of pink'. But nothing mattered. She'd make the best of her wedding day, come hell or high water, because it offered security for her and her baby, and a decent man on her arm, and that's all that mattered, in her eyes.

'What are you doing, Harry?' Lizzie looked at Harry while he sat writing in the dim light of the oil lamp. 'It's nearly midnight. Are you not coming to bed?'

'I'm reminding that pig-headed fella over in Appersett about all the times he's got things wrong. And I've also reminded him that his wedding was a bit hurried, if I remember rightly; and that he married below his station, as Agnes was only a scullery maid. The self-righteous hypocrite! He'd be nowt if it hadn't been for his father and grandfather working their fingers to the bone. He's been privileged from the day he was born, and now he's going to spoil his lass's special day. The day she needs her mother and father, not an old fella who isn't even related

340

walking her down the aisle. I'll send it with the post lad first thing. Happen Tom will see sense and at least let Agnes come to the wedding.' Harry sat back and looked at Lizzie. 'I know Mary would have understood both my needs and Meg's. I just wish Tom realized how lonely he will be without his only daughter in his life, when she and her new family could make it so full for him. And I've told him to help them out with some money. The tight old bugger can't take it with him – there's no pockets in a shroud.'

'Well, you'll be lucky if he ever talks to you again,' Lizzie exclaimed.

'It's what he needs, a good squaring up. And I'm the man to do it,' Harry growled.

'The sun's shining. There's one or two clouds in the sky, which look as if they could threaten snow, but at least it's not raining.' Lizzie opened the back room's shutters and turned round to look at Meg, who had just come down the stairs. Her long, dark hair was still wrapped in the rags that Lizzie had insisted she curl it with, to form ringlets for her special day. 'Your wedding day is here, Meg. Another few hours and you will be Mrs Alderson, and you will have your own home and your whole future in front of you.' Lizzie giggled.

'Is Uncle Harry opening the shop today? He'll not want to lose trade; after all, it's a Saturday and we are always busy. I can work behind the counter until twelve.' Meg yawned and looked across at Lizzie, who seemed to have abandoned her lodging house for the comfort and company that the shop offered.

'You'll do no such thing! We have your hair to see to, and this morning you need to relax and look forward to your wedding. Harry is opening the shop until dinner time, and then he says he's going to the King's Head for a gill of Dutch courage before he walks you down the aisle. I think his nerves have got the better of him. He regards you as the daughter he never had.' Lizzie smiled and made Meg sit down next to the fire, which was still banked up, with embers glowing from the previous evening.

'He's not the only one. I feel sick this morning, and my stomach is churning.' Meg watched as Lizzie put a pan of milk on the fireside to make porridge. 'I don't want anything to eat.' She nearly gagged at the smell of the warming milk.

'That's only to be expected, as the baby is making you feel like that, along with nerves. A slice of buttered bread will do you no harm, though. You've got to eat something.' Lizzie looked with concern at Meg.

'I don't want anything. I just wish I weren't having this baby and that I'd not been so foolish. Everybody is being so kind, and I don't deserve any of it. In another few years Jack will regret the day he married me, especially when he's struggling to make a living and sees a child that isn't his getting under his feet and demanding to be fed.' Meg hid her head in her hands and cried. She'd not slept all night, thinking of all the things that could go wrong, and they were swamping her with fear.

'Now, young lady, pull yourself together. You hold

your head up high, and you marry the lad who worships the ground you walk upon. He'll love that baby as if it was his own, don't you worry. And aye, you might never be millionaires, but there's a lot that are in the same boat in this dale and they make do. Now, breakfast, and then we'll look at your hair. Harry's already in the shop. He's seen the baker and he'll be wanting something to eat himself, so stop all this self-pity; it will not get you anywhere.' Lizzie folded her arms and tried to look fiercely at Meg, but she couldn't. She knew that what Meg had said was probably going to be true, if she and Jack didn't have any support from Meg's family.

'Now, look at you! How can Jack not help but love you? Those ringlets are perfect and the flowers are just the right colour. By, you are a bonny bride.' Lizzie stood back from her handiwork, then looked at Meg and sighed.

'A bonny bride with only three guests at her wedding,' Meg said and felt tears welling up in her eyes. 'I thought perhaps my mother and father would appear. They must have heard that it's my wedding day, as gossip travels like wildfire around here.'

'Now forget them. Today you are marrying Jack – that is, if Harry gets his arse out of the King's Head. He said he'd be back by half-past one.' Lizzie looked at the mantel clock and shook her head. 'I bet Jack is already waiting at the chapel for you. Do you think his mother will have made her way there, or is she another who's more stupid than I think?' She stopped spouting as Harry, a little worse for drink, opened the back door and grinned at them both.

343

'I've nobbut had a couple, before you both start. Just to celebrate the happy couple.' Harry went over and kissed Meg on the cheek. 'Tha's a bonny lass. If I were forty years younger, that Jack would not stand a chance,' he slurred as he linked arms with Meg. 'Should we?' he said, pointing to the open doorway. 'I've seen Jack and his mother go into the chapel, so he's not done a runner.'

Lizzie looked as black as thunder at Harry, then kicked him on the shin in a bid to shut him up, as he walked unsteadily down the road to the chapel. Villagers looked on from outside their houses, wanting to see the young lass from the shop who was to wed one of the Alderson lads. They wished her well as she walked over the bridge and down the road, a biting northern wind making Meg shiver in her thin wedding dress.

Harry and Meg stood for a second before entering the chapel, both gathering their nerves as they walked down the aisle, with no music playing and no guests except Jack's mother, sitting alone in the pew next to her son. Lizzie quickly rushed to a pew in front of them. This was not the wedding Meg had dreamed of as a young girl; there were no frills and no flowers, but worst of all, there was no sign of her parents. She felt sick inside, and if she could have run, she would have done. But she owed more loyalty than that to Jack, who turned and smiled at her as the minister urged her to come forward.

Jack rose from his pew as Meg, escorted by Harry, walked to his side. 'Are you alright? You look beautiful,' he whispered and smiled at her, silenced only as the minister started the wedding proceedings.

He was stopped in his tracks as the chapel door clattered and was pushed open by two guests.

Jack, his mother, Lizzie, Meg and Harry turned to see who the late arrivals were.

Meg gasped and nearly cried, as her father and mother walked down the aisle and took a seat. The look on her father's face was not one of pleasure, but her mum smiled as she sat down. Please don't let them say that I cannot marry, Meg prayed, as the minister asked the small congregation if there was any just impediment preventing the marriage from taking place. But no objections were to be heard, and the service continued.

Meg heard herself making her vows as if in a dream, and smiled as Jack placed the wedding ring on her finger. She was married and there was nothing anybody – especially her father – could do about it now. She kissed Jack and whispered 'Thank you' as he held her tight. And then she turned to look at her parents, noticing her mother in tears, as she took Jack's hand to leave the chapel.

'We nearly didn't make it, as the road was icy and our way was slow.' Agnes looked at her daughter and smiled, before hugging her as they stood outside the chapel. 'You look wonderful, and Jack looks so handsome.'

Meg kissed her mum and felt her heart swell as she held her hand and smiled.

'Aye, Jack's a grand lad. You should be glad he's joined your family,' Harry butted in.

'You can hold your noise. Writing bloody letters to me to make me feel guilty. What with you telling me what you thought of me, and Agnes here telling me there was a baby on the way, I haven't slept for bloody nights. Anyway, I'm here to make it right. Here, this will help. I can't see my lass struggling and her baby going hungry, so I've done this for you.' Tom pulled a folded parchment out of his breast pocket, passing it to Jack. 'The Rash is your farm – you own it now; you are not renting. I came to an arrangement with Dick Turner, the owner. It's in your name, because from what Harry told me, we owe you. And there's twenty sheep and another milking cow in our home field, waiting to be driven over. That should get you going.'

'I don't know what to say, sir. Both of us can't thank you enough.' Jack reached for Meg's hand and smiled at her as she wiped away the tears.

'Thank you, Father. We didn't expect anything, but I'm so glad you are here.' Meg put her arms around her father's neck and kissed him.

'Aye, well, you can thank this old rogue here. Is this your fancy piece, then? I've known for a while that you've not exactly been behaving yourself.' Tom turned and looked at Lizzie, who thankfully had not heard herself being called a 'fancy piece' as she talked to Jack's mother.

Agnes shook her head in disbelief at Tom's straight talking.

'Aye, this is Lizzie. And before you say anything else, we are to be married in spring,' Harry said quickly.

'About bloody time. You've been going with her long enough, from what I heard. Poor Mary used to despair of your long walks. Thank God she never knew what you were about – and me neither, come to that.' Tom shook his head. 'While we are here, Agnes wants to visit Mary's grave, so we will go there now and then we can all have a drink in the King's Head to celebrate. Although you may already have done enough of that, Harry, by the look of that nose of yours. It's as red as that robin redbreast over in that holly tree.' Tom grinned as he took Agnes's arm and they walked along the path to the small chapel graveyard where both Mary and Sam lay. Meg, Jack and everyone else followed them and stood looking down on the two graves, with those they loved inside them.

'I'll share my bouquet between Mary and Sam,' Meg whispered to Jack, and he nodded in agreement as she split the few chrysanthemums between the graves, nearly crying as she willed thoughts of love to Sam.

Tom and Jack turned their faces up to the sky as the first snowflakes of winter came slowly and gently down to earth.

'A blessing from heaven, that is, lass. They are telling you that they love you and are wishing you happiness,' Tom said quietly.

Meg smiled and hid her tears. She hoped her father's words were true, but time would tell. For now, she'd try and make her heaven on earth, with her husband and their child. Sam might be the baby's true father, but the love Jack had shown her over the last few weeks was everlasting and she knew it.

'Reeth Bartle Fair'
by John Harland (1806–68)

This mworning as I went to wark
I met Curly just coomin' heame;
He had on a new flannin sark
An' he saw at I'd just gitten t' seame
'Whar's te been?' said awd Curly to me
'I've been down to Reeth Bartle Fair.'
'Swat te down, mun, sex needles,' said he,
'An' tell us what seets te saw there.'

'Why, t' lads their best shoon had put on,
An' t' lasses donn'd all their best cwoats;
I saw five pund of Scotch wether mutton
Sell'd by Ward and Tish Tom for five grwoats.
Rowlaway had fine cottons to sell,
Butteroy lace an' handkerchers browt;
Young Tom Cwoats had a stall tuv hissel,
An' had ribbins for varra near nowt.

'Thar was Enos had good brandy-snaps,
Bill Brown as good spice as could be;
Potter Robin an' mair sike-like chaps
Had t' bonniest pots te could see.
John Ridley, an' awd Willy Walls,
An' Naylor, an' twea or three mar,
Had apples an' pears at their stalls,
An' Gardener Joe tea was thar.

'Thar was scissors an' knives an' read purses,
An' plenty of awd cleathes on t' nogs,
An' twea or three spavin'd horses,
An' plenty o' shoon an' new clogs.
Thar was plenty o' good iron pans,
An' pigs at wad fill all t' deale's hulls;
Thar was baskets, a'n skeps, an' tin cans,
An' bowls, an' wood thivies for gulls.

'Thar was plenty of all maks o' meat,
An' plenty of all sworts o' drink,
An' t' lasses gat monny a treat,
For t' gruvers war full o' chink.
I cowp'd my black hat for a white un,
Lile Jonas had varra cheap cleath;
Jem Peacock an' Tom talk'd o' feightin',
But Gudgeon Jem Puke lick'd 'em beath.

'Thar was dancin' an' feightin' for ever,
Will Wade said at he was quite griev'd;
An' Pedley tell'd 'em he'd never
Forgit 'em as lang as he leev'd.
They knock'd yan another about,
Just warse than a sham to be seen,
Charlie Will look'd as white as a clout,
Kit Puke gat a pair o' black een.

'I spied our awd lass in a newk,
Drinkin' shrub wi' grim Freesteane, fond lad;
I gav her a varra grow leuk;
O, connies, but I was just mad.
Sea I went to John Waites's to drink,
Whar I war'd twea an' seempence i' gin;
I knaw not what follow'd, but think
I paddl'd through t' muck thick an' thin.

'For to-day, when I gat out o' bed,
My cleathes were all sullied sea sar,
Our Peggy and all our fwoak said
To Reeth Fair I sud never gang mar.
But it's rake-time, sea I mun away,
For my partners are all gain' to wark.'
Sea I lowp'd up and bade him good day,
An' wrowt at t' Awd Gang tell 't was dark.'

For the Sake of Her Family

DIANE ALLEN

It's 1912 in the Yorkshire Dales, and Alice Bentham and her brother Will have lost their mother to cancer. Money is scarce and pride doesn't pay the doctor or put food on the table.

Alice gets work at Whernside Manor, looking after Lord Frankland's fragile sister Miss Nancy. Meanwhile Will and his best friend Jack begin working for the Lord of the Manor at the marble mill. But their purpose there is not an entirely honest one.

For a while everything runs smoothly, but corruption, attempted murder and misplaced love are just waiting in the wings. Nothing is as it seems and before they know it, Alice and Will's lives are entwined with those of the Franklands' – and nothing will ever be the same again.

OUT NOW

For a Mother's Sins

DIANE ALLEN

It is 1870 and railway workers and their families have flocked to the wild and inhospitable moorland known as Batty Green. Here they are building a viaduct on the Midland Railway Company's ambitious new Leeds to Carlisle line.

Among them are three very different women – tough widow Molly Mason, honest and God-fearing Rose Pratt and Helen Parker, downtrodden by her husband and seeking a better life.

When tragedy strikes, the lives of the three women are bound together, and each is forced to confront the secrets and calamities that threaten to tear their families apart.

OUT NOW

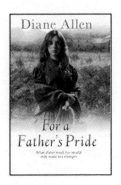

For a Father's Pride

DIANE ALLEN

In 1871, young Daisy Fraser is living in the Yorkshire Dales with her beloved family. Her sister Kitty is set to marry the handsome and wealthy Clifford Middleton. But on the eve of the wedding, Clifford commits a terrible act that shatters Daisy's happy life. She carries her secret for the next nine months, but is left devastated when she gives birth and the baby is pronounced dead. Soon she is cast out by her family and has no choice but to make her own way in the world.

When further tragedy strikes, Daisy sets out for the bustling streets of Leeds. There she encounters poverty and hardship, but also friendship. What she really longs for is a love of her own. Yet Daisy doesn't realize that the key to her happiness may not be as far away as she thinks . . .

OUT NOW

Like Father, Like Son

DIANE ALLEN

From birth, Polly Harper seems destined for tragedy. Raised by her loving grandparents on Paradise Farm, she is unknowingly tangled in a web of secrecy regarding her parentage.

When she falls in love with Tobias, the wealthy son of a local landowner of disrepute, her anxious grandparents send her to work in a dairy. There she becomes instantly drawn to the handsome Matt Dinsdale, propelling her further into the depths of forbidden romance and dark family secrets.

But when tragedy strikes, Polly is forced to confront her past and decide the fate of her future. Will she lose everything, or will she finally realize that her roots and love lie in Paradise?

OUT NOW

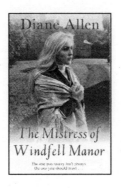

The Mistress of Windfell Manor

DIANE ALLEN

Charlotte Booth loves her father and the home they share, which is set high up in the limestone escarpments of Crummockdale. But when a new businessman in the form of Joseph Dawson enters their lives, both Charlotte and her father decide he's the man for her and, within six months, Charlotte marries the dashing mill owner from Accrington.

Then a young mill worker is found dead in the swollen River Ribble. With Joseph's business nearly bankrupt, it becomes apparent that all is not as it seems and Joseph is not the man he pretends to be. Heavily pregnant, penniless and heartbroken, Charlotte is forced to face the reality that life may never be the same again . . .

OUT NOW

The Windfell Family Secrets

DIANE ALLEN

Twenty-one years have passed since Charlotte Booth fought to keep her home at Windfell Manor, following her traumatic first marriage. Now, happily married to her childhood sweetheart, she seeks only the best for their children, Isabelle and Danny. But history has a habit of repeating itself when Danny's head is turned by a local girl of ill repute.

Meanwhile, the beautiful and secretive Isabelle shares all the undesirable traits of her biological father. And when she announces that she is to marry John Sidgwick, the owner of High Mill in Skipton, her mother quickly warns her against him. An ex-drinking mate of her late father who faces bankruptcy, Charlotte fears his interest in Isabelle is far from honourable. What she doesn't realize is how far he's willing to go to protect his future . . .

OUT NOW

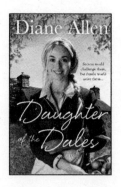

Daughter of the Dales

DIANE ALLEN

The death of Charlotte Atkinson, the family matriarch, at Windfell Manor casts a long shadow over her husband Archie and their two children, Isabelle and Danny. With big shoes to fill, Isabelle takes over the running of Atkinson's department store but her pride – and heart – is tested when her husband James brings scandal upon the family and the Atkinsons' reputation.

Danny's wife Harriet is still struggling to deal with the deaths of their first two children – deaths she blames Isabelle for. But Danny himself is grappling with his own demons when a stranger brings to light a long-forgotten secret from his past.

Meanwhile, Danny and Harriet's daughter Rosie has fallen under the spell of a local stable boy, Ethan. But will he stand by her or will he cause her heartache? And can Isabelle restore the Atkinsons' reputation and her friendship with Harriet, to unite the family once more?

OUT NOW

The People's Friend

If you enjoy quality fiction, you'll love
"The People's Friend" magazine. Every weekly
issue contains seven original short stories and
two exclusively written serial instalments.

On sale every Wednesday, the "Friend" also
includes travel, puzzles, health advice, knitting
and craft projects and recipes.

It's the magazine for women who love reading!